A NOVEL

SILENCED

THE WRATH OF GOD DESCENDS

JERRY JENKINS

TYNDALE HOUSE PUBLISHERS, INC.
WHEATON, ILLINOIS

Visit Tyndale's exciting Web site at www.tyndale.com

Designed by Dean H. Renninger

Edited by Ken Petersen

Published in association with the literary agency of Vigliano and Associates, 584 Broadway, Suite 809, New York, NY 10012.

1-4143-0283-5 (international edition)

Library of Congress Cataloging-in-Publication Data

Jenkins, Jerry B.
   Silenced : the wrath of god descends, a novel / Jerry Jenkins.
     p. cm. — (Underground zealot series)
   ISBN 0-8423-8410-3 (hc) — ISBN 0-8423-8411-1 (sc)
   1. World War III—Fiction. 2. International organization—Fiction. I. Title. II. Series.
   PS3560.E485S55 2004
   813'.54—dc22   2004007010

Printed in the United States of America

10 09 08 07 06 05 04
7   6   5   4   3   2   1

To
STANLEY C. BALDWIN
*from whom I learned more
than from any other mentor*

Thanks to
DIANNA JENKINS
DAVID VIGLIANO
RON BEERS
KEN PETERSEN
THE TYNDALE TEAM
TIM MACDONALD
and
MARY JO STEINKE

With gratitude to
JOHN PERRODIN
for research assistance

AT THE CONCLUSION OF WORLD WAR III

in the fall of 2009, it was determined by the new international government in Bern, Switzerland, that beginning January 1 of the following year, the designation A.D. (*anno Domini*, "in the year of our Lord," or after the birth of Christ) would be replaced by P.3. (post–World War III). Thus, January 1, A.D. 2010, would become January 1, 1 P.3. This story takes place thirty-seven years later in 38 P.3.

AFTER THE THIRD WORLD WAR, a holy war that resulted in the destruction of entire nations, antireligion, antiwar factions toppled nearly every head of state, and an international government rose from the ashes and mud. The United States was redrawn into seven regions, the president deposed, and the vice president installed as regional governor, reporting to the International Government of Peace in Bern, Switzerland.

When he completed his graduate studies, **Dr. Paul Stepola** dreamed of a corporate job. But when his Ph.D. in religious studies didn't open those doors, his wife, **Jae,** urged him to pursue the National Peace Organization. Jae's father, **Ranold B. Decenti,** a retired army general, had helped build the NPO from the ashes of the FBI and the CIA. Like the CIA, the NPO is a foreign intelligence force—though a skeletal one, since in the postwar world the United Nations oversees global peacekeeping. And like the FBI, it handles interstate crimes—which these days were as likely to be international—such as fraud, racketeering, terrorism, and drug trafficking.

Paul trained at Langley, Virginia, then spent his first few years in Chicago on the racketeering squad where, surprisingly, his graduate work found purchase. Studying the world's major religions had introduced him to a broad range of cultures, background that proved invaluable when investigations drew him or his colleagues overseas.

When the NPO initiates a new task force, the Zealot Underground, to expose and eliminate religious influence in the USSA, Chicago NPO bureau chief **Bob Koontz** taps Paul to provide intelligence and analysis of the underground. Paul leaps at the opportunity.

Becoming a key member of the Zealot Underground, Paul becomes enmeshed in the NPO's covert operations. He is the decorated sole survivor of a raid on a small house church in San Francisco where he shoots and kills the leader, a widow. In a Texas investigation of oil-well sabotage he witnesses the stoning to death of an underground Christian. In a subsequent oil-field fire, Paul loses his sight.

While recovering and contemplating the possibility of never seeing again, Paul meets **Stuart "Straight" Rathe,** a volunteer at the hospital. Paul asks for the New Testament on disc so he can brush up on the beliefs of his targets in case he is ever able to work again.

The combination of his exposure to the New Testament and to Straight, a secret believer, leads to Paul's dramatic conversion and the restoration of his sight. Paul cannot tell Jae, fearing she will tell her father and expose him to a death penalty. Straight introduces Paul to the leaders of the Christian underground, one of whom challenges Paul to become a double agent, staying in the NPO while secretly aiding the resistance.

Paul is able to appear committed to the NPO by arresting phony people of faith. Then the NPO calls his father-in-law out of retirement to head Special Projects, and he presses Paul into service for a major thrust against the Christian underground in Los Angeles.

In Los Angeles—where Paul and Ranold are staying at the opulent estate of movie mogul Tiny Allendo—Paul must appear loyal to the NPO while secretly warning underground Christian groups about the operation, led by top agent **Bia Balaam.**

One of the underground groups distributes a manifesto calling believers to ask God to prove Himself by drying up the Los Angeles water supply unless the extermination of Christians stops. Ranold and his Special Forces respond by planning a massive strike that will wipe out the L.A. underground.

Jae arrives in Los Angeles, further complicating Paul's double agency, and settles in with Paul at Allendo's mansion. While Jae shops on Rodeo Drive, Straight informs Paul by phone that the media has picked up the Christian manifesto. At Allendo's mansion Paul can only wait . . . and pray.

THEY ARRIVED AT THE ALLENDO ESTATE a few hours before dinner and strolled the grounds in the sweltering heat. Jae kept her distance from the fountain so it wouldn't ruin her hair, but she stared at it from inside the fence that separated the pool from the rest of the grounds.

"Who are all the young women?" she said.

"Party favors," Paul said.

"And did you—"

"No."

"And Daddy?"

"Don't ask."

Paul found himself silently praying every spare moment. . . .

Allendo was resplendent in his usual black on black, gold-mirrored shades in place. Tiny didn't seem to sweat, while Paul felt as if he were swimming. The governor's entourage arrived at ten to six, when Ranold also made his appearance for pictures and handshakes. He proudly introduced Jae to all the dignitaries. The governor's wife appeared relieved to see Jae and insisted on staying at her side and sitting next to the Stepolas at dinner. . . .

Jae whispered, "There's sure a lot of laughter for what

should be a sober day. You'd think they were planning a surprise party."

"Peculiar, considering people might die," Paul said.

The governor's wife agreed. "I know we're targeting terrorists, but I find it hard to approve of jocularity at a time like this."

Paul and Jae sat at the far end of the table, nearest the pool. Tiny's "party favors" continued to cavort in the water during dinner, and Paul envied them, longing to plunge in and cool off. The servers kept the wine flowing, but Paul concentrated on his tall glass of ice water.

What if there were more targets than Straight's people had been able to reach? What if he had to go along and see his brothers and sisters killed? He fought to hold fast to his faith. He had to believe God would heed an entire nation's prayers and make Himself known.

• • •

"So," Juliet Peters said, as the waiters came around with dessert, "have we all been sufficiently warned of the judgment of God?"

She smiled and sipped water from her glass.

The others laughed.

"Yes," Ranold said, sounding on the verge of a guffaw, "better stock up on water!"

"Indeed," Allendo said. "I bought extra-long straws so we can drink out of the pool if necessary."

Paul could hear the rush of the fountain from the front of the house, which showed high above the roof, and the splashing of the young women in the pool. *Spare us*, he prayed.

. . . Juliet Peters coughed. Someone cried out, and Paul looked up just in time to see one of the women at the pool plunge down a slide and slam into the dry bottom of the pool with a sickening thud. Her friends screamed.

The fountain had ceased.

The water glasses on the table were not only empty, but also dry. Even the sweat on the glass serving pitchers was gone.

Tiny Allendo jumped up so quickly his chair pitched backward. He stared at the pool, then whirled and looked at the fountain.

Paul studied the table. Even the liquid in the food had evaporated. The fruit tart had shriveled. The sorbet was colored powder. The wineglasses held a gooey residue.

Tiny's voice sounded weak and timid. "Bottled water!" he croaked.

Waiters ran into the house, then came out, looking stricken. "The bottles are unopened, sir, but empty."

Paul looked at the grass on the beautiful sprawling lawn under the lights. It was withering. By tomorrow it would be brown.

. . . Ranold stood, fingers fluttering, lips trembling. Tiny called out to his people. "Get to the store. Bring back all the water you can."

But Paul knew what they would find. More empty bottles. God had more than answered the prayers of the faithful. He had done more than shut off the water supply to Los Angeles.

The mighty Lord and creator of the universe had withdrawn every drop of water in the wicked city. The word would spread throughout the land, and underground believers would rise up with confidence and strength, boldly proclaiming the message of faith. The powers that be would stop killing the people of God, or they would all wither like the grass and die.

• • •

The miracle would be known around the world within minutes. To those aboveground, it marked the beginning of what would become known as the Christian Guerilla War. To those under-ground, this was clearly the beginning of the end, the mark of what—and who—would be coming.

Soon.

PROLOGUE

IT TOOK LESS THAN A MONTH for every United Seven States of America and International Government agency to concede that Los Angeles was not fixable. Initially the various heads and undersecretaries pointed at each other, insisting that one or another must act first before their own experts could wade in. As the foliage withered and services—particularly medical—shut down for lack of water in any form, eventually everyone reluctantly pulled out.

It was hard for the public to imagine life without water. Nothing to drink. Hardly anything to eat. Toilets wouldn't flush. People couldn't bathe. Anything and everything that in any way relied upon H_2O became worthless. Thousands died. The rest, reluctantly but fast losing hope, slowly migrated elsewhere. The largest city in the world, by landmass, became a barren ghost town.

Except for people of faith. The underground became the sparse populace that had the run of the place. The endless miles of freeway pavement, once the crippled cars of the judged were moved aside, became a playground for the formerly oppressed.

They had running water. Their bottles were full. Their machines had fluids and lubrication. And when they assumed control of the dead vehicle of a banished victim, it sprang back to life.

Unable to explain such a catastrophe to the populace, the government resorted to threatening to obliterate life in the greater Los Angeles metropolitan area. This was met with a furious outcry. What about the landmarks, the homes, the office buildings? If a cure were ever found, what would there be to return to? Was this not admitting that the majority had lost to the minority?

Worse, there were those who—given the poverty of the government's ability to explain, let alone rectify, the situation—suggested that the claim of the rebels must be true: God had sent this plague on Los Angeles because of the slaughter of innocents. And should the government compound its culpability by attempting to wipe out the rest of them, what would stop Him from expanding the scope of the disaster?

This proved the greatest nightmare for the government since religion had been banned internationally more than three and a half decades prior. The year 38 P.3. (which would have been known as 2047) was shaping up to become the year of the underground, of the rebels, of the resistance. In all the USSA's regions, underground factions seemed to take heart from what had transpired in L.A. It was as if God had had enough of the carnage, the persecution. Secret believers came to hope that He would not abandon them, that they might grow bolder and be able to count on His protection, even His vengeance against their pursuers.

In Columbia—formerly the nation's capital—people who were found bearing the flat, smooth, white stones that identified them as believers were suddenly feared. While the NPO had a mandate to round the believers up and prosecute them—the sentence, death—private citizens suddenly quit turning them in. Rather, the populace looked the other way when they happened upon a rebel planting literature in a public place. Some even risked stealing a glance at the printed material, though none dared being caught with it on their person.

In Atlantica, where the underground carried ailanthus leaves that marked them, some believers in the office buildings of New York City were bold enough to establish hybrid groups made up of some from one cell and the rest from others.

In Gulfland, medallions depicting the Bible were left at scenes of what otherwise might have appeared to be industrial sabotage. Yet officials refused to follow leads that might have pointed them to the resistance.

In Heartland, particularly in Chicago, bold rebels were actually seen wearing crown-shaped pins on their lapels in public. Yet not one was followed to a gathering place of believers.

In Sunterra, where San Francisco was soon named the capital, replacing the ghost town to the south, it was commonly known that house churches—much like the one that had been destroyed—were springing up all over. Ancient Lincoln-head pennies identified believers there.

In both Rockland and Pacifica, rumor had it that underground believers were having tiny tattoos applied on the ankle. Insurrectionists in Rockland chose crosses; in Pacifica the ichthus, sign of the fish, was the choice. Authorities broadcast far and wide that such decisions were self-inflicted death penalties and announced rewards for information leading to the capture of anyone so bold as to sport such a sign. Yet no news of an execution came forth.

Eventually the government seemed to decide that noisy retaliation was not worth the risk of another Los Angeles. While some agencies continued to feverishly study a way to remedy the situation there, the new national modus operandi became to hearken back to the propaganda of wartime—to the rhetoric that had resulted in the banning of religion.

The government fought fire with fire. Every attempt by the underground to establish that God was alive and well and that He might soon return was met with a barrage of information from Columbia. With a flurry of e-mail and Internet broadcasts, television and radio pronouncements, messages broadcast to every personal digital assistant in the country, the USSA was reminded by its leadership of the new core values that had resulted in more than thirty-six years of peace on earth.

"Remember," citizens were told, "that war results from religion. The propagation of fairy tales, of promises of pie in the sky by and by, devalues the human mind and reduces men and women to puppets, automatons, sheep. Ask yourself what ultimate positive effect religion has ever had on a society. Eventually, extremists arise, mutually exclusive sects emerge, and war and bloodshed follow."

The tactic seemed to work, at least temporarily, in the USSA, which had been embarrassed globally by becoming known as the nation of civil unrest. Elsewhere it appeared there was no underground, that the international community had succeeded in bringing entire nations into line. Human goodness and intellect were revered; religion was an ugly stepsister of the past.

By early January of 38 P.3., the USSA was on the cusp of becoming a model of how to quell such uprisings—largely with a docile response to the underground and eschewing real confrontation.

•   •   •

Charlotte Ian, twenty-two, left the suburban London flat she shared with four other young women at a quarter past six the morning of Thursday, January 10, 38 P.3. She hadn't had time to do her hair the way she liked, but that was less important than being on time. Mr. Woodyard, the supervisor of guides at Stephen's Tower (formerly St. Stephen's Tower) had remarked in her most recent performance review that he expected her uniform to be "clean and crisp," her hair "fashionable but done in a way that doesn't draw attention to itself," and "most important, that you never be one minute late again. I'm serious, Miss Ian. This is a plum position if I may say, and many wait eagerly in line behind you. You must be here, in place, and ready to go when the first tour is scheduled. I should also like to warn you not to let your plumpness get the better of you. We like a tidy image and your uniform should fit appropriately."

Her uniform was only slightly askew, though embarrassingly tight—thus she toted a very light lunch, and while her hair was up in back like a prancing horse's tail, Charlotte believed her top priority was reaching the tube early enough to make it to the tower in time to be ready. She had no doubt she had her lines down, and Mr. Woodyard had corroborated this. "You have a loud, clear, pleasant enough voice, and it's plain you have well memorized the patter, though I must say it doesn't sound rehearsed. I would like you to stay on, so please attend to these other areas, promptness being the major one."

Charlotte arrived at the clock tower of the Houses of Parliament in the Palace of Westminster ten minutes before her day was to begin. Her first tour group consisted of twenty people. "How many Brits?" she asked, and about half raised their hands. "Americans?" Six more. "Others?" One couple was from France, another from Russia.

That told Charlotte that she would be giving statistics not only in metrics but also in feet, tons, and miles. As she led her charges through the structure, she began, "This tower was completed some hundred and ninety years ago in 1858. You may know that the original Palace of Westminster was nearly destroyed by fire twenty-four years prior. The tower stands ninety-six meters tall, and for you Americans, that calculates to three hundred sixteen feet."

"Is it the clock or the bell that is called Big Ben?" the French woman said.

"Actually Big Ben is the name of the bell, the clock, and the tower. The name first referred to the bell, and tradition tells us it may have been named after Sir Benjamin Hall, London's commissioner of works at the time the tower was constructed."

Charlotte recited the weight of the clock, the diameter of the four faces, the lengths of the hands, the height of the numbers, and added, "The bell has been heard from as far away as fourteen kilometers, or nine miles."

By her three o'clock tour, Charlotte had been through this seven times, and the hard-boiled egg and two ounces of chicken breast she'd scarfed at noon had long since worn off. She was breezing through her recital of facts while talking herself into an ice cream on the way home in two hours when Mr. Woodyard passed with a smile and a thumbs-up that made her day.

Twenty seconds later she and her tour group, plus four hundred and sixty-three people in the adjacent palace, two hundred and seventeen at street level, and dozens of others passing by, lay dead under rubble. Charlotte had coached her people on how to cover their ears completely when the more than ten-thousand-pound bell sounded the hour, but no one had been prepared for the much louder blast of the bomb that would eventually be traced to a newsstand on the ground floor.

1

NOTHING HAD PREPARED Paul Stepola for living a double life, and there were days when he wondered how long he could go on. That wasn't like him. He had been military, a man's man, a decorated operative in the National Peace Organization. But he had seldom been called upon to work under cover. He had always been a straightforward representative of the government of the United Seven States of America. Paul relied on his bearing, his presence, his intellect, his communication skills. Pretending to be someone else had been fun on the few occasions his assignment called for it, but those had always been short-term, means to ends.

Now his whole life was an elaborate deceit. Paul was a mole within his own agency, within his own family. He had undergone the greatest transformation a man could, and he could think of nothing he would rather do than tell his wife and children and include them in his new life. But he could not.

Without knowing in advance Jae's reaction, or whether she would tell her father, Paul could not risk it. The truth in the wrong hands meant death for him and perhaps for his family as well. And the NPO would settle for nothing less than being led to whatever underground factions had compromised their star.

It was one thing to show up at the Chicago bureau office and be lauded as a premier enemy of the underground while secretly supporting the rebels. It was quite another to be unable to even tell your wife what had caused the change in your personality. For all Jae knew, their reconciliation and renewed attempts to repair the marriage were her ideas. He was finally ready and even equipped to make the changes, but she had to wonder why. If only he could tell her.

Wintermas of 37 P.3 was an ordeal, another visit to Jae's parents in Washington, this time with her obnoxious older brother in attendance. Berlitz (who had named these people?) had brought along his third wife, Aryana—yet another he complained of aloud who wasn't "likely to pop me out any progeny."

Aryana looked crushed and was stony the rest of the time, which at least made her fit the family. Jae's father, Ranold B. Decenti, wore his usual scowl, formally acknowledging the children when noticing them at all. He couldn't hide his disgust over his only son, who had, he said, "never succeeded at anything except graduating high school."

It was all Paul could do to get through the long weekend. When they sang and ate and opened gifts, he wished he could sing what was in his heart, that he could pray aloud, that he could celebrate the birth of Christ rather than "the bounty of the season." For Jae's part, she seemed genuinely appreciative of the new Paul. She commented more than once about his getting along with the difficult personalities and his attentiveness to her and the kids.

"It's not me," Paul wanted to say. But all he could do was smile. How could he know if she was genuine? Was she onto him, looking for ways to trip him up? Why the sudden change in her? He had never felt so precariously on the edge of an abyss. The pressure affected his sleep, threatened to make jagged his new personality. It was as if he teetered all the time.

Late at night, as was his custom, Ranold liked to debrief, as he called it, the events of the day with the "menfolk." But the short, dark, spiky-haired Berlitz, eager as he seemed to share a drink in Ranold's den, had little to offer. He was from another world, a salesman on commission.

"Do you not even watch the news, boy?" Ranold said, reddening. "Do you not keep up at all?"

"Some," Berlitz said. "Not like you two, I guess."

"I guess not! Do you not care what goes on in the world?"

The adult son shrugged, sitting. Paul couldn't imagine what it must have been like growing up in that home. For now he was grateful Berlitz was taking the attention off him. Paul's every word had to be weighed. He had to be constantly on guard and appear to give the party line. All the while he was privately celebrating the events in Los Angeles, but of course that could never come out.

As Berlitz and Ranold consumed more alcohol, their inhibitions, never well controlled, seemed to evaporate. "This one," Ranold would begin, nodding toward his son before launching into an assumption about how the man thought.

"Yeah, speak for me like you always do," Berlitz would say. "At least you're givin' me credit for having a thought in my head."

"My mistake," Ranold said.

"Thanks, Dad."

"For giving you credit, I mean."

Berlitz flipped his father an obscene gesture.

"I ever did that to my dad," Ranold said, "I'd have been star-ing at the ceiling."

"You wanna try something with a forty-year-old man?" Berlitz said.

Ranold waved him off.

Merry Christmas, Paul thought.

"One more for the road," Berlitz said, rising to pour himself another.

"Where you going?" Ranold said.

"Just to bed. Can't get rid of me that easy, pops."

"You need booze to sleep?"

"I need booze for a lot of things."

Ranold seemed embarrassed when his son was gone. "Don't let Connor grow up to be like that," he said.

Paul couldn't imagine it. He was just grateful the discussion topic was not business for once. "How do I ensure that, sir? What would you have done differently?"

"Put him on his can when I was able," Ranold said. "I bought into all the 'let 'em be' bull. Look what that produced."

"He's all right."

"He's nothing. Not like you."

Paul fought a double take. Ranold hadn't liked Paul much in Los Angeles. At times they were at each other's throats. In the end, though, the result seemed to take heat and suspicion off Paul. He couldn't have been behind the drought phenomenon, and that turned Ranold's ire from him to the underground. He was still seething.

"I don't like the way NPO brass and the government kowtow to the rebels," Ranold said.

Paul raised an eyebrow. "You *are* NPO brass, sir."

"Not really. But 'slong as I've got any clout, I'm going to do things the old-fashioned way. I catch one of these yahoos from the underground, I'm not looking the other way, I'll tell you that."

"Not afraid of a judgment from God?" Paul said, pretending to tease.

"Nah. You?"

"No, sir." That was no lie.

"I see big things ahead for you, boy."

"Big things?"

"In the organization."

Here we go. "I don't know, sir."

"I do. They like you. I like you. You've succeeded where many have failed."

Paul studied the old man. Maybe the alcohol had already done its work on him the way it had on his son. But he was good. Could he already be onto Paul, flattering him to see if he could cause a misstep? Was Ranold really so naive about the difference between a real person of faith and the charlatans Paul had exposed? If that kind of success made him look effective, well, so be it. But after decades of espionage, Ranold had to be more astute than he was letting on.

On the other hand, Paul's father-in-law had seemed to flip from bemusement to real respect when Paul had been honored after being blinded in action. They'd had their ups and downs since, but it appeared Ranold looked for reasons to be proud of Paul.

• • •

Jae still didn't know what to make of the new Paul. She was grateful, no question. They had not raised their voices to each other in weeks. She had almost talked herself into believing that—while he had been unfaithful to her in the past and deserved whatever she dished out—perhaps her more recent suspicions were unfounded. He seemed to be trying to prove he had changed, and now his attitude—toward her at least—appeared truly different.

He had helped get the kids to bed and kissed her good night as she settled in to wait for him, all the while knowing that her father expected him and her brother in the den. Those sessions seldom went smoothly, and the addition of Berlitz did not bode well. Big brother was the type of guy who frustrated the daylights out of an overachiever like Paul. In the past they had merely tolerated each other, so Jae had been surprised during the flight from Chicago when Paul had expressed actual eagerness to see Berlitz again.

"Really?" she said. "Why?"

"He's harmless. Charming in his own way."

"His weird way, you mean."

"You said it, Jae. Not me."

"I know Berlitz is a strange bird," she said, "but I love him."

"And that's reason enough for me to as well."

Jae had cocked her head at Paul.

"What?" he said.

"You love Berlitz too?"

"And your parents, because I love you."

"And your name again is—?"

He acted playfully hurt, but she sensed he had been sincere. How did that happen? Paul had always displayed good manners with her, acted chivalrous, did the things a husband was supposed to do in public. But she could always read in his look and body language that his motive was guilt over indiscretions or simply a sense of duty. Or he had just been doing what he had to do to keep the peace. Heaven knew she often made him work for it.

But this trip, he was truly deferential, helpful, kind, as he had been since their return from California. Frankly, she found it disconcerting. It wasn't that any weakness revealed itself. He wasn't throwing aside his maleness. He was being a different kind of man, not too big to keep an eye on the kids, help with the luggage, take charge by serving her, doing for her.

It had made her want to do her part too. She recalled many times having stood waiting, giving him an expectant stare as if silently demanding to know whether he was going to shoulder his part of the load or let her do everything. It was no wonder he seemed to do it begrudgingly. But now she didn't have to wait or wonder, and thus there was no need for the look. Upon landing he was out of the seat, reaching overhead for her stuff, corralling Connor, advising Brie, getting them from the plane and onto the road in the rental car without incident. Maybe his new friend Straight was having a good influence on him.

Paul had even adjusted his relationship with Straight, restricting their time together to when the kids were in bed and any other family responsibilities had been met. Straight seemed to enjoy playing with the kids for a few minutes before he and Paul settled in for some chess. Jae appreciated that now they played late at night if at all. Once she had overheard Straight exhorting Paul to treat his wife the way he wanted to be treated. Of course she wanted Paul to do that on his own, but whatever it took. Straight had been responsible for the loss of his own entire family, so perhaps the motivation behind his counsel was grief and regret. But his words reaped benefits in Jae's family, and one day she would have to tell Straight that.

She also knew that one of the contributors to a better marriage and home life was that since Paul's Las Vegas and California assignments, he had been home more. Jae didn't expect that to last. He had become a prize, in demand, sought by other bureaus for his expertise. For now she would enjoy his being home at reasonable hours. And if he could keep up this new attitude, she would resolve to give him the benefit of the doubt when he was away. It all made Jae more than ambivalent about the shocking discovery she kept to herself in a safety deposit box at Park Ridge Fidelity in the Chicago suburbs.

When Jae heard weary footsteps on the stairs at her parents' home that Wintermas, she hoped it wasn't Paul knocking off early because of some offense by either her father or brother. She heard the tinkling of ice in a glass as the unsteady gait moved past her door. Peeking out, she saw it was Berlitz.

"Little sister," he said, seeming to force a smile.

"Hey, Berl," she said. "You guys solve all the problems of the world already?"

He stopped and leaned against the wall, as if weary. His eyes were bloodshot, which they had not been at dinner. Jae had never known him to be a problem drinker, but clearly he wasn't holding his liquor well that night. Of course, Daddy stocked only the good stuff. A shot or two of that was like a whole bottle of anything else.

"Ah," he said. "You know Dad. I *am* one of the problems of his world. Always comparin' me to Paul. Paul this and Paul that."

Jae knitted her brow. "He did that with Paul there?"

"Not in so many words. C'mon. You know how he is. Oozing disgust for the no-account son."

"That must've made Paul terribly uncomfortable."

"*Paul?* What about me? I was the target. Paul is the model."

"But Paul didn't contribute, did he? That doesn't sound like him."

Berlitz took a sip and sloshed the liquid in circles in the glass. "Paul's all right, you know? I've always liked him. He must think I'm—"

"He thinks you're all right too, Berl." When he squinted she said, "He does! He told me on the way here he was eager to see you again."

Berlitz swore with admiration. "For real?"

She nodded. "And I like your new wife too."

"Do ya? I'm not sure I do yet."

"What? You—"

"I'm not sayin' I don't love her and all that, Jae. But loving and liking are two different things. She's starting to get quiet all the time, like Mom, like she's just tolerating me."

"Well, that's more than you can say for your first two choices."

"Don't remind me." He muttered a label for them under his breath. "Sorry."

"Frankly, I can't argue. Never liked either of them."

"But you like this one? Honest?"

"I do."

In truth, Jae just hoped Aryana would settle him, smooth him out. He could be an okay guy if he would just focus on his work and his relationships. When she was little he'd been a good brother—protective, parental in many ways. Then it became clear that he was not going to be the kind of son her father had hoped for, someone who would follow in his footsteps. Daddy had been unfair in that, she concluded. Berlitz would never be his father, and she wished Ranold could accept that.

As she returned to bed, grateful Paul had found reason to stay and talk with her father, she had to chuckle at her own brother's name. It was her father's mother's maiden name, but still . . . to lay that on an unsuspecting son and expect him to deal with it his whole life. Well, it spoke volumes about her father.

When Paul finally came to bed, he closed the door quietly and changed in the dark, as if he thought Jae was asleep.

"You survived?" she said.

"Oh yeah," he said, sliding in beside her. "It was okay. Your dad's exercised about how soft the government and the agency have become. And poor Berlitz. He'll never measure up. He bailed early."

"Couldn't you encourage him, Paul?"

"I could try. I don't want to offend him though. He's older than I am, you know."

Who was this sensitive, new man? Jae loved him.

• • •

Back in Chicago the week after New Year's, Paul successfully deflected a plan to reward him with a bigger, more opulent office. He told his boss, Bob Koontz, "Half my success is owed to blending in. I need to do that here too. First sign I'm getting too big for my britches, all of a sudden I don't get what I need from other departments to do my job. I've already got nice views, lots of room, and the best secretary in the bureau. Now if you wanted to promote me or give me a raise . . ."

Koontz laughed. "A bigger office was supposed to be like a raise without pay."

"You should be in propaganda. Talk about doublespeak."

"Well, let the record show, you turned me down."

"So stipulated, Your Honor."

"And as for that secretary of yours," Koontz said, "you know I have dibs on her when mine retires."

"Doesn't she get a say in that?"

"Only if it's yes."

"Don't count on it. I treat her right."

Tall, black, and direct, Felicia was the kind of woman with whom Paul would discuss such a matter—mainly to nip it before it blossomed.

The next day, Thursday, January 10, at just after nine in the morning, Felicia said, "You don't need to worry about that. I wouldn't work for Bob Koontz unless you died."

"That's comforting. What do you have against Bob?"

"That was a compliment to you, not a rap on him. Fact is, I wouldn't work for *any*body else 'less you died."

"He's a good guy."

"Maybe so," Felicia said, "but women talk."

"His secretary bad-mouths him?"

"How would I know? I don't listen to gossip."

Felicia's headset chirped. She held up a finger and took the call. "Yes, ma'am," she said. "Right away." She clicked off. "Speak of the devil. You don't think this office is bugged, do you?"

"'Course it is," Paul said. "We're the NPO. Bob want me or you?"

She pointed at him. "And right now. Sounds urgent. Remember everything."

"No need. You don't listen to gossip."

Of course, it wasn't gossip and it had nothing to do with secretaries. By the time he arrived in Bob's office, the International News Network was broadcasting on one of four big screens on the wall, and Koontz was teleconferencing with Washington—Ranold Decenti—and NPO International in Bern.

Within seconds Koontz's office was filled with heads of other departments. There was no small talk, just coarse language and grunts of surprise when INN showed simultaneous disasters on a split screen. Black smoke billowed from a crater where London's Big Ben had been, emergency vehicles noisily swarming. In Rome, the former zoological gardens (which for fifty years had been a Bio Park containing endangered species) had been nearly obliterated, the animals killed or scattered, and hundreds of visitors killed or wounded.

"A Norwegian whom authorities have been as yet unable to

identify has claimed responsibility for both attacks," INN reported. "He calls himself Styr Magnor and has announced from an unknown location that he represents, quote, 'the millions of underground believers throughout Europe, brothers and sisters to the oppressed in the USSA, and followers of the one true God who had judged the wicked of Los Angeles.'

"Magnor threatens more reprisals if the International Government does not lift its ban on the freedom of citizens to practice religion. Head of the International Government in Bern, Chancellor Baldwin Dengler, had this response: 'We have not, do not, and will not negotiate with terrorists. End of story.'"

The chancellor's combative response spurred the room to cheers. Paul had to join in, despite his own waffling on whether this Magnor character was from the true Christian underground.

Paul traded glances with others and knew they were all thinking the same about the chancellor. He had never seen Dengler so outwardly upset. The man's jaw was set, his eyes level, and his tone severe.

This would be called an act of war, and it would be blamed on religion. Whatever gains the USSA underground had made would be dashed. The dichotomy was not lost on Paul. Usually, inside these walls, he tried to keep himself from thinking like the double agent he was. Not thinking for or about the believers kept him from blurting anything that might give him away.

"What time is it over there?" Paul said.

"Middle of the afternoon in London," Koontz said. "After three. An hour later in Rome. Thus all the casualties. Brassy. But who is this Magnor?" A dozen faces folded into scowls as they tried to place the name. Koontz snapped his fingers. "Who is he? Come on! Somebody has run into this kook in some case or another. Paul?"

He shook his head. "I can check the files, but no. Nothing. No idea. I doubt the underground connection though."

"Why? Is this so different from L.A.?"

"Bombs and carnage?" Paul said. "Hard to blame on God."

"If that was God in Sunterra, He snuffed a lot of people there too. Not just government or NPO. Innocent bystanders, just like here."

Paul could only shrug. "You have a point."

"We're Code Red," Koontz said. "Ultimate security. Everybody on this until we know what we've got and can advise Washington and Bern."

AT TIMES LIKE THIS, Jae longed to be working again. She heard the news from Europe while out running errands, and she expected a call from Paul telling her he had been called over there. She had no doubt he would be, and at the worst possible time for them. Things were going so well. Part of her wanted a pledge from him that he would remain faithful to her, but another part of her knew that if she still had to require that, they weren't healthy.

She resolved to bury her worries and suspicions and concentrate on loving and supporting him. If he remained the new Paul, he would be in frequent communication with her, and she would be able to tell from the sound of his voice whether he was behaving himself. The more she told herself she would give him the benefit of the doubt until proven otherwise, the more she knew she was lying to herself. The fact was, he had so far succeeded only in softening her and persuading her that he was trying. If he cheated on her again, she would not be able to forgive him, even if she wanted to.

Jae made sure the kids were occupied when Paul got home that evening, and she steeled herself to avoid an accusatory tone. She wanted to demand to know why he had waited to tell her about the trip when he had to have known that morning. But that he hadn't called also gave her a glimmer of hope that perhaps he would not be sent overseas.

He looked preoccupied when he walked in, and she knew. "Where will you be and how long will you be there?" she said.

"Better sit down," Paul said. He draped his heavy coat over a chair and laid his hat atop it, kicking off his boots.

"You see?" she said, dropping onto the couch. "This is what happens in the name of religion. Who is this kook anyway?"

"The one taking credit? He's new to us. Might not even be true. He was only the first to claim responsibility. You had to like Dengler's response though, eh?"

"'Never have, don't, and never will'? What else could he say?"

"He didn't have to say that much. I was proud of him. I've always found him a little soft."

"Oh, Paul! We were just getting back on track. Didn't you think so?"

"That doesn't have to change, Jae."

"I won't change," she said, regretting it as soon as it came out of her mouth. Without accusing him in so many words, she was, well, accusing.

"I won't either," he said, looking directly at her. "But let me say it before you do: actions speak louder and all that."

Jae was angry with herself. Could she not just once have an unexpressed thought, if only to keep the peace? She would never again allow herself to take the blame for Paul's indiscretions, but she knew a bad attitude on her part had to contribute. That didn't justify anything. He had given *her* plenty of reasons to roam during their marriage too, and she never had. She took vows seriously. She bit her lip to keep from saying even that.

Jae wanted to push, to ask if it were possible that Paul imagined her not worrying about this all day. But he had his way and his timing for such announcements, and though she knew the inevitable was coming, she would just have to wait. She imagined herself saying, "I could deal with this—or start dealing with it—if I could just get my mind around the scope of it. Where and for how long?"

But she held her tongue.

Paul began with a sigh. "The initial posture is to wait, to see whether the response from the chancellor cools things. Face it, he laid down the gauntlet. If he will not negotiate with this terrorist, what *will* he do? Dengler is the ultimate peacenik. Could be whoever's behind this will push him to violence, even to war."

Peacenik. How long had it been since Jae had heard that archaic term? "And if he takes the bait, forces Dengler's hand?"

"Then I'm to be over there within hours."

Jae crossed her arms and stared out into the late-afternoon blackness. How she hated the short days of winter in Chicago, especially at times like this.

"It's not my choice, Jae, and I didn't volunteer."

Jae started at the edge in his voice, something she hadn't heard for a while. She quickly moved to his side. "I'm not blaming you, sweetheart," she said. "I just hate that you'd have to go now. What if it's this weekend?"

"We'll see. Maybe I won't have to go at all."

"Be serious. Anyone with the cheek to attack London and Rome has to respond to Dengler's challenge."

"You've got an amazing mind, you know that?"

"Don't change the subject, Paul."

"I'm serious. You could work in our bureau. What you just said was the consensus today. If there was an office pool, we'd all be tied, predicting another attack."

Jae appreciated his attempt at flattery, but agreeing with NPO strategists on this wasn't brain surgery. "So Dengler called him out. Maybe that wasn't so wise."

"Maybe not. My gut tells me you're right, Jae. We don't know when, of course, but this isn't over. When whatever happens happens, I go to Bern."

"To meet with NPO International?"

"Eventually."

"What, then?"

"I'm to meet with the man himself."

"Dengler?"

Paul nodded.

Much as she hated the thought of his going, she was unable to hide that she was impressed. "What's the purpose?"

"Humility forbids . . . ," Paul began.

"Oh, stop! He asked for you?"

"Not by name."

"He asked for the best, didn't he?"

"He did."

"Well, I can't argue with that. You *would* have to be good enough to be the only choice."

"Yes, I would."

Jae punched him playfully. She was proud of Paul, making it even harder to resent his having to go. "How long? What's your guess?"

"Truthfully, I haven't even thought about it. I'm hoping that if this is really the work of this Magnor guy, he'll blink and my going will be moot."

"Be real, Paul."

• • •

Gabriela Negrutz of Romania and her nine-year-old twin sons, Radu and Nicolas, were in France on holiday as her husband, Lucien, conducted business in Paris. She had been counting the days until today, Friday. Lucien had promised to spend the day with them in a park called the Champ-de-Mars near the Seine River, site of the rebuilt Eiffel Tower.

The original tower, built by structural engineer Alexandre Gustave Eiffel in 1889 for the World's Fair, had been destroyed in World War III before Gabriela was born. The rebuilt tower, made of gold-plated steel and iron and porcelain, was three times the height of the original and had become *the* tourist attraction in Europe. Critics of its garish look and monstrous size called it the Awful Eyeful. A marvel of modern technology, it rose more than half a mile into the heavens.

The boys were more interested in the park itself, which boasted donkey and amusement-park rides. Gabriela was relieved to find that in response to the terrorist attacks in London and Rome, the park would enjoy tightened security, but it would not be closed. She promised the boys they could enjoy whatever they wanted as long as they were on the glassed-in jetvator, soaring to the top of the tower, by eleven in the morning. The family would eat in the rotating restaurant at the top.

Gabriela had over packed for the unseasonably warm day in Paris. She and Lucien shed their coats and sat on a blanket, watching the boys cavort. At times Lucien joined in the fun, and

Gabriela howled when he awkwardly followed them on a donkey ride.

Earlier, the boys had ogled the tower but had resisted standing in the long lines waiting for a ride to the top. They insisted that the wait at the top for lunch would be even longer, and indeed looking at the jetvator line confirmed their fears. Every person, item of clothing, and package was being thoroughly searched by a cadre of guards before anyone was allowed onto the jetvators, making the process several times slower than normal.

Now, as they inched toward the jetvator cars, they passed several shops and restaurants and stands built into each of the four colossal feet of the tower. Gabriela herself grew impatient and began feeling guilty as the line crept along ever so slowly. Was she being selfish to expect the boys to endure this? She considered acceding to their pleas that the family just eat somewhere else, but Lucien overruled them. "Your mother has been planning this day for months, and this is the one thing we will do together that she wants to do. Frankly, all this security makes me feel safer."

Gabriela was touched by Lucien's sensitivity. She only hoped the jetvator ride would be worth the wait. It promised to be fast and provide one of the great panoramic views in the world.

When they finally boarded the overcrowded car, the boys complained that they could see nothing. So Gabriela and her husband jockeyed until the twins had their noses pressed to the glass, waiting for takeoff.

Gabriela noticed small signs printed in several languages informing passengers that the car was programmed to stop due to any minor malfunction, including a change in weight or balance or trajectory. It also stated that the jetvator shaft had a series of brakes every so many meters, and the car was designed not to drop more than two meters, regardless. "Should the apparatus stop, do not panic and do not attempt to leave the car. Notification will have already been sent to Security. Help will appear momentarily."

That made her feel better, and the boys' expressions of delight let her know they had forgiven her. They whooped, and it was all their mother could do to keep from squealing when the jetvator took off, making her feel as if her stomach had dropped to her knees. She felt Lucien's arms around her waist, and she turned briefly to smile at him. He looked pale but had pasted on a brave smile.

Gabriela turned back to the view. The farther the jetvator rose, the more of the park came into view. Thousands milled about in the sunshine. The sky was brilliant with just a few wispy clouds, and Gabriela believed she could see a hundred miles, maybe more. It felt as if the car was picking up speed and that they would soon shoot through the top of the tower, but a voice announced in several languages that they had just reached the halfway point. She could tell from the *ooh*s and *aah*s that most, like her, could hardly believe they would actually go higher, but all the while, the ground receded and the clouds seemed to move down.

Gabriela heard a horrific explosion and instinctively grabbed for her sons when the entire jetvator shaft rocked as if in an earthquake. People cried out as the massive brakes slowed the car to a quick stop. People tripped and fell into each other, screaming and grabbing one another, trying to stay upright.

The entire tower pitched toward one corner, and Gabriela felt the weight of all the other bodies pressing her into her sons, whose cries were quickly muffled. She watched in horror as full carloads around her suffered likewise, with terrified, vacant, helpless eyes staring back at her as the tower began to tip. The great beams groaned and screeched as an incongruous voice came over the PA system. "Please do not panic. The jetvator has stopped due to the computer sensing a slight malfunction. Do not attempt to leave the car. Help is on its way."

But by now the world's tallest structure had tipped more than forty-five degrees and was heading to the ground. Gabriela was now flat against the glass, the crushed bodies of her own children beneath her. She felt her ribs and pelvis give way. She could not breathe. Glass broke and bodies fell from other cars. Her last sight, before asphyxiation claimed her, was of thousands of panicking people in the park beneath her running for their lives.

3

AT 4:30 A.M. IN CHICAGO Paul was awakened by a sound audible only to him through an implant in one of his molars. He left the bed quietly, hoping not to wake Jae or alarm her if he did. He shut the bathroom door for his hushed conversation with Koontz.

Paul's hope that Jae might assume he had simply risen to relieve himself was dashed when he tiptoed back out to find her sitting on the edge of the bed, her reading lamp lit. Her dressing gown was wrapped around her shoulders, and while her head was bowed, she raised her eyes expectantly.

He sat next to her and put his arm around her. She embraced him, pressing her face between his neck and shoulder. "It's nearly noon in Paris," he said.

"Paris?"

"Yeah. About fifteen minutes ago, Bern was warned. Guy

claiming to be Styr Magnor said the next bit of news they heard should be interpreted as his response to Baldwin Dengler's challenge."

"He called it a challenge?"

Paul nodded.

"Don't tell me it was the tower again."

"It was, Jae."

"Full of tourists?"

"And customers and workers. It's unseasonably warm there today. Nearly sixty degrees. I can't imagine the final death toll."

"Bombed?"

Paul nodded again. "The front right leg took a massive hit. The thing shifted to that side, of course, then disintegrated and fell in seconds. Koontz thinks Magnor, or whoever, designed it to make sure it didn't fall into the Seine."

Jae shook her head. "What about the play areas, the attractions for kids, all that?"

He looked at Jae sadly. "Half a mile of iron and steel fell into the Champ-de-Mars."

"And this in the name of God."

"So Magnor says," Paul said. He hoped and prayed that Christians weren't really behind this. Who could justify that? It seemed a little out of character for Jae to state the obvious, but he didn't have the emotional resources to pursue it. "My flight to Bern leaves in four hours."

"You going to try to get more sleep?"

"No. I've got meetings first."

• • •

It was all Jae could do to keep from hammering at the religious angle. Paul couldn't suspect that she had found the letter his father had written him when Paul was born. It had to have humiliated Paul, learning that his father had been covertly religious, but there was no way that influenced Paul now. No wonder his late mother had squirreled it away and never shown him. If only his mother had destroyed it. Jae decided that was what she herself would have to do. As soon as Paul was gone, she would rid herself, and him, and especially her children, of it for good.

Paul had been raised the way she had, and if what had happened in London, Rome, and Paris over the last two days didn't prove the validity of their stand against religion, she didn't know what did. She was proud of Paul, leading the way to ridding the world of such a menace. How such a dangerous belief system had been able to rise from the ashes of World War III after so many decades, she couldn't compute.

Brilliant, she thought. *Try to win the right to practice your religion by murdering thousands of civilians. Yes, that's the kind of thing we'd like to see more of.*

• • •

Paul parked his Chevy Electrolumina and walked three blocks to Straight's apartment, not far from PSL Hospital (formerly Presbyterian-St. Luke's). With his head and ears covered, scarf over his face, and gloved hands thrust deep into the pockets of his coat, Paul still had to brace himself against the single-digit temperature and the bitter wind. His feet were warm, but having only one layer of clothing on his legs left his thighs, knees, and shins raw as he pushed the button over the name *Stuart Rathe.* He was grateful Straight buzzed him in immediately.

At six-four and well over two hundred pounds, the rawboned black man looked imposing in a ragged robe, even hobbling slightly on his prosthetic foot. Having just turned sixty, white and gray had begun to invade his hair. Paul had long been impressed by Straight's magnificent skin, which usually made him look younger. But this early in the morning his eyes showed fatigue and his cheeks sagged.

The apartment was small and sparse, but it was warm. "Nothing wrong with vinyl and linoleum," Straight often said. "It served several generations of Americans. Can't wear it out." The former University of Chicago professor kept the place tidy, and his shelves were jammed with the great writings of the world on thousands of discs.

Paul pulled off his hat and loosened his scarf, but he stayed in his coat and boots as he sat, receiving a large mug of coffee with both hands.

"Jes' the way you like it," Straight said, sitting heavily across from Paul.

"Just the way *you* like it, old man," Paul said, detecting not a hint of cream or sugar.

"Already had mine," Straight said. "Ready to get down to business. What do you know for sure about where you're going to be?"

"I start in Bern, with the chancellor."

"There's no underground—that we know of—there."

"That's amazing in the cradle of Calvinism."

"Maybe you can start one."

Paul looked into Straight's eyes to see if he was serious.

"Or at least be an underground of one," the older man said.

"Any idea how lonely this is?"

"I can only imagine, Paul. The underground here will be with you, you know."

"Be judicious about who you tell."

"Naturally."

"And you'll look in on Jae."

"Of course. She suspicious?"

Paul studied the ceiling. "I can't tell. I'm suspicious of every-body, and though she's not trained like her father is, I could read something into everything she says and does."

"You ask her about the letter yet?"

"I can't do that. Unless she comes right out and admits she has it, how will I know she's telling the truth?"

"That document doesn't have to be incriminating as it stands. It doesn't have to reflect on you that your father was a be-liever."

Paul stood and paced. "If she's seen the letter, she has to wonder when I became aware of it. Nothing I said or did in the first ten-plus years I knew her could have hinted anything. Had I known of it, I think that would have come out, and at that time I would have distanced myself from my father and his notions."

"And now?"

"Well, she's noticed a change in me. How could she not? But would she tie that to his letter? Just because I'm a better husband doesn't make me a Christian."

"No. It's the other way 'round."

"Well, you and I know that, Straight, but that would be a mighty big leap for her. If she believes I've become a Christian, she has to also believe I'm a traitor, a liar, and worthy of execu-tion."

"All true, under this government."

Paul sat again. "You really know how to comfort a guy."

"That's my gift," Straight said. "You wanna pray?"

The big man slowly knelt on the hard floor and Paul joined him. "Lord, encourage this brother," Straight began. "Lead him to whoever he needs to be led to, give him the words to say, and plant a protective hedge of fire around him."

Paul could not speak. He could pray only silently, and when

he felt Straight's hand on his shoulder, he knew his spiritual mentor understood.

Presently Straight looked at his watch. "You're leaving at eight out of Daley?"

Paul nodded. "Got to be out of here in ten minutes."

"Dengler going to send you to the attack sites?"

"Likely."

"Commit this to memory. Head of the French underground is Chappell Raison. Goes by Chapp. He will not be easy to connect with, but he knows you may be coming."

"Was that wise?"

"Wise as serpents; gentle as doves. If you want to see him, he's got to know. You won't find him unless he's also looking for you. If and when you get to Paris, you talk to me and only me by secure connection, and I'll give you a location and a code phrase."

"Why not give it to me now?"

"I know nothing until I need to know it, and neither should you."

"And Italy?"

"In Rome you want Enzo Fabrizio. Same setup."

Paul repeated the names. "Got it."

"I have something for you," Straight said. He picked around behind a row of discs on a high shelf and brought down a black, leather-bound book. "The whole Bible on paper."

Paul held it gingerly, treasuring it. "Old Testament too, eh? This must be valuable."

"Dangerous is what it is."

"But I've got reasons to be studying these ancient texts."

"Just don't tell anybody where you got it. And God be with you."

The 4,400-plus-mile direct flight to Bern would take a tick over two hours.

. . .

As soon as Jae dropped the kids off at school she drove straight to the bank in Park Ridge. She knew it was only her imagination, but she feared every car following her until it turned off. She felt watched even as she walked to the entrance of the bank. An iris and a fingerprint scan opened her lockbox, from which she pulled the letter to Paul from his father, which she had found in the basement of Paul's late mother's home.

Her fingers trembled as she stuffed it in her purse and carried it to the car. How to dispose of it? Fire was the only way. There was no question Paul had seen it; that had been clear from the way everything in the basement had been arranged. Some stuff was still covered in dust. The letter was among things that had been perused.

Was it the first time he had seen it? And what would it have meant to him? Back in her car, Jae checked her mirrors and pulled the letter from the heavy, cream-colored vellum envelope that still carried the residue of a blob of wax on its flap. Was it possible Paul had been the first to break the seal? Unlikely. If his mother had hidden it from him all these years, it had to be because she knew what was inside.

On the front, in heavy, dark ink: "For My Son on His Twelfth Birthday."

From the date on the letter, Paul Stepola Sr. had written it the day Paul was born.

My beloved son,

Your birth today was a miracle, filling me with a joy greater than I have ever known or thought possible. Holding you for the first time, I felt blessed with the ultimate earthly gift. One day you will hold your own child and understand the profound depth and breadth of a father's love.

The day you read this letter you will turn twelve. On the threshold of manhood, you will be old enough to understand another kind of love—the love of God.

Jae remembered her horror and revulsion the first time she read that.

It is a much maligned love at the time I write. There have been persecutions and terrorist acts around the globe—supposedly undertaken in the name of God, as different groups construe Him—which have drawn us into world war. Many, your mother among them, have turned away from a God they see as the root of the world's misery. But you must not turn away, Son. First, God's love transcends all earthly gifts, even the gift of your birth for me. God so loved the world that He sacrificed His perfect, only Son, who died on the cross to save us. Accepting that love has been the most important and fulfilling decision of my own life.

The second reason is that God's Son has promised to return in glory to gather up those who believe in Him. The Bible tells us "He will lead them to springs of life-giving water. And God will wipe away all their tears."

But those who have rejected God will face a very different fate: punishment and suffering beyond anything we can imagine or have ever managed to inflict upon each other. The end of the Bible, the book of Revelation, describes in vivid and terrifying detail what will befall those who incur God's wrath.

This may happen in your lifetime, Son. Many scholars see our current world conflicts as the fulfillment of the Bible's ancient prophecies. The Gospels tell us that we must be ready at all times, "for the Son of Man will come when least expected." And in Revelation, the Lord Himself reminds us several times, "I am coming soon."

*I hope to be at your side when you read this letter. But if
I am not, I hope I will at least have had time to educate you
in these things as soon as you were old enough. Otherwise,
you must seek the truth for yourself. I urge you to open your
heart to the truth—to become not just a man but also a man
of God.*

Your loving father,
Paul Stepola Sr.

The first time Jae had read the letter, her eyes had raced
across the page and the words had sickened her. She had driven
straight to the bank to secure it in hiding. In the ensuing months
Jae had recalled that the thrust of the letter was that Paul's father
had been a Christian and intended to make his son one too. It
had flown in the face of everything she knew and believed, and
at her core she wondered if it compromised Paul's role with the
NPO. Could a man whose father believed like this be trusted to
carry out his duty? Would there not be a temptation for him to
sympathize with people of faith, knowing that his own father
had been such a person?

Paul's record showed otherwise. He had had to kill underground zealots. He had been lauded for his work.

And somehow, this read-through of the letter was different.
Jae was not so uptight. She had been merely eager to destroy it so
it would not influence her own children. But this time she had
been able to read between the lines, to catch the emotion and
feeling of a new father. This was a picture she had never had of
the man who would have been her father-in-law.

Wrong. Misguided. Delusional, surely. But how he loved his
son! Naturally Paul could tell her nothing of his father, as he
died when Paul was an infant. And his mother said little about
him, even while showing ancient photos. She seemed respectful

and deferential, admiring of his military record. But her stories of Paul Sr. had always seemed formal, somehow distant. Jae realized she had never heard their love story, anything touching really.

She knew she should head back home and burn the document in the privacy of her own kitchen. And yet . . .

Jae read it through once more, this time slowly and deliberately. She could not identify with Paul Sr.'s language, with his manner of expression, with what he was saying. She was diametrically opposed to his worldview and beliefs. And yet he reached her—even though she was not the object of the letter—with his love for his child. She knew what it was to love a child. And she knew what it meant to love *his* child. She loved Paul with all her heart, in spite of everything.

Would it be right, fair, to destroy this precious piece of her husband's past? There was no evidence it affected Paul in any negative way. If there was, Jae would have no qualms about sharing it with her father. He would know what to do. Ranold B. Decenti always knew what to do.

As Jae stepped back into the bank to first photocopy the letter and then to replace it in her box, she felt a hollowness in the pit of her stomach. What niggled at her was that by even considering what her own father would do with such a conundrum, she had forced herself to compare him with a man she had never met. And her father had been found wanting.

Had her father ever loved her the way Paul Sr. clearly loved his son? Perhaps. But had he ever expressed it in such a heartfelt way? Had he ever expressed it at all?

Jae was not raised to be an emotional woman. She cried infrequently, and then only because of frustration and anger. And her husband had most often caused that. Well, he had done nothing to make her weep lately except to leave for an undetermined period in Europe. Yet she found herself overcome as she drove home. In fact, she could hear the splats of tears as they leaped from her face to her lap, even over the crunching of the frigid snow beneath her tires.

Jae didn't know what had gotten into her. All she knew was that she already missed Paul and missed him desperately. The thought of spending much of the rest of the daylight hours alone at home, waiting for the kids, caused a cavernous grief and loneliness to overtake her.

She used to laugh with her friends about how sometimes—even though they knew better—they found themselves tempted to pray. For help. For rescue. For someone or something to take care of their loved ones. Now all she could do was wish and hope that Paul would be all right, that he would not be gone long, and that he would come back to her the same loving man she had discovered him to be.

4

JUST ENOUGH SUNLIGHT REMAINED west of Bern to bathe the Jura Mountains in yellows and oranges. That beauty gave the illusion of warmth, but Bern proved only slightly warmer than Chicago. Paul was grateful to be met at the gate by an international government aide who said another waited behind the wheel at the curb.

The man who met him was cordial, welcoming him to Switzerland "on behalf of Chancellor Dengler. You will find him most inspiring."

"I'm sure I will," Paul said, hurrying out into the deep freeze and climbing into the car with him.

While the heater blasted inside the car, the driver—who had black curly locks peeking out from under a stocking cap—seemed as chilly as the weather. "So this is *Doc*tor Stepola. The expert."

"Nice to meet you," Paul said, extending his hand. Paul knew Curly had seen it, but he plainly pretended not to. "Hey, maybe you can tell me something. How did Bern get to be the international capital? I mean, Switzerland makes sense, but why not Zurich?"

"Bern is the capital of Switz—," the driver said.

"Sure, but—"

"Have you been here before?"

"To Zurich, but never to Bern."

"Then why would you say it shouldn't be the world capital?"

"I didn't. I was just wondering—"

"The minute you set foot in our city, you disparage it? Zurich is bigger, so Zurich is better?"

"You must be from here," Paul said, which he knew was not true of Chancellor Dengler. The head of the International Government was from Berlin.

"What of it?"

"It's inspiring to meet someone so loyal to his hometown."

"Aren't you?"

"You bet."

"Where you from, Doctor? Washington? New York?"

"Chicago."

"Same thing."

That was hardly true, but Paul wouldn't bite. "Well, you sure have a lovely city here."

"That's why it's capital of the world."

"No doubt."

The light was fading fast, the sun having dropped nearly all the way behind the mountains, but the lights of Bern made it sparkle in a light snowfall. A quarter of a million people lived here, Paul knew, twice that in the greater metropolitan area.

The Aare River looked black in the twilight, but near its banks tiny flashes of white showed it was flowing furiously.

The city's midsection boasted ancient buildings with new facades and arches that vaulted over sidewalks. Paul stared at the beautiful fountains, idle in the below-freezing temperatures. "Does the *Zeitglockenturm* run in this weather?" he said.

The driver laughed, pulling off his cap and shaking out his curls. They stopped just below his ears. Regulation. "For more than five hundred years now. No coffee breaks. You want to watch?"

"If we have time."

"I get it."

In a few minutes the driver pulled within sight of the famous clock tower. "The dancing bears, the wood figures, and the knight appear on the hour," he said. "But that is forty minutes from now. The chancellor is expecting you."

"Yes, thanks. We should go."

Not far south of the clock tower lay a more modern area that housed four museums near Helvetia Plaza. "*Helvetia* is the Latin name for Switzerland," the driver said.

"I know," Paul said. "Learned it in graduate school. Religious studies. This used to be quite the hotbed for—"

"But no more," the man said. "See all the buildings that look like churches? Years ago they had crosses and such. Now they are all shops and office buildings."

Sad, Paul thought, but he couldn't say so.

Just west of the museums and across the Aare lay the massive headquarters of the international government, bordered on the east by Damaziquai, on the west by Marzilistrasse, and on the south by Monbijoubrucke. A three-block-long structure of fifteen stories, it sat gleaming in the artificial light of the Swiss evening. Cars streamed from the parking lots and poured across the bridges.

"End of the workweek," the driver said. "Except for you and the big boss, of course."

. . .

Jae had forgotten to eat. It was coming up on 1 p.m. in Chicago, and the kids wouldn't be home from school for three hours. She pulled leftovers from the refrigerator and sat at the kitchen table near the window, where the sun glared off the blanket of snow in the yard. She picked at cold chicken, which was no more appetizing than it looked.

And she phoned her father, reaching him at NPO headquarters in Washington. "I'm so sorry to bother you, Dad," she began.

"Nonsense, Jae! Always a pleasure. Tell you what. I'm proud of our boy, probably meeting right now with Dengler. That's somethin', hey? Never would have figured. Even I haven't met the chancellor."

"I miss Paul already, Dad."

"Well, that's good, isn't it? You two have had your, you know . . . so things are better?"

"Too good to be losing him to his job just now."

"Oh, Jae! This is more than a business trip. It would be selfish of us to deprive him of this opportunity, and to deprive the world of his expertise."

"He's really that unique, Dad? No one else could do this?"

"No one I know. Paul and I tangle at times too—you know that. But he's got it, Jae. He's got the goods. He's intuitive, sharp, quick. Wise. We need him right where he is."

"But for how long?"

"Well, let me answer that by tellin' you what I'd do with an expert consultant. I'd use him up. This won't be one meeting where the chancellor gives him his blessing and introduces him to NPO International. For one thing, Paul probably knows those people better'n Dengler does. No, I see ol' Baldwin sending Paul to Paris, Rome, maybe even London, hooking him up with authorities there. The top priority is going to be getting a bead on this Magnor fella. We've got to know whether he's for real, what his agenda is, find out where he hides, and root him out. Nobody better for that than Paul."

It was worse than Jae thought. "How long, Dad?"

"'Fore he comes home? I won't lie to you. Could be weeks."

She sighed. "Could it be longer?"

"Could be."

"I've got to tell you," she said, "this is going to drive me crazy."

"You'll talk to him every day."

"Of course, but you know I'm no housekeeper or homemaker. I need things to do so I don't go bats. I mean, I loved it when the kids were home, but now they're gone all day, and—"

Jae could tell from even her father's breathing that he was fast wearying of her whining, and he had never been comfortable talking about things he found inconsequential. What she really wanted was a little sympathy, but it was obvious Ranold was waiting for his opportunity to jump in and fix things. He always had solutions. No commiseration. Just answers. He didn't disappoint.

"You want to do something in numbers again, like you did at the Board of Trade?"

"Well, sure, if I was really going to look for something, I'd want to use my training, yes. But I'm just venting, Dad. I—"

"I could use a numbers person here in D.C., Jae. It's not a long-term deal, and I can let you go when Paul gets back. How about that?"

"Oh, Dad, no. Now that sounds like charity, and anyway—"

"Charity! You know me better than that!"

"Well, no, I appreciate it. But I can't yank the kids out of school and—"

"'Course you can! Your mom would love to help with them. And they never get to see their uncle. Not that Berlitz would be any kind of influence on 'em. But that new wife of his—what's her name?"

"Aryana."

"Yeah, she seems nice enough."

How would you know? "Well, Dad, thanks. I can't really think about doing something like that, especially when I'm just into the first day of this. But I appreciate your hearing me and think-ing of me."

"I'll e-mail you the particulars. You know we pay well, even for temporary full time. Put yourself away a little nest egg."

• • •

Paul was ushered into the great marble-floored lobby of the gov-ernment building, where from the looks he got from security per-sonnel it was clear he was expected. As someone took his coat and hat, which he would retrieve later outside Chancellor Dengler's office, he was told, "Your luggage will be delivered to your hotel, where it will be unpacked, your clothes pressed and hung, and your room readied for your arrival after dinner. You will stay near the old train station at the Trump Einstein."

Talk about an oxymoron.

"Ah, sir," Paul said, "could you instruct whoever's going to do that that the clothes in the plastic, uh, garbage bag are not to be washed, pressed, or hung?"

"Certainly, sir."

They were his stash of disguises, and some needed to be as wrinkled and dirty as they came.

A five-minute procedure in a hermetically sealed booth gave

building guards bioreadings on Paul that were matched with the NPO database. His iris scan, fingerprints, DNA, even facial-construction data were coded onto an identification chip that was painlessly embedded under the fingernail of his left pinkie.

"Merely expose that finger to the scanner at any secure site on these premises," he was told, "and you will be admitted."

A minute later a man and a woman in severe but natty uniforms whisked him via jetvator to the north end of the top floor, where he was transferred to the care of similarly clad aides. Eventually he was delivered to Baldwin Dengler's personal executive assistant, then to his chief of staff, and finally to Dengler himself.

Subordinate staff were excused when the chancellor met Paul in an alcove between his office and that of his assistant. Hers alone was opulent enough to have convinced Paul it was Dengler's. The chancellor was as tall as Paul, sixty-five years old, slim, trim, tanned, with thinning gray-and-white hair. He extended a hand, and when Paul shook it, Dengler clasped his other hand around Paul's too. *Exceptionally long fingers,* Paul thought.

His voice was mellower than Paul had remembered from broadcasts, when the leader often spoke forcefully. Dengler breezed through the formalities of how glad he was to meet Paul, how grateful he was for the assistance, how much he'd heard about him, how sorry he was for the short notice, and how he hoped the flight was uneventful. Paul found his English as impeccable as his light gray suit, with only a trace of a *Schwyzerdutsch* (Swiss-German) accent. The man had a spring in his step and his eyes were alive. His workout routine was legendary, and it was borne out in his bearing.

Dengler led Paul into an office that covered the entire northeast end of the floor. The bank of windows behind the massive mahogany desk looked out upon the city over a bend in the Aare.

With the snow coming harder now and lit by the streetlights, the scene was surreal, as if from an expensive Wintermas card.

"Beautiful," Paul said.

"Thank you," Chancellor Dengler said, as if he himself had created the masterpiece and was used to being acknowledged for it. "Please." He pointed to a deep, soft, leather chair at one end of a small table, facing an identical chair on the other side. When Paul had sat, Dengler sat facing him across the table. "Are you hungry, Dr. Stepola?"

It would have been easy for Paul to say no. He could get something at the hotel later, and he had had a light snack just after takeoff. But the truth was he was famished, and he had learned that men of real power appreciate honesty. "Actually I am," he said, imagining the two of them being whisked to one of Bern's fabulous restaurants.

"I have arranged for a most unusual repast," Dengler said, fingering a button beneath the lip of the table.

The door swept open and a quartet of young people, two boys and two girls in formal-service attire, hurried in behind a rolling cart. They nodded politely to Paul and quickly set the table, beginning with a lace cloth. Bone china and silver completed the layout, and one of the young men draped linen napkins over each of the men's laps. "Apple cider?" a young woman whispered, and Paul was certain he had not heard correctly.

"I'm sorry?" he said.

"Apple cider, sir?"

Paul stole a glance at Dengler, who looked on with amusement. He was nodding. "Please, Doctor. I have taken the liberty of exposing you to some of our delicacies."

"By all means," Paul said, and the girl poured a wineglass half full of the pungent, dark liquid. Onto each of their china plates was placed a lunch-sized paper bag, but they were any-thing but brown sacks. The paper was thick and glossy and yellow and tied at the top with a braided string.

Paul wondered if he was expected to open his bag, but when Dengler remained with his hands in his lap, Paul did the same. Servers simultaneously opened the men's bags and set on each plate a gleaming green apple, a triangle of Swiss cheese the size of a piece of pie, a two-inch-square block of chocolate, and what appeared to be a large wrapped sandwich.

"Shall I open yours, sir?" the young woman asked.

Paul looked to Dengler, who said, "No, please. We will open our own, thank you. That is all. You are dismissed, and thank you very much."

The young people bowed and scurried away.

"Do you smell that, Doctor?" Dengler said.

"Sir?"

"Can you smell your sandwich?"

"I can. If I were in America, I would guess it was summer sausage."

"Trust your senses, young man!" Dengler said with a huge smile. "Were it the middle of the day, we would have taken this feast into the mountains, climbed to an intermediate level, sat on rocks in the most heavenly scenery on earth, and enjoyed it in the open air."

"Sounds fantastic."

"Please enjoy."

Paul unwrapped his sandwich and found the thin-sliced summer sausage piled an inch and a half high between two ridic-ulously thick slices of fresh, soft white bread with moist, chewy crust. He also noticed a thin layer of brown mustard and a gener-ous dollop of mayonnaise.

"Follow each bite with a slice of the apple," Dengler

suggested, "and the occasional piece of cheese. Save the chocolate for dessert."

Maybe it was the heady company, maybe nerves. Maybe it was the exotic combination of foods he wouldn't have predicted in a million years. But Paul found the meal the best he had ever tasted. Everything was perfect. Chancellor Dengler beamed throughout and proved an enthusiastic eater. "The meat is more indigenous to my country," he said, "but everything else is a specialty of my adopted home here."

"This is a magnificent city," Paul said.

"First time?"

Paul nodded.

"I wish I could say you would have time to get to know it. But I plan on keeping you busy."

"That's what I prefer."

"That is what I have heard."

Dengler signaled the waitstaff to come and clear the table, and then he and Paul moved to a couple of chairs and a smaller table in a corner of the office. He asked his assistant to bring in the latest information from Intelligence. When she handed Dengler the folder, she also passed him a single folded sheet, which he read quickly, his face clouding. He held the sheet before his assistant and pointed to a name. "Get him on the phone for me immediately."

They sat and Dengler pressed a disc from his folder into a tiny slot in the table. A large, flat screen appeared on the wall, but before anything showed, the chancellor said, "I may have to break momentarily, should she succeed in placing that call."

"I'm at your disposal, sir."

"Let me ask you, Doctor, has anyone on my staff been inappropriate to you in any way since your arrival?"

The question took Paul wholly by surprise. "Not really, no."

"That was a bit equivocal."

Paul racked his brain. "Everyone has been most helpful and engaging," he said, suddenly remembering the borderline surliness of his driver.

Dengler sat and studied the paper. "'Sarcasm in using Dr. Stepola's title. Defensive. Argumentative. Disrespectful.' Does that refresh your memory?"

"I was not offended, sir."

"One aide tells his superior that another was other than deferential to you. Let me put it to you this way: normally, such issues do not reach me, of course. That I was meeting personally with you caused this manager to believe I would want to be made aware of this."

"Really, it was nothing. I certainly wouldn't want a man to get into trouble over something I have already put behind—"

"Begging your pardon, Doctor, but I am going to come at this from one other direction, if you will indulge me. Were you in my position and had been informed of such conduct by one of your people toward an honored guest, would you ignore it, based on the graciousness of the victim?"

"My personality is such that I did not feel particularly victimized, Mr. Chancellor. I suppose my self-esteem is healthy enough to weather that type of—"

"Pardon my persistence, sir, but I asked you to put yourself in my shoes, not back in yours."

"Point taken." Was Paul being tested? Again, men at Baldwin Dengler's level had little patience for the obtuse. "Yes, I would have wanted to be made aware of it, and I would have made clear it would not be tolerated."

"That is my feeling precisely. Thank you."

"But, Mr. Chancellor, I would feel terrible if I got a man in trouble for something that barely registered with me."

"Oh, please, Doctor. Surely you do not believe that you are in any way responsible for the consequences of this man's actions."

"Well, I have the feeling that my corroboration—"

"Merely clarifies. You should not allow this matter to trouble you further."

"In truth, it barely troubled me at all."

"That says more about you than about the offender; would you not agree?"

Against his better judgment, Paul merely shrugged. He feared he was not impressing his host.

Dengler held up a hand, stood, and said, "Excuse me." He moved about ten feet from Paul and with his back to him took a call, apparently on an embedded device. "Not at all," he was saying. "I very much appreciate your bringing this to my attention. The eyewitness was in the car and heard all this himself? . . . And you have no doubt as to the veracity of the information? . . . The driver is to be terminated immediately—no recourse, no appeal, no grace period, no severance. Yes. That is correct. And thank you very much again for dealing with this forthrightly. I appreciate your service to me and to the international community."

Paul felt awful and couldn't hide it. When Dengler rejoined him at the table, Paul was staring at the floor. "Dr. Stepola, allow me to conclude this distasteful bit of business by offering my sincerest apology."

Paul thought about protesting more or at least again expressing his own regret, but he did not want to offend. Many much bigger issues were at stake. His suspicious mind wondered if the whole thing had been a setup to impress upon him the decisiveness of the chancellor and the finality of his decisions. In truth, Paul was impressed, though he doubted he would have taken such extreme measures. *Maybe that's why I'm not king of the world.*

When Baldwin Dengler pointed a laser at the wall to trigger

the holographic projector, Paul slipped a pen and a tiny leather-bound notepad from his pocket.

"This is all we know about the name *Styr Magnor*," the chancellor said. "And you will find it is precious little."

"If, in fact, the man is even using his real name," Paul said.

"Precisely."

• • •

By early evening when Brie and Connor were about to get ready for bed, Jae had pushed from her mind her father's ridiculous idea. She couldn't deny it had worked on her mind during the lonely last hour before the kids arrived home. Would the days only get longer, knowing Paul would not be pulling in after work as he had for weeks? The more Jae obsessed about it, the worse it got. She had to do something. Maybe there was work in the Chicago area. Maybe even at the bank in Park Ridge where she kept her private account and her safety-deposit box.

Jae was grateful the kids got along. They already missed their dad and said so, but something Brie raised put Jae on a whole different thought track. "Does this mean we won't see Mr. Straight either until Daddy gets home?"

"Not necessarily," Jae said before thinking. "You want to see him?"

"Yes!" she said, and Connor echoed her. "We like him! He likes us."

It was true. The man who had been so good and so strong for Paul when he needed a friend—when not even Jae could give him what he needed—had always been wonderful with the kids. They loved his basso profundo, his big expressive eyes, his silly magic tricks. He called them by name, lifted and swung them in circles, sometimes pretended to chase them.

In fact, there had been times when Jae wished Straight

would pay her half as much attention. It was as if she intimidated him, though she couldn't imagine why. Yes, she had at times been difficult with Paul—with reason, she believed—in front of Straight. But he should have been able to see that she had her points and that she was under tremendous stress. She hadn't known whether her husband would ever see again, let alone work and be able to provide for his family. And while he may have had a right to be self-possessed at a time like that, Paul had been downright surly and selfish. She would not have respected herself had she not countered that, act by act and verbal jab by jab.

Straight had not seemed to lose respect for Paul during that time, so why had it seemed to Jae that perhaps she had fallen some in his view? He was always courteous and chivalrous, but she sensed distance as well. He was wise; there was no question of that. And a servant. In Jae's book, anyone who turned his own tragedy and handicap into something positive was worthy of a pedestal. The man seemed a master at encouraging patients, and he had worked wonders with Paul. If the kids wanted to see him, she wanted them to. Maybe that would give her a chance to connect with him on a more even plane too.

Once the kids were finally down, Jae settled into a funk she feared would not lift. She didn't have the energy to climb the stairs to an empty bed. She left the TV on as she leafed through the paper, realizing she wasn't really reading but was rather simply willing the clock to move to where she would be too tired to think and able only to sleep. Her greatest dread was that her melancholy would not allow her to sleep, and she was already sick to death of herself.

When the phone rang she leaped off the couch, hoping it was Paul. But he wouldn't call at that time of the morning in Bern. Though it was just past 9 p.m. in Chicago, it was after 4

a.m. in Switzerland. They had agreed he would not likely call until the next day.

The caller was her brother, and he was excited. "Tell me it's
true, Sis."

"What, Berl?"

"Mom says you told Dad you wanted to move to D.C. until
Paul gets back, and he might not be back for a half year or so."

"*A half year?* First, he'll be back long before that or I'll go get
him. Second, that wasn't my idea; it was Dad's. And third, it's
about as likely as you going to Mars."

"Hey, I've got friends on Mars."

"Well, are *you* going?"

"No, but—"

"There you go."

Berlitz swore.

"What's the problem?" Jae said.

"I wanted it to be true, that's all. Aryana liked you. Says she
could enjoy getting to know you."

"Well, I liked her too, but—"

"C'mon, Jae. I'm usually on the road Monday through
Thursday nights. Your man is gone all the time, for now. You
know Mom wants this or she wouldn't have told me about it."

"Did she really say it was my idea?"

"Nah, I was just foolin' with ya. But she wants it to be your
idea."

"Did she put you up to calling me?"

"Hmm?"

"You heard me."

"You mean, is she waiting by the phone to find out what you
said? Yeah. Fact, I'm in Cincy tonight, Cleveland and Toledo tomorrow, and then home, and I've already heard from Mom,
Dad, and Aryana. We want you out here, Jae."

"The kids are back to school. They have their friends here. It would just be—"

"Do you never think of me anymore?" Berlitz said. He sounded suddenly more than serious. "Brie and Connor are the only thing close to kids I'll ever have. And I hardly ever see them."

"You were sure good with them over the holidays."

"I'm depressed about getting old, Jae. You wouldn't really deprive me of my niece and nephew, would you? I might start drinking more, being a worse husband—if that's possible—neglect my ma, who is also your ma, you remember. I might not even keep trying to be the son Dad wants me to be. I'll be a drunk, old orphan, divorced three times, and it'll be all your fault. You could save me with this one little decision."

At least he had made Jae laugh.

5

PAUL HAD SPENT the entire evening with Chancellor Dengler, willing himself not to look at his watch. It wasn't that he didn't find the whole meeting interesting, but he knew the man wanted to call it a day as much as he did. And he wanted to call Jae if at all possible. But it wasn't.

The brief show would not have passed muster in college. It was much ado about little. The greatest intelligence corps in world history had amassed a short list of every Styr Magnor they could find, most of them—of course—residing in Scandinavia. Over the course of the next forty-eight to seventy-two hours, teams of midlevel NPO operatives would make contact with as many of them as humanly possible, eliminating them from the data bank by their alibis.

"We really have nothing, no leads, do we?" Paul said.

"Not a thing," Dengler said. "But Monday you will meet

with NPO International here—many of whom I assume you already know. Something wrong?"

Paul had not been able to hide his concern over the delay. "Should we not take advantage of the weekend? I mean, I hate to put people out, but—"

"As it is, our field staff will be canvassing the Magnors of the world. If there is another incident, Doctor, everyone on the executive staff is on call to come in immediately. Perhaps I should have marshaled them for tomorrow and Sunday, but I did not. I thought you might appreciate the rest."

"I do, but—"

"You may rest assured that every tidbit of information we have will be funneled to you. And once we have met Monday, until we get something that points us to the right Styr Magnor, I assume you too will want to be in the field."

"At the scenes of the attacks."

"Right. Any specific order?"

Paul was still reeling from the decision to waste the weekend. Why had he not just waited and flown in Sunday night? "Yeah, uh, I thought I'd start in Rome, then Paris, then London."

"South to north," Dengler said softly. "How much time in each place?"

"As long as it takes."

"We are on the same page as far as the disposition of this madman, I assume."

Paul chose to flash his powers of recall. "'No recourse, no appeal, no grace period, no severance.'"

Dengler raised his eyebrows and smiled. "Well done," he said. "You forgot 'terminated immediately,' and I did not mean losing his job."

"We are together on that, Chancellor."

"Excellent."

Paul stood, assuming the meeting and the evening were over. He was wrong.

"I thought we would spend a few more moments and get acquainted," Dengler said. "But you are tired and I am imposing."

"Sir, again, I am here at your disposal. There is nothing I'd rather do—short of being home with my family—than whatever you wish."

"Ah, a family man," Dengler said, settling in, which obligated Paul to do the same. "You may or may not be aware that I am a man who boasts a long marriage. More than forty years. Four grown sons, many grandchildren."

Paul had heard. He nodded and smiled.

"Do you smoke?" the chancellor said.

"No, sir. No thank you."

"Cigars, I mean."

"No, sir."

"Do you mind if I—?"

"Not at all, please."

The way Dengler enjoyed a fine cigar, even the smell, made Paul wish he smoked. So far he actually liked this man. He would have to talk with Straight about that. There had been little question that his friend was uneasy about his being in the lair of the enemy.

"People thought it ironic that the chancellor of a country like Germany—with her checkered record of human rights—had become chancellor of a new international government of peace," Dengler began.

Paul knew he was in for a long evening. "You have done quite a job, sir."

"Dr. Stepola, I—"

"Forgive me for interrupting sir, but, please call me Paul."

As Dengler studied him, Paul couldn't read whether he was bemused or miffed. "When you are ready to call me Baldwin."

"Dr. Stepola will be fine, Mr. Chancellor."

Dengler laughed, took a discreet puff, and carefully exhaled away from Paul. "As you will be reporting to me for a time, allow me to acquaint you with my mind-set. Frankly I thought it a stroke of genius to house the International Government in a nation with a three-quarters of a millennium tradition of peace and freedom. If you know your history—and I know that you do—you know that Switzerland remained neutral throughout all three world wars."

"Frankly, Mr. Chancellor, I've always thought it ironic that the best-known army knife in world history comes from a country that has been militarily neutral for centuries."

Dengler howled. "The Swiss penchant for peace is an amazing record, but I confess that it frustrated me. I was in my mid-twenties during the last war, and at that time I had little more regard for the Swiss than I did for the French. France was hardly neutral, but she was so capitulatory—as she had been toward Hitler in World War II—that she might as well have renamed herself Geneva. I still feel that way toward France, Doctor, but as you can imagine these are not sentiments I can voice in public."

"Oh, sir, you may be certain that anything said within these walls—"

"If I were worried in the least about that, you would not be here. In the interest of full disclosure, I am compelled to add that I had my frustrations with Switzerland as well."

"Their pacifism?"

"No, no. I admired their constancy in that. The Swiss were not ready to surrender to or coddle dictators the way I believed the French were. They merely remained free and out of the fights, offering venues for peace talks. What so frustrated me about the history of this little landlocked island was how slow they were to come round on issues of civil rights. Do you realize that women were not allowed to vote in national elections here until 1971? Think of it! A mere seventy-six years! Blacks in America were voting long before that."

"Civil rights are important to you."

"Of course. And should be to all men of peace. I am most fascinated by your educational background, Doctor, and here is why: I am wondering if you, as I do, see the beauty and—how shall I say it?—the wit of Switzerland being home to an essentially atheistic world government."

Paul smiled, hoping only he was aware of his increased pulse. *"Essentially?"* he said.

Dengler leaned forward and delicately shaped the hot end of his cigar on the edge of a crystal ashtray. He dipped his head. "All right, a wholly atheistic world government."

"You say 'beauty and wit' because of Switzerland's having been the cradle of Calvinism?"

Dengler nodded. "Excellent. But of course you also know that the Reformation resulted in the fracturing of Switzerland into religious armies—Protestant and Roman Catholic. They actually warred against each other."

"Four times in less than two hundred years," Paul said.

Dengler was plainly impressed. "So when a country like this agrees to a total ban on religion for the sake of peace, the rest of the world must take notice. And it did. I simply find the dichotomy refreshing and telling."

"It is that," Paul said.

"It may surprise you to know, Doctor, that I am sympathetic to the yearning of the human soul for something beyond itself."

"That does surprise me."

"You will not report me, will you?"

Paul laughed. "To whom?"

Dengler suddenly fell serious. "I have no illusions as to why man created religion. I have not studied all the religions as you clearly have, but when one delves into them at any depth, it becomes no wonder why they swept up so many millions. There are beautiful tales, truths really, in so many of the belief systems, much we can learn and much we should put into practice.

"The sad fact is, people are people, and their religious codes of conduct were unable to corral their basest instincts. Rather than mold them into loving, others-minded, altruistic beings, their very beliefs caused them to fight to the death over who was right. And of course, the bottom line is that none of it was true. That must be seen as the saddest fact of antebellum history: that so much of the globe literally believed in the ethereal immaterial." Dengler seemed genuinely saddened by this.

Paul nodded, purely from politeness. The stress of sitting here a traitor nearly consumed him, and yet he had to maintain his edge. Faltering here, revealing himself to the leader of the new world, would have unfathomable consequences even compared to his being discovered by his wife or father-in-law.

"Yet you say you understand that longing of the human soul," Paul said.

"Oh, of course. I would not deny even feeling it myself. How wonderful it would be if there really were a supreme being of love and peace and goodness, who watched over us and could help us. But people who believed that wound up killing each other in the name of that being, proving beyond all doubt that their faith had been misplaced. And over the last nearly four decades, I believe we have made greater strides than ever in the history of humankind. We have shown that the eradication of religion results in true peace. We have proven, at least in my mind and in the minds of right-thinking people, that the true source of honor and goodness is found within oneself. My religion? Humanity. Worship the human mind and heart and soul and potential."

"You do believe in a living soul then?"

"Oh, certainly. It is the conscience, the inner person."

"So the conscience, in effect, worships itself."

"Yes! Very good! There is nowhere else to look, and rightfully so. Men and women are, at their core, loving, giving, caring, achieving people. I would say selfless, and in the sense of thinking of others before oneself that would be accurate. But in fact I know I am talking about selfishness in the best sense. For the selfish person adores the best parts of his own inner being. He sees his own potential and rises to it."

Paul wanted to play devil's advocate, to ask about people who follow their base natures and commit crimes and put themselves above others. But he couldn't risk it. The discussion would lead back to Styr Magnor and be blamed on evil in the name of God again. And without having met Magnor, Paul would not be able to argue. Whether Magnor was a true brother or a madman, what he had done had almost irretrievably set back the cause of the underground.

Dengler stood, signaling the evening was finally coming to an end, and Paul was relieved. The older man put a hand on Paul's shoulder and walked him to the door. "Let me tell you what I consider the greatest stride humankind has made since the war. It has been in the virtual eradication of racism. This from a German who carries the burden of a hundred years of national shame over Nazism. Religion was not the only felon. Nationalism, imperialism, racism. These were religion's illegitimate children."

As soon as Dengler opened the office door, an aide rose with

Paul's coat and hat. "It's colder and snowier now, sir," the aide said. "I'll have you to the Einstein in just moments."

Dengler moved between the staffer and Paul and whispered, "I have enjoyed this immensely, Dr. Stepola. It is so refreshing to converse with a man of letters. Get the rest you need, and when you arrive Monday you will have access to anything and everything you need to catch this enemy for us." He offered Paul a team of six rotating bodyguards for the rest of his time in Europe, but Paul declined. That was the last thing he wanted. How could he fulfill his own agenda and that of the underground with all those eyes on him?

• • •

The following Monday, January 14, after the loneliest weekend she could remember, Jae was about to call Straight when he called her. He said Paul had asked that he check in on her. She was struck that he sounded so kind, not as if he were merely following through on a promise to a friend.

"So," he began, "how are you doing?"

She was tempted to offer a polite lie, but she sensed sincerity in his tone. "To tell you the truth, Mr. Rathe, I'm struggling."

"How so? Missing your man?"

"Exactly. That may be a surprise to you after what you've witnessed in our home, but—"

"Oh no, ma'am. I understood well all the pressures you both were under, and besides, Paul has kept me up to speed on how things have changed around there in the last few months. And of course I noticed that too."

Jae was nearly speechless. Had she overestimated the distance she'd felt from this man? Or had he just been shy? Having seen him in action at the hospital poked holes in that theory.

Jae told Straight that Paul had called her twice over the

weekend. "I was wondering, sir, if you would care to come visit, perhaps for a meal."

"Beg pardon?"

"The kids. My kids. Brie and Connor miss you already, and I think it would help with their dad being away."

"Oh, certainly, yes. Well, I'm at the hospital just now, calling you on break."

"They get home from school late in the afternoon, and we have dinner at six. Can I count on you tonight?"

"Yes, ma'am, and thank you."

"I do hope you can stay awhile. I'd like to talk to you privately."

"Whatever you wish."

"And do you have any dietary restrictions or preferences?"

"Well, ma'am, as long as you asked, I love fish."

"Any particular kind?"

"Fish."

"What type?"

"Fish."

She chuckled. "So I can't go wrong."

"Not with fish, ma'am, no. Now if the children don't care for it, I'm easy. I'm sure I'll enjoy whatever you prepare."

• • •

After an entire day and most of the evening with NPO International, Paul returned to his hotel exhausted.

"Would you like to be accompanied inside?" his driver asked.

"Thanks, no. I'll be fine."

Paul hesitated off the lobby near the twenty-four-hour restaurant he had tried the day before—excellent steaks—but decided on room service instead. It seemed less lonely somehow. After ordering and while waiting for his meal to be delivered, he called Jae. It was after 11 p.m. in Bern, just after four in Chicago. He should be able to talk to the kids.

Jae told him how excited they all were about Straight's visit in less than two hours. The kids were both shy with Paul on the phone, but it was good to hear them. When Jae came back on, he told her, "I'm headed for Rome in the morning. International seems more than willing to let me shoulder the load over here. I guess their priority is Magnor."

"Well, it would help you if they find him."

"Sure, but local authorities at these attack sites are not going to welcome a one-man detective agency nosing around."

"You'll win them over."

Paul heard a knock at the door.

"Room service! May I come in?"

"Yeah!"

The door opened, and as his tray was pushed in Paul was about to turn away to continue his conversation when he recognized the deliveryman as his curly-haired driver from the airport Friday. Unless this was his twin, Paul could be in mortal danger.

"Jae," he said calmly, only half turning from the man to keep him in his peripheral vision, "let me call you back."

"Everything okay, Paul?"

Paul rang off. As he turned toward the rolling cart, he planted his foot and lunged toward it, grabbing his end with both hands and propelling it into the thighs of the man. It drove him back into the door, spilling food all over him. Paul leaped over the cart and atop the man, pinning him to the floor. "You armed?"

"No!" the man spat. "I just wanted to talk to you! I wanted to thank you for getting me fired."

"You went to all this trouble for that? I doubt it." Paul searched him and found a fifty-caliber handgun. He raised it as if to strike the man in the head.

The man flinched, pulling away. "Think for a minute, man. Before you call anybody, hear me out."

Paul held the weapon on him. "*You* got yourself fired, friend. Don't put that on me. Do you know the penalty for assault on an International Government agent?"

"I didn't assault you, sir. You assaulted me."

"What, you moonlight here in room service and just happen to carry a gun?"

"For a smart guy, you're pretty dense." His head was against the door, constricting his voice. "Can I at least sit up?" Paul backed off and let him rearrange himself. "Thanks. Didn't you think I was being too obvious when I drove you to headquarters?"

"Too obvious?"

"Mistreating an honored guest?"

"Frankly I figured you were an idiot and didn't give it much thought."

"It didn't surprise me when I got fired. Shouldn't have surprised you."

"What are you getting at? I could put a bullet through your head and not a question would be asked. Dengler himself knows you had a motive to come after me."

"If I wanted to kill you, I'd have come in shooting, wouldn't I?"

Paul froze. That was true.

"I wasn't even drawing down on you when you attacked, Doctor. What do you make of that?"

Paul sat on the bed, the man's gun still at the ready. "Keep talking."

"He is risen."

Paul blinked slowly. "What?"

"You heard me. If you can't respond to that, you might as well shoot me and tell the story any way you want."

Paul's mind raced. He could barely take in the possibilities. Could the entire scenario have been planned by International, based on suspicions in America? Could they get him to commit, do him in, and tell his wife he mysteriously disappeared? The only proper answer to the man was "He is risen indeed," but Curly had been right: Paul had blundered at least twice already. As a surly driver, the man *had* been a bit much. And the bumbling approach with his weapon tucked away should have told Paul there was more here than met the eye.

"So you're part of the Swiss underground?" Paul tried.

"I know you were told there wasn't one. That's because your guy was told the same by the people who told me you were coming. He is risen."

Paul set his jaw. He could respond, test the waters. If he was wrong he'd know soon enough and could still kill the man. "He is risen indeed."

"Call me Gregor," the man said, moving to rise.

"Just stay right there for now, Gregor," Paul said. "I'm still processing this."

"You can trust me," Gregor said. "We are brothers."

"Yeah, well, that may be. But I won't trust you just because you say so."

"It doesn't make sense to you that your contact isn't aware of the Bern underground?"

"For starters, yes."

"My contact is Abraham from the Detroit underground. Your man, Straight, is on a need-to-know basis about us. By the time you next talk to him, he will have been informed."

Or arrested.

"May I stand?" Gregor said.

Paul nodded. "I'll be hanging on to the fifty-caliber."

"Suit yourself, but it should feel a little light."

Paul popped the clip and found it empty. No shell in the chamber either. He sighed and shook his head and tossed it to Gregor.

"You're going to be looking for Enzo in Rome and Chapp in Paris. Now, how would I know that if I weren't on your side? If I were working for Dengler and we knew that much, the European resistance would be through, wouldn't it?"

For the first time, Paul relaxed. But he couldn't force a smile, couldn't match Gregor's enthusiasm. The adrenaline rush from a death threat always left him nearly incapacitated.

"I'm here to encourage and help you," Gregor said. "Sorry if I alarmed you."

"Well, there's the understatement of the century. What now?"

"You go to Rome tomorrow as planned. I'll see you there. I can save you a lot of time."

Paul helped clean up the mess and sent Gregor out with the rolling table so as not to create any more attention from room service. Finally Paul called Jae back and apologized. "They screwed up my order" was all he dared tell her.

Paul's dreams were filled with underground meetings gone awry, room-service waiters with high-powered weapons meeting him at every turn. There had been times when he was younger when he worried that such dreams revealed his true cowardice. Yet he had always functioned at the peak of his abilities. Maybe his weakness when unconscious made him concentrate more when he was awake. A man could hope.

6

JAE FOUND A BANQUET of frozen fish in the bottom of her freezer—everything from scallops and shrimp to lobster and mahimahi. This she thawed, stir-fried in garlic sauce, folded with generous amounts of three different cheeses, and baked as a casserole. The kids loved it, she supposed because it was close enough to macaroni and cheese. Straight had two large helpings and was effusive in his praise.

Problem was, the fish was old. Had Jae sampled it during the stir-fry stage she might have noticed the rubbery quality of especially the scallops and shrimp. But good cheese, not overcooked, apparently overcame the texture malfunction, and unless Straight was a better actor than Jae knew, she had scored.

The kids ate half their desserts and toyed with the rest, so Jae was inclined to let them go when they singsonged, "May I be excused?"

"You may," she said. "Mr. Straight and I would like to talk, and then he can come play with you."

"Whoa," Straight said, smiling. "Now just a minute here. You two are going nowhere!"

"What?" the kids squealed, Brie appearing to sense some sort of a tease and Connor looking to her for a clue.

"What kind of guest would I be if I let you kids get away without helpin' your mama? You—" he said, pointing at Connor—"carefully take your dish to the sink and scrape off the extra food into the garbage. And you—" pointing at Brie now—"do the same and start the hot water running. Get me some soap in there. We'll all clear our own places; then I'll wash and Mama will dry. Fair enough?"

Connor looked unsure until Brie cheered. Then he was in.

"Thank you, Straight," Jae said. "I could have handled it all after you'd gone."

"No need for that," he said. "Maybe they'll get the idea to help you all the time."

"I should be so lucky."

Later, after Straight roughhoused with the kids and helped Jae get them ready for bed, she insisted he wait downstairs while she tucked them in.

"As you wish," he said. "I'd better get going soon anyway."

"Read the paper or watch TV," she said. "I'd just like a little time with you."

Jae was preoccupied as she put the kids down. She didn't dare mention Paul's dad's letter. She couldn't imagine Paul ever having mentioned that, even to his best friend. She wanted insight on Paul, though, and she couldn't think of anyone better to get it from.

When finally she sat across from Straight in the living room and he put the paper down, she realized he was nervous again.

What was it? Her? He didn't seem to want to maintain eye contact. Maybe it was something about being alone with a woman. But he was nearly thirty years her senior.

"Straight," she said, "first I just want to thank you for everything. For coming tonight. For putting up with the kids."

"I love those kids."

"I know you do."

"For not mentioning my rubbery fish."

He threw his head back and laughed. "That's the way I like it. I wondered how you knew!"

"But mostly I want to thank you for what you've done for Paul."

"Oh, no—I . . ."

"You came into his life when he needed someone the most. You went way past your role as a hospital volunteer, and you became his friend."

"I'd like to think we're friends, yes."

"Well, I should say you are, and I know you don't have the time to get involved in the lives of all the patients you must see every day."

"No, that's true. Fact is, I don't believe I have a relationship with anyone else outside the hospital. A few kids I keep up with with birthday cards and pictures, you know. But Paul captured me. He's a very special person. 'Course, you know that better than I."

Jae leaned forward, elbows on her knees, peering at this magnificent man. Still, she could not get him to look at her for longer than a second. It was charming, really, his shyness. "That's just it," she said. "I think I've learned from you to view Paul in a new way. And somehow that makes him seem like a different man."

"He *is* a different man," Straight said. "I mean . . . ah . . . that he, uh, is sure a different person than when he came home from the hospital."

"Straight, he's a different person than he *ever* used to be. He's a better man than the one I fell in love with years ago. Do you know we'll celebrate twelve years of marriage this summer?"

"I do know that," Straight said. "Paul talks about it."

"He does?"

Straight smiled and looked away. "I shouldn't be tellin' tales out of school."

"What?"

"Well, he admits that not all twelve years are worth celebrating, especially for you."

"He said that?"

"I didn't make it up. Doesn't it sound like him?"

"No. It sounds like me. He's right, of course, and has himself to blame. I'm not saying I've been perfect in all this, but I was always faithful to him."

Jae realized she had just told Straight, if not in so many words, of Paul's affair and assorted flings. "I've said too much."

"Not at all," Straight said. "Paul and I talk about these things."

"You *do? He* does?"

Straight nodded. "If it makes you feel any better, he takes all the blame. Says you never gave him cause. Oh, you could be a tough one when you caught him, and sometimes he used that to fuel his own rationalizations, but even then he knew he was wrong. He really loves you, ma'am."

"Six months ago I'd have laughed at that," she said.

"I might have too. You remember he didn't treat me all that kindly at first."

"He wasn't treating anyone nice at first. I wouldn't have predicted you two would have become friends."

"Me either," Straight said. "And now I can't imagine otherwise."

Jae sighed. Straight was stirring as if ready to go. She didn't want to keep him past his comfort point, but she sensed she hadn't really gotten anywhere yet. "Straight, what do you make of Paul? What's happened to him?"

"Ma'am?"

"All this we've been talking about. It's as if I'm married to a different person all of a sudden."

"I don't hear you complaining."

She laughed. "Of course not. I just want to understand it. If I did or said or acted any differently and that brought it about, I want to keep doing it."

Straight pursed his lips and stared at the ceiling. "Frankly I believe this was an inner change, ma'am. More his doing than yours. Oh, your response triggers more of the same. Anybody responds to positive feedback."

Jae rested her chin in her palm. "You don't suppose he's covering, do you?"

"Ma'am?"

"Feeling guilt over something?"

Straight hesitated. "Such as?"

"Another involvement. I don't guess it would be fair to ask you to tell me if you knew anything like that."

"I don't mind saying, ma'am, that if I suspected that, while I might not tell you, I would no longer be his friend."

Jae flinched. "Seriously?"

"I don't go in for that. I was not a good citizen when my wife was alive, but I never cheated on her once—no, ma'am, not ever. I have no respect for people who do that to one another, husband or wife. I never let Paul get away with even coming to the edge of justifying what he used to do."

"I know you counsel him on how to treat me, Straight, and I appreciate that more than you know and more than I can say."

"Just common sense," Straight said.

"Well, it may make sense, but it's not common enough. Listen, I know you want to get going, but can I ask one more thing?"

"Of course."

She told him of her father's idea and the enthusiasm for it that was shared by her mother, her brother, and her brother's wife. "I have a lot of reasons not to do this," she said. "The kids mainly. But I have to confess it intrigues me. The days get lonely. I get squirrelly."

Straight had a strange look. She didn't know what to make of it. "Well," he said, "I'd miss the kids."

"It wouldn't be for long. Only until Paul returns. What do you think?"

"I don't know. You want an honest answer, I just can't say. At first blush, I'm not sure it's wise. Can't tell you why. Just makes me uneasy. But let me think on it. I shouldn't be the one to help you decide anyway. Paul should. But you asked."

• • •

Jae sat in her dark living room for more than an hour after Straight left. She had thoroughly enjoyed the evening with him, until the end. That she couldn't make compute. She had even enjoyed getting a little private insight into Paul, and her mind was put at ease, at least for now, about his roving eye. Who knew how long that would last when he was this far away for who knew how long?

But Jae had fully expected Straight's support for her temporary move to Washington. When she posed the question she thought she was genuinely looking for input, but when he was—there was no other way to say it—essentially cold to the idea, it stunned her. She realized immediately that she had really wanted and fully expected his approval. He had asked for time to think about it, but that was just his way of avoiding rudeness; she was sure of it. He didn't like the idea, didn't know why, or wouldn't say. And that was that.

Worse, Jae knew now that she would disappoint Straight if and when she went to Washington. And she was pretty sure she would be going. As she sat there she was distracted by the fact that more cars seemed to pass the house at that hour than she was used to. Or was it the same car?

Jae stood by the window in the darkness, waiting. She was about to go up to bed when a car pulled slowly past. She tried to study it, to get a bead on the make, but she could not. When it did not return she went upstairs, changed, and slid into bed, missing Paul more than ever. So before she let her mind disengage, she went to the closet to find his robe. As she pulled it off the hook she caught sight of the cache of discs of the New Testament Paul had used to familiarize himself with his target. He had taken a few with him, but several were left.

Might listening to these give her some insight into him or at least something they could discuss? She pulled down a handful she could listen to in the house or in the car after dropping the kids off at school. They would be archaic, she knew, and full of legends and fairy tales and, what else, poetry? But perhaps they would make her feel less alone, more involved in what Paul was doing.

• • •

Paul was up at five-thirty Tuesday morning and already regretting it. He had arranged an early commercial flight to Rome, not really expecting to have been up so late the night before. The meeting with NPO International the day before had been largely perfunctory and nearly interminable.

And while he finally persuaded himself he had actually met a brother in Gregor later, the man's tactics and approach were so disconcerting that Paul was still reeling from the encounter. He wasn't entirely sure the advantage of Gregor's saving him time connecting with the underground in Rome would be worth the risk of his bumbling. When he considered the numerous ways he could have been exposed by the fiasco last night, Paul could only shake his head.

He had showered, shaved, and was wolfing a light breakfast from room service when a call came from Baldwin Dengler's office. It was his executive assistant.

"You're in early, ma'am."

"Every day," she said without humor, though he had found her most pleasant in person. "I just wanted to tell you of a slight change of plans."

"I'm on my way out the door. Flight to Rome at seven, you know."

"Your driver is aware of the change, Dr. Stepola. He will bring you here for a brief private meeting with the chancellor."

"Well, all right, but I'll have to change my flight. I—"

"I have already taken the liberty of doing that, sir. You will be transported to Rome privately via government charter."

"Oh, well, then. Very good. What time would that be?"

"Well, Doctor, they won't leave without you. That's the beauty of a charter. Your driver should be there now. Are you available for the meeting with the chancellor?"

"On my way."

When Paul reached the lobby the tone from his molars signaled a call. He pressed his thumb to his pinkie. "Stepola here."

"Straight. Debriefing after a most interesting time with your family this evening."

"What time is it there, Straight?"

"After eleven. I waited as long as I could. Hope I didn't call too early."

"No, I'm up and running. How'd it go?"

"There's stuff we need to discuss, Paul. You seem distracted."

"It's a bad time, frankly. I'll be in a car with a driver and then in a meeting."

"Thought you were on your way to Rome."

Paul explained quickly. "I'm about to get in the car, Straight. Did you know, by the way, that you were wrong about a Bern underground?"

"I told you there wasn't one."

"Yeah, well, there is. I'll call you from the plane in a few hours. Meanwhile, you'd better talk to Abraham."

"It's an hour later in Detroit, Paul."

"This will be worth waking him for."

• • •

"Terribly sorry about upending your morning, Doctor," Dengler said, briskly shaking Paul's hand and leading him to a chair. "There have been a couple of developments I wanted you to know about so you would not feel blindsided. First, our staffer, the one we fired for being inappropriate with you upon your arrival, was apprehended at your hotel last night."

"What?"

"He has been sentenced to twenty years in prison for assault."

"On whom?"

"On you, sir."

"I was not assaulted."

"His plan was clear. He paid a room-service worker to allow him to borrow his uniform. Did you order a meal last night?"

"Yes. I—"

"He told the original waiter it was a prank, but what he paid was so extravagant that the waiter regretted it as soon as he lent the uniform. He tipped off local police, who found him near the elevator on your floor. He was armed. An identification trace led them to our personnel database, and they turned him over to us."

Paul shook his head. "And he has been tried already?"

"This was a clear-cut case, Doctor. We have broad powers."

"Apparently."

"I thought you would want to know."

"Yes, thank you."

"That could have been tragic."

"Yes."

"I wish you would reconsider my offer of a cadre of body-guards for the duration of your stay."

"I appreciate that, but—"

"I understand," Dengler said. "I hate them too."

"Frankly, I thought you were bringing me here to tell me you had a bead on our terrorist." Paul privately hoped he would find Magnor first, of course, in the unlikely event that he was a true believer.

"I am aware only that our people have eliminated many of the Styr Magnors of the world. You know, it's ironic that the name seems to suggest he is Scandinavian. No doubt you re-member that the only serious recall I ever had to survive came from a Norwegian."

"I do remember that," Paul said. "But he had support from outside Norway. Somewhere in the British Isles, wasn't it?"

"Probably from elsewhere too," Dengler said, his mind al-ready clearly onto something else. "The other issue of which I wanted to make you aware is something I trust you will agree should help your cause. This was in process when first we met, but I was not at liberty to mention it then. It will not be announced until next Monday, and there will undoubtedly be minor adjustments in the wording before then, but I wanted you to see it."

The chancellor moved to his desk, from which he pulled a leather notebook. This he handed to Paul, who opened it to find a single sheet on International Government stationery with Chancellor Baldwin Dengler's seal affixed and a line on which the reader could sign. It read:

> By order of the Supreme Council of the International Government of Peace, headquartered in Bern, Switzerland, and dated this Monday, January 21, 38 P.3, it is resolved that within sixty days, or by March 22, 38 P.3, every citizen of the world community who has reached the age of eighteen years shall be required to stipulate by signing this document and having it on public record, thus:
>
> "Under penalty of life imprisonment, or death in extreme cases, I hereby pledge that I personally support the global ban on the practice of religion. I am not affiliated with any group, organization, or individual who acts in opposition to the ruling of the international government on this matter, and I stipulate that if I become aware of any citizen violating this ordinance, I am under obligation to report the same, failure to do so resulting in the same punishment."

Paul had trained himself to look collected at times like this. What in the world was he going to do when required to sign? Had he just been given the term limit on his own role with the NPO? Was there a chance government personnel were exempt? At the time of his hiring years before he had vowed—orally and in writing—his allegiance to the tenets of the government.

"I'm, uh, not versed in legal wording and the like," Paul said.

"And I am not asking for that kind of input, Doctor. I just wanted you to know of our progress and assure you we were not working on something of this magnitude behind your back."

No, we wouldn't want to work behind each other's backs.

"I trust," Dengler continued, "you agree that this puts on notice the subversives who threaten to overthrow our way of life. Silences them, really. I am not so naive as to believe it will bring a man like Styr Magnor to his senses. The point is that it gives us the freedom to round up anyone who cannot sign in good conscience, and in this way we break the back of the rebel resistance."

"It does have the capacity to effect that," Paul said.

"You are less than enthusiastic."

"I'm just wondering about the logistics, the manpower and bureaucracy required to accomplish this within the time constraint."

Dengler offered a closemouthed grin. "This government is efficient above all else."

"May I take a copy?"

"A souvenir? Certainly. I'll even sign it. I would ask that you not share it with anyone outside the government before the announcement."

Paul nodded.

"In fact," Dengler added, signing with a flourish, "this scene will be repeated a week from today as I become the first to officially sign. It is redundant to those of us within the government, but I will ask that no one be exempt. It should be a powerful statement of unity and loyalty; do you not agree?"

"It certainly will."

As Paul was leaving, Dengler put an arm around his shoulder. "I would like you to know my personal hotline number, Doctor, should something absolutely crucial come up that demands my attention. Can you commit it to memory?"

. . .

Later, on the plane, it was Paul's turn to ask if he had phoned too late.

"I won't sleep tonight anyway," Straight said. "Paul, I am so sorry, and none too happy, to have been left out of the loop about the Bern underground. It may have been too hot for you to make contact without detection there anyway, but you have to know I had no idea . . ."

"Of course I knew. But you can imagine my surprise and chagrin when I learned of it. You've heard, I suppose, of the disposition of Gregor by now."

"Of his murder? Sure. Needless to say, that's a message from—"

"His *murder*?"

"You didn't know?"

"No! I was told—"

"You were told he had been sentenced to a prison term, right?"

"Right."

"The party line is that he tried to overtake the guard on his way to prison, and they were forced to shoot him."

"Does Dengler know?"

"Paul. There's no question Dengler ordered it."

Paul couldn't speak.

"You still there?" Straight said.

"Yeah. How much does Dengler know?"

"You mean about you? We think he's still in the dark, but he may suspect. Thus this murder."

"Does he know Gregor made contact, was in my room? Word I got was that they had caught him in the hall on my floor and nothing was said about my knowing he was there."

"All I know is that you should not ask Dengler about it or he could trace you to the underground. The government informed only his family, so it would expose you if you proved you knew that much."

"I'm as good as dead, Straight. They've got me in their cross-hairs. Wait till you see the document Dengler gave me this morning."

"Document?"

"You mean I know something you don't?"

"What is it?"

"Only the death knell for the underground if it's carried out. Let's not risk talking about that now. How's Jae?"

"Curious, that's how she is."

"The new me is boggling her mind?"

"For sure. She's seriously considering her father's invitation to go and work for him in Washington."

"I can't let that happen, Straight. But it has to be her decision. If Ranold suggested it because he suspects me, it can't appear I forbade it."

"I told her I didn't like the idea, Paul, but I don't think I made much of an impression. Why would I have a problem with it?"

"What'd you tell her?"

"Just that it didn't seem the right thing to do. I told her I needed to think about it."

"Good. Get back to her in due time and tell her you really have a bad feeling about it. Can you find her work, volunteering in the hospital or something, anything to keep her occupied?"

"Hadn't thought of that, but I can always use help. I don't get the impression she wants to do this for money."

"No. She's just going stir-crazy with me gone. And her family is applying pressure."

"Well," Straight said, "I'll see if I can apply some of my own, but I have to tell you, Paul, her bags are already mentally packed."

7

THE LEARJET XXX MADE the 425 miles from Bern to Rome in half an hour, most of that on takeoff and landing. After talking with Straight, Paul barely had time to even analyze the overwhelming sadness that overtook him. He had not known Gregor, of course, and had developed zero respect for anything about the young man except his faith. He would certainly have been mostly a liability in covert operations. And yet the death of a brother was always a loss, and Gregor *had* been trying to help. Paul could only imagine the grief and sense of helplessness of his family.

As the luxurious craft began its descent, Paul pulled from his bag one of the minidiscs containing the Gospels. Knowing he would have little room in his schedule or his luggage, he had left the rest of the New Testament home. With his regular listening over the last several months, he had developed a memory for key

passages. He quickly found Matthew 5:11, the reference he had
been reminded of with the death of Gregor. It quoted Jesus:

> *God blesses you when you are mocked and persecuted and lied
> about because you are my followers. Be happy about it! Be very
> glad! For a great reward awaits you in heaven. And remember,
> the ancient prophets were persecuted, too.*

But what followed puzzled Paul.

> *You are the salt of the earth. But what good is salt if it has lost
> its flavor? Can you make it useful again? It will be thrown out
> and trampled underfoot as worthless. You are the light of the
> world—like a city on a mountain, glowing in the night for all
> to see. Don't hide your light under a basket! Instead, put it on a
> stand and let it shine for all. In the same way, let your good
> deeds shine out for all to see, so that everyone will praise your
> heavenly Father.*

What could that possibly mean in the context of the world in
which Paul found himself? Soon he would be forced to declare
himself, and he didn't anticipate anyone but those who were already his brothers and sisters lauding him for "letting his light
shine" for all to see. He would be stripped of his job, his freedom, likely his life. The only ones praising the heavenly Father
for that would be those who shared Paul's faith.

• • •

The Lear pilot had steered clear of Leonardo da Vinci Airport in
Fiumicino, southwest of Rome, and landed instead at Ciampino
Airport to the southeast. Paul was met on the tarmac by a navy-
suited woman of about sixty, who introduced herself as Alonza

Marcello, Rome's chief of detectives. Her salt-and-pepper hair was short and feminine, but her grip was strong and tight. "I hate weak handshakes," she said, "especially from women, but men have no excuse." Trim and fit, tall and thin, she led Paul to a limousine where they both sat in the back.

Ms. Marcello's not unkind brusqueness was almost funny. "Welcome to Rome, good to have you, hope you had a good flight, and hope you don't mind working alone."

"I don't mind," Paul said. "In fact, I prefer it."

"Good, because it shouldn't come as a surprise that we have had so-called experts before—even some from the USSA—but almost every one sent to us by International has proved a royal pain."

Paul might have smiled had it not been for all that was coursing through his brain. "I'm only here to help."

Alonza flashed a knowing look. "You'll excuse my saying I've heard that before. Of course, in your case, since I assume you don't claim expertise in crime-scene investigation—"

"I don't."

"—which happens to be my and my team's specialty, you're here to give us some insight into the mad bombers."

"I'll do my best. Uh, did you say *bombers*, plural?"

"That's what our evidence shows so far, as you will see. Of course, our focus is on the man behind the bombs, not the detonators themselves. Religious extremist, that much is clear."

"It appears so."

She cocked her head and gave him a look. "*Clear* and *appears* - don't jibe, Dr. Stepola. The man's message was unequivocal."

"Perhaps too much so? I should think your team might have considered that."

"I'll let you ask them. The ones not canvassing witnesses are at the Bio Park, trying not to contaminate the crime scene. We'll marshal them for a session with you. I don't mind telling you, they resent the intrusion. I have warned them they must behave, but I can't make them like you."

"I can only be my normal charming self. I'm not here to get in their way or tell them how to do their jobs. If a religious faction is behind this, I might be able to shed some light."

He had lost her attention. "*Cinecitta*," she said, pointing out the window. "Cinema City. If we drove due west, you might be interested in the Catacombs. Sealed off now, of course, but still somewhat a tourist attraction. Certainly you know that Vatican City is long gone. A brief memorial to the history of the place lasted only a few months before the ban on religion. You can imagine how long it took to effect that in a country like this. The former Vatican is a community park now. The Sistine Chapel, which some believed was miraculously spared, is now a shopping bazaar. Have you heard the new name?"

"Tell me."

"The Sister's Château."

"That's awful."

"Rome, as you know as well as I, used to be *such* a religious city. When I was a child it seemed there was a church on every corner. Those became landmarks for a short time, then they were converted into retail shops, restaurants, malls. It's sad, really."

Paul studied her. "How so?"

"Just a part of my personal history, that's all."

"You had a religious background? I ask only because—"

"It's your area, of course. Yes, I was raised Catholic. I grew up in central Rome, which we are approaching now. Not far off the New Appian Way sat the Church of St. Mary Major, which is now a Harrods of London." She shrugged. "I buy clothes where once I endured catechism classes, accessories where once I made my confessions."

"You were devout? You believed?"

"Not really. When I was a child, yes. You take on the beliefs of your parents. In my case, my mother. Church every day for her."

"You don't say."

"My father enjoyed the Communion alone, if you get my meaning. It was not hard for him to give up what little faith he had. He didn't have to give up the wine, after all. For my mother, more of an ordeal, but she managed."

"It must have been difficult for her. Religious conviction runs deep."

They hit traffic and the limo crawled.

"She was a smart, pragmatic woman," Chief Marcello said. "The war seemed to suck the life from her. She feared God had abandoned the world, and it wasn't long before that brewed into her wondering if there was a God at all. Eventually she decided there was not. She still crossed herself in private, but the religious icons, the prayers, the rosaries, they all disappeared over time. Mother is gone now, but she died a patriotic atheist."

"You must find that a little sad too, no?"

"No. I became disillusioned with the church at about the onset of adolescence. It seemed to have nothing to say about what was happening to my mind and body. The war soon followed. I didn't agree at first that all war had originated with religion, but I was glad for a reason not to have to suffer through interminable ceremony and teaching I didn't really accept anyway. I was a quick and willing convert to the worship of the state and the self."

"You never missed God?"

She shook her head. "God was not personal to me. Always up there, out there, somewhere, hanging on a cross or—I imagined—staring disapprovingly at me from beyond the clouds."

She fell silent until the limo reached central Rome, and then she began pointing out the former religious sites. "That used to be the Church of St. John Lateran. We'll pass the Arch of Constantine near the Colosseum. Your studies must have included Constantine."

"Oh, of course. First Christian emperor of Rome. Gave Christians freedom to practice their religion. Ironically, the arch was a pagan monument."

Alonza furrowed her brow. "What's the old phrase? What goes around comes around? It's now called the Arch of Humanism."

"If I may be frank," Paul said, "I expected the city to be brighter. The sun is high in the sky, and yet it seems so dark."

"That is the soot of the centuries on the buildings. It has its own charm."

"Not to me," Paul said, which he would have kept to himself had she herself not been so direct. On the other hand, he didn't want to disparage a city the minute he stepped in it, as he had with Gregor in Bern. "What's with all the porn?"

Ms. Marcello leaned to look out the window as if seeing for the first time the gigantic holographs and billboards depicting all manner of hard-core activity. "Oh, that," she said. "I hardly notice anymore."

"It makes Rome seem so decadent," Paul said.

"According to what standard?" she said with such incredulity that Paul had no response.

But as they proceeded deeper into central Rome the streets became narrower, the blackened buildings taller, and the limo a claustrophobic amusement-park car in a haunted-house ride. Soon every place of business reminded Paul of Amsterdam, live nudes in the windows, offering every kind of fleshly heterosexual and homosexual pleasure to all. Bars, nightclubs, strip joints, houses of prostitution, tattoo parlors, drug-shooting galleries—everything was legal.

Paul wanted to ask the chief if this made her proud of her city, if she preferred this to the prewar days when churches dotted the landscape. But she seemed wholly unruffled by it. This was life in Rome now, and as she implied, there was no standard to which it could be compared. What was the problem with people being exposed to anything they wanted? They didn't have to buy or indulge. These were merely options for an enlightened populace that had long since cast off any shackles of propriety—which, after all, was only in the eye of the beholder anyway.

As they passed through the Arch of Humanism and came upon the Colosseum—fully restored thirty-three years in advance of its two-thousandth anniversary—they eventually drew within sight of the ruins of the Domus Aurea. "The palace of Nero, you know," Chief Marcello said. "*Domus Aurea* is Italian for 'golden house.' The ruins are massive and mostly underground. That's the Column of Marcus Aurelius. It's been there almost two thousand years."

"What happened to the top?" Paul said. "In grad school we learned a statue of St. Paul stood atop it since the sixteenth century."

"That's been gone since just after the war," she said, "thirty-five years or so. It was big news at the time. Former soldiers who were to become pacifists were allowed to shoot at the statue until it crumbled. When it finally fell, spectators had miscalculated the direction, and it was a wonder no one was killed. Several were injured by little bits of St. Paul smashing onto the pavement and flying through the gawking crowd, as if he were protesting this turning against all he stood for."

When finally they reached the expansive and lavish Villa

Borghese in the northern part of central Rome, Paul was drawn to its beauty.

The driver parked, and as they disembarked, Ms. Marcello told Paul, "Villas like this used to be the estates of the wealthy, but they were turned into public parks. This one has been open to the public for nearly two hundred and fifty years." She gestured grandly, pointing to an area cordoned off by police tape. "That is where much of the bomb damage was done. Almost every Renaissance master had a work in the Borghese collection. This is a loss that can never be replaced.

"The rest of the damage was at the Bio Park, which was once a typical zoo. It became an interactive center where the public could get closer to the animals and where the experts could study endangered species. Again, devastating."

"Not to mention the loss of human life," Paul said.

"Of course."

Paul had not noticed Chief Marcello communicating with anyone else, but by the time they reached a one-story stone building that had somehow escaped damage between the two bomb sites, some eighty or so plainclothes detectives were taking an espresso break, and everyone, it seemed, was enjoying some sort of pastry. The noise abated quickly as she strode to a small lectern and microphone. Paul decided against making a joke about American cops and donuts, worried it would be lost on this audience.

"Ladies and gentlemen," Alonza Marcello said, "please welcome from the United Seven States of America, with the blessing of International Government Chancellor Baldwin Dengler, Dr. Paul Stepola."

She paused, Paul thought, as if hoping or even expecting polite applause. Such was not forthcoming. Her prediction that these people might not welcome an outsider was on the nose. Mostly they stared and continued to eat and drink.

"I remind you that Dr. Stepola is here solely in his capacity as a consultant and adviser, specializing in the religious background of terrorists such as the one taking credit for this attack. Dr. Stepola."

"Greetings and thank you," Paul said. "First allow me to thank you for your service to the global community and of course to your own. This has to be difficult, painstaking, and unsavory work, and I applaud your efforts."

Still nothing.

"I wish I were an expert in an area that would aid you in crime-scene investigation, but I am not. My specialty is religious studies, and as the responsibility for this attack has been claimed by a man who uses religious rhetoric, that puts it in my bailiwick.

"Perhaps you have heard that the real Styr Magnor, if he exists, has not yet been identified. I am happy to tell you that under Chancellor Dengler's auspices, a vast canvassing force is carefully eliminating men of the same name who have alibis. We hope to report soon on the locating of this criminal.

"Meanwhile, I will be following leads and staying out of your way. But if there is anything I can help with in the way of information, I am happy to answer any questions."

"That's it?" a man called out. "You came all this way to open the floor for questions?"

"Yes, sir. If I knew more, I would share it."

"We probably know more than you do!"

"There is little question of that," Paul said. "But if I studied the crime scene, I wouldn't be able to interpret it the way you can anyway. If you have no questions for me, perhaps I should ask what you have found so far."

"We *do* have questions for you, Sherlock!"

Paul laughed with the rest, but he'd rather have left the lectern. He didn't need or want this any more than they did. Imagine if they knew he was also there to connect with the underground, and not for the purpose of arresting believers. Paul had to play this game, had to establish himself as part of the team. Then they would leave him alone and he would be free to make the contacts he really needed.

A scruffy-looking, older detective stood, his pastry and coffee in one hand, his other raised. "What should we be looking for then, sir, given that this was likely the act of a religious madman? So far we've been sifting through animal body parts and human remains. It's ugly business, and we know no more today than the day it happened. Two explosives, both from suicide bombers, were triggered almost simultaneously."

Before Paul could answer, a younger man stood. "Yes, we're not finding religious artifacts." That brought another wave of laughter, as if they imagined an incendiary full of crucifixes or Stars of David.

"Well, if you'll indulge me," Paul said, "despite the claims of this Styr Magnor character that he is a brother of underground Christians in America, experience tells me such people are averse enough to suicide that they would not likely have carried it out in this manner."

"*Because* of their religious beliefs?"

"In my opinion," Paul said. "Many Christian believers, Catholics for instance, consider suicide a mortal sin."

He noticed nodding and heard murmurs of assent, as if they might have actually heard something constructive.

Someone called out, "So if it *was* some crazy religious faction, it would more likely be Muslims, who think they're going to earn seventy virgins in the afterlife?"

A few chuckled. A man shouted, "Or one seventy-year-old virgin!"

With that the chief took one step forward and the place quieted. Paul was impressed at her silent control. "Any more questions?" he said.

When there were none, she took the microphone. "Thank you, Doctor," and with that came a smattering of applause. "I will get your number so my division commanders and I can keep in touch if we think of other things you may be able to help with."

Paul felt the way the original questioner had, wondering if he had really come all this way for only that. But privately he couldn't have been happier. He would help as he could, but it appeared he would have the time and space he needed to do what he really wanted.

The chief said her good-byes and had her driver take Paul to the luxurious Venito Hotel, equidistant from the University of Rome, the National Library, and the Termini Station. "An unmarked staff car has been issued you for the duration, Doctor," she said. "Please let me know if there is anything you need, and I'll be in touch, as I said, if we have more questions."

Paul would use the staff car only, naturally, for his NPO work. If he was being watched, International would know that car. He would do on foot what he had to do regarding the underground, and if he needed to rent a car, he could do it under one of his many aliases.

By the time he checked in, it was two in the afternoon, making it 7 a.m. in Chicago. Paul would give Jae time to get the kids up and off to school before he called her. He spent the next two hours cruising the city, getting the lay of the land. Staying within an approximate four-square-mile box and crossing and recrossing the Tiber River several times, Paul was struck anew at the depressing state in which he found what many had described as one of the most beautiful cities in the world. Would Paris, which also competed in people's minds and hearts for that title, look as debauched?

He called Straight, who sounded groggy but insisted it was okay to talk. "We're getting word to your contact that you're in the city," the older man said. "I'll get back to you with instructions. Tell me something about his name that assures me you remember it."

Enzo Fabrizio. "His first and last names start with consecutive letters of the alphabet."

"Too early in the morning for me to ruminate on that. Hmm. Yeah, I guess they do. Very good, grasshopper."

After having covered most of central Rome, Paul found himself parked in an alley just south of the Baths of Caracalla. "You ever been here, Straight?"

"Rome, yes, years ago on a U of C faculty-and-student exchange trip. Those Baths still just a tourist spot?"

"Looks like it. I'm not going in. They appear to have been refurbished, but, man, this whole city is depressing, depraved."

"*Degenerate* is the word you're looking for, Paul."

"Exactly."

"The USSA isn't much better. You're just used to it. Remember your reaction to Vegas and L.A."

"God needs to do something here, Straight."

"He *is* doing something there, friend. You."

Paul checked his mirrors. He had no feeling of being followed or watched, but perhaps NPO International was just that good. Part of him wanted to believe that everyone at every level in every country still saw him as a top, crack, loyal agent. But he wasn't that naive. Even if they weren't onto him yet, he had to live as if they were.

He told Straight, "I'm beginning to see why New Testament believers were always sent out at least in twos."

"Lonely already?"

"Missing Jae, sure, but there's an isolation here I feel more keenly even than when I'm living my big lie in the bureau. I could sure use a Barnabas."

"Well, if you're thinking about me, I could never keep up with you."

"Ah, you could work me into the ground and you know it."

"Jes' trying to be humble, Paul."

Paul sighed, not wanting to get off the phone but sensing Straight needed to get going. "Tell you one thing: I'm getting a lesson in what's happening to me here."

"How's that?"

"This is the kind of place that would have turned my head not that long ago."

"You'd be tempted, you mean?"

"Big-time."

"And now?"

"This all disgusts me. I mean, I can tell I'm different at home. Even Jae sees it. But I didn't know how I'd do in this situation—away, alone, homesick. That would have justified a lot of mischief in the past."

"Don't get overconfident now, Paul. You're still a man."

"A lustful male, you mean."

"That's what I mean."

"Pray for me."

"Constantly."

On his way back to the hotel—Paul wanted to talk to Jae from there—he wondered where the Rome underground might be located. There seemed myriad possibilities. Every ancient site, especially the ruins, had underground features. Not all could be open to tourists. If he were leading a rebel faction here, he would look into appropriating some long-closed-off and forgotten belowground location, perhaps right in the middle of the city.

Maybe he was way off and they were in various locations in the suburban areas, as they had been in Los Angeles. He guessed he'd find out soon enough.

ON THE PHONE BACK AT THE VENITO, Paul found Jae un-
usually chipper. "I can't help it, Paul. I miss you terribly and it's
hard on the kids, but I'm taking action and making decisions,
and we're going to be all right."

"That's great, babe. I miss you too, but I'm keeping busy." He
told her of the initial meeting with the Rome detectives. "The
site is ghastly. I don't envy them that work. So, you're keeping
busy?"

"I soon will be. Paul, I'm accepting a job with Dad, and the
kids and I are moving to Washington until you get back."

Paul closed his eyes. That's all he needed.

"Paul? Are you there?"

"I'm here."

"You don't sound happy."

"Can't say that I am."

"Oh, Paul, I need this. It'll be something to do all day, and it'll be in my area of expertise. Mom will help with the kids, and I'll be able to get to know Aryana better—you know, Berlitz's wife."

"I know. But uprooting the kids? Why not just find something to do in Chicago?"

"I just told you. My family being there makes the difference. That's the real draw."

"What if I finish up quickly over here? You're going to have just started with your dad and then leave him in the lurch."

"He understands that's a possibility. Frankly, I hope that's what happens."

"That's nice to hear."

"Well, there's no question, Paul. Ideally I want you home with us in Chicago, but this is clearly the next best thing."

It wasn't so clear to Paul. While Jae had—to his knowledge—never been trained in espionage, he couldn't know for certain that she herself wasn't already onto him. He didn't want to be paranoid, but he had to keep an edge, maintain his equilibrium. Her plan to work not just in Washington but also with the NPO and with Ranold could be part of an elaborate scheme for them to set him up. Maybe they had enough on him already to call him in and put him on trial for treason. But if they played him, he might lead them to a wide circle of the underground. Paul decided he'd rather die than take any part of the underground church down with him.

Again, the tightrope. If he tried to forbid Jae, she would defy him, no question. Plus he would look terrible. If they only suspected him at this point, such an action would tip the scales against him. "No way I can talk you out of this, Jae?"

"I told the kids' teachers this morning, Paul. They'll finish out the week and we'll leave after school Friday. I start work

Monday the twenty-first. I so want you to be happy for me and proud of me."

Paul couldn't bring himself to say either. January 21 was announcement day, when Chancellor Baldwin Dengler would go on worldwide television and reveal the plan to require a signed expression of loyalty to the international government and its long-standing policy against religion.

• • •

Jae had been through a lot with Paul and their rocky marriage, but somehow she had endured with her optimism intact. The rest of the day proved a downer for her because of his response to her plan. She had been disappointed enough at Straight's initial reaction, but she really wanted Paul to be behind her. Deep inside she believed that if she remained upbeat on the phone with him, once they were in Washington, he'd come around.

Washington. It seemed a respite from her troubled mind. Was it what she was listening to or the frustration of feeling that eyes were on her? The Mother Bear in her wanted to emerge when she worried that if she was being watched, so were the children. Jae had seen no one and nothing concrete . . . yet. She did not recall this paranoia during Paul's other trips. She was no expert, and Paul had long since assured her that if professionals were trailing her, she would not know it.

When Straight called later in the day, suggesting she volunteer at PSL Hospital with him, she believed Paul had put him up to it in a last-ditch effort to thwart her plan. Straight was even more dead set against her going, telling her he had a very bad feeling about it. On the other hand, he accepted her invitation to dinner on Thursday night and offered to help get her and the kids ready for the trip.

Jae had never read or heard one word from the Bible. Her only exposure to what Christianity was about was from brief conversations with Paul when he was trying to explain what he was learning about the enemy. But he hadn't said much about that in a while, though she knew he was still frequently listening to the New Testament. She could also tell from the discs and the documentation that came with them that he had taken with him the first four books of the New Testament and that they were called the Gospels.

That afternoon Jae slipped into the player the first of the minidiscs Paul had left and listened to the first chapter of The Acts of the Apostles.

Dear friend who loves God:

The opening salutation told her this was a letter, but what a quaint phrase—"friend who loves God." Not only did she not love God, but she had also been taught—and had always accepted—that there was no God. She had expected this experience to be strange, but she had not anticipated this. So these people, the writer, and apparently whoever was reading his letter, believed in God. And loved Him.

In my first book I told you about everything Jesus began to do and teach until the day he ascended to heaven after giving his chosen apostles further instructions from the Holy Spirit.

During the forty days after his crucifixion, he appeared to the apostles from time to time and proved to them in many ways that he was actually alive. On these occasions he talked to them about the Kingdom of God.

In one of these meetings as he was eating a meal with them, he told them, "Do not leave Jerusalem until the Father

*sends you what he promised. Remember, I have told you about
this before. John baptized with water, but in just a few days
you will be baptized with the Holy Spirit."*

The Holy Spirit? She had heard the term, also the term *Holy
Ghost.* Both sounded more than bizarre. This crucifixion and resurrection had been referred to in the letter from Paul's father.
This must be a common theme among believers in God: letters
expressing their views.

Jae thought this was one of the strangest things she had ever
heard. The only thing she could relate to it was the classic
A Christmas Carol by Charles Dickens, in which ghosts or spirits
of Christmas appeared to Scrooge. She found the phrase "baptized with the Holy Spirit" so off-putting that she was tempted to
turn off the machine. She decided to give it a few more minutes,
mostly to see if it grew even weirder.

*And another time when he appeared to them, they asked him,
"Lord, are you going to free Israel (from Rome) now and re-
store us as an independent nation?"*

The mention of Rome stopped her. How ironic that Paul was
there even now. How old was this text? How different was Rome
today from the Rome of the New Testament?

*"The Father sets those dates," he replied, "and they are not for
you to know. But when the Holy Spirit has come upon you,
you will receive power and will tell people about me
everywhere—in Jerusalem, throughout Judea, in Samaria,
and to the ends of the earth."*

*It was not long after he said this that he was taken up into
the sky while they were watching, and he disappeared into a*

cloud. As they were straining their eyes to see him, two white-robed men suddenly stood there among them. They said, "Men of Galilee, why are you standing here staring at the sky? Jesus has been taken away from you into heaven. And someday, just as you saw him go, he will return!"

All right, that was more than plenty. She shut it off. Jesus talked about His own death and resurrection then floated up to heaven? Men in white, maybe white coats, said he would return? Now she was reminded of the old movie *It's a Wonderful Life*. Now, come on, that had an angel in it and conversations in heaven, but everybody—and she meant everybody—knew that was a fairy tale, a parable.

Did people actually buy this stuff, believe it? Paul had told her that the antigovernment forces believed Jesus was coming back soon, as prophesied in the New Testament. They really, truly believed this enough to risk their freedom and their lives to defy the International Government of Peace. It was as if Jae were suffering sensory overload. It was way too much to deal with. She started packing.

Strangely, the words kept working on her. She shuddered. So peculiar. Why should ancient texts bother her so? Jae turned the machine back on. Words couldn't hurt her.

According to the disk, after Jesus left, his followers went back to Jerusalem and had a prayer meeting that went on for several days. *Several days?* The term *prayer meeting* was self-explanatory, Jae thought. They met to pray for days? Surely that was an exaggeration.

During this time, on a day when about 120 believers were present, Peter stood up . . .

A hundred and twenty people? Jae shook her head, talking

to herself. *This is told as if it actually happened!* Peter talked about a traitor who had died, and then he suggested that he be replaced.

> *"So now we must choose another man to take Judas's place. It must be someone who has been with us all the time that we were with the Lord Jesus—from the time he was baptized by John until the day he was taken from us into heaven. Whoever is chosen will join us as a witness of Jesus' resurrection."*
>
> *So they nominated two men: Joseph called Barsabbas (also known as Justus) and Matthias. Then they all prayed for the right man to be chosen. "O Lord," they said, "you know every heart. Show us which of these men you have chosen as an apostle to replace Judas the traitor in this ministry, for he has deserted us and gone where he belongs." Then they cast lots, and in this way Matthias was chosen and became an apostle with the other eleven.*

This Matthias, Jae decided, must be the main character of the rest of this part of the story. He replaced the bad guy, because . . . ? Maybe she would listen to a little more as she worked, just to see if the story got better or there was some kind of character development.

● ● ●

Paul took a call from Alonza Marcello just before dark. "I thought it went well today," she said.

"Did you? I felt a little chilly."

"Don't say I didn't warn you. Listen, one of our men found graffiti in a women's toilet just outside the range of the damage of the first bomb. I'll read it to you, but I imagine you'll want to see it."

"Yes, or a picture of it."

"We have that. If that will be sufficient, I'll have it transmitted as we speak. It was written in English on a stall door in lipstick. Here's what it says:

"*Long live the USSA. Long live the City of Angels. Long live Jonah. European resistance arise.*"

"Mm-hmm," Paul said.

"Mean anything at first blush?"

"Possibly. I'll study the image. It's difficult to say whether this group is really connected, but all four references refer to underground religious groups. The USSA is where most of the underground activity has heretofore originated. The City of Angels—"

"Is Los Angeles, of course."

"Right, and you understand the Jonah reference?"

"Vaguely," she said. "Wasn't that your case?"

"Yes."

"In Reno or some such?"

"Las Vegas." Paul didn't want to say too much. His superiors and the press and public believed the Jonah character was just another underground Christian. Paul scored major credibility points for single-handedly bringing him down, and the case helped establish Paul as *the* go-to guy within the NPO. Of course, the real person behind the Jonah pseudonym was as far from a true believer as a man could be. That shed some real light on Styr Magnor, if his suicide bombers were instructed to associate their acts in any way with Jonah's. It was to Paul's advantage if the public painted all underground rebels with the same brush. As long as he knew the nuances, it would help his cause.

"Jonah was the leader of that Christian underground, wasn't he?" Chief Marcello said.

"Right. Now what about the encouragement to the European resistance? Do you know anything about that, ma'am?"

"There's no real resistance, especially here. Of course, there is evidence of some pockets, but the worst they've done is circulate printed material trying to win converts. These show up in public places, but so far no one has been caught putting them there, and frankly, it's insignificant enough that we haven't made it a priority."

"Probably wise," Paul said. The image had come through on his computer. "You might want to have a handwriting expert take a look at this. It's printed, but there could be a hint at a nationality here."

"I had that same thought," Alonza said. "Something about it just didn't look Italian."

"Were you guessing American?" Paul said.

"Seemed logical."

"Can't blame you, but I'd wager we're not going to find Styr Magnor in America."

"Because he says he's Norwegian?"

"Partly. I don't know. Just a gut feeling."

"You're known for that, Doctor. But isn't the northern middle west almost an enclave of Scandinavians in your country?"

"What used to be Minnesota? Yes."

"That's where I'd look."

"You may be onto something, Chief, but if you're right, Chancellor Dengler has a whole lot of people in the wrong place. I know you don't need to be reminded of this, but just to cover the bases, don't allow this to be leaked to the press. Once it's been publicized, we'll never know who the real Styr Magnor is."

• • •

The period between lunch and when the kids got home had proved the longest and loneliest stretch of Jae's day. But this day, despite her less-than-favorable interactions with both Paul and

Straight, she was motivated to stay busy. Jae believed in traveling light and was certain she could put everything she and the kids needed into one suitcase each. She was driving the seven hundred miles herself, and she planned to average just under a hundred miles an hour—to be safe and take into consideration the rush hour while trying to get through Chicago after school. She didn't want a car laden with heavy stuff.

Jae kept half an eye on the front picture window, again unnerved because it seemed that slightly more traffic passed than she was used to—or had been aware of. She shook her head and dismissed her fears. Had she really kept a subconscious tally of the number of cars on her street? How would she really know if there were more . . . even one more?

While she selected what the kids would take to Washington, Jae listened to another chapter of Acts:

On the day of Pentecost, seven weeks after Jesus' resurrection, the believers were meeting together in one place. Suddenly, there was a sound from heaven like the roaring of a mighty windstorm in the skies above them, and it filled the house where they were meeting. Then, what looked like flames or tongues of fire appeared and settled on each of them. And everyone present was filled with the Holy Spirit and began speaking in other languages, as the Holy Spirit gave them this ability.

There was that reference to Jesus' resurrection again. These people didn't consider this just something figurative. Jae would have to ask Paul if he thought the New Testament was supposed to be taken as a historical record. That didn't make it true, of course—she certainly didn't believe it—but if modern people bought into this with the same enthusiasm as those of that time apparently did, she could see why they would be so zealous.

The talk about tongues of fire made Jae want to turn off the machine again. How could anybody believe this stuff? Yet each time she heard something strange and disconcerting like that, she was less shaken by it. She was going to hear this out. In some intriguing way it made her feel closer to Paul. They would have something to talk about; she could be a more vital part of his work. For a long time she had wondered why everyone was so upset about underground cells of nuts who still believed in the old ways. Were they essentially harmless, proven by the silliness they believed in? But hearing this persuaded her at least that there was a long history of people who were into the same thing, and this, plainly, was the story of how it all began. But speaking in other languages? *Oh, please! What in the world is that all about? The Holy Spirit, this ghost of Christmas past, gave people the ability to speak in other languages? They were probably just drunk.*

> *Godly Jews from many nations were living in Jerusalem at that time. When they heard this sound, they came running to see what it was all about, and they were bewildered to hear their own languages being spoken by the believers. . . .*
>
> *They stood there amazed and perplexed. "What can this mean?" they asked each other. But others in the crowd were mocking. "They're drunk, that's all!" they said.*

Jae started at this, feeling peculiarly affirmed that she was not alone in her conclusion.

> *Then Peter stepped forward with the eleven other apostles and shouted to the crowd, "Listen carefully, all of you, fellow Jews*

and residents of Jerusalem! Make no mistake about this. Some of you are saying these people are drunk. It isn't true! It's much too early for that. People don't get drunk by nine o'clock in the morning. No, what you see this morning was predicted centuries ago by the prophet Joel:

'In the last days, God said, I will pour out my Spirit upon all people. Your sons and daughters will prophesy, your young men will see visions, and your old men will dream dreams.

'In those days I will pour out my Spirit upon all my servants, men and women alike, and they will prophesy.

'And I will cause wonders in the heavens above and signs on the earth below—blood and fire and clouds of smoke.

'The sun will be turned into darkness, and the moon will turn bloodred, before that great and glorious day of the Lord arrives.

'And anyone who calls on the name of the Lord will be saved.'"

Jae had heard Paul mention something about how the zealot underground put a lot of stock in ancient prophecies, but again, that only made her think less of them. With the death of religion and spirituality and the onset of a healthy, new brand of humanism, no thinking person really believed in Nostradamus or fortune-telling or even horoscopes anymore. They were fun and people dabbled in them, and sure, money was to be made by charlatans at the hands of the gullible.

But couldn't these prophecies of the Bible be debunked? Weren't they vague and couldn't they mean anything a person could read into them, much like those of Nostradamus? Jae had to admit that she didn't know. Here were references to the prophecies and even the recitation of one of the them. If they were *not* credible, at least to the writers and readers of the New Testament, how had the Bible lasted for so long? Would it not have been cast aside as fanciful thinking long before World War III?

The best part of this, Jae decided, was that something about it reminded her of her good days in college and grad school. She had not been the type of student who hangs on for dear life. She would grab onto a subject, especially one like this—something not in her area of expertise—and not let go until she had thoroughly researched it.

Jae had to chuckle at herself. No way was she going to all of a sudden become a New Testament buff, the way her father was a Civil War aficionado. Puzzling and crazy as listening to this was, it was sort of fun. When was the last time she had been exposed to something so wholly outside her realm of experience, not to mention her comfort zone?

People of Israel, listen! God publicly endorsed Jesus of Nazareth by doing wonderful miracles, wonders, and signs through him, as you well know. But you followed God's prearranged plan. With the help of lawless Gentiles, you nailed him to the cross and murdered him. However, God released him from the horrors of death and raised him back to life again, for death could not keep him in its grip.

This must have been a known, historical event, Jae decided. She had quit packing and was just sitting and listening now.

King David said this about him: "I know the Lord is always with me. I will not be shaken, for he is right beside me.

"No wonder my heart is filled with joy, and my mouth shouts his praises! My body rests in hope.

"For you will not leave my soul among the dead or allow your Holy One to rot in the grave.

"You have shown me the way of life, and you will give me wonderful joy in your presence."

King David? Jae didn't know much about the Bible, but she knew David was not a contemporary of Jesus. He had died long before the New Testament was written, hadn't he?

David was looking into the future and predicting the Messiah's resurrection. He was saying that the Messiah would not be left among the dead and that his body would not rot in the grave. This prophecy was speaking of Jesus, whom God raised from the dead, and we all are witnesses of this.

We? Who's we? The apostles saw Jesus after His death?

Now he sits on the throne of highest honor in heaven, at God's right hand. And the Father, as he had promised, gave him the Holy Spirit to pour out upon us, just as you see and hear today.

So Jesus sent the Holy Spirit. Jae was still in the dark, but certain things were coming together. Jae found herself saying with the people who heard Peter, "What should we do?"

Peter replied, "Each of you must turn from your sins and turn to God, and be baptized in the name of Jesus Christ for the forgiveness of your sins. Then you will receive the gift of the Holy Spirit. This promise is to you and to your children, and even to the Gentiles—all who have been called by the Lord our God." Then Peter continued preaching for a long time, strongly urging all his listeners, "Save yourselves from this generation that has gone astray!"

That's what Paul Stepola Sr. had been talking about. That's what he had done. And he wanted Paul Jr. to do the same. Paul had to have seen that letter. What did he think? How had he responded to it? What would he do if he knew Jae was aware of it? A wave of guilt washed over her, but she was in too deep. If she ever revealed to Paul that she had the letter, it would be on her own terms and in her own time.

Those who believed what Peter said were baptized and added to the church—about three thousand in all. They joined with the other believers and devoted themselves to the apostles' teaching and fellowship, sharing in the Lord's Supper and in prayer. A deep sense of awe came over them all, and the apostles performed many miraculous signs and wonders.

They must have been as confused as I am, Jae decided. *Now if I could only see some miracle!* Paul said the believers in Los Angeles claimed the drought was a miracle. Was it possible? The underground had survived, maybe even flourished. But was that God's idea of a miracle? Something that hurt and killed so many people?

And all the believers met together constantly and shared everything they had. They sold their possessions and shared the proceeds with those in need. They worshiped together at the Temple each day, met in homes for the Lord's Supper, and shared their meals with great joy and generosity—all the while praising God and enjoying the goodwill of all the people. And each day the Lord added to their group those who were being saved.

Jae wondered if that had happened within the underground. They didn't enjoy anyone's "goodwill," not that she knew. Were they having any impact on the public at large? And if they were, who would risk their lives by admitting it?

Jae called Straight. "Can you talk?" she said.

"For a minute. What's up?"

"Do you know anything about the Bible?" she said, noticing a man on the other side of the street, striding as if he knew where he was going. He did not look toward her or even at the house, but she did not recognize him. *Stranger Danger?* She chuckled to herself. But it would be no laughing matter if he was still around when the kids got home.

Straight didn't respond at first and she wondered if he had heard her or if they had a bad connection.

"The Bible?"

"Yes, you know. Old Testament, New Testament."

"Know anything about it? I know Paul used the New Testament to bring himself up to speed on the thinking of—"

"Yeah, but do *you* know anything about it?"

"Like what?"

"Like Old Testament prophecies about the birth and death and resurrection of Jesus."

"Oh, boy."

"Don't worry, Straight. I won't get you in trouble if you do."

"Thanks."

"But I thought maybe when you were a professor, you know, you studied ancient texts or something."

He hesitated again. "Well, yes, I've had some exposure to such things. Why?"

Jae told him she had been listening to Paul's discs and how puzzling yet fascinating she found them. "I just have a lot of questions, that's all."

"Try me. What do you want to know?"

EAGER TO MAKE A FORAY into the Rome night, Paul was frustrated when he reached only Straight's answering device. When his friend finally called back, he said, "Paul, between babysitting you and Jae, I'm getting precious little of my own work done. Good thing I'm not on salary. I'd have been fired today."

"You were on with Jae?"

"Yeah, and know what? She's listening to your New Testament discs."

"Uh-oh."

"Seems innocent enough, honestly." Straight told him of Jae's curiosity about references in the New Testament to prophecies from the Old.

"I should have left the Gospels there for her. That's where she should start."

"God knows, Paul. And listen, when you're praying about this, remember what God Himself says about the Bible."

"I'm listening."

"In Isaiah 55:10 and 11 He says, 'The rain and snow come down from the heavens and stay on the ground to water the earth. They cause the grain to grow, producing seed for the farmer and bread for the hungry. It is the same with my word. I send it out, and it always produces fruit. It will accomplish all I want it to, and it will prosper everywhere I send it.'"

"But, Straight, Jae was raised as I was. It has to sound as strange to her as it did to me."

"You turned out all right."

"But look at all the complicators with Jae. Her father. My work."

"She's got more complications than you do?"

"Well, no, but look what I had to go through before I could see the light."

"Yeah, you're right, Paul. I think Jae is too much for God to deal with. Probably hopeless."

"All right, Straight."

"Paul, we do have a problem. Our guy there isn't sure he wants to risk seeing you."

"What? Why? I face as much risk as he does, if not more."

"Not in his mind. The Bern situation has swept the underground there. And a lot of the predrought tragedies of L.A. have too."

"So they deduce that where I go, trouble follows."

"That's hard to argue, Paul."

"Tell me about it. But c'mon, I've got to make contact. What do I have to do to break the logjam?"

"Abraham and his people are still working on Enzo. Apparently Enzo knew Gregor or at least knew of him. Thought highly of his contribution."

"Now wait a minute, Straight. I told you that story. I appreciated the young man and his commitment, even his bravado. But his contribution was not good and wasn't going to be. He was way too thoughtless and reckless. He came very near to exposing me. I feel terrible speaking of a martyr that way, but what does it say about Enzo if he admired a kid like that?"

"This is second- and thirdhand, Paul. I didn't say he admired him. I said he appreciated him and his commitment, and I'm telling you only what I've heard. They're hurting. There's division in the ranks over what this Styr Magnor has done. Some applaud the overt attacks. Others, naturally, say there's no way he's really one of us."

"Where do you stand, Straight?"

"With you, of course."

"You know where I stand on Magnor?"

"I know where you'd better be standing, Paul. He's not one of ours, and if he is, we ought to eliminate him ourselves."

"Wow, you feel strongly about this."

"Caught that, did you?" Straight said. "Tell me you're not thinking the same thing. You want a guy on our side who kills innocents? I don't. That's not of God. Even in L.A., God struck down the opposition. His own were spared. We lost brothers and sisters in the Bio Park there, and also in Paris and London."

"How many?"

"No one knows yet."

"Then why doesn't Fabrizio mourn them and cut me some slack? Does he seriously wonder if I'm for real?"

"You can't blame him for being careful."

"I don't blame him, Straight. But if he honestly thinks I'm a phony, that means I have the full backing of the International Government and the NPO to infiltrate the underground."

"Naturally."

Paul sat on the bed. "Honestly, Straight, I'd think more of the man—provided he truly believed that—if he agreed to meet with me tonight and put a bullet through my brain."

Straight sighed. "I know where you're coming from, Paul. But why don't we let Abraham try to calm him and—"

"I'm dead serious, Straight. The man has a chance to eliminate the most dangerous enemy he could ever have, so why doesn't he do it?"

Straight didn't answer, and Paul immediately realized that was what he loved so much about him. He had to know Paul was venting and that there's no reasoning with an angry man.

"You finished?" Straight said finally.

"Yeah, I think I am."

"Don't give up the ship. In my personal opinion, Enzo ought to meet with you, and the sooner the better. If we can still arrange it for tonight, you in?"

"'Course I'm in. I'll be waiting."

"And hey, Paul?"

"Yeah."

"I might have been followed home tonight."

"By?"

"Not sure. It was just a feeling."

"Well, if it was obvious enough that you knew, it's no one to be worried about."

• • •

By 10 p.m. Paul had despaired of anything developing that night. He turned off the lights and opened the drapes before the great picture window that looked out to the northwest. A heavy rain made the traffic slow, but millions of lights shone through the mist and made the City of Hills—which he knew to be dark and corrupt—hearken back to its legendary beauty. The way pedestrians rushed about, shoulders hunched and collars up, told Paul it was unseasonably cold.

To his far left, beyond and over the Termini Station, he could see the opera house. Scanning right he spotted the National Roman Museum. And to his far right he could make out the Piazzale Porta Pia and the National Library.

Not having to venture out into such weather was just fine with Paul, and he allowed the fatigue created by his schedule and exacerbated by the tension of his double life to wash over him. It invaded the back of his neck, the tops of his shoulders, and traveled down his spine. He put one foot forward and bent his knee, placing his palms high on the window and hanging his head.

The cool moisture on the glass confirmed the nastiness outside. And the tone sounded in his molar.

"Stepola."

"Straight. You ready?"

"You bet. For what?"

"Well, maybe not Fabrizio, at least initially."

"He's still scared of me?"

"Who isn't? C'mon, Paul. Put yourself in his shoes."

"I can't even put myself in his presence."

"Well, here's the first step. You know where Trevi Fountain is?"

"Saw it today. I can find it."

"Supposed to be within two miles west of your hotel, between the Pantheon and the Quirinal Palace. Be there at half past. Sit on the edge of the fountain with your back to it, facing east. They'll find you."

"Got it. Like a sitting duck. Who am I supposed to meet?"

"Two of Fabrizio's men. They're giving us only first names. A big, bald guy named Baldassare and a small, thin man with a limp. Calls himself Calvino. You much of a linguist, Paul?"

"What? No."

"Baldassare's the bald guy, making his name easy to remember, but Calvino means 'bald,' and he's not."

"You're a fount of useless information, Straight."

"Just here to serve."

"I'd better get going."

"Unarmed," Straight said.

"You serious?"

"Of course. And they're reserving the right to search you."

"And they'll be unarmed too?"

"No."

"We're getting off on the wrong foot, Straight. I'm risking my life, and they're treating me like an infiltrator."

"Stop fighting everything, Paul, or I'll start wondering about you myself."

"Straight—"

"Stop it, Paul. You know I'm with you and USSA underground is counting on you. The people over there have hardly any history with us, let alone you. Let 'em have their caution. Win them over."

"Yeah, whatever."

"You can't expect to waltz in there like a hero."

"I said yeah, Straight. And I've got to get moving. It's raining and I've just about enough time to get there."

• • •

Paul dug through his stuff, finding a plastic coverall that would protect him, including his head. He didn't like the smell or the confining nature of it, but it would keep him dry and out of the wind. He was sorely tempted to plant a weapon at his ankle, but he didn't want to give these fragile Italians cause to kill him.

Besides making his way to Trevi Fountain, Paul knew he had to allow time to check for any tails. Legit as he was, carelessness could lead International or Rome police right to the rebels. He had found Venito Hotel personnel personable and friendly, so he decided not to leave through the lobby. They'd wish him the best, ask if he needed anything, and definitely remember having seen him leave.

He got off the elevator on the second floor, walked down a back stairway, and exited into the parking lot at the rear of the hotel. He walked around the block twice, alert for foot or auto traffic that might be shadowing him. Persuaded he had been un-noticed, he headed west toward the fountain, avoiding main thoroughfares. With two taps of his thumb to the tips of both his ring and middle fingers, he set the phone receivers embedded in his molars to privacy mode. He didn't need a call in the middle of this meeting.

Paul began to warm as he quickly strode the several blocks toward his destination. The plastic allowed no wind to reach his skin, except where it sneaked in at the neck. He had to keep ad-justing the hood, and the rustling of the material was louder than the storm. Twice he stepped in puddles that pushed icy wa-ter above his shoes and into his socks. He was going to be in a mood when he met Baldy and Limpy.

Paul had to admit he was impressed that he saw neither of his contacts as he came within sight of the fountain. That showed some proclivity for this kind of work. He had half ex-pected them to be standing in plain view. Paul circled the foun-tain. Pedestrians passed through the area, but no one stopped to admire a water show on a night like this. The wind added the fountain's spouts to the rain, which drummed onto Paul's hood.

Finally he found his spot, facing east, smoothed out the length of his rain gear the way his wife smoothed her skirt before sitting. He sat there, hands deep in his pockets, reminding himself of the people he had seen from his hotel-room window, hunched against the cold.

Paul's begrudging admiration for his contacts' abilities took a hit when he saw them coming from more than a block away. He squinted through the downpour to make out Mutt and Jeff, big and small, striding and limping. To their credit they didn't slow or stare at him, but Calvino did stop to light a cigarette. That told Paul there were likely more than two of them. Who tries to smoke in the rain? It was clearly a signal. And when the little man put out the smoke and coughed, then laughed, Paul could only shake his head.

The two moved past him at the fountain without turning their heads, reached the next corner, took a right, then another, then came directly toward him. They sat on either side of him.

"Get your signal sent, Calvino?" Paul said.

"That?" the little man said. "Yes." He chuckled.

"Something funny?" Paul said. "I mean, funnier than the three of us sitting next to a fountain in a cold rain?"

Calvino laughed. "I don't smoke. It was a dumb signal."

"And who were you signaling?"

A bigger, more serious voice now, from Paul's other side. "You know who," Baldassare said.

"The only other name I know here is your boss's," Paul said. "So that's encouraging. You're like the king's food tasters, eh? If you don't die from your encounter with me, he feels safe?"

Calvino was still grinning. "That's about it, yes."

"We have to search you," Baldassare said. "You mind?"

"Of course I mind, but I agreed to it."

"Stand up."

"What? You're going to do it right out here in public?"

"Nobody's watching."

"They will if you start frisking me, man."

"Well, we can't take you to Fabrizio until we know you're unarmed."

"Then let's find a place where you can make sure."

"Sounds good to me," Calvino said, rising unsteadily.

"Just hold on," Baldassare said. "We have to maintain control here."

"How's that working for you so far?" Paul said. "Come on, guys, really. Look, there's an alley." Paul pointed behind them and to the left. "It's even lit, but it's out of the view of traffic. Go there and wait for me and I'll be along in a minute. Then you can give me a root canal if you need to."

Calvino laughed aloud, and Baldassare shushed him. "Yeah," the big man said. "We get over there and you come in shooting. Then where would we—?"

"Sir, think a minute. The fear here is that I am not what I claim to be. If that were true, which I assure you it is not, what would I gain by taking out you two? I wouldn't have access to Fabrizio. I wouldn't know where you assemble. I would have nothing."

"That's a relief," Calvino said.

"You don't think it'll look a little strange," Baldassare said, "two guys walking into an alley?"

"No stranger than you two walking down the street together."

"Then you and I will go into the alley," Baldassare told Paul, "and Calvino can keep an eye on you from behind and join us in a minute."

"And what if I do you in before he gets there?" Paul said. It was like teaching Espionage 101.

"Like you said, even if you're an infiltrator, that gets you no-where."

"Now you've got it, big man. Good plan. Let's go."

"Just a minute," Baldassare said. "I'm a better shot. You two go and *I'll* follow."

"Anything to move this along," Paul said, rising.

"Wait," Calvino said. "We were supposed to ask him the questions."

"Ask him on the way."

Calvino limped alongside Paul as they headed for the alley. "Do you believe Jesus Christ came in the flesh?" he said.

"I do."

"He is risen."

"He is risen indeed. Hey, Calvino, you want to have some fun?"

"I'm not sure. I'm kinda scared right now."

"Trust me, you'll enjoy this, and so will Baldassare."

"I don't know. He doesn't enjoy much. But what?"

"When we get in the alley, you search me and persuade your-self I'm unarmed. Then let's move out onto the next street and let him wonder what happened to us."

"Oh, I don't know. I don't even know about searching you, because that takes two hands and if you *are* armed, you could get the drop on me."

"Truth be told, Calvino, I could get the drop on you right now." Paul turned and saw the smile fade on the smaller man.

"Baldassare has my back," Calvino said.

"Then why are you scared?"

"Because I don't know who you are. You're trained and an expert and all that. We're just underground believers."

"Let me tell you something, sir. I am your brother in Christ.

I am no more interested in harming you than the man in the moon."

"I'd sure like to believe that."

"You can, and you will, soon enough. Guess I can't talk you into pretending to scream out in terror as soon as we're out of Baldassare's sight, can I?"

Calvino flashed him a double take, then grinned. "Just for fun, you mean? To scare him?"

"Of course."

Calvino laughed. "Nah. No. We might give him a heart at-tack. He takes this all pretty serious, you know. I do too, even though it might not look like it. I laugh when I'm nervous."

"You don't say."

"It's true. Baldassare didn't even think I was a good choice for this."

"You're doing fine." Paul only wished he'd had a mark this easy when he was really working under cover.

When they got into the alley, Paul raised both arms and spread them.

"You can wait on that," Calvino said. "We'd better do this by the book and wait for Baldassare."

The big man entered less than a minute later, and Calvino immediately chuckled.

"What *is* your problem?" Baldassare said.

Calvino, between guffaws, told him Paul's idea of scaring him just for fun.

Baldassare was not amused. "I'd have shot you both."

"I believe you would have," Paul said, assuming the position to be frisked. This only tickled Calvino more.

Baldassare turned on his partner. "Hold your gun on him, would you? I'm going to be totally vulnerable doing this."

"Very good," Paul said.

"Don't patronize me, man. I mean it."

"I was dead serious. That's by the book."

Baldassare patted Paul down but reached only his shins. When he stood, Paul said, "Sir, just a word. If I were to bring a weapon, I'd probably strap it to my ankle."

The big man sighed and squatted again, checking. Finally satisfied he phoned Fabrizio. "In an alley west of the fountain, sir. Oh, you saw us. . . . Well, we couldn't search him in public. . . . No, we took precautions that would keep him from doing that. . . . Yes, sir. Right away."

Baldassare led Paul out of the alley. "We're to take you to a little espresso shop south of here, and he'll join us. His driver will wait in the car."

"Sir," Paul said, hesitating, "what if I am being tailed by International or even local authorities? How do I explain you three?"

Baldassare shrugged.

Calvino weighed in. "Tell 'em you're succeeding. You're infiltrating."

Paul shook his head. "Then they identify you as underground and eventually follow you to the others."

Baldassare and Calvino looked at each other. Baldassare got back on the phone and explained the conundrum to Fabrizio. "Yes, sir, he's clean. . . . At the corner. Right."

"They're picking us up two blocks south."

"Now you're thinking," Paul said. Really, these guys were charming bumblers. In a way they reminded him of Gregor, who had been different only in how seriously he took himself. The underground had a huge disadvantage against the government. They weren't cut out to be surreptitious. It was a wonder more had not been caught. Paul only hoped Enzo Fabrizio was in charge for a reason. Surely he had some savvy.

Paul was not disappointed. What a relief to finally meet the head of the Rome underground. Fabrizio waited in the backseat of a black Hydro van, and while the other two climbed in behind the crew-cut driver, Fabrizio leaned forward and grabbed Paul's outstretched hand with both of his, pulling him in beside him. Paul was impressed that the windows were tinted black and the inside light was set not to come on when the doors opened.

"He is risen," the stocky, thirty-fiveish man said. He had long, black hair, olive skin, perfect teeth, and shining dark eyes.

"He is risen indeed," Paul said, immediately at ease. His plan to lecture Fabrizio on his treatment vanished as his host launched into an abject apology.

"First, let me say how sorry I am about the way we connected with you. Frankly, there is sometimes as much politics within the church as without, as you may already know. I have factions who actually support the acts of terrorism, even though we still don't know whether Magnor is truly a brother or not."

"I'm fairly certain he's not," Paul said, "but we can get into that later."

"And I also want to apologize to you, Doctor, for any implication that you are not truly a brother. That was not me either. I will not mislead you; there are those among us who are very suspicious and who may be hard to sell."

"Understandable."

"Yes, but also faithless, untrusting, and rude."

"Imagine if they were right though, brother."

"Well," Enzo said, "there is that. All this to say that all these machinations were designed to set at ease the minds of those who fear we may be opening our secret home to the enemy."

"I completely understand. Truth and time walk hand in hand." Paul surprised himself at how quickly he had gone from the offense of how he was "welcomed" to empathizing with the cautious ones among the underground. He only hoped he wasn't being swayed too easily by the most engaging Enzo Fabrizio.

10

THE KIDS HAD, AT FIRST, seemed to like the idea of moving to Washington for a few weeks or months. But now Jae found them, especially Brie, on the verge of changing their minds. Her daughter had raised the issue as soon as she got home from school, and Jae hauled her into another room.

"Let's not discuss this in front of Connor, if you don't mind. I don't need to fight you both on this."

"But all my friends are here! And what are we going to do when Daddy gets back? We'll come back here, right? Then I'll have to start all over with my school and my friends and everything."

"Look at the advantages in Washington, honey. Grandpa and Grandma and Uncle Berlitz and Aunt Aryana . . . " Jae caught herself wanting to mention that there was also the matter of living without a man in the house. But there was no way she would even suggest danger to her daughter, and neither did she want to exhibit weakness just because she was a woman.

"Grandpa doesn't like me, and Aunt Aryana doesn't even know me."

"That's why it'll be good to be out there. You and she can—and, hey, your grandpa loves you."

"Maybe, but he doesn't like me."

"He just has a different way of—"

"And what school will we go to, anyway? We'll be the new kids, and—"

"Grandma's looking into that, and she'll get you started next Monday."

"This is going to be awful!"

"No it's not, Brie. Now let's assume the best."

But Jae wasn't so sure herself. Why was she doing this to the kids? Just because *she* was lonely? Scared? Feeling watched? What kind of self-possessed mother was she? Even Paul and Straight were against this. It was four-to-one against now, unless she counted the votes of her family. That made it five-to-four in favor. If she wasn't sure, why was she going?

Jae got the kids settled into their predinner activities and turned on the New Testament discs. This time she wore headphones. Brie and Connor didn't need to hear this foolishness.

Jae picked up from Acts 3, where Peter and John met a crippled beggar:

Peter and John looked at him intently, and Peter said, "Look at us!" The lame man looked at them eagerly, expecting a gift. But Peter said, "I don't have any money for you. But I'll give you what I have. In the name of Jesus Christ of Nazareth, get up and walk!"

Then Peter took the lame man by the right hand and

helped him up. And as he did, the man's feet and anklebones were healed and strengthened. He jumped up, stood on his feet, and began to walk! Then, walking, leaping, and praising God, he went into the Temple with them.

All the people saw him walking and heard him praising God. When they realized he was the lame beggar they had seen so often at the Beautiful Gate, they were absolutely astounded! They all rushed out to Solomon's Colonnade, where he was holding tightly to Peter and John. Everyone stood there in awe of the wonderful thing that had happened.

Jae couldn't deny that's the way she felt when Paul's sight was restored. But no one had healed him, had they? Surely not God.

Peter saw his opportunity and addressed the crowd. "People of Israel," he said, "what is so astounding about this? And why look at us as though we had made this man walk by our own power and godliness? For it is the God of Abraham, the God of Isaac, the God of Jacob, the God of all our ancestors who has brought glory to his servant Jesus by doing this. This is the same Jesus whom you handed over and rejected before Pilate, despite Pilate's decision to release him. You rejected this holy, righteous one and instead demanded the release of a murderer. You killed the author of life, but God raised him to life. And we are witnesses of this fact!"

Jae couldn't remember where, but she had heard that story. Pilate had tried to talk Jesus' enemies out of crucifying Him, saying he found no fault in Him and washing his hands of the responsibility. Was it possible this was an actual historic event? It didn't have the earmarks of a fable or fairy tale. It had a documentary quality. Jae reminded herself not to get sucked in, despite the eyewitness accounts of seeing Jesus after His crucifixion and resurrection. Unless the New Testament was assumed by all to be a fanciful account, why had there not been an outcry against these claims?

The name of Jesus has healed this man—and you know how lame he was before. Faith in Jesus' name has caused this healing before your very eyes.

Friends, I realize that what you did to Jesus was done in ignorance; and the same can be said of your leaders. But God was fulfilling what all the prophets had declared about the Messiah beforehand—that he must suffer all these things. Now turn from your sins and turn to God, so you can be cleansed of your sins. Then wonderful times of refreshment will come from the presence of the Lord, and he will send Jesus your Messiah to you again. For he must remain in heaven until the time for the final restoration of all things, as God promised long ago through his prophets.

Jae was jarred every time she heard a reference to the ancient prophecies; maybe because she knew it was in these that the underground rebels put so much stock. But what had strangely gripped her even more was the part about changing one's mind and attitude about God and turning to Him. And why? So He could cleanse your sin and send you refreshment from His presence.

Jae wondered why that should sound so sweet. If there was anything she had known about stubborn hangers-on to religion, it was that they either believed their good works outweighed their bad or that they were fundamentally wicked and only God could save them. She had never felt either until now.

Was she sinful? What was sin? And what was it measured against?

She could be selfish, rude, greedy, short-tempered, even lustful. Though she had always been faithful to Paul, she couldn't say she hadn't been tempted. If these discs were going to make her feel bad about herself, even guilty, maybe they weren't worth listening to after all.

Moses said, "The Lord your God will raise up a Prophet like me from among your own people. Listen carefully to everything he tells you." Then Moses said, "Anyone who will not listen to that Prophet will be cut off from God's people and utterly destroyed."

That sounded more like what Jae had heard about religion. Get in line or get destroyed. That didn't sound like a loving God.

Starting with Samuel, every prophet spoke about what is happening today. You are the children of those prophets, and you are included in the covenant God promised to your ancestors. For God said to Abraham, "Through your descendants all the families on earth will be blessed." When God raised up his servant, he sent him first to you people of Israel, to bless you by turning each of you back from your sinful ways.

There it was again, the sin thing. She would have a lot of questions for Straight Thursday night. Maybe even before then. Jae wished she didn't have to wait to see him. She felt safer when he was there.

• • •

Paul was impressed that Enzo Fabrizio had his driver circle Rome twice before heading back into the central part of the city.

Enzo also was proving collegial. He asked the driver and
Baldassare and Calvino if they agreed there was no tail. The
driver agreed. Baldassare apologized for not having been on the
lookout, and Calvino said the same.

"Doctor?" Enzo said.

"I worried about one vehicle for a while," Paul said, "but no."

"The one that exited toward the airport?"

"That's the one."

"Me too." Enzo called out to the driver, "Directly to the compound."

Enzo wanted to know Paul's story, all about how he became
a believer, what had happened in Las Vegas and Los Angeles, and
especially how things went with International Chancellor
Dengler. Finally they talked about Gregor.

"I loved that young man," Enzo said, "but I have to admit,
when I heard he had actually gone to work for International, I
had misgivings."

"Why?" Paul said.

"The very things you cited. He was passionate and devout,
but subtlety was not his gift. I grieve his loss, but frankly I am
glad he is not in a position to give away the underground. I don't
know how it works in the USSA—other than the little I've heard
from my Detroit and Washington contacts—but here we do not
actually live underground. We meet and plan and prepare
underground, but we live in society."

Paul was intrigued, but the mention of Washington caught
his attention. "You know the Washington underground?"

"Only the leadership, which has been cut in half, as you
know. I knew the Pass brothers. I mean, I never met them, but
Detroit connected us and we talked by phone and private message. Andy was a tragic loss, and I don't think Jack has been the
same since his brother was murdered by the NPO."

"You know I had a long history with Andy, and a recent history with his daughter."

"I didn't know," Enzo said. "You know Angela?"

Paul nodded. "You?"

"Only by name. I know she's something special."

Paul fell silent, trying to keep track of his surroundings but distracted by being thrust back into his memory banks and the magnetism of the lovely young widow, Angela Pass Barger. Somehow the thought of her made Paul miss Jae all the more. Well, that was encouraging at least.

"Here's what we do, Doctor," Enzo said. "When we reach our destination—a ground-level door built into an electrical transforming station with dire high-voltage warnings and all the rest—we park in one of the largest apartment-complex lots in Rome and wait in the van sometimes as long as half an hour to be sure we have attracted no attention. When there are no cars or pedestrians, one by one we slip out and down the street past the transforming station, then circle back to the door. As you can imagine, especially on a night like this, you must be very careful to stay away from the transformer unit itself. You need be only as close as ten feet for millions of volts to arc between you and the contraption. Only your smoking bones would be found."

"That's comforting."

"I would chaperone you in, but we have a strict policy that only one person enters every five minutes, and the people inside know in advance who is coming, so an intruder would feel less than welcome."

"How much less?" Paul said.

"We kill them," Enzo said.

"You do?"

"We do. If you have a better solution, I'm open to it. And don't get me started on the ethical and theological ramifications.

I can't say we are unanimous in our thinking on this, but look at it from our perspective: Anyone who goes through what we must go through to get to our compound has to know where he is going and be going there on purpose. If an intruder shows up and gets past the first two doors without identifying himself, he means to expose us. Far too many lives are at stake, and we are at war."

"Has this happened?"

"Sadly, it has. A Rome policeman came nosing around, and we still have no idea why. Had he seen one of us enter? Had someone left the door ajar? That happens to be my theory, because he didn't have a key, and needless to say, the door is securely locked. Our sensors picked him up immediately, but we did not intercom him to identify himself because insiders know that is the responsibility of the one entering. We will tell you about a station where you must use the intercom to identify yourself or risk being met with force."

"And you murdered this man, Enzo?"

"We did. He was a casualty of war. Think about it, Dr. Stepola. Could we risk being exposed?"

"Were there no other options? Could you not have held him until you could move your site? And what about the ethics of sending a lost man to hell?"

"We did share our faith with him. Of course, he realized immediately that he was not going to leave the place alive, and to his credit he did not pretend to convert just to save his skin. Had he done that, we would have had to keep him around, imprisoned until he proved himself. But of course he had checked in with police headquarters and was known to be in that area before disappearing, so we would have been inviting the full force of the Rome police to come looking for one of its own."

"And so?"

"We pleaded with him to give his heart to Christ. Then we sedated him, humanely injected him with enough phenobarbital to kill a thoroughbred racehorse, and he died peacefully. We then transported him to the parking lot of another apartment complex in the area and phoned in an anonymous tip. The mystery made news for days and was, of course, never solved."

"And you're okay with that?"

"Interesting you should ask, Doctor. The death of that man haunts my dreams. I don't know what God will have to say to me about it, but my conscience speaks volumes. I do know this—and I am not rationalizing as much as trying to explain—the police in Rome have a mandate to execute religious believers upon sight, based on any real evidence. They have asked people outright if they are atheists, and with a witness hearing the perpetrator deny it, they are allowed to 'terminate them with extreme prejudice' on the spot."

"And that has happened to your compatriots?"

"You will see the memorial," Enzo said. "We have had more than thirty executed by Rome police alone."

Paul told him of his conversation with the chief of detectives who pooh-poohed the influence of the underground in the city and said their existence was negligible.

"That is the impression they like to give," Enzo said. "And by quietly eliminating us one by one, they are, of course, trying to make us inconsequential. But our little literature efforts pay off, Doctor. We circulate tracts, which we will show you tonight. They are mostly Scripture, but the Word of God will not return void."

"That's the second time I've heard that today, not in so many words."

"People come to faith through the truth of the Bible," Enzo said. "Many of our members find us that way."

"How about you?" Paul said. "What's your story?"

The driver had pulled into the apartment-complex parking lot and turned off the engine. The rain pelted the van and the wind whistled. Despite the unparalleled insulation of European-made vehicles, Paul felt the draft. The temperature was dropping, and the men seemed to close in upon themselves, sitting on their hands or folding their arms.

"It was my wife," Enzo began, "whom you will meet tonight. She's one of the bravest women I've ever known."

"And one of the most beautiful," Calvino said, giggling. "If I may say."

"I won't argue with you, Cal," Fabrizio said, "but that was not what attracted me to her. It was her smile and her infectious radiance. We met at the university fifteen years ago."

"My wife and I also met in school," Paul said.

"We hit it off right away," Enzo said, "and once she got to know me and believed I really cared for her as a person, she came right out and told me. Or I should say, she asked me. She said, 'What would you say if I told you I was a secret believer in God?'

"I said, 'Tell me where to sign up.'

"She said, 'Don't be facetious because I'm serious, and the fact is, you'd *have* to sign up if there's a future for us. Or you could turn me in and that would be the end of me and us.'

"Well, I told her I wouldn't turn her in, but I'd like the opportunity to try to talk her out of this dangerous craziness. Dr. Stepola, she didn't even get mad at me. When I think back about how important this had to have been to her—because, of course, it's as important to me now—I can hardly imagine the chance she took. But she was just in my face about it. She told me she loved me but that she could never be unequally yoked. I had never heard the expression before. And she told me that as much as she loved me, God loved me more.

"I've got to tell you, the only thing I knew about God was that He was not real and did not exist. I didn't know what people who believed in Him thought about Him, other than that He *was* real and *did* exist. I had never even heard the idea that they believed He also loved them. I had always had the impression that He probably didn't love anybody. If He was real, He was a grumpy old guy, always frowning on people and holding them to a standard they couldn't live up to."

"I can identify with that," Paul said.

"Maura was raised by her grandparents after her parents were killed in the war when she was a baby. She's a few years older than I am. I was born just after the war. Anyway, her grandparents were Christians, and they resisted the effort to ban religion, at least in their own home. I don't know where Maura got her courage, because they were very secretive and warned her never to tell another soul that she was a believer. They had a Bible they locked in a cabinet in the basement, but when she was allowed to hear it read and then read it for herself, she did not, she said, find anything in it about keeping your faith a secret. As she grew up she became judicious, of course. That's why she didn't tell me about herself until we were serious about each other.

"But then she put the pressure on. We argued, we debated, we discussed, but mostly she prayed. Doctor, I can't even tell you when or why I went from not believing in God to believing that He was pursuing me. All I know is that when that happened, it was as if He was as relentless as she. I felt chased, pursued, wooed. Eventually, when I ran out of arguments, I confessed my sins and received Christ. God and Jesus became as real to me as they were to Maura. It has been quite an experience, raising a family, holding a job—I am a tour guide by day—and being trained to be a spiritual leader in a society that makes such a goal punishable by death."

"How have you done it?"

"Technology, brother. The greatest resource of theological works and instruction is housed in the Detroit underground."

"I've been there."

"So I've heard. You saw it? The collection of discs."

Paul nodded.

"They transmit those all over the world to students who can be verified as worthy candidates," Enzo said. "It's taken me more than ten years, but it's as if I have a seminary education."

Baldassare cleared his throat. "Beg your pardon, boss, but it's coming up on midnight."

"Yes, we'd better get going," Enzo said. "You three go ahead, five minutes apart. Then I'll send Dr. Stepola, and I'll bring up the rear."

Five minutes after the last of the other three had left the van, Enzo instructed Paul on how to get to the compound. "When you get to the edge of the parking lot, slip through that row of trees and look to your right. You'll be able to see the transformer station two and a half blocks away. Being sure no one is around, following or watching, walk past the station, turn left, and circle back to it."

Enzo handed Paul a key. "There is a dead-bolt lock on the door that puzzles even electrical workers. It unlocks in the opposite direction of a conventional lock, and it must first be triggered from inside. If you are not expected, your key will not work. Once inside, immediately shut the door behind you. It will relock automatically. Don't make the mistake of moving too quickly in the dark. You will be standing on a wood ledge, about a half-meter platform at the top of narrow wood stairs.

"Obviously, we can't risk anyone seeing light from inside, so the passageway to the compound is unlit all the way. You'll find it harrowing, especially the first time. The steps will take you about twenty feet belowground. Eventually you'll come to another heavy metal door with even more warnings on it, but these can be seen only if someone has brought a flashlight, which you will not. Feel around the right side of that door for an intercom, press the button, and hold it as you say your name in a conversational tone. Watch for a tiny green light to shine, indicating you have five seconds to open the door. You will hear no response or buzz, so be alert.

"Shortly after you have passed through that second door, the tunnel makes a ninety-degree right turn and leads two blocks to beneath the Baths of Caracalla. We meet in an area far from where the tourists visit, and it's insulated by several feet of earth and stone."

Paul raised his eyebrows. "Well, it's not the abandoned salt mines of Detroit, but it's something. And that one cop is as close as you've been to being found out?"

Enzo nodded. "As far as we know. On the other hand, we could have been infiltrated. We give polygraph tests and we ask the right questions. Normally people are associated with us and working with us a full year before they are allowed to join us in the compound. That's why there are those who believe what I am doing with you tonight is suicidal."

11

JAE FOUND STRAIGHT maddeningly circumspect on the phone that evening. She couldn't tell if he was upset because she had ignored his advice and wishes about her move to Washington—and surely he and Paul had discussed the fact that Paul didn't want her to go either—or if he simply thought she was calling him too much. After all, he was also coming for dinner Thursday night.

The kids were down and she had asked if he had some time. Though he said he did, his answers were short and noncommittal, almost curt. If she didn't know better, she'd have wondered if he had something to hide. Was it possible he actually worried that she would get the wrong impression because he seemed to know a thing or two about the Bible? Even if she thought he knew too much to be a loyal atheist, it wasn't as if she would have him investigated. Of course, with her connections, she could. She certainly, however, did not view Straight as a threat to the USSA.

She told him what she had been listening to and asked whether he knew if the Bible was considered a nonfiction historical record.

"I thought we were going to discuss this Thursday night," he said.

"Well, we are, but that's just been bugging me all day. What do you think?"

"I don't know what I think. Are you asking if *I* believe it's true, or . . . ?"

"I'm asking if you know whether people who are believers see the Bible as truth or just some sort of allegorical guideline or something. Because it's sure different than what I expected."

"What had you expected?"

He's stalling! "Well, I don't know, sir. I guess I always thought the Bible was full of legends and poetry and psalms, hymns, that kind of thing."

"I don't think there are hymns, outside the Psalms, of course."

"And so?"

"Well, I don't see how I can speak for what other people think. Who knows whether they took it literally or figuratively?"

Jae was actually growing irritated with him. She had assumed he would have been the type of professor she would have enjoyed. Until this. Jae tried her postulation on him that if it were not true, it shouldn't have stood the test of time that it did. "I mean, in just the few chapters I've listened to, there's some pretty bizarre stuff. Unless there's some deeper meaning, people either had to buy this stuff whole or pass it off as a joke."

"They didn't seem to do that, if history is a barometer."

"My point exactly, Straight. So this is a true, historical record."

"I can't decide that for you."

"But it was for them?"

"For whom?"

"For believers!"

"Well," he said, "I think you just answered your own question."

Jae was tempted to ask him flat out what he personally believed. Why else would he be so elusive? She was off the phone with him much more quickly than she had expected, but she got the impression he was relieved when they were through. She hadn't even followed through on broaching the subject of mysterious cars and people in the neighborhood.

Jae hoped he wouldn't change his mind about coming for dinner. Brie and Connor could talk about nothing else.

She sat to read but couldn't concentrate. She tried TV and quickly tired of it. She wasn't in the mood for more from the New Testament right then, but she had to wonder why this had become so important to her. Just because it was strange? Novel? Phrases and verses and stories had come to her mind throughout the day. There was something magnetic about it, though she could not imagine ever buying into it. People who did intrigued her. Maybe that was it. She was gaining insight into the minds of people from a whole other culture.

• • •

No way in the world Paul would have ever gotten near the transformer station in central Rome had he not known what was waiting for him underground. The signs began on the sidewalk and the fence and were pervasive every step of the way toward the door: Danger. Keep Out. High Voltage. Fatal or Debilitating Injury Possible. Authorized Personnel Only.

He checked his watch. Knowing he was expected, he inserted the key Enzo Fabrizio had given him and at first turned it the wrong way. Was his memory getting that bad? No. He was just a creature of habit. Quickly turning it the other way, the door popped open.

He stepped in gingerly, careful to not move too far as he shut the door behind him. Paul had experienced darkness before, but never anything like this. There were no handrails on either side, so as he carefully reached out with his toes, he rested his hand on the cold concrete at the right side of the staircase. With nearly every step, he imagined the next would be the bottom, but he didn't dare walk ahead as if on flat ground. Each succeeding step seemed a surprise. And if it was possible, the darkness in the shaft seemed to grow thicker—and colder—the deeper he got.

Finally he found flat ground. What came next? He should have memorized it. Moving along in pitch-black, not knowing when he might run into something, was just as harrowing as going down steps and not knowing which was the last. He moved slowly, hands in front of him, as if sleepwalking.

Finally Paul felt something solid and metallic. Though he was expecting it, feeling for it, it still jolted him. He felt around on the wall to the right and finally located a button. He pressed it and leaned close, and not knowing why, felt the need to whisper his name. Almost immediately a tiny dot of green appeared, and he opened the door.

Enzo had told him that soon after he passed through that door he would have to take a right turn, but he did not tell him how soon. With one step Paul hit a concrete wall. He felt to his left and found the same. The door shut and he suddenly felt claustrophobic. There was space to the right, and he would take Enzo's word for it that it was at a ninety-degree angle.

As he carefully moved that way, hands in front of him again, Paul felt panic rise. Nobody had told him the reason only one person entered at a time was that there was room for no more. His plastic rain gear scraped both sides of the tunnel, and unless it was only his imagination, the walls seemed to get closer in spots. Even at their widest, he was still brushing both sides. If he met another barrier, he feared he would not have room to turn around. He would have to back all the way out, and he had no idea how far he had come since the second door. It was supposed to be two city blocks, but how could he tell how far he had come without counting his furtive, baby steps, which he had not thought to do?

Paul knew it was only his imagination, but he was certain the air was getting thinner too. Besides his racing heart, his respiration increased. Despite how cold it was this far belowground, his plastic cover made his body overheat. He was miserable, blind, and scared. Just when he was about to cry out for help or just stop and wait for Enzo to catch up with him, Paul reached another door.

Now what? He felt a knob, which was locked tight. He felt a keyhole, for which he had not been instructed to use his key. He felt for a button but found none. Was he to knock? Call out? He clumsily tried his key, and while it fit, the lock would not turn either way. He knocked quietly.

"Identify yourself," he heard. A woman's voice.

"Paul Stepola," he said, a frog in his throat.

"Say again, please."

He nearly shouted it and the door swung open, the light from inside, though relatively dim, making him squint. The woman embraced him and he held her tight, mostly from relief. "I'm Maura Fabrizio," she said, "and you look terrified."

"I'm all right now," Paul said as she helped him shed his rain gear. He was soaked through his clothes. "Enzo told me about you."

About thirty people milled around in a generous-sized, concrete-walled room with rudimentary lightbulbs strung about the ceiling. Enzo had told him that hundreds could congregate down here, so Paul knew it had to lead into other larger areas. Cheap folding chairs were grouped here and there, but few were using them. Large coffee urns sat on card tables in two corners, and the aroma of strong, black espresso overwhelmed Paul.

The chilly reception Paul was warned of began immediately. A few people asked to be introduced and seemed warm. But most kept their distance, eyeing him warily, mostly when they thought he wasn't looking. Paul had developed a technique that allowed him to quickly shift focus and catch someone staring. He found it strangely comforting to see Baldassare, Calvino, and the unnamed driver. They nodded, clearly not claiming him as a friend just because they had been responsible for getting him here. Paul hoped Enzo's endorsement would go a long way with this understandably suspicious crowd.

The leader arrived a few minutes later, put his arm around Paul, and led him through the anteroom to a larger area, where a hundred or so people were waiting. It was furnished the same as the other room, sans the coffee stations.

Here were the ones who didn't even care to get a peek at him when he first arrived. And Paul had thought the Rome detectives were tough. These were supposed to be brothers and sisters. Of course, he couldn't blame them. If they themselves were not allowed here until they'd proved themselves for a year, who in the world did he think he was?

Enzo called everyone around and asked them to find a seat. There were not chairs for all, so the younger and hardier sat on the cold, unforgiving floor. Enzo and Paul had not discussed what was to happen here, and Paul wished he had a little more time to compose himself. He had no idea what he looked like to these people. Disheveled, he assumed. And what if Enzo called on him to encourage them? He had planned nothing to say. Straight had made a big deal about how with his trip to Europe he could mirror the ministry of his namesake, the apostle Paul, and minister to the church in its various forms. "You could build them up," Straight had said.

Well, here he was and here they were, and he was the one who needed encouraging. For one thing, he wasn't the apostle Paul. He was a baby Christian who didn't have the history or the training of Maura Fabrizio, let alone Enzo. These people didn't need him, and he had nothing to offer. Paul had never felt so inadequate.

"Ladies and gentlemen," Enzo began, "let us welcome in the name of Christ our brother and compatriot from the United Seven States of America, Dr. Paul Stepola."

There was zero applause, and as far as Paul could tell, not even a smile, except from the pleasant-looking Mrs. Fabrizio. He could tell she had been a knockout in her day, but years of living a double life in an atheistic society had worn itself into the lines of her face. She looked radiant but tired. And Paul missed Jae all the more.

He had calculated that Maura was not quite forty yet, but she looked fifty. Paul tucked her welcoming look into the back of his mind, hoping it would carry him through this frigid reception.

"As you know," Enzo continued, "Dr. Stepola is a new believer and remains an operative with the National Peace Organization. USSA underground assures us that he is the highest-placed mole we could have, and possibly our only one. Neither he nor I are unaware of the suspicion with which many of you must view him. I thought it would be good to start by allowing you to ask him anything you want. Anyone?"

Enzo turned and beckoned Paul to his side. He stood there

awkwardly, wishing he could will them to accept him. But he would have responded the same way to an interloper who could get them all executed.

A middle-aged woman raised her hand. "Assuming you are who and what you say you are, how long before NPO International discovers you're a turncoat? I mean, they are—"

"The best espionage outfits in the world, yes. Frankly, I don't know. So far I have been able to keep them off my track by succeeding in rooting out underground charlatans that appear like people of faith only to the uninitiated. NPO doesn't know the difference, painting all of us with the same brush. Our hope and prayer should be that Styr Magnor is not a true believer and that I will be able to apprehend him."

"Magnor?" a young man said. "He's done more for our cause than you have."

"I haven't done much yet, I confess," Paul said. "But I respectfully disagree that Magnor has done us any good. Terrorist acts like those for which he takes credit are not of God. If we can succeed in bringing him down, *that* will be a benefit to the underground church here. It will take the spotlight off you."

The room fell silent. Then a man: "Can you give us any inside information, something that will persuade us you're not loyal to your employers?"

Paul had to think twice about simply bad-mouthing the NPO. He looked down, then hit upon a strategy. "Let me tell you two inside things. These might show you I'm on your side." He spoke both of the highly confidential lipstick warning in the women's toilet at the Bio Park and of the plan to require all citizens to pledge their loyalty in writing on Monday.

"We're dead," someone said.

"Wait," another said. "What's the significance, in your view, of the lipstick warning?"

"To me it shows that Magnor is not one of us. Had any of us heard of him before? No one in the USSA had. Then when he tries to identify with us he shows no more discernment than the NPO. He lauds the L.A. drought, which was clearly an act of God. Yet he also identifies with Jonah, the phony in Las Vegas whose philosophy of free love and drugs caused several deaths. This is not a man we want to embrace or have embrace us."

Paul hoped it wasn't wishful thinking, but he sensed a different tone and body language from these people already. How long had it been since he had been in the presence of this many brothers and sisters? Without even knowing them, he longed to connect with them.

"What do we do about next Monday's announcement?" someone called out.

"Well, I for one will not be signing it," Paul said.

"None of us can, of course," someone else said. "But then we become instant fugitives."

Others began jumping into the discussion.

"Does the government have the manpower to track down everyone who refuses to sign?"

"Depends on how many there are."

"We need a miracle like they had in Los Angeles."

"Let's not get ahead of ourselves. We're taking this man's word for this so-called inside information, and we haven't even confirmed he's legitimate."

Paul was wounded to see how many in the crowd seemed to agree.

"Can I speak to you a moment from a personal standpoint rather than as a Christian mole within the government? I know you may still not choose to believe me, and I can't say I'd be any different if I were in your shoes. But maybe we can begin getting onto the same page if you know that I am just like you . . . same worries, same struggles, same cares. Before I get into this, I suppose I should ask Enzo whether it's fair to keep you here any longer. I understand that no one lives or even stays here and that most of you have work in the morning."

He looked to Enzo who put it to the people. "If you must go, feel free. Otherwise, there is value in hearing out our brother."

To Paul's relief and encouragement, no one left. He told them his story, how he had begun as an enthusiastic persecutor and even killer of underground believers. He covered his injuries, his blindness, meeting Straight, listening to the New Testament, being healed, and finally coming to faith. "That's when the fun began," he said, "and I assumed I would have to immediately resign and get into some other line of work. Underground Christians in the USSA believed I could be more valuable to the cause if I stayed put. I'm still, frankly, not so sure. Because, you see, I'm not just a rogue agent. My father-in-law was one of the founding fathers of the NPO. His daughter, my wife, is still in the dark about what has happened with me."

"Your wife doesn't know? You have kids?"

"My wife and my daughter and son cannot know until I know they will react favorably. I cannot risk her talking to her father, exposing me, taking the kids to protect them, all that."

Paul's voice caught as he mentioned his family, and though he had not done it intentionally, he sensed he had suddenly captured the imagination and sympathy of these brothers and sisters. "Maybe," he said, "the drive for citizen-loyalty signatures will finally force the issue, even in my own home."

When the meeting finally broke up and people began the slow process of leaving one by one, several shook Paul's hand. Others embraced him. Many told him they would be praying for him and his family and said they thanked God that someone like him was now part of their cause.

A woman tugged at his hand until he followed her into a corner, in full sight of everyone but far enough away that they could not hear. "I know you're a relatively new believer," she said. "And perhaps this language is new to you. But when you were speaking of your wife, the Lord really laid her on my heart. Do you know what I'm saying?"

"I think so."

"He's nudging me to pray specifically for her. I am fully aware that I might simply be overcome by emotion, but I do feel this is of God. Tell me her name again."

"Jae." He spelled it. "And your name?"

"Ysabel. I believe God wants to do something in Jae's life, which would be a great benefit and blessing to you too, of course."

"Of course. I appreciate this so much. I—"

"I will pray fervently and regularly for her. And I will ask friends to do the same. One day I hope to meet her as a sister in Christ. If not here, then up there."

"Thank you, ma'am," Paul said, his throat constricted. He was overcome with regret over how infrequently he himself prayed for Jae, specifically for her salvation.

"Also, sir, Enzo asked that I show you our memorials."

"Yes, please."

Ysabel led him down a narrow hallway into a small room that apparently was dedicated exclusively to honoring their martyrs. Small photographs dotted the walls, each captioned with basic information: name, birth date, death date, how killed. There were thirty-one, and all had been executed by Rome police when they refused to renounce their faith.

"This is my son," the woman said. Paul stepped behind her and looked over her shoulder at a round, beaming face. "Innocenzio."

Paul noticed that Innocenzio had been killed within the last year. "He was a beautiful boy. I hope that was an old picture. Surely he was older than that when—" But he noticed the life span and quickly did the math. "They murdered a thirteen-year-old boy?"

She nodded, her eyes full. "They may have thought he looked older. . . ."

Paul could not speak. They *were* at war.

• • •

Paul spent the next few days concentrating on the Bio Park case and interacting with International on their progress toward getting to the real Styr Magnor. While they had succeeded in eliminating dozens of possibilities, the real perpetrator continued to prove elusive.

Rome's Police Chief of Detectives Alonza Marcello got back to Paul on the handwriting of what they assumed was one of the suicide bombers. They met in the Venito Hotel coffee shop.

"Don't ask me how," she said, "because I don't know what they look for in block printing, but the graphologist we used believes it was written by a woman—I know, good thinking because of where it was found—and that she could be British."

"Did the expert know the Styr Magnor connection? I would have guessed she was Norwegian."

"The expert knew, so in my mind that makes this all the more credible. But get this, Doctor. The remains of the bomber were so nearly vaporized that we cannot harvest DNA to help identify her, if it is a she. But the other bomber, who wrote no note that we have found, may have left part of a hand."

"How in the world could they determine it was the hand of the bomber in all that carnage?"

"My question exactly," Chief Marcello said. "They tell me

they have had experts on this since it happened, and they have used computerized imaging, satellite technology, trajectory studies, and even bomb-residue analysis. If it's true, it's the luckiest break we could have hoped for."

"There has to be plenty of DNA in part of a hand," Paul said.

"It's being tested now and will be cross-matched with the NPO International database. Cross your fingers."

"That's not funny."

The chief looked up in surprise. "Oh," she said, smiling. "It wasn't meant to be. Sorry."

12

STRAIGHT WAS WONDERFUL with the kids again Thursday night, and Jae was grateful. He even encouraged Brie to simply do what her mother said, to respect her and trust her, and she would be back to her own school and friends before she knew it.

But Straight did not accept Jae's invitation to stay later like he had the time before and answer more questions about what she was hearing in the book of Acts. He persuaded her to get to bed early so she would be fresh for the trip the next afternoon. Jae knew this was the better part of wisdom, but she was frustrated anew. She still couldn't read Straight. She had no doubt of his character. He was a wonderful man, a loving person. And he was smart. Wise too. But she wasn't able to pin him down long enough to take advantage of that.

Had she offended him? Was he too shy without Paul here? Or was he hiding something? Jae simply didn't know. So she was on her own, trying to interpret what she was hearing. The kids would read and color and play and sleep on the trip. That would give Jae a few hours to listen to the discs in the car with earphones. Anything to pass the time as she sped toward Washington.

She had planned so well that she was able to pack the car even before taking the kids to school, leaving her the rest of the day to prepare to close up the house and plot her route. Once finished, she merely had to wait until it was time to pick up the kids and get going. And while she waited, she listened some more. By now she was up to Acts 4, and the Temple police had seized Peter and John for talking about Jesus' resurrection.

That's sort of Paul's job now, Jae thought. *The NPO is like the Temple police.* But what was so wrong about claiming that Jesus had risen from the dead if they really believed that—and why wouldn't they when they said they had seen Him? No one else was forced to believe it, and if they did believe it, did it cause them to break any laws?

Then Peter, filled with the Holy Spirit, said to them, "Leaders and elders of our nation, are we being questioned because we've done a good deed for a crippled man? Do you want to know how he was healed? Let me clearly state to you and to all the people of Israel that he was healed in the name and power of Jesus Christ from Nazareth, the man you crucified, but whom God raised from the dead. For Jesus is the one referred to in the Scriptures, where it says, 'The stone that you builders rejected has now become the cornerstone.' There is salvation in no one else! There is no other name in all of heaven for people to call on to save them."

Save them from what? Jae wondered. *Sin?*

So they sent Peter and John out of the council chamber and conferred among themselves.

"What should we do with these men?" they asked each other. "We can't deny they have done a miraculous sign, and everybody in Jerusalem knows about it. But perhaps we can stop them from spreading their propaganda. We'll warn them not to speak to anyone in Jesus' name again." So they called the apostles back in and told them never again to speak or teach about Jesus.

But Peter and John replied, "Do you think God wants us to obey you rather than him? We cannot stop telling about the wonderful things we have seen and heard."

The council then threatened them further, but they finally let them go because they didn't know how to punish them without starting a riot. For everyone was praising God for this miraculous sign—the healing of a man who had been lame for more than forty years.

If this is a historical record, Jae decided, even the enemies of Jesus and the apostles here corroborate the miracle. This is the same as what the NPO does today. Jae found herself strangely pulling for the underdogs in the story.

As soon as they were freed, Peter and John found the other believers and told them what the leading priests and elders had said. Then all the believers were united as they lifted their voices in prayer: "O Sovereign Lord, Creator of heaven and earth, the sea, and everything in them—you spoke long ago by the Holy Spirit through our ancestor King David, your servant, saying, 'Why did the nations rage? Why did the people waste their time with futile plans? The kings of the

*earth prepared for battle; the rulers gathered together against
the Lord and against his Messiah.'*

*"That is what has happened here in this city! For Herod
Antipas, Pontius Pilate the governor, the Gentiles, and the
people of Israel were all united against Jesus, your holy servant,
whom you anointed. In fact, everything they did occurred according to your eternal will and plan. And now, O Lord, hear
their threats, and give your servants great boldness in their
preaching. Send your healing power; may miraculous signs
and wonders be done through the name of your holy servant
Jesus."*

Jae couldn't ignore that the prayer seemed to describe the
current world government and its opposition to people of faith.
And these people shared their lives and belongings—when was
the last time Jae had heard of people taking care of each other
like that? It seemed today it was everyone for himself. What was
so wrong with people of faith, even if we disagree with them?
They don't hurt anybody. In fact, they help the needy.

Just before it was time to leave to pick up Brie and Connor,
Jae reached Acts 9 and found herself riveted.

It was the story of Saul, who would become Paul, and how
he threatened believers with every breath and wanted to destroy them. He requested from the high priest cooperation in
arresting Christians and bringing them to Jerusalem in chains.

*As he was nearing Damascus on this mission, a brilliant light
from heaven suddenly beamed down upon him! He fell to the
ground and heard a voice saying to him, "Saul! Saul! Why
are you persecuting me?"*

"Who are you, sir?" Saul asked.

And the voice replied, "I am Jesus, the one you are perse-

*cuting! Now get up and go into the city, and you will be told
what you are to do."* . . .

*Now there was a believer in Damascus named Ananias.
The Lord spoke to him in a vision, calling, "Ananias!"*

"Yes, Lord!" he replied.

*The Lord said, "Go over to Straight Street, to the house of
Judas. When you arrive, ask for Saul of Tarsus. He is praying
to me right now. I have shown him a vision of a man named
Ananias coming in and laying his hands on him so that he can
see again."*

Straight Street? What were the odds? And Saul regaining his
sight? This was too much. Ananias argued with God because
Saul had been so brutal to Christians, but God told him,

*Saul is my chosen instrument to take my message to the
Gentiles and to kings, as well as to the people of Israel. And I
will show him how much he must suffer for me.*

• • •

Late Friday night, Paul visited the underground one more
time for a private meeting with Enzo Fabrizio. As he moved
through the dank, tight tunnel, Paul busied himself praying for
Jae and the kids, who would be on the road to Washington
by now.

"I'm leaving in the morning for Paris," he told Enzo. "But I
have an idea for trying to flush out Styr Magnor. What if you
and your people put out the word in your own circles that you
wanted to meet the man? Imply that you have been impressed
by what he accomplished and that you would love to entertain
ways you might work together with him and his people."

Enzo's face clouded over. "I would have to make clear to my

compatriots that this is a ruse. I already have small factions who support what Magnor has done, and obviously I don't want to be associated with that."

"Of course. Now listen, brother, if you or yours have any Norwegian connections, that is the place to start. He may be crafty, may be trying to mislead, but so far everything points to his originating there and perhaps headquartering there too."

"Norway," Enzo said. "Got it."

Paul wanted to get going, but it was clear that Enzo had something on his mind. "I hope to be back to see you all," Paul said, "but with this announcement coming and the likelihood of all of us having to take a bold stand—"

"It may be impossible. I understand. I think you won over most of our people, Doctor. The personal touch made the difference. You became human to them with your concern for your own family. Many are praying for you and your wife and your kids."

"I know."

"Who are you going to connect with in Paris? Chappell?"

"Yes."

"Met him once. As intense a man as you'll ever want to know. Deep mood swings. A fighter. You'll have to keep a very cool head around him, but he can be brought to his senses."

"That's good to know."

"And now, brother Stepola, may I pray for you?"

"Please."

Enzo slipped from his chair to the hard, cold floor, and Paul felt obligated to do so as well. The Italian put a hand on Paul's shoulder. "Father, thank You for this servant who has so encouraged us. We claim his wife and children for You and we plead Your care over him as he completes his dangerous mission."

Enzo paused and Paul wondered if he intended that Paul pray aloud too. He did not feel led, so he just remained quiet.

Finally, Enzo spoke again, exhorting and blessing him: "Dear friend, build up your life ever more strongly upon the foundation of our holy faith, learning to pray in the power and strength of the Holy Spirit. Stay always within the boundaries where God's love can reach and bless you.

"Try to help those who argue against you. Be merciful to those who doubt. Save some by snatching them as from the very flames of hell itself. And as for others, help them to find the Lord by being kind to them, but be careful that you yourself aren't pulled along into their sins. Hate every trace of their sin while being merciful to them as sinners.

"And now—all glory to Him who alone is God, who saves us through Jesus Christ our Lord; yes, splendor and majesty, all power and authority are His from the beginning; His they are and His they evermore shall be. And He is able to keep you from slipping and falling away, and to bring you, sinless and perfect, into His glorious presence with mighty shouts of everlasting joy. Amen."

• • •

By the time Jae had endured the rush-hour traffic and was into Indiana, the kids were sound asleep and she was already near the end of the thirteenth chapter of Acts. She thought she had been paying attention to the story and all the exciting things recorded, but she really perked up at the words of the apostle Paul as he preached in Antioch. He had just established that prophecy had been fulfilled with Jesus' death and resurrection.

But God raised him from the dead! And he appeared over a period of many days to those who had gone with him from

Galilee to Jerusalem—these are his witnesses to the people of Israel. . . .

This is what the second psalm is talking about when it says concerning Jesus, "You are my Son. Today I have become your Father."

For God had promised to raise him from the dead, never again to die. . . . Brothers, listen! In this man Jesus there is forgiveness for your sins.

Jesus is still alive? Is that what the underground believers mean when they say He is coming back soon? Back from where? Back from where He lives now? There was the sin thing again, too. Ever since Jae had first heard it, she had been obsessed with her own short-comings. How much easier life had been when she never thought about this! She skipped ahead and heard the apostle Paul defending himself before a king.

Authorized by the leading priests, I caused many of the believers in Jerusalem to be sent to prison. And I cast my vote against them when they were condemned to death. Many times I had them whipped in the synagogues to try to get them to curse Christ.

This could be about my father and my husband, Jae thought. She hoped with all that was in her that Paul had never had people whipped. Dare she ask him?

I was so violently opposed to them that I even hounded them in distant cities of foreign lands.

Now this was hitting a little too close to home. Jae had to turn off the disc a moment. It didn't appear this Paul had even been seeking God. In fact, it was clear he was God's enemy. And yet God invaded his life.

Later, Jae put in a new disc and found herself in the book of Romans, a letter Paul had written to the believers in Rome. She was particularly struck by several different passages.

> *For I am not ashamed of this Good News about Christ. It is the power of God at work, saving everyone who believes—Jews first and also Gentiles. This Good News tells us how God makes us right in his sight. This is accomplished from start to finish by faith. As the Scriptures say, "It is through faith that a righteous person has life."*

Everyone? How many did that include since this was written? And exactly what is this Good News about Christ? Was the underground church as small as her father believed? Or might it be a strong force that had never surrendered?

> *For all have sinned; all fall short of God's glorious standard. Yet now God in his gracious kindness declares us not guilty. He has done this through Christ Jesus, who has freed us by taking away our sins. For God sent Jesus to take the punishment for our sins and to satisfy God's anger against us. We are made right with God when we believe that Jesus shed his blood, sacrificing his life for us.*

Jae's head was full of new ideas. Who knew all this was in the Bible? She couldn't wait to talk with Paul. If Straight wouldn't satisfy her curiosity, surely her husband, new man that he was, would want to discuss it.

Several minutes later she found herself especially intrigued again.

Therefore, since we have been made right in God's sight by faith, we have peace with God because of what Jesus Christ our Lord has done for us. Because of our faith, Christ has brought us into this place of highest privilege where we now stand, and we confidently and joyfully look forward to sharing God's glory.

Peace with God? Peace with a God Jae wasn't even sure existed? *God has something specifically in mind for us? for me? Surely not.* Jae found her mind wandering as she pondered this, but the text grabbed her again when the apostle Paul summarized:

What can we say about such wonderful things as these? If God is for us, who can ever be against us? Since God did not spare even his own Son but gave him up for us all, won't God, who gave us Christ, also give us everything else?

Can anything ever separate us from Christ's love? Does it mean he no longer loves us if we have trouble or calamity, or are persecuted, or are hungry or cold or in danger or threatened with death? (Even the Scriptures say, "For your sake we are killed every day; we are being slaughtered like sheep.") No, despite all these things, overwhelming victory is ours through Christ, who loved us.

And I am convinced that nothing can ever separate us from his love. Death can't, and life can't. The angels can't, and the demons can't. Our fears for today, our worries about tomorrow, and even the powers of hell can't keep God's love away. Whether we are high above the sky or in the deepest ocean, nothing in all creation will ever be able to separate us from the love of God that is revealed in Christ Jesus our Lord.

No wonder these people are willing to put their lives on the line for something they believe in! The Bible itself acknowledged that they might face death for this decision. Is it fair for a government, a world system, to tell people who they can and cannot believe in? Jae worried she was becoming sympathetic to the enemies of the state.

13

BECAUSE THE INTERNATIONAL GOVERNMENT charter plane had been pressed into service for the Styr Magnor investigation, on Saturday morning, Paul flew commercially the nearly seven hundred miles from Rome to the heart of northern France. Paris remained its capital and largest city, some fifteen million living in the greater metropolitan area.

Paul landed at Le Bourget Airport and breezed through customs on the strength of his top-level clearance ID. He was met in the terminal by a swarthy, balding, sixtyish man who looked uncomfortable in a tight white shirt, tie, and suit, carrying a trench coat over one arm. He was about five-ten, and Paul guessed him at close to two-hundred-fifty pounds. The man introduced himself as Karlis Grosvenor, Paris bureau chief of NPO International. He shook hands firmly but briefly and led Paul to an idling sedan at the curb, his large, expensive shoes echoing throughout the terminal.

Paul was impressed that Grosvenor was alone. No aides or lackeys for him. "I am not going to waste your time, Doctor, by arranging a bunch of meetings with my division heads. First, they are all busy, as you can understand. Second, I like to stay totally informed in an investigation such as this, so I can tell you anything they could. They are all working today and taking tomorrow off, which I would like to do as well. Unless you have other needs, plans, or questions, I will take you on a driving tour of the city, ending at the attack site. Then I will deliver you to your hotel, where we have provided a fleet car for your use."

"That sounds perfect, Chief. Thank you."

As they passed the city of Denis on their way south into the city, Grosvenor pointed at a skyscraper in the distance. "That's your hotel."

"Really, out here? Pardon me for saying so, but it seems a bit remote from the city."

Grosvenor, who seemed to eschew eye contact—or any kind of enthusiasm as far as Paul could tell—said, "All those arrangements were handled through Bern."

Paul tucked that away. Having decided a small dose of paranoia might keep him alive, he had to wonder if he had been lodged so far from Paris (only a few miles, really) so he could be more easily observed. "It's sure a tall one; I'll say that."

"You won't see many that tall within Paris proper. After the Maine-Montparnasse Tower, which is nearly sixty stories, was finished almost seventy-five years ago, people didn't like how it looked on the skyline. The city council put a ten-story limit on new construction, and it's still in force."

"Except for the Eiffel, eh?"

Grosvenor nodded. "That was the exception. And when you see what a half mile of rubble looks like, you'll understand why there's an outcry to not rebuild it again."

Paul did not respond.

"First time in Paris?" Grosvenor said.

"No. I flew through here once. Didn't see much but Orly Airport and the hotel there."

"Well, you can't tell in the daytime, but come this evening you'll know why it's known as the City of Light."

"I understand it's one of the most beautiful cities in the world."

"Used to be," the chief said, not elaborating. Soon Paul was able to tell why he'd said that. "We'll take the Boulevard Haussmann to the Arc de Triomphe, then head southeast on the Champs-Élysées all the way past the Louvre to the Bastille, staying on the right bank of the Seine. Then we'll cross the river to the left bank on Boulevard Germain—formerly Boulevard Saint-Germain—and come back northwest past the Île de la Cité, the Island of the City, to Bourbon Palace. That's where the government is housed and where we have our offices. From there it's a short drive to the Champ-de-Mars. After that you will be on your own, but I will remain available."

"Thank you. Isn't the Island of the City where Notre Dame stands?"

Grosvenor nodded. "Of course it's not called that anymore, and the crosses are long gone. It houses the University of the Self-Movement now."

As they reached the Arch de Triomphe at the western end of the Champs-Élysées, Grosvenor finally turned enthusiastic tour guide and bragged that it remained "at nearly fifty meters, the largest arch in the world."

"Largest triumphal arch maybe," Paul said, unable to hold his tongue.

"I beg your pardon?"

"Chief, the St. Louis Arch has to be nearly four times the size of this one."

Grosvenor made a dismissive sound. "That is a mere novelty. This is a magnificent work of art, more than two hundred years old and decorated with the figures in relief."

Paul couldn't argue with that.

While Grosvenor circled the great arch, Paul counted twelve wide avenues extending from the square in all directions. His host headed southeast on the Champs-Élysées, soon passing the Place de la Concorde, the Square of Peace. Paul noted the famous chestnut trees dotting the landscape, but the beauty of this once-regal city had been compromised by the same blight that marred Rome. Decades of thumbing their noses at anything relating to God had somehow driven every moral standard to its lowest common denominator. Grosvenor failed to point out the houses of ill repute, the women of the evening working in broad daylight, the drug trafficking in full view of the public. *Corrupt*, Paul thought. The whole city reeked of corruption. He wondered if that embarrassed Grosvenor or if he, like Chief Marcello in Rome, was so used to it by now that he didn't even notice.

To the credit of the French, the great Louvre had been left intact and unblemished. Paul had not expected it to be so large, extending nearly half a mile, bordered on the south by the Seine and on the north by the Rue de Rivoli. They soon came within sight of the Island of the City and the former Notre Dame Cathedral to Paul's right, but Grosvenor said they would get a better view after they turned around at the Bastille.

Crossing the Seine to the left bank, Paul got a full view of the great cathedral with its famed flying buttresses standing on the Island of the City in the Seine. Only the absence of the crosses, which had not been addenda but rather part of the fabric of the design, detracted from the beauty of the place. He couldn't even figure out how they camouflaged the crosses, but an enormous sign clarified that the structure was now the University of the Self-Movement.

To his left, Grosvenor pointed out the Panthéon, the University of Paris, and Luxembourg Palace. About a half mile farther up Boulevard Germain they passed what Paul said looked as if it too had once been a church.

"Very good," Grosvenor said. "The former namesake of this boulevard, the Saint-Germain-des-Prés Church. It now houses the original documents of the Humanist Manifesto and draws nearly a million visitors a year."

Just before they reached Bourbon Palace, Grosvenor turned left, and they soon came within site of the devastation of the Eiffel Tower at the Champ-de-Mars. Guards recognized Grosvenor and his car immediately, saluting and waving him through. It had been a week since the tragedy, yet to Paul it appeared as fresh as hours ago. Thousands of forensics experts still combed the place. As Grosvenor carefully picked his way around great recognizable chunks of the famous landmark, now scattered over half a mile, he gave way to dump trucks, garbage trucks, front-end loaders, cranes, and all manner of emergency vehicles.

Finally, in a spot where Paul could take in almost the entire expanse of the once-great tower, Grosvenor pulled over and parked. He sighed and wiped his head and face with a handkerchief. "Here is what we know from eyewitnesses," he said sadly and paused as Paul quickly dug through his bag for his notebook.

"As you might imagine, there were very few survivors close enough to the epicenter of the blast to provide useful information. The best we can determine, it was one bomb. A couple of eyewitnesses corroborate something we picked up on a closed-circuit surveillance camera."

Grosvenor pulled a small player and disc from his glove box

and turned it on for Paul. "I apologize for the poor quality and also that the activity in question is not centered on the screen. But who knew where this camera should have been pointed?"

The disc showed that the camera was intended as a record of the lines waiting for the elevators within the tower. "Naturally, because of what had happened in Rome and London the day before, local authorities were being most careful. The lines were slow, and we worried that tempers would flare and fights would break out. Ironically, none of this occurred, but here, look, right there at the top right of the image area. A bakery truck pulls up, you see?"

Paul nodded. "Henri Foods," he read from the side, which also depicted loaves of bread and platters piled with croissants.

"We have determined that the truck was phony. Though there are three bakeries in Paris with similar names, none uses that style or picture or even that model truck, a year-old Benz. There, see, the driver gets out, goes round to the back, and begins stacking, meter by meter, wheeled flats of bakery goods until the pile is two feet higher than he is. Notice how heavy that tray is, right there, as he pulls it from the truck. You see?"

"I do."

"That, we believe, carried the incendiary. Not only is it clearly several times heavier than any of the other trays, but the driver also places it gingerly atop the others."

"Yes, and he seems casual and even reckless with the others."

"We believe he may have actually had bakery-truck experience, because other than that one suspicious tray, he appears to do this habitually, methodically, easily."

"You've had bakeries view this to see if they can identify him?"

"Of course, Doctor," Grosvenor said, pausing the disc.

"Sorry, silly question."

"Not at all, but yes, we have been pursuing every avenue." He started the disc again. "Now watch—he pushes the tall stack of fresh-baked goods toward the bistro located in what we call the front-right foot of the tower. We have compared this footage with the work of other bakery-truck drivers, and the only difference is the amount of effort it takes him to get the stack moving. Even a large rolling supply like that is not very heavy if it is made up mostly of bread and rolls and some pastries."

"The bomb makes the difference."

"That is our conclusion. But notice that someone from the bistro, the man in the green apron, meets him. We're only guessing, of course, but it appears he is disputing that an order is due that day. In fact, he seems to look with confusion at the truck, as if he doesn't recognize it. The two are arguing here, see? The driver pulls a sheet of paper from his pocket, opens it, shows the man, slaps it with the back of his hand. It's as if he's insisting he has an order and he's determined to deliver it. Green-apron man is now gesturing wildly as if to say he wouldn't know where to put it. This becomes graphic, Doctor."

As Paul watched, the driver balls up the order form and throws it at the man in the apron. It bounces off his chest. The driver then runs to his truck as the man picks up the paper and seems to rear back to throw it at the driver. The driver appears to turn the key in the truck, and the stack of baked goods vaporizes. The last image for several seconds is the bistro man flying through the air from the image area. The truck is obliterated in the blast, as are hundreds of people standing in line, most of whom never even noticed the altercation.

As the dust settles and the camera wobbles, it shows the great tower shaking, leaning, and falling. Remarkably, the camera continues to record as it lies on the ground, until debris and dirt and a great dust cloud fill the frame.

"I think it's fairly self-explanatory," Paul said, "but what have you deduced from it?"

"Just speculating, of course," Grosvenor said, "but I believe the driver thought he could get the goods and the bomb into the bistro somehow. It would have done its damage more directly from there, but obviously it was large enough to accomplish its work anyway.

"It was clearly triggered by the ignition of the truck, so the driver had to initiate the receptor as he was lifting that tray out. We don't think he ran to the truck thinking he could avoid the blast but rather simply to do the deed before the restaurateur made enough of a scene to draw authorities."

"So plainly a suicide mission."

Grosvenor nodded. "But what an elaborate scheme, eh? All the detail on the truck. And those baked goods appear to be the real thing."

"I don't mean to insult you, but I assume you checked—"

"These pictures with Parisian bakeries to see if anyone sold the goods to this man in this truck? Of course."

"Sorry."

"No apology necessary. I know this is not your field, Doctor. But then I don't imagine anything you've just seen gives you any insight into the religious nature of this crime."

"No."

"Pity."

"You say there were surviving eyewitnesses? I can't imagine."

"As often happens, even in heinous events like this, blind luck finds someone standing behind the right girder or falling beneath the right bodies and somehow avoiding death. They might as well have died for the horrific memories they'll live with, but out of hundreds we did have a half dozen survivors actually under the tower. Two of them have a vague recollection of the confrontation, and one believes he heard part of the conversation. That's poignant, I must say, as it's touch and go whether he'll ever hear another thing as long as he lives."

"What did he hear?"

"He claims the driver shouted, 'Long live Jonah' as he threw the wadded-up paper at the other man."

"You know the significance of that, don't you, Chief?"

"I've been briefed on all the findings in Rome, yes. And we were all aware of your Las Vegas case."

"Might I get a few minutes with that witness?"

"Sorry. Have to say no on that one. He's been so traumatized that his lawyer refuses to let him talk about it anymore. Waiting for money from the entertainment industry, if you ask me. But also, I'm satisfied that we got out of him everything he knew. And what we know, you know."

· · ·

Jae had pulled up to her parents' Georgetown brownstone late the previous evening, the kids sound asleep. She was disconcerted to find cars in the driveway and on the street, the light burning in her father's den. Jae's mother answered the door in her bathrobe. She embraced Jae and carried Connor up to bed while Jae lugged Brie inside. Neither child stirred.

"Where's Dad?" Jae asked as her mother followed her back out to the car to help with the luggage. "You shouldn't have to do this."

"Big meeting. He says to say hi and he'll see you tomorrow."

"Can't even break to greet his daughter."

"Now, honey, you know how important these last-minute meetings can be."

Once the luggage was inside, Jae's mother asked her if she was hungry or thirsty.

"No," she said. "I need to get to bed and so do you. Thanks for everything."

Her mother tried to express how thrilled she was to have Jae and the kids, but Jae shushed her and nudged her toward her bedroom. Then Jae hurried back out to the car and grabbed her disc player and pulled the disc from the dashboard. She was exhausted and ready for sleep, but there were a few things she had heard during the last hundred miles that she wanted to hear again.

Finally in bed, she attached the earphones, looked at her hastily scribbled notes, and found the verses. In First Corinthians she had heard:

> It is this Good News that saves you if you firmly believe it—unless, of course, you believed something that was never true in the first place.
>
> I passed on to you what was most important and what had also been passed on to me—that Christ died for our sins, just as the Scriptures said. He was buried, and he was raised from the dead on the third day, as the Scriptures said.

Jae had no idea why these verses gripped her so, but she felt compelled to memorize that last one, beginning with "Christ died for our sins . . ." She played it and replayed it until she was able to recite it without aid. Then she found the passage in Ephesians that had also made her make a note:

> God is so rich in mercy, and he loved us so very much, that even while we were dead because of our sins, he gave us life when he raised Christ from the dead. (It is only by God's special favor that you have been saved!) For he raised us from the dead along with Christ, and we are seated with him in the

heavenly realms—all because we are one with Christ Jesus. And so God can always point to us as examples of the incredible wealth of his favor and kindness toward us, as shown in all he has done for us through Christ Jesus.

God saved you by his special favor when you believed. And you can't take credit for this; it is a gift from God. Salvation is not a reward for the good things we have done, so none of us can boast about it.

Jae didn't intend to memorize that, but she wanted to hear it again and again. So she set the coordinates and programmed the player to repeat, and she listened to the passage all night, six or eight times before she drifted off.

• • •

"Would you care to take a walk-through?" Grosvenor said. "Not too many will get the privilege, if you can call it that."

"I'd be honored," Paul said. "I'd regret it if I didn't."

"I'm going to pass, if you don't mind. Once is more than enough, believe me." Grosvenor gave him a pass to clip to his coat. "Take your time, and I'll be parked near the École Militaire at the other end."

Paul started at the base of the tower. Forensics personnel told him that the mostly intact bodies had been removed, but that this team was now collecting body parts. Everyone wore surgical masks and rubber gloves, and they all looked dog tired as they picked through the debris with small brushes, placing tiny fragments in plastic bags.

The three remaining legs of the tower were silhouetted in surreal relief against the late morning sky. From where he stood, looking at the gold girders strewn across the length of the park, Paul could not see the end, the top of the tower, which had whip-cracked, according to authorities, and actually catapulted over the École Militaire.

As Paul walked the more than half mile from the base to the waiting Karlis Grosvenor, he was overcome. He felt the presence of evil, of grief and tragedy. Death here had an author, and though he knew that somewhere Styr Magnor was likely rightly taking credit for it, the real source of these casualties was the enemy of God himself. Straight and what he had heard of the New Testament over the past several months had taught him that much.

He couldn't forget the passage in the book of John where Jesus Himself spoke of Satan as the thief: *"The thief's purpose is to steal and kill and destroy. My purpose is to give life in all its fullness. I am the good shepherd. The good shepherd lays down His life for the sheep."*

Paul's molar emitted a tone and he took a call from Alonza Marcello. "Thought you'd want to know," she said. "DNA and actually part of a fingerprint from the second suicide bomber traces to a Scot named Philip McCandlish, a penny-ante mercenary lowlife NPO International had in their files. Used to be in jail all the time. Hasn't been arrested for more than ten years."

"Never heard of him."

"Neither have we, but we thought it significant that he's not Scandinavian."

14

BRIE AND CONNOR SEEMED to have forgotten their aversion
to Washington and woke Jae with their roughhousing. Actually,
what woke her was her father barking at them. They quieted immediately, and Jae assumed they were scared of him. Why
shouldn't they be? She always had been.

Jae called down the stairs, "Dad, just give me a minute to get
a shower and I'll take over!"

"Your mother has already taken over. They're going to the
zoo."

"Have her wait for me! I'll go along. The kids are going to be
without me enough during this visit."

"No! I need some time with you, Jae. They're on their way
out the door."

"Did they eat?"

"They're getting fast food."

That, Jae assumed, would make everything worth it.

When she finally dressed and headed downstairs, Jae smelled pancakes and sausage, her father's specialty and one of her childhood favorites. It had taken her years to catch on that his fixing this breakfast was always a means to an end. It was his way of apologizing for a slight or an overreaction. It could also be his way of telling her he loved her or respected her or even liked her—things he had never been able to put into words. Often this morning ritual was a way of breaking down Jae's resistance to some scheme or another.

Wonder what he wants.

As usual, her burly father dominated even their expansive kitchen. Wearing corduroy trousers and a thick, flannel shirt, and padding around in woolen socks, he had set her place, with every utensil where it ought to be. He kissed her on the cheek but didn't embrace or touch her because he had a mitt on one hand and a spatula in the other.

How convenient.

"S'pose I've told you before," he said, his shock of white hair gleaming under the kitchen chandelier, "but I had to learn etiquette when I studied protocol for overseas duty."

She nodded. *Only a million times.*

"Sit right here, princess," he said. He had set a place for himself directly across from her. "You remember this breakfast, don't you?"

"Of course I do. My favorite."

"You can have it every morning if you want."

"Yeah, and I can go back to Chicago weighing five thousand pounds."

He wasn't listening. Nothing new. "Not that *I'll* fix it every time," he said. "Your mother does a passable job, and you can cook it for me once in a while. We'll be riding to the office together, needless to say."

"We will?"

"'Course! I can't wait. Commuting with my favorite daughter."

"Your only daughter, Dad."

"My favorite child then, all right? There, I've said it."

"You've said it before, Daddy, and you know you shouldn't. I hope you've never let Berlitz get wind of that."

"Agh!" he growled, waving her off with the spatula. The very mention of her brother's name had clouded him over.

Jae had never minded needling him. "You ought to get *him* a job with the NPO," she said. "He might surprise you."

"Surprise me? *Surprise* me! I'd be amazed if it weren't the end of the republic as we know it."

As always, everything was hot and done at the same time, and Ranold Decenti piled the plates with food and set them out like a pro. "Got something I want to talk to you about, honey."

What a shock.

For all his manners and etiquette, Jae's father had a penchant for talking with his mouth full when he was excited. Jae never ceased to be amazed at how he could pull it off without offending. Somehow he was able to tuck his food deep in a cheek somewhere and sound as articulate and passionate as ever.

"You're not really coming to work for me as a numbers gal," he said.

"What?"

"Now don't get your linens in a bind," he said. "It'll look like that's what you're doing. You'll have spreadsheets on your computer and all that, but I've got much more important work for you."

"But, Dad, I'm not trained in—"

"Bip, bip, bip," he said, "don't start fighting me on this before you even hear what it is."

She hadn't lifted her fork yet. He pointed to her food. "Enjoy, enjoy. You'll like this idea."

· · ·

"Do you feel like a light lunch," Paris NPO Bureau Chief Karlis Grosvenor said, "or did your walk spoil your appetite?"

"Both," Paul said. "I was a baby when the war ended, you know, so to see this and the Rome thing inside a few days . . . whew. How do you deal with it?"

"I don't know," Grosvenor said. "I *am* old enough to remember the war, so I saw the original tower before and after. It was nothing like this, but the TV images from around the world? A lot worse then. Makes me want to be the guy to kill Magnor though."

"I know what you mean."

Grosvenor pulled up to a huge, ornate, white building atop Paris's tallest hill at the north edge of the city. It was called Coeur de Paris. "The Heart of Paris," he said. "Besides the upscale shops, there's a great little bistro here. As you can imagine, I know them all."

Paul was not in a mood to kid the chief about his girth, even if Grosvenor had raised the subject. As they walked through the parking lot, Paul stared at the onion-shaped dome and bell tower of the magnificent structure. "This had to have been a church once too."

Grosvenor nodded. "Basilica du Sacré-Coeur. The Basilica of the Sacred Heart. Yet another gaudy monument to the so-called sacred heart of Mary, mother of the God who allows things like the bombing of the tower. If that doesn't disabuse these lunatics of their ideas—but of course, it was the crazies who did this! Or at least they want the credit for it. Does that make a bit of sense to you, Doctor?"

"Not a bit," Paul said.

"We'll just have appetizers," Grosvenor said as they were seated, which sounded just right to Paul. But while he ordered a small plate of snails in garlic butter sauce, the big man ordered pastries stuffed with chicken and cream sauce, plus mushrooms in a thick wine sauce. Still he finished long before Paul and was soon bouncing a knee and quietly drumming the table.

"Sorry to keep you," Paul said. "We can go. I can even get a cab to my hotel."

"It's not that far," Grosvenor said. "I'm ready when you are."

Paul was eager to be alone so he could check in with Straight and find out how he was to connect with the head of the Parisian underground tonight. But he didn't want to appear too eager to be free of Grosvenor, even though the chief didn't hide that he was ready to get back to his own affairs.

"We'll stay out of your hair," Grosvenor said as he dropped Paul off at his hotel. "And we'll expect to hear from you only if you have insight that will help our case."

Paul found it interesting that he was assigned a room on the fortieth floor. Had he been in charge of that—assuming International was making sure their inquiring eyes had plenty of time to pick up his trail every time he left the hotel—he would have at least tried to throw off the target by giving him a fancy suite and blaming the high floor on that. But he had a normal room, still spectacular and with an awe-inspiring view.

On the phone Straight told him that Chappell Raison was eager to meet him and had been waiting for a couple of hours already.

"Waiting? Waiting where?"

"You'll need to record this."

"Meet him in broad daylight? I don't know, Straight."

"It's remote. Trust me."

"Yeah, but I still have to get there. How remote?"

"A little more than a hundred miles southwest of you. You recording?"

"Just a minute."

Paul pressed his index, middle, and ring fingers to his thumb tip simultaneously and heard within his skull a woman's voice. "Recording."

"Fire away," he said.

When Straight finished reading the directions, Paul turned off the mechanism. "I can't take an International car. I'll have to rent."

"There's a rental agency within walking distance of the hotel," Straight said. "And here's Raison's number."

Paul took it but said, "You call him. Tell him I'll be a couple of hours."

"A couple of hours for a hundred miles? What century are you living in, Paul?"

"I've got to get the car, and I don't know the terrain. I'm just saying . . ."

"I'll tell him."

"You can also tell him I don't like the idea of doing this during the day."

"Already did," Straight said. "You want to hear why he thinks it's important, or you want to let him tell you in person?"

"In person."

. . .

"Jae, we're on the cusp of a very exciting adventure, maybe one of the most important missions in the history of the NPO. Are you in?"

"I don't know, Dad. I didn't exactly sign on for this. I came here so I wouldn't go crazy with Paul being away. I wanted to help where you had a need, and I wanted my kids to get to know my family a little better. You can't say you've been a terribly involved grandfather."

He ignored that, again no surprise. "But, Jae, listen; your country needs you. I need you. I'm going to let you in on some highly classified information, and I need to know you can handle it. You're smart, you're patriotic, and I've always known you to be a loyal citizen. Does that still apply?"

In spite of herself, even knowing that her father was flattering her for his own purposes, Jae lived and died for positive input from him. "Of course, Dad. If there's something you think I can help with—"

"It's more than something to help with, honey. It's top secret, classified, for-your-eyes-only kind of stuff, and frankly you were the first person who came to my mind for the assignment."

Now he was really shoveling deep. A founding father of the National Peace Organization, having worked with the best minds in international espionage, intelligence, and security for decades, and *she* was the first person he thought of for—what had he called it?—one of the most important missions in the history of the agency? Please. "Why me?"

"Finish your breakfast and we'll talk in the den."

Uh-oh. This has to be about Paul.

• • •

Paul closed the drapes to within six inches of each other, then set timed triggers on his television and lights. While he was gone it would appear he was still here, and anyone monitoring his window would see the flickering of channels changing and lights going on and off in various rooms every few hours. The question was whether he could slip out unnoticed.

He took the jetvator down to the thirtieth floor, walked

down two flights and moved to the other side of the tower, taking another jetvator to the fifth floor. From there he took escalators to the second, then a jetvator to the parking level. He headed back up to ground level via two staircases at the back of the place and walked directly to the car-rental agency. Using the automatic kiosk under an alias he had never used before, he rented the smallest, most inconspicuous car he could find. Top speed was only a hundred and twenty miles an hour. Anyone who knew him would not be able to imagine him in an economy car.

From the kiosk came a computerized voice. *"Danke, Herr Koen. Guten Tag."* How nice of the French to make a German feel at home.

The middle of the afternoon foot traffic in the city confirmed Paul's suspicion that Paris had to be one of the most crowded capitals in the world. He didn't feel he could open up the hydrogen engine until he had passed the exit to Orly south of the metropolis and the city of Palaiseau. Playing back the recording of Straight through his cranium, Paul proceeded to rocket southwest toward the Loire River near Tours. He checked in with satellite weather and found that the temperature in Paris had been five degrees Celsius and that Tours would be six. *Forty-one and forty-two Fahrenheit,* he calculated.

Paul soon was at top speed, but he had to concentrate as headwinds buffeted the tiny car. He continually checked his mirrors for tails and was certain there were none.

•   •   •

Jae had a bad feeling as she settled into her father's own chair in the den. He was pulling out all the stops. Had he asked if she'd wanted a Scotch, she'd have scolded him for suggesting such a thing so early in the day. But when he simply poured her a tall one, straight, not even on the rocks, she took it gratefully with trembling fingers. She found it significant that he abstained.

"Had quite a meeting here last night," he began.

"Did you?" she said, sipping and trying to sound nonchalant.

He sat across from her and leaned forward, elbows on his knees. "I'm going to tell you things you don't want to hear."

"About Paul?"

"Yes."

She set down the drink and clasped her hands. She didn't want to know, and yet there was nothing she'd rather know. "Women?"

"Likely."

She swore. "Worse?"

"In my opinion. Of course, there's little worse in this world than violating one's vows to a spouse. . . ."

Oh, please. You don't think I know your own past?

"But you've been through that before and found it in your heart to forgive and start rebuilding."

"Like a fool, apparently. Get on with it, Dad."

"Well, this latest is worse than a little marital trouble, which is not easy to say to the victim of that trouble. It points to treason, Jae."

She couldn't breathe. It must have showed.

"Take another sip, honey."

She did. "Treason?"

"Paul has always had a penchant for working alone."

"How well I know. But not alone enough apparently."

"I'm off the marital thing now, Jae. Stay with me."

"Treason, yes."

"The reason he was so susceptible to temptation on the other issue was because he's not a team player. He goes on assignment, gets briefed by locals, then goes out on his own."

"That used to be his strength." Jae was seething, already eager to do whatever her father was asking if it meant nailing Paul. Did she not care what that would mean to her, to the kids? Frankly, no. He would get what he deserved and they would all be better off without him. How quickly she had turned. So he *had* been covering something, and not just other women but something that threatened the very security of the USSA. She'd help with this operation—whatever it was—even if she wasn't married to the perpetrator.

"Jae are you familiar with Stockholm syndrome?"

"Where a hostage becomes sympathetic to the kidnapper?"

"In a nutshell. Being as generous as possible, that's what we think may have happened with Paul."

She closed her eyes and shook her head. "You've lost me."

• • •

Intense. That was all Paul had heard about Chappell Raison. He didn't even know what the man looked like. He couldn't wait to meet him, broad daylight or not. Normally Paul would have enjoyed the beautiful scenery. But the rolling plains and the heavily wooded plateaus and hills hardly registered as he concentrated on the road ahead and behind. He saw sheep and cows grazing, but his eyes couldn't linger. Straight's directions told him to watch for a famous example of French Renaissance architecture, the Château de Chenonceau that spanned the River Cher. "Chappell says you'll know it when you see it. Unique, I guess."

Unique was right. As the dazzling structure came into view, Paul wished he had a camera. Jae would love this. Nine parapets at the base of the roof level topped two stories of windows over four wide archways and a narrower one, all designed, it appeared, to allow boats through beneath the château. On the far right end was a series of cathedral-like towers, but Paul couldn't tell if the building originated as anything religious, as any carved ornate symbols now bore the seal of the International Government of Peace.

Three miles past the château, Paul was to look for a right turn onto an unmarked two-lane road between a dairy farm and a cattle farm. Straight's recording said, "If you see any traffic whatsoever, it should be farm machinery." Paul encountered none, and to the best of his knowledge, no one had followed him into the country.

Two more miles and another right turn took him to a grove of trees, one of which had a large white scar in its trunk, as if it had once had a chunk of bark ripped off by a car or truck. Paul was to drive slowly past the tree, looking for his contact.

15

"BEFORE I GET INTO SPECIFICS, Jae," Ranold B. Decenti said, "I must discuss something of the utmost importance with you."

"As if Paul's infidelity, not to mention *treason,* is not important."

"You and I have had our differences, and like most people of your generation, you probably think me and others of my generation are largely out to lunch. But listen; I pick up on things. I understand subtleties and nuances, though no one would likely assume that of me."

"Hardly." But Jae knew it was true. You didn't get to his station in the intelligence community by being as bullheaded and close-minded as he seemed.

"You've made it clear lately that you've been encouraged about your relationship with Paul. After what I tell you, you might begin to understand why that has happened."

I think I'm already understanding it.

"But because you're encouraged—and I know you are because you're missing him so—"

I was. Right now I don't care if I ever see him again, except to kill him.

"—I imagine you're in frequent contact with him. I hope I don't have to belabor this point, Jae, but you can understand how crucial it is—"

"I know."

"You know?"

She nodded. "Mad as I'm going to be, betrayed as I feel, I can't let on that anything has changed."

"There! You see? You're perfect for this assignment."

Jae knew she should care more about the treason than the infidelity, but if she had it her way, she would force her father for every detail of Paul's indiscretions. What a delicate word for a disgusting practice. She wanted to ask who? when? where? for how long? Were these his typical one-night stands, or was he actually interested in someone for once?

And Jae couldn't decide which would be more acceptable. Either made her murderous. The nerve! To come on like he was a new man, a changed guy, as eager to backhoe and fill and work on the marriage as she. Jae had actually looked forward to the rest of their married life together, allowed herself to imagine how much healthier Brie and Connor were going to be growing up in a happy home. Now Paul was going to have to sue her to see his own kids. If he wasn't behind bars or put to death. The latter was too good for him, unless she got to give the injection herself.

"Dad, I'm going to need a minute."

"Jae, I haven't even told you anything yet."

"You've told me enough. Not that I don't want to hear it all.

But I just . . . just . . . I'll be right back." She hurried from the room, then spun and came back, grabbing the Scotch.

"Don't be long," he said. "I have people waiting for us at headquarters."

"You what?"

But she didn't stay long enough to hear him repeat it. He must have known this would push her over the top, would eliminate any hesitancy on her part about working with him against her own husband. She fled upstairs, set down her drink, and threw herself onto the bed, burying her face in the pillow and screaming.

When she thought she had it out of her system Jae rolled over and sat up, reaching for her glass. There it sat, next to her minidisc player and her New Testament discs. What a laugh. She had actually begun to wonder if perhaps Paul had been influenced—for the good, no less—by these ancient texts. Was that what her father meant by Stockholm syndrome? Did they actually suspect he had flipped to the side of the rebels? That was the very definition of treason.

Throwing back a big swallow, she sloshed liquor on her sweater. Great, she would have to change or go to NPO regional headquarters with booze on her breath *and* on her clothes. She finished the drink, changed her top, gargled with mouthwash, and headed back downstairs as if to her own execution. Jae had gone up to let off some steam, but by the time she reached the den again and heard her father murmuring about her on the phone—"She's ready; she's going to be gold, and we've hardly scratched the surface"—she was ready to burst.

• • •

As Paul slowly rolled along the grassy path between pastures, he saw a redhead poke out and then duck back in behind foliage.

Paul stopped. If that was his contact, Paul would wait until he showed himself again and gave a signal. He wasn't going to simply drive up to a hiding person.

Soon the head poked out again and then the torso, beckoning vigorously with a wave. Paul parked, got out, and walked toward the man, who now stepped out and showed himself. He was almost Paul's height, maybe an inch shorter at six-two. And he looked about the same age—midthirties. He appeared to be in shape, but not from working out. More, Paul guessed, from being the type of person who lived life on the edge, a man with a galloping metabolism and too much to think about and do to worry about overeating. Pale and fleshy without being heavy, he had light blue eyes and a long, aquiline nose with a deep crease between the nostrils. His teeth were too small for his generous mouth.

"You're Paul, right? 'Course you got to be Paul 'cause only a person who knows where he's going comes here. I gave the directions to a guy I trust, and he passed them on to your guy, Straight, a guy *he* trusts, so unless we've got a serious breach of security, you're Paul. You are Paul, right?" He talked a mile a minute.

"He is risen."

"Well, there you go. He is risen indeed. Nice to meet you, Paul."

Chappell Raison shook Paul's hand, his elbow bouncing as he did. And before letting go he embraced Paul, then tugged him into a nearby nondescript, one-room house that looked as if it had been fashioned out of a chicken coop. The screen door slapped behind them. "Better shut the storm door too," Chappell said. "Is it this cold in Paris?"

"About the same," Paul said.

"Let's sit by the fire."

The plastic chairs and table by a tiny gas stove made Paul think of lawn furniture in the USSA. Talk about sparse. "This is the underground?" Paul said. "You couldn't fit more than eight or ten people in—"

"Oh no. Truth is, there is no real underground in France. Physically, I mean. I know of Detroit and Rome and other places where they literally meet underground. Makes me jealous, if you want to know the truth. But here we have the famed Sûreté Nationale. They're under the Ministry of the Interior, which reports directly to NPO International, as you well know."

"I do, Mr. Raison."

"Chappell, please. Better yet, Chapp. My point is, brother, that the Sûreté Nationale gendarmes overstep their bounds. They are supposed to serve as military police and cover the rural areas as well. But naturally, because of the chain of command— all the way to International—every one of them is trying to impress the next level. They give us no end of trouble."

"You lost family, Chapp. Is that right?"

"Wife and two children, a son and a daughter."

"I'm sorry."

"Thank you. I'm sorry too. Every day."

"I can only imagine."

"Well, no you can't, Paul, unless it's happened to you. You don't mind me calling you Paul, do you, because I can just as easily call you brother or Doctor or Mr. Stepola or anything else you want. It doesn't matter to me, but I don't want to offend."

"It doesn't matter to me either, Chapp. Call me anything you want."

"It means a lot to me, to the leadership here, that you have come. We long for news from other groups, and we want to know the latest from the USSA. I get only a little from phone calls. You're like a living, breathing ambassador from our brothers and sisters. I've got the rest of the leadership team coming just after dark, and you're right, we'll fill this place. Can you stay and greet them and give us an update, anything to encourage us?"

Paul looked at his watch. "I think so. I'm to check in with International in the morning to see where they are on the Magnor search."

Raison made a sound. "Magnor."

Paul froze. "What?"

The redhead wouldn't look at him. "I've got to talk to you about him. That's why I had to see you right away."

• • •

Jae let herself drop again into her father's chair and looked at him expectantly.

"Feel better?" he said.

"Hardly. But listen, Dad. Do me a favor. I want both barrels, nothing held back for my feelings. Understand?"

He nodded.

"I'm serious. Maybe you're too close to this. Maybe you ought to have someone else debrief me. Someone who knows all the details and won't try to spare me any grief. If I'm to do this, if I'm to help, I have to know everything."

"Fair enough," he said. "But I can handle telling you."

"You sure?"

"You kiddin'? There's no love lost between Paul and me, not after what he's done to you."

"I thought you were genuinely proud of him. Or was that all playacting?"

"I *was* proud of him! He had won me over there for a while. He was a decorated operative. He's that good, honey. He even fooled me. I don't know how he does it, but just when we're as suspicious as we can be and ready to move in on him, he pulls off a big bust and we assume he's legit. One of the rebels in L.A. tried to tell us he was on their side, even described him and his car and everything. I confronted him on it, and he didn't deny it. But you know what I thought? That he'd gone too far in infiltrating, had stepped outside his authority. I mean, he had the right to do it, but not without telling Bia Balaam or me. He could have got himself killed by either side, and if he *was* acting in NPO interests, we never would have known. Like an idiot, I gave him the benefit of the doubt."

"What's changed your mind?" Jae said. "What's convinced you he's turned?"

"It's not so much what we know as what we don't know," Ranold said.

Jae squinted. There had better be more than that. Just because Paul was still operating independently didn't mean he had flipped. He might still be pretending to be an insider with the underground rebels. If her father got her all exercised with no more than this—

"What don't you know?" she said evenly.

"Where he is. Who he's with. We've got some of our best people on him, and so far no one believes he's aware. He makes and keeps appointments, talks with contacts, never reports in. We're not even telling International yet, because we don't want it to get back to the chancellor. If he started suspecting Paul, he'd just yank him out of the field, charge him with treason, and put him to death."

"What would be wrong with that, if you're right?"

"We want to play this out, Jae. Use Paul. Let him lead us to the heads of the European resistance. We thought we had problems in this country. And we do. But if the Europeans are going to resort to terrorist attacks—in the name of God, of course— that's where we need to concentrate."

Jae sighed. "Tell me you've got more on his infidelity than you have on his treason."

. . .

"Wait," Paul said. "Whoa, hold on, and time out. You've *met* Styr Magnor?"

Chappell Raison nodded. "He visited me here, not long after I lost my family three years ago."

"Where'd he say he was from?"

"Norway, of course, but you want to know the truth? Though he looked Norse, I always thought he was faking the accent. And since then, on the phone, he doesn't sound Norse at all. I can't place it, but he talks like a brother. He's angry, but of course so am I."

"Why didn't I know about this?"

"I told no one."

"No one? None of your contacts in the USSA? No one else in the underground anywhere?"

Chappell shook his head. "Just my leadership team here."

"But why? What about after the attacks? You know the world is looking for him."

"When I realized what he really was, I was embarrassed to have met with him."

"So you were embarrassed! If only you'd have—"

"And I realized long ago he was no friend of the underground, Paul. He predicted these attacks, you know. He told me, 'It may take years, brother, but I will avenge your family.'"

"And you didn't report that? Don't you realize what you could have stopped?"

Chappell stood and paced. "Yes! I'm guilty! Why do you think I'm telling you? I know you're assigned to find and stop him, so I'm telling you now."

"But it's too late for all those innocents in Rome and Paris!"

"Don't you think I live with that twenty-four hours a day? But what could I do? Who would I have told? The authorities would have demanded to know what he wanted with me. I couldn't give up the people here. When years passed and nothing happened, I tried to tell myself he had just been talking. I didn't think he would ever go through with anything."

"How did you know he wasn't a true brother?"

Chappell sat again. "For one thing, he never mentioned the name of Christ. That is a dead giveaway, you know. A lot of God talk and a lot of revenge talk, but no evidence of a real relationship with Jesus. He did not pray with me. I asked him to pray for us, and he asked if I would please do it. I didn't think much of that at the time, but it all added up later."

"Are you still in contact with him?"

"I could be. He tries to contact me."

"He doesn't know you are onto him?"

Chappell shook his head. "It confirmed for me that he was not really one of us when he railed against the USSA NPO for capturing the Jonah character. You were behind that, weren't you?"

"I was, and any discerning believer should have been able to tell that Jonah was a charlatan."

"Of course."

• • •

Jae wasn't the intelligence expert her father was—who was?— but she found it disconcerting when the earnest eye contact she had enjoyed while he was trying to woo her to his side against Paul for treason was now absent as she pressed him for details of Paul's misplaced affections.

"Too much time unaccounted for," Ranold said. "That kind

of thing. You know he's on the prowl, Jae. Leopards don't change their spots."

"You're telling me you have no hard evidence? You can't tell me of all-night visits, frequenting sex shops, that kind of thing?"

"We will be able to soon."

"What are you talking about?"

Now he was clearly nervous, not merely avoiding her gaze but also looking at the floor, out the window, anywhere but at her. "We're going to set him up."

"Entrap him, you mean?"

"That's a strong word, Jae."

"You're going to entrap him!"

"If he's clean, he can't be entrapped, can he?"

"That's true, but what if he wants to stay clean? He keeps himself out of those situations, stays in contact with me. And then while he's weak and tired and homesick you put a woman within reach? Dad, I can't guarantee what I would or wouldn't do with an available young hunk if you tried to entrap me at the wrong time."

"Jae, that's disgusting."

"No more disgusting than trying to entrap one of your own people."

"If you forbid it, we won't do it. But if I were you, I'd want to know how he reacted."

Jae couldn't deny that she definitely would want to know. "Who's in charge of this?"

"Ms. Balaam."

"I met her in L.A. Scary. Paul doesn't like her much."

"That's been clear."

"She's a little old for him, isn't she, Dad?"

Ranold laughed. "She wouldn't be the plant, Jae! We have our choice of, of—"

"You don't have to say it, Dad. I get the picture. Is Balaam going over there?"

"Soon. She's got a son home from college who goes back in a few days."

"So I'll see her today? She'll be at this meeting?"

"She's looking forward to it."

"I'll bet she is."

16

FOR THE FIRST TIME since he'd left the States, Paul was onto something. "You willing to help flush Magnor out for me?"

"Why do you think I told you?" Raison said.

"I'm still trying to understand why you never told anyone else."

"What was there to tell, Paul? He was encouraging to me, trying to support me, to share my grief and anger and sense of vengeance. When I thought he was a brother and he was vowing to get revenge, I was not in a position to argue. In my heart I knew it wasn't right. I know vengeance belongs to the Lord. But what could I say? I would have murdered the gendarmes myself, the ones who executed my family—not just my wife, herself an adult rebel, Paul, but children! Children not yet ten!"

"I understand."

"Do you?"

"Chapp, I know I can't really put myself in your shoes, but I too have a young girl and boy, and I love my wife. I would feel the same if someone took them from me."

Chappell sat in silence a moment. Then, "When I came to my senses and finally understood I was dealing not with a brother but a madman, I was more ashamed than ever. My people here were helping me work through my pain and suffering, and they agreed it would be best to leave Magnor alone. If we exposed him, to whom would we do that? It would only turn the focus on us, because the natural question would be why he turned to me. That is a door, I am sure you agree, that we do not want to open."

Paul thought a moment. "We have to come up with a plan, something foolproof, to draw him out. You're sure he is not aware that you are onto him?"

"Unless my silence has already given me away. But I have never challenged him, never told him how I feel. And he still tries to make contact."

"Would you be willing to thank him for what he has done?"

"What?"

"Get word to him that you are rejoicing in how he has vindicated your family?"

Chappell covered his mouth, then pulled his hand away just enough to be understood. "That makes me ill, Paul. It would take every bit of fortitude I have to be able to express that." His eyes were red and full. "But if the leadership here agrees it is the thing to do and it will in any way avenge the tragedies in England, Italy, and France, I will do it." With that, Chappell Raison broke down.

Paul felt deeply for him, impressed that he had mentioned avenging the terrorist attacks and not even his own family.

He put a hand on Chapp's shoulder and felt his heaving

sobs. "Listen to me," Paul said. "I memorized this from something Straight gave me. It's from the Psalms:

> In times of trouble, may the Lord respond to your cry. May the God of Israel keep you safe from all harm. May he send you help from his sanctuary and strengthen you from Jerusalem. May he remember all your gifts and look favorably on your burnt offerings.
>
> May he grant your heart's desire and fulfill all your plans. May we shout for joy when we hear of your victory, flying banners to honor our God. May the LORD answer all your prayers.

Raison slowly raised his head. "Thank you, my brother. I can't wait until you meet my team."

• • •

By late morning in Washington Jae had been proudly escorted by her father to a lavish boardroom at NPO regional headquarters. She remembered the building from her childhood, but she had never noticed the ornate opulence. Back then it was just where Daddy worked, but now she saw it for what it was: a monument to materialism. With its European-like carvings in the outside granite walls and similar renderings deep in the mahogany inside, it shouted wealth and success and achievement. Her father had long said that this was a place not where someone started but rather where a person finished, "a place to aspire to." Of course, it was built as the national headquarters of the NPO and now merely served as a regional site.

Ranold introduced Jae to various department heads, many who responded to her with friendly smiles before apparently realizing why she wasn't returning their expressions in kind.

"Good to have you here," they would say. "I understand how difficult this must be for you."

The rawboned Bia Balaam, whom Jae would have described as the woman with no lips, seemed overdressed for the occasion. This was a Saturday meeting, off-work hours, and she was dressed in a copper lamé dress and heels, pushing her well over six feet tall, her silver hair up and festive. And those eyes. Jae decided that if she had eyes that matched her hair color as eerily as did Ms. Balaam's, she certainly wouldn't do a thing to try to enhance them.

While formally introducing everyone around the table, Ranold made an issue of his regret over pulling "Chief Balaam away from her college-age son."

"He's probably relieved," Bia said with a smirk. "I tend to dote on him."

Though Jae had had an aversion to the woman since they met, and while her comment seemed self-serving and inappropriate to the tone of the meeting, Jae had to admit that somewhere within her own core, she could identify with doting on a child, regardless of age. Just the knowledge that Bia Balaam was a mother slightly softened Jae's impression of her lack of humanity.

Ranold began to drone on about how he didn't want to keep them long and was eager to get down to business. Jae had learned his rhythms and cadences and knew when to tune him out. All she could think of was that if these people were wrong, if they had misread Paul's motives and intentions and actions, too many people suspected him by now to get the cat back into the bag. Innocent or not, Paul's reputation had been irretrievably soiled.

Ranold's secretary took lunch orders. Jae declined. How could she eat now? How could she do anything but drink? That was the irony of it. Jae probably drank wine twice a month, hard liquor maybe once a month, and always only as a nightcap. She still had a light buzz from the Scotch and wished she'd had more. What could be worse than this? Sitting with eager agents, their teeth into one of the most important internal investigations in their careers, all expecting her to help take down her own husband.

A huge screen was lowered at one end of the room and the lights went down. Then came gigantic projected images of Paul, persuading her that her father, at least, had suspected him for a lot longer than she knew. First came shots of him as an almost gawky military man before they had even met. No body fat. All arms and legs and muscles. Interacting with Delta Force Command Sergeant Major Andrew Pass.

"This was his idol," Ranold said. "There is no evidence that Pass was an underground rebel at this time. Intelligence tells us they doubt it. When Pass turned, we do not know. His brother, John—goes by Jack—is known as a leader of the resistance in our own district. Andrew's daughter, Angela Pass Barger—a widow—is shown here speaking at her father's funeral. Notice that Agent Stepola also attended—*click*—spoke—*click*—and interacted with Ms. Barger."

Jae was stung by the body language and expressions of those two. Paul didn't even seem to be trying to hide his attraction to the woman. This had been a year ago at Wintermas. Had Jae been so cold that day that Paul was on the prowl?

Next came a slide of Paul with a flamboyant-looking redhead Jae did not recognize, even after Ranold identified her as Trina Thomas, head of the Chicago bureau forensics lab. "You'll see later evidence of inappropriate activity between them, but even here you can tell there's interest on his part. Forgive me, Jae, if I'm reading into this."

Jae wanted to hide. Why must she be subjected to this? Here were surreptitious pictures shot within the very walls of Paul's workplace! Would not an agent of his stature realize he was fair game in his own office building? And why was she defensive for him? This Thomas woman looked like a floozy, and yet again, his attraction and flirtations were undeniable.

"Mrs. Thomas, a happily married woman by the way, triggered the remote shutter herself on these. To Paul's credit, at this time he resisted her advances, though his excuse was he was leaving on assignment the next day and could not accept her offer of lunch in exchange for a favor. The favor, she says, was that he was asking her to examine something for him personally. As you'll see, he eventually accepts that offer."

Jae lowered her head and covered her eyes. How bad was this going to get? She looked up again when she heard Ranold rattle a paper and announce that it was Trina Thomas's report of the contact. He read from it: " 'Paul told me it was, and I quote, "A personal favor actually. For Jae." I asked if Jae was ready for me to take him off her hands. He said, "Afraid not. No, it's more of a—it's a genealogy project, I think. She came across some document and wondered if its age could tell her who in her family produced it." ' "

Ranold looked to Jae. "Can you confirm this? Any recollection?"

She shook her head. *What in the world? The letter from his father? Does Paul know I've seen it? I hadn't at that time! Why would Paul lie to this woman?*

Her father set the paper down and continued: "Paul shined in an assignment in San Francisco, killing the woman who headed an underground zealot cell there and himself winding up seriously wounded, the only survivor of that raid. His first day back at work we have these images of him again with Trina Thomas."

These were worse than the first ones. Mrs. Thomas was pulling out all the stops. Jae could tell, even if the Washington-based people couldn't, that Trina was sitting on Paul's secretary's desk, her legs crossed and a high heel dangling from one toe. Paul was under surveillance in his own office! It seemed unfair and invasive, and yet he was getting what he deserved.

Ranold read from Trina Thomas's report again: "'I flirted with him unabashedly and got him to commit to the lunch. And I told him what I had determined about the scrap of paper he had given me. It was part of an envelope, at least thirty-five years old, high quality. High organic content, wood pulp, even cloth fibers. Made me as curious as all get-out, but he never mentioned it again, even though I asked several different ways. All he told me was that it came from one of Jae's relatives during the war at around the turn of the century. I told him I was surprised her relatives couldn't identify it.'"

Ranold looked to Jae again, and she shook her head. "I gave him no such document. This had to be something of his own." Never had she been more tempted to tell her father about Paul's father's letter, but she wasn't about to do that in front of these people.

Ranold projected more images on the screen, almost enough to make Jae leave the room. But she could not pull away. Here was Paul in the dark corner of an elegant restaurant with Trina Thomas. They were eating, leaning into each other, laughing. Now enjoying wine. And more wine. And more. Finally, Paul sat with his arm around her, as if he was about to fall asleep. She looked drunk. And finally an amorous kiss.

Ranold read from her report: "'It was a three-hour lunch, and my assignment was to see if I could get him to, you know, prove he was the same old Paul Stepola.'"

"Assignment from whom?" Jae interrupted.

"Guilty," Ranold said. "I wanted to know if he'd cleaned up his act, and if he hadn't, I would have told you."

"If he hadn't?"

"Listen to this: 'That was as far as it went, and he has avoided me since.'" Ranold looked up. "So that was encouraging."

"To you, maybe. What I just saw was enough." Boy, was it. Lucky for Paul he was not within striking distance. How she would be able to interact with him by phone without letting on that something was wrong was beyond her.

Ranold reported that Paul went on to succeed on yet another assignment, this one in Gulfland, where suspicious oil-well fires appeared to be terrorist acts by the Christian underground. "Paul arrested one of the ringleaders, then risked his life to save the man who had stoned his prisoner to death. Paul lost his sight and wound up in the hospital.

"One of our most encouraging signs about Agent Stepola came about this time when Paul asked me for a disc version of the New Testament. Plainly, he expected to regain his sight and rejoin the ranks of the NPO, and he wanted to be ready and up to speed on his targets. He had majored in religious studies in graduate school, but nothing, he told Koontz, had struck him as so pervasive among devout believers that would cause them to be as zealous as he was finding them now."

Click.

Jae was surprised to see a photo of Straight.

"Here is a man we have yet to figure out," Ranold said. "Name's Dr. Stuart Rathe, now age sixty. He's a former professor at the University of Chicago who lost his job and his family, and a foot I might add, in a car wreck in 28 P.3 while he was drunk. Seems to have tried to put his life back together and assuage his guilt by volunteering at PSL Hospital in Chicago, where he met Agent Stepola. They have become fast friends, have attended chess tournaments together, and appear to keep in touch. He accompanied Agent Stepola here when Paul was still blind and received the Pergamum Medal. I met him when he dropped Paul at our place. Seemed most congenial. We did photograph him lunching with Agent Stepola and the widow Barger on their way out of Washington. Not knowing whether Ms. Barger is associated with the underground the way her father was and her uncle is, we were unable to draw any conclusions about Mr. Rathe. Jae, I assume you know this man, as he has been seen frequenting your home."

"He is a dear friend of the family."

"Any evidence of subversive activity? underground connections?"

"None."

"He has visited you even in Paul's absence, has he not?"

Jae noticed double takes on the parts of some around the table. "I said he is a dear friend of the family. He's wonderful with the kids. And I resent the idea that my home is under surveillance."

"It's for your own protection, honey."

Jae stared hard at her father, who quickly moved along.

"Dr. Raman Bihari, an eye specialist at PSL, reports that the restoration of Paul's sight was as close to miraculous as anything he has encountered in medicine. The NPO was merely grateful to know that Paul would eventually be back to full strength. He was next spotted in Toledo at a chess tournament with Mr. Rathe, and while we suspected an inappropriate sexual dalliance there—a suspicion shared by you, Jae, if you recall—"

If I recall?

"—we were unable to confirm that. Paul completed successful operations in New York and Las Vegas, though we began to suspect him in earnest then. In New York he met with a woman from the offices of Demetrius & Demetrius, who had ties to the underground, but we determined he was merely interrogating her.

"In Las Vegas the aforementioned Ms. Barger reappears and works closely with Paul on the infamous Jonah case. The outcome of that investigation is one of the feathers in Agent Stepola's record. However, as these pictures show, if he was not involved with Ms. Barger, the relationship was clearly overly familiar.

"I personally met Paul in Las Vegas and scolded him on that very issue. He insisted that he merely used her as a means to an end—an end we were pleased with. And there has been no evidence of continued contact with her. He accompanied me to Los Angeles, and you all know the outcome there. My suspicions of Agent Stepola crescendoed there, when I first feared he had flipped allegiances, then decided that he had merely pretended to flip as a bold, undercover move. He did this, however, without the knowledge of Ms. Balaam, his immediate superior, or me, whom it would have been logical to inform."

Jae wondered how much longer she could take this. On one hand, of course, she was ready to throttle Paul. On the other, she was finding it excruciating to give up the promise his new attitude had given her for the future of their lives together. She had never even heard of Trina Thomas, yet who knew what her and Paul's history—or future—might include? Desperate to hold out some hope in the far reaches of her imagination, Jae tried to tell herself that these encounters with other women, though clearly within the last year, predated the change she had detected in Paul. And yet, perhaps they were the reason for his new behavior, at least in front of her. For all she knew, he was seeing both these women regularly and feeling guilty enough about it to treat Jae with more deference and respect than she had enjoyed for years.

Of one thing she was certain so far: the NPO had little on Paul in the matter of flipping. He would appear the same either way. If he had switched allegiances, he would spend time interacting with the zealot underground. If he was still the best espionage man in the world in the area of religious rebels, he was likely to do the same. How would anyone ever know unless he declared himself or was found to aid and abet the enemy?

"The best we can determine," Ranold concluded, "is that Agent Stepola is in familiar form in Europe. He very much impressed Chancellor Dengler in Bern, and unless and until we are ready to bring him in and file charges, we want to keep it that way. Stepola's fall from grace will be noisy and embarrassing to the NPO and to the USSA. He continues to make initial contacts with local authorities, make cursory investigations of the affected sites, and begin his own investigations independently."

"That's always been his modus operandi," Jae said, knowing she sounded defensive and sensing pity on the parts of others, who had to believe she was in denial.

"True," Bia Balaam spoke up. "But we're about to shadow him much more closely. If he is becoming too familiar with the underground, for purposes other than setting them up for apprehension, we'll know. And while his personal indiscretions are none of our concern—other than if they affect the quality of his work—those will become obvious to us as well. And thus to his father-in-law. And thus to you."

"Which will make me all the more eager to help nail him on the NPO side," Jae said.

"That is a very healthy attitude in the midst of a most unfortunate set of personal circumstances," Chief Balaam said.

Jae almost thanked Bia out of habit but caught herself. What was she thinking? *Was* she in denial? She couldn't argue that part of her wanted to defend Paul, to find him innocent on every front. If whatever happened between him and Trina or Angela *was* in the past, why should he be expected to dredge it up and lay it on her? Best-case scenario, something had happened that made him clean up his act, and he was doing everything in his power to be a good citizen at home and on the job.

Yeah, and I'm the tooth fairy.

"I know how this sounds," Jae said, "so let me assure you all in advance that I am neither blind, nor have I lost my mind. But indulge me. Let's say I deal with the domestic issues. They're my business anyway. Putting those aside, is there any scenario in which Paul might prove that you have misjudged him? What would exonerate him and convince you that he is a patriot, that he has not flipped? His methods may be unorthodox, not by the book, not the way they were done in your day, Dad. But in many of the instances you cited, he was successful."

"If I may jump in here again, General Decenti," Bia said, irritating Jae but clearly impressing Ranold by using his military title.

"Please," he said.

"This is just my personal opinion, but I daresay it is shared around this table. The only way Agent Stepola could redeem himself within the NPO and the international intelligence community now would be to personally bring down Styr Magnor."

17

CHAPPELL RAISON'S COMPATRIOTS began arriving singly over the next few hours, and by nightfall five more men and three women had joined him and Paul in the tiny meeting room. Meanwhile, Paul had taken a call from Enzo Fabrizio in Rome.

"I have good news and bad news," Paul's new friend reported. "The good news is that my people were most encouraged since your visit. While there may be a holdout or two here or there, the vast majority consider you a brother and are glad to have you where you are."

"I appreciate that," Paul said, "but they realize that is only temporary, do they not? I cannot imagine my staying in place with the NPO long after Monday's announcement."

"Oh, they know," Enzo said. "In fact, that's the bad news. We have not yet decided what to do when the announcement comes. Those few who are still suspicious of you concede that they will find you entirely credible if the announcement is made as you predicted. But they, and the rest, agree that such an eventuality would give the entire global underground church sixty days' worth of marching orders. Unless we do something drastic, true believers who would never denounce their faith will face death."

Of course Enzo was right. But . . .

"Here's the rest of the bad news, brother," Enzo said. "None of us here has any connection whatever to Styr Magnor or any underground in Norway—or anywhere in Scandinavia for that matter, not that we doubt there is one, maybe a real one. Even those few here who laud what Magnor has accomplished have no ties with him or anyone who knows him.

"I presented to our people your idea of helping to draw him out, and I have to tell you, Paul, it was soundly voted down. And not just by the majority against Magnor. Fortunately I didn't have to vote, but I'll tell you, brother, I must agree that the threat of this International decree Monday hangs over us like Damocles' sword. I'm not inclined to go against the wishes of the body and put our efforts into a dangerous mission when we have so much on our plate already. If and when the announcement comes, as you can imagine, we will feel the pressure of time like never before."

"I understand," Paul said, unable to hide the disappointment in his voice.

"Do you? That is a great relief to me."

"I didn't want to burden you, Enzo. I just need help, that's all."

Paul heard his friend sigh. "There are few things as important as bringing Styr Magnor to justice, Paul. But I have to agree with my people that we are already engaged in two of them. One is to get the message of Jesus to the masses while we still can. The other is finding a way to unite and fight this decree. The only possible way of surviving it is to show the International Government that there are enough of us that we should be heard. Our very act of not signing is a declaration *for* the Lord. I have to believe He will honor that and protect us."

"But, Enzo, you all have been living underground for years. It has been like this for decades already."

"Yet the government feels this need to put us on the spot. We have made inroads, Paul. Why else would there be this stepped-up effort to force our hand? Do you think this is entirely attributable to Magnor? Yes, we have lived under the shadow of being lawbreakers and answering to a higher authority all our lives. But now, if you are right, not only would we lose our jobs and homes and any privileges that come with citizenship, but we would also lose our freedom and likely our lives."

"True."

"What will *you* do, Paul? This has to be even worse, more dangerous for you."

"No question. And I have no idea. But I know this: Nothing will make me sign."

"Praise the Lord. But what about the disposition of your wife and children?"

Paul hesitated. It wasn't that he hadn't thought about this; he simply had never articulated it. "I have already put them in God's hands," he said. "If the only thing within my power to save them was renouncing my faith, I would not do it. I could not. I would only pray they be drawn to God through my example."

"We'll pray with you, but you know what often happens in those situations, especially if your stand comes as a surprise to loved ones."

"Of course I know. Jae would be shocked and assume I was

crazy. I am trying to live in such a way that she will at least be sorry to lose me."

"Brother," Enzo said sadly, "I have a passage for you. May I read it?"

"Please."

"It's from the first chapter of Ephesians:

So we praise God for the wonderful kindness he has poured out on us because we belong to his dearly loved Son. He is so rich in kindness that he purchased our freedom through the blood of his Son, and our sins are forgiven. He has showered his kindness on us, along with all wisdom and understanding.

God's secret plan has now been revealed to us; it is a plan centered on Christ, designed long ago according to his good pleasure. And this is his plan: At the right time he will bring everything together under the authority of Christ—everything in heaven and on earth. Furthermore, because of Christ, we have received an inheritance from God, for he chose us from the beginning, and all things happen just as he decided long ago. God's purpose was that we who were the first to trust in Christ should praise our glorious God. And now you also have heard the truth, the Good News that God saves you. And when you believed in Christ, he identified you as his own by giving you the Holy Spirit, whom he promised long ago. The Spirit is God's guarantee that he will give us everything he promised and that he has purchased us to be his own people. This is just one more reason for us to praise our glorious God.

• • •

It had been years since Jae was in her father's office, and she was frankly surprised that he had been reassigned the one he had left when first he had retired.

"Yes," he said, "they bring back an old dog and give him the same house, bone, and bowl."

"Some house," she said, admiring the deep, rich woods, the marble floor, the tasteful decorating that he, obviously, had had little to do with. "They let Mom in here, or did you have professionals decorate?"

"Doesn't look like my handiwork?" he said, smiling. "Is that what you're saying?"

"Exactly."

"I hardly notice it. Too busy. But yes, if you must know, your mother worked with inside people."

Jae felt superficial even commenting on it. She didn't care and it was hard to pretend she did. But anything to keep from talking about the elephant in the room. Eventually, of course, she had to. "Dad, even you have to know how excruciating that was for me in there."

He sat behind his desk in a high-backed judge's chair, leaning on his elbows. For the first time in a long while he didn't have an immediate answer. He looked at her with what she took as sympathy and pity, and in spite of herself, she was buying it. He actually looked sincere. He shook his head. "I can't imagine. And I'm sorry, honey."

She wasn't so sure of that. Much as he loved her in his own way, nothing was more exciting or fulfilling to him than nailing someone. Even if that someone was her husband, his son-in-law. Things looked bad for Paul, and much as Jae told herself to avoid creeping toward denial for her own selfish reasons, she couldn't allow herself to totally turn her back on him.

But why not? Look at what Paul had done to her in the past. And those pictures! They didn't lie. The other stuff was thin and circumstantial, but her dad and the others clearly had some plan whereby they could confirm or deny where Paul stood on his loyalty to the USSA and the International Government. The question was where she came in.

"Can you hide what you know from your conversations with Paul, Jae?"

"I have to."

"Yes, you do. And can you do whatever is necessary to help us, if he's turned on us?"

"To be perfectly honest, Dad, you haven't proved that to me yet. But if you could, of course I would do whatever was necessary. What kind of a person, citizen, mother would I be if I wouldn't?"

"That's my girl."

My biggest fear: I'm Ranold B. Decenti's girl—no more, no less.

• • •

Paul found Chappell Raison's leadership team supportive from the get-go, as explained by his right-hand man, Lothair Manville. A short, stocky, soft-spoken man in his midtwenties, Lothair had come to faith through the persistent influence of Chappell. "His selling the rest of us on you reminded me of those days," Lothair said with a smile. "He argued his case from all angles, shooting down our arguments before we could raise them."

"But you weren't simply beaten down till you had to concede, were you?" Paul said. "Because I am willing to field any questions. And we have a saying in America: 'A client sold against his will remains unsold still.'"

Lothair laughed with the others, and a woman said, "You should know this about the French, Doctor. We love to debate, and at high decibels. If we conceded that Chapp was right about you, we had to have been genuinely convinced. For one thing, the time is short and we cannot waste it continuing to debate your veracity. If you are a wolf in sheep's clothing, we are all dead anyway. So let us assume the best and move on."

"The time is shorter than you know," Paul said. And he told them of International's announcement due in two days. He did not see another smile the whole evening. Naturally, it had to be hard for them to concentrate on anything else while imagining the ramifications. They were already leading dual lives, hiding the truth about themselves to most others in their spheres. Now their rebellion against the government, against atheism, could be hidden only through overt deceit and a denial of their faith.

Before they continued—and Paul had much he wanted to discuss—they insisted on praying. Everyone knelt in the drafty little room, and for more than an hour they pleaded with God for wisdom and direction. Paul lost track of how many times he heard someone admit, "We don't know what to do, Lord."

• • •

On the way back to the house, Ranold asked Jae the question she dreaded but knew had to be coming. "Is there anything else you can tell me that will help? Anything at all?"

She didn't want to lie to her father, but she wasn't ready to cave on Paul just yet either. Silently she chastised herself. *Why protect him? What cause has he given me? Even his new attitude— his loving, caring, listening, others-oriented personality—could be just a ruse to cover what he's really been up to.*

But what if he was for real? What if he had really changed? Did that mean he had flipped? Had all this nonsense from the New Testament reached him somehow? Was he a victim of Stockholm syndrome? And would that be so terrible?

What was she saying? Would it be so terrible if he had become a believer in God like his own father? Well, yeah. It would make him a turncoat. A traitor. A liar. A double agent. Worthy of death. Was it possible? Could the very thing that made him a better husband have also made him an international felon?

"Dad," she heard herself say, as if from a hollow room somewhere deep in her soul, "I do have something you need to see."

•   •   •

After prayer, as they returned to their chairs, it was getting late and Chappell's people were glancing at their watches. "I don't want to keep you," Paul said, "but there is an urgent matter. Chapp and I have discussed his exposure to Styr Magnor. If we can work together to capture this man, imagine the several-pronged benefits to the cause."

Paul had already almost lost them; he could tell. They paled, looked at each other, gazes darting. "Don't worry," he said. "I would no more expose you people than—"

"Expose us?" someone said. "If you're right about Monday, we'll already be exposed. Once the sixty days are up, what will we do? Live here?"

"There's no perfect scenario, but consider this: Magnor needs to be brought to justice. Even if we weren't looking at this as Christians, he's still a murderer, a coward. The international community may make strange bedfellows for us, but on this we must agree. Regardless the offense, regardless the differences, the answer is not the obliteration of innocent people."

"Which is what they're planning for us," a woman said. "Are you sure it's not the answer?"

"We're disagreed on Magnor?" Paul said with incredulity.

"No," she said. "Not at all. We're just talking. It's how we think. Aloud."

"Then consider this: If somehow I can be central in apprehending him, I once again eliminate suspicion about me with the very agency I serve."

"That's the benefit to *you*," someone said.

"Besides that, he gets to stay alive," another said.

"I get to keep working under cover in an agency devoted to destroying you," Paul said.

"But for how long? You could bring in Magnor and still be required to sign the decree, right?"

"Of course. And as I've said, there's no scenario I can imagine in which I would do that. Now I live a covert lie. By what I don't say and what I imply, they think I'm with them. If I am asked outright to deny God, to deny faith, no."

"So you'll also have sixty days from Monday, regardless. Even if you bring in Magnor."

Paul thought a moment. "Right. And during that time, while I do everything in my power to evade the issue, I'll remind myself of the value of seeking justice for the innocents and protecting the future from Magnor."

"Worthy," one said, "but not our primary goal."

"Or responsibility," another said.

"We're going to be living hand to mouth until we're caught. How can we worry about Magnor?"

"How can we not?"

Chappell held up a hand. "I want to be careful not to browbeat anyone into agreeing—"

"Sure you don't."

"No, seriously, I don't. But let me tell you where I am on all this. As I've told brother Paul, I feel a tremendous guilt, a horrific sense of responsibility for the lives lost in Rome and London and here. I know it's not my fault, but I sensed Magnor was dangerous. Eventually I knew it. There's no question he's not a true brother. We know that. The least I can do is help Paul get him. It may not do anything but make me feel better and buy us some time. But it should protect the world from more senseless attacks, and that's something, isn't it? No one else here has to cooperate. I'm the one he wants to communicate with, so I say let him. I'll tell him whatever he needs to hear to persuade him we can help. And then I'll work with Paul on putting him out of circulation."

• • •

Jae asked her father to come to the guest room where they had put her. Her plan was to find her copy of the letter from Paul's father, but she had forgotten that the first things her father would see were the New Testament discs.

"What's this?" he said.

"Like my husband, I'm just trying to see what these crazies are all about."

"You're trying to see what's got into Paul, aren't you?"

"That too."

He sat heavily on the bed. "Come to any conclusions?"

"Well, hardly the ones you and your team came to."

"What, you thought he had merely turned over a new leaf?"

She nodded. "Frankly, yes. It happens."

"It happens but it doesn't last. We are what we are, Jae. New leaves are like New Year's resolutions. The only one I ever kept was the year I resolved to make no resolutions."

He laughed. She didn't.

"People don't change, Jae. My mother told me on my fiftieth birthday that I was no surprise to her. I kicked in the womb, came out screaming—and kicking. Got in trouble in pre-school—no less—for, guess what?"

"Kicking?"

"Kicking. Then I was king of the hill, Eagle Scout (in spite of myself), class president, scholarship football player, ROTC—you name it. You know the history."

"Of course I do."

"No surprise to Mama. She said I was the same at fifty as before I was born. Kicking, screaming, and running the show."

"Have I never changed either, Dad?"

He appeared to study her. "Can't say that you have, honey. You were always sweet and pretty and smart. That 'bout sums you up, doesn't it? You were mostly obedient, didn't challenge authority. That still cover you?"

Unfortunately, yes, Jae decided. And that had to be why she found the New Testament stuff so impactful. She had never been taught to question, to investigate. Studying was one thing. Learning. Expanding your base of knowledge. But the man who had made a life of kicking and screaming and running the show had ingrained in her—with the implicit support of a docile wife—that certain things simply were the way they were. You didn't question that religion was a farce, that God was a creation of man, that anything spiritual or outside the realm of the material was akin to fairy tales but not so harmless. People didn't change. How could they? The only values worth fighting and dying for were humanism and the preeminence of the state.

"You were going to show me something, Jae."

"Yeah," she said, ashamed of herself and regretting it before she even started looking for the letter. She was going to do this thing, and there was no way around it. This single act didn't have to reflect on Paul. After all, he merely read the letter; he didn't write it. How could he be held responsible for something his father believed in? What would it prove? Surely not that he had flipped. Not necessarily.

On the other hand, under the current circumstances, what Jae had decided to do could also carry enough weight to cost Paul—and her—everything the two of them ever held dear.

18

PAUL KNEW IT WAS FOOLHARDY, but time was short. Circumstances called for bold measures. What was the worst that could happen to him? He might be suspected, lose respect in the eyes of Chancellor Dengler. In two months his standing with the International Government and intelligence community would be moot anyway. On the drive back to his hotel, he put in a call to Dengler's office. Naturally, he wound up, late on a Saturday night, speaking to someone at the security desk.

"I wouldn't even know where to begin to get a message to the chancellor over a weekend," the man said. "He knows who you are?"

"Yes. Patch me through to his secretary's phone, and I'll leave a voice mail, or—"

"Not allowed to do that."

"I don't see the harm," Paul said.

"You're not sitting where I'm sitting. Best I can do, I think, is leave that voice mail myself. Give me all the information again, and I'll put it on her phone and his chief of staff's phone. How's that?"

Paul told him to simply say that Dr. Stepola had an urgent need to speak with the chancellor as soon as possible.

• • •

The letter from Paul's father shook in Ranold's hand. He turned colors, rose, paced, slammed his fist on Jae's bedside table, making the New Testament discs bounce.

"How long have you known about this?" he said.

"Awhile. Paul doesn't—"

"And you didn't think I needed to know?"

"—know I have it." Jae felt like a little girl again, cowering before her father.

"This proves it, Jae! Don't you see?"

"No, it doesn't, Dad. It proves nothing. Just because his father happened to—"

"How long has Paul known about this? Since he was twelve?"

"No! I'm sure he's been aware of it only a little longer than I have. It had to have the same effect on him that it's had on us."

"He always idolized the memory of his father, Jae, even though he never knew him. This had to affect him deeply."

"I'm guessing it embarrassed him, Dad. Humiliated him. Otherwise, why would he have hidden it?"

"This had to be what he was having Trina Thomas evaluate! He wanted to know if it was real. Well, I know real when I read it. Stepola Sr. bit on the Christian thing hook, line, and sinker. But didn't you—or he—tell me his mother was not just an atheist but also antireligion?"

Jae nodded. "She was."

"Wasn't it she who talked Paul into religious studies? Was that just a sham, covering for her own secret beliefs? Is it possible Paul was raised in this? That he's been a plant in the NPO since day one?"

"Now you're getting paranoid, Dad. I would have known that. He couldn't have fooled me all these years. Anyway, if it were true and he had been devout, how do you explain the other women?"

"I don't know, but—"

She waved him off. "No, there's no way. I know Paul. If he's turned even sympathetic toward the rebels, it's been only in the last half year or so."

"Don't start covering for him now."

Jae started, catching her father involuntarily glancing at her New Testament discs. "Yeah, I'm a secret believer too, Dad. We're all out to ruin your life, overthrow the USSA, and take over the world for Jesus. We've brainwashed Brie and Connor and they're working on Mom right now. Please, Dad. If I had anything concrete on Paul, do you think I'd have even shown you that letter?"

Ranold held up a finger as if getting a call. He stood and turned his back to Jae. "Yes, yes sir. When was this? . . . No, no. He knows protocol. . . . No, we're sure not ready to expose him just yet, though I'd say we're closer than we've ever been. . . . If I had to guess, I'd say a week to ten days. Let me call Paul. Far as I know he suspects nothing. . . . Rumors of what? . . . You don't say. Well, something like that would sure put the spotlight on who's with us and who's agin' us, wouldn't it? And this is supposed to happen Monday? Got to say I love it."

• • •

Paul was within sight of his hotel when a light, cold rain began. When the tone in his mouth told him he had a call, he hoped it would be someone close enough to Dengler whom he could persuade to get the chancellor on the phone this very night. But it was his father-in-law.

"Just checking in, Paul. How're things?"

"Things are good, Dad. Jae and the kids get in all right?"

"Yeah, yeah. Great to have them. You're a lucky man."

Paul hesitated. "Sir?"

"Yes?"

"We've known each other too long for me to buy that you're just checking in."

"What," Ranold said, "I don't ever make social calls?"

"No, you don't."

"Well, you know me better than most. There is a . . . ah . . . rather delicate issue that's arisen here, and I need your take on it."

"Shoot."

"USSA NPO brass got a call from someone high in the chancellor's office saying you're trying to reach Dengler by phone this weekend."

"True."

"Now, Paul, I know you impressed the chancellor in your meetings with him, but you know as well as I do that that doesn't make you guys buddies. There is protocol, which has always been one of your strengths. I don't have to tell you that just because I have a healthy give-and-take meeting with the regional governor at the White House doesn't mean he and I are going to chat by phone a day or two later."

"What're you saying, Ranold? Dengler is offended that I want to talk with him personally?"

"I doubt he even knows of the request. If I were on his staff, I wouldn't tell him. I'd do what this person has done and check with your superiors to see if they're aware of this breach."

"Breach?"

"Are you not listening, Paul? It's a breach of protocol—at the very least a breach of etiquette or common courtesy (common sense, if you ask me)—for you to think you have the standing with the chancellor of the International Government of Peace that allows you to ask him to call you."

"So unless I had something of a life-or-death nature, something that concerned the security of the world, I shouldn't even consider such an approach?"

"Exactly. And what embarrasses me, Paul, as your mentor, is that you *know* this. You teach this. I've heard you counsel others on chain of command."

"You're right."

"I am?"

"Of course. I know protocol as well as anyone in international service."

"Then you'll apologize for this and—"

"No."

"What? Why—?"

"No, sir. I will not."

Ranold swore. "What is not getting through that thick skull of yours?"

"Ranold, I know what constitutes an issue worthy of the chancellor's personal attention, and I believe he knows that I understand such things. I need to talk with him by phone or in person as soon as humanly possible, and I am confident that if he knew that, he would not be tattling on me for asking but would give me the benefit of the doubt and accede to my request. If you still have the clout you seem to think you do, maybe you could put it to good use by wiping the nose of whatever brat in his office spends more time whistle-blowing than getting the man to call me. Can you do that?"

"Who do you think you're talking to, Paul?"

"To a man who once had the power to do just what I'm asking. I believe you still do, and I know *you* believe you still do. So prove it. Dengler asked for the best man the USSA had for this job, and he got me. So they ought to start treating me that way."

"Paul, what in the world is so important that you have to discuss it with Dengler himself?"

"If I could tell you that, I would have. Now can you get him to call me or not?"

"I can sure try."

"Thank you."

• • •

"That boy's on thin ice," Ranold said.

"Dad," Jae said, "what is going on?"

Ranold told her, including the rumor of the decree coming from International requiring citizens to pledge their loyalty in writing. "Then Paul scolds me for taking the side of Dengler's staff, who are naturally offended that someone at his level casually calls and asks to speak with the man himself."

"Paul understands all that stuff," Jae said, as they walked downstairs. "Must be important."

"It had better be huge, but if it is, shouldn't we know about it?"

Ranold took a call and told Jae that her mother and the kids would be home within the hour. "I've got another call to make," he said.

Jae was intrigued to see her father in action, playing to his strengths. And part of her was proud of Paul for not caving in to the pressure. At least it sounded like pressure. Her father had acted insulted that Paul had spoken to him with impudence, yet now she believed Ranold was using the very words—or at least tone—Paul had recommended.

Mr. Decenti called back the NPO contact who had informed him of the issue. "Listen," he said, "you tell that snot-nosed meddler in Dengler's office that if the best guy we have to offer says he needs to talk to the chancellor, then he ought to get the message to his boss. Our guy is seasoned enough to know when something's important enough to go to the top. If it turns out to be a waste of Dengler's time, I'm sure he'll let Stepola know that, and he'll have to suffer the consequences. . . . No, just don't take no for an answer. Get the ball back in their court and see if they snub us."

• • •

Paul was in his room for half an hour when he got a call from Dengler's chief of staff. "First, sir," the man said, "I want to apologize for the delay. I take full responsibility."

"No problem."

"No, Doctor, it was my responsibility to get your message to Chancellor Dengler immediately, and I dropped the ball."

"Let's put it behind us."

"Thank you, sir; that's most generous of you. Now I can transfer you directly to the chancellor's line, or he is willing to meet with you personally, if that would be more convenient."

"You realize I'm in Paris."

"I informed him of that, Doctor. He assures me that if you feel a face-to-face is mandatory, he will be happy to come your way or to rally a charter to bring you here."

"Speaking by secure phone will be sufficient."

Seconds later, Dengler came on. "Hold for a moment, Dr. Stepola, while we confirm that the scrambler is initiated. . . . There we go. First, I assume you know that if we had a lead on Styr Magnor, you would be the first to be informed."

"Of course."

"All right, then. How may I help you?"

"First, Mr. Chancellor, I'm sorry if you had to go back to the office to do this."

"Think nothing of it."

"All right, let me be as brief and direct as I'm able. I hope you know that if I thought anyone else could make this decision and take the action I'm recommending, I would not have bothered you with it."

"One more apology, Doctor, and I am going home."

Paul chuckled. In spite of himself, he almost liked this man. "Sir, I have made significant progress, inroads into rebel factions."

"Excellent."

"I am actually to the point where I may be just days from personal contact with Magnor himself."

There was a pause, as if Dengler was letting this sink in. "So he *is* part of the zealot underground."

"It appears that way."

"How can we help?"

"Needless to say, my wish is to keep all my contacts, sources, and locations classified. The fewer who know, the better."

"I would not even want to know and can imagine no scenario in which my knowing would benefit anyone."

"I wouldn't want to burden you with it, Mr. Chancellor. What I need and want are these two things: One, if and when I can arrange a meeting between myself and Magnor, I would like to inform International intelligence and NPO International as close to the contact time as possible."

"To avoid any leaks or any activity that might spook the target."

"Precisely."

"And so they can make the arrest an overwhelming success."

"Right again, sir."

"And second?"

"This, I realize, is a long shot, but I'm wondering if you would consider delaying Monday's announcement."

Silence.

"Sir?"

"I am here, Doctor. Puzzled, but here."

"Your plan may be brilliant, Chancellor Dengler, and it wouldn't surprise me if it is the noisiest and most significant action of your tenure."

"And yet you would like it postponed."

"Again, so as not to scare off the prey."

"Hmm."

Paul waited. He knew what he was asking.

"Regardless when the announcement is made," Dengler said, "citizens will have but sixty days to comply. At the end of that period, International enforcement will require monumental amounts of man-hours and dollars."

"Is that not an argument for delaying?" Paul said.

"Good point. The fact is that the plan is known throughout the intelligence committee, and try as we might, there will be no containing it. News of the upcoming decree is already undoubtedly sweeping the globe, and a delay would signal weakness on our part, wavering."

Paul took a deep breath. "I guess the decision, then, comes down to how important it is to actually capture Magnor."

Dengler was silent again for a long moment. "I could sure use you in my office."

"Sir?"

"You have a way of cutting to the heart of an issue."

"Thank you," Paul said.

"You believe the announcement could jeopardize your ability to personally connect with Magnor. Why?"

"It will mark the boldest move yet by the International Government against the underground, against terrorists, and let's face it, against Magnor."

"Um-hmm." Dengler was plainly thinking again. Paul waited, praying. While his request was sincere and largely for the reason he stated, the benefit of giving believers even a few more days was at the heart of it.

"I will tell you what I will do, Doctor," Dengler said. "If you believe you have a serious inroad to Magnor, I will call off Intelligence and put them on the underground at large."

Ouch. "Okay."

"That will keep them from scaring off the prey, as you say."

"True."

"But I am not going to delay the announcement. We are much too far down the track with this. While I hope it comes as a pleasant surprise to the global community, my fear is that too many people already know about it—enough that if it were delayed, it would reflect poorly on us as the international government."

"I understand," Paul said, knowing when to push and when to let go.

"You do not sound as if you understand."

"I'm disappointed, sir. Obviously, it's the opposite of what I wanted. But I understand your reasoning."

"You are a good soldier."

Oh, I hope so.

"And, Doctor, the hotline number I gave you would have eliminated a lot of the delay in reaching me. I answer that one myself. I trust you not to abuse it."

19

JAE WAS ALREADY FEELING GUILTY that she was spending less time with Brie and Connor than she had in Chicago. They didn't seem to be suffering, though, as her mother lavished attention on them. Saturday evening Berlitz and Aryana came over, and while neither seemed to know how to interact with kids that age, their interest alone eventually won over Brie and Connor.

Of course, Ranold used the opportunity to speak privately with Jae yet again. "The chancellor himself may be onto Paul," he said.

Oh no. "Why?"

"You know what Paul wanted from Dengler? Rather transparent, if you ask me. Wanted him to delay the announcement of the pledge of loyalty."

Jae cocked her head, trying to make sense of it. "What possible reason could Paul have had for that?"

"See," Ranold said, "you're thinking like me now."

"But seriously, Dad. Even assuming Paul has flipped to the other side, would he not know how obvious that request looks? Surely there had to be something else behind it."

"To his credit, Dengler turned him down flat. And in all fairness, the chancellor did not report on the full extent of the conversation."

"Did he indicate any suspicion?"

"Well, I didn't talk to him personally, of course, but he told the head of USSA NPO he thought Paul was a brilliant thinker."

"Then why do you think Dengler's onto him?"

"I said he 'may' be. It's not what is said that is as important as what is not said."

Typical male thinking, Jae thought. *Or at least typical Ranold thinking.*

• • •

Late that night Paul was drowsy, and despite his failure to talk Baldwin Dengler into delaying Monday's decree, he felt strangely at peace. The next day he was scheduled to talk with Jae. And he would also strategize with Chappell Raison about Styr Magnor.

Collapsing into bed, he slipped his book of John disc into the player and listened to a few verses before drifting into a sound sleep. It was a passage from the twelfth chapter, where Jesus tells His disciples that the time has nearly come for Him to return to heaven.

"The truth is, a kernel of wheat must be planted in the soil. Unless it dies it will be alone—a single seed. But its death will produce many new kernels—a plentiful harvest of new lives.

Those who love their life in this world will lose it. Those who despise their life in this world will keep it for eternal life. All those who want to be my disciples must come and follow me, because my servants must be where I am. And if they follow me, the Father will honor them. Now my soul is deeply troubled. Should I pray, 'Father, save me from what lies ahead'? But that is the very reason why I came! Father, bring glory to your name."

Then a voice spoke from heaven, saying, "I have already brought it glory, and I will do it again."

• • •

In the wee hours of the morning Paul roused. Had there been a tone in the chip embedded in his molar? Yes. But for how long? Had he already missed the call? He sat up quickly and saw it was 3:30. He pressed his fingertips together and answered.

"Doctor Stepola?"

"Yes. Who's this?"

"Lothair."

"Lothair, what's up, man? Everything okay?"

"He is risen."

"He is risen indeed. What's the trouble?"

"Chapp's really upset. He can't even talk. This brings back all the memories of what happened to his wife and kids."

"What does?"

"One of our women was hauled in by the gendarmes under suspicion of running a house church. The thing is, she never ran one. She's part of us, but she never did anything overt except show up to our meetings. I mean, she planted literature at a couple of malls and a park near where she works—"

"What's happened, Lothair?"

"Yeah, sorry. She never got caught for that, or even suspected, as far as we know. But somebody turned her in for something, because they charged her with carrying out illegal religious activity."

"Go on."

"Her family doesn't know she's a believer, so they went down to deny the charge for her and plead with authorities to let her out. One—her uncle—said he saw her bound and gagged and demanded to know what the purpose of that was."

"Was she hurt?"

"He thought she was, but he didn't see any marks on her then. She looked terrified. Then later the Sûreté called and told the relatives to come back because she had died. This time her parents saw her and said she was covered with cuts and bruises on her head and face, hands, and one leg."

"Sûreté Nationale killed her?"

"Of course they killed her."

"What can I do to help?"

"There is nothing we can do, Doctor. We don't dare do or say anything with the announcement coming Monday. That's so frustrating; we're climbing the walls here. But Chappell wanted me to tell you that he has changed his mind about helping with Magnor."

"No! Now, he can't—"

"I am just passing on the message, Doctor. He will get back in touch with you when he is able to speak."

"When will that be? I'll wait up."

"No. Not before tomorrow. I am sorry to have to bring this news."

• • •

By early evening Jae already found herself exhausted from one of the worst days of her life. She thought it had been bad when first she had heard that Paul was not the man she had married. To have him admit to flings—again, such a light word for a nearly lethal injury to their relationship—seemed to suck the life from her. It had taken her more than a year to deal with that, and in many ways it was never far from her. And just when she thought she had gotten over the hump, he would "slip" again. Why wasn't there appropriate terminology for heinous decisions and actions that nearly killed her?

But this. This was the worst. Just when she had more hope than she'd had in a decade, it turns out Paul may be worse than a philanderer. The kids were busy with Grandma and seemed content, so Jae stole upstairs and sat on her small bed, cheeks resting on her fists, staring out the window at a light snowfall. She was chilled and yet she chose not to don a sweater. She deserved to be cold, deserved to suffer for her blindness and stupidity.

Strangely, though, some small part of her remained loyal to Paul. What was that? Where did it come from? She was an intelligent woman. She wouldn't protect him for no reason. She didn't want him at any cost just so her kids could have a live-in dad. Jae would throw him over in a second if all of what the NPO suspected was true.

And it might be. But if they couldn't convince her beyond reasonable doubt, the woman who had been betrayed by this man enough times to have justified dumping him years ago, would they trash his career anyway?

Jae already deeply regretted having shown her father the devastating letter. What was this need she had to pour fuel on an already raging fire? Did she need the points with her dad? For one thing, Ranold needed no more ammunition. His mind was clearly made up.

Jae stretched out atop the covers, fully clothed. She lay staring at the ceiling, her mind racing. The New Testament discs seemed to magnetize her. What drew her back to them, especially after a day like today? She reached for them and several fell on the carpet. She grabbed them, selecting one blindly, and fed it into the machine. When she inserted the earplug and hit the button, she found she had chosen a letter from the apostle Paul to a man named Philemon.

The first words said Paul was writing the letter while in prison for preaching. *That happened back then too?*

> *I am praying that you will really put your generosity to work, for in so doing you will come to an understanding of all the good things we can do for Christ. I myself have gained much joy and comfort from your love, my brother, because your kindness has so often refreshed the hearts of God's people.*

Faith that will grip others too. Is that what's happened to my Paul, if anything? Jae had to wonder if anything about her had ever refreshed anyone's heart. That, she decided, would be a worthy goal.

> *That is why I am boldly asking a favor of you. I could demand it in the name of Christ because it is the right thing for you to do, but because of our love, I prefer just to ask you. So take this as a request from your friend Paul, an old man, now in prison for the sake of Christ Jesus.*

Talk about manipulation, Jae thought. This Paul put her father to shame. Who could deny this request, regardless of what it turned out to be?

> *My plea is that you show kindness to Onesimus. I think of him as my own son because he became a believer as a result of my ministry here in prison. Onesimus hasn't been of much use to*

you in the past, but now he is very useful to both of us. I am
sending him back to you, and with him comes my own heart.

Asking a favor on someone else's behalf! It wasn't self-
motivated at all. And he did this while enchained in prison? No
wonder her husband's father had named him Paul. Mr. Stepola
had wanted a son like this. "With him comes my own heart"—
what a way to say that!

I really wanted to keep him here with me while I am in these
chains for preaching the Good News, and he would have
helped me on your behalf. But I didn't want to do anything
without your consent. And I didn't want you to help because
you were forced to do it but because you wanted to.

Jae had to smile. No, Philemon would feel no pressure at all!
In the rest of the letter, Paul admitted that Onesimus was a run-
away slave who wound up in prison with him. The apostle asked
for Onesimus's freedom, reminding Philemon that he owed
him "his very soul."

Yes, dear brother, please do me this favor for the Lord's sake.
Give me this encouragement in Christ. I am confident as I
write this letter that you will do what I ask and even more!

How could Philemon do anything but? Paul expected to be released
soon, and he asked Philemon to prepare for a visit from him.
Even if she never shared this Paul's faith, there was much Jae
knew she could learn from him.

20

UNABLE TO SLEEP NOW, Paul decided to call Jae. It would be the middle of the evening in Washington. Regardless of the international situation, he could not let anything keep her from being his first priority.

Besides loving her and caring more deeply for her and the kids than he ever had before, Paul sensed that when the truth came out, if she didn't run from him—which was, of course, entirely possible—she had the potential to be his greatest ally. If there really had been a noticeable change in him, if she had seen anything that would help convince her that he was now living in the light of eternal truth, he trusted that God would confirm it to her and that she would become a believer too. The price of that, naturally, was that she and Brie and Connor—like Paul—would soon become fugitives. It would not be beyond

Ranold Decenti to go to any length, in his way of thinking, to rescue the kids.

Ranold had never cared that much about them before, but Paul knew the man was capable of attacking his own daughter and son-in-law at their most vulnerable point. The kids would be merely chips he would play to get his way.

At sunrise, Paul would make arrangements to get together with Chappell Raison again. What the man had to be going through was beyond Paul's ability to understand. Chapp would resist Paul's attempts to talk him back into helping catch Styr Magnor, but everything depended on that. There were so many reasons to do it—despite several compelling arguments for why it would be more convenient not to—that Paul hardly knew where to begin. He had an idea how to talk Chapp into at least getting together, but past that, Paul was in no-man's-land.

• • •

Jae and the kids were finishing a bedtime snack with her parents in the kitchen. Brie and Connor were excited about going to a Washington Native American football game with Uncle Berlitz and Aunt Aryana the next day, though neither had ever shown the slightest interest in the game.

"Berlitz never liked football either," Ranold said. "I ought to go so the kids at least learn something."

Margaret rose to answer the phone, calling back over her shoulder, "Berl said he had only four tickets, so . . ."

"Bet Aryana would love a reason to stay home," Ranold said.

"Jae," her mother called out, "it's Paul calling from France."

Jae surprised herself at how eager she was to hear his voice, as if she had forgotten what she'd really like to say to him.

"Can I talk to Daddy?" Brie squealed.

"Me too, me too," Connor hollered.

"You two can talk to him down here until I get on the phone upstairs," Jae said, hurrying toward the stairs.

Her father was following her. She stopped on the steps and spun. "Dad! Do you think I can do this without you hovering?"

"I just wanted to remind you, Jae." He tapped his temples with his index fingers. "Focus."

"Well, maybe if you just go back to the kitchen, I can."

Jae rushed up the stairs so quickly she had to stop and catch her breath before picking up the phone. Brie was still on with Paul, and Connor was begging her to hurry. Jae waited until Connor got on and ran out of things to say.

"Tell Daddy good-bye, Connor," she said. "You can talk to him again soon."

"Hi, sweetheart," Paul said, and he sounded so sincere that Jae had to slow herself. She didn't want to get sucked in, but neither did she want to give anything away. She was not great at playacting.

"Hang up the phone, Connor," Jae said, still hearing downstairs sounds.

"Grandpa!" Brie said. "Don't listen in!"

"Hi, Ranold," Paul said.

Click.

"Sorry about that, Paul," Jae said.

Paul was chuckling. "He really thought he could get away with eavesdropping in front of the kids?"

"I guess. You know Dad."

"NPO born and bred. Jae, it's good to hear you. I love you, and I miss you so much it hurts."

"I miss you too, Paul." She did not have to fake that. Could he be this good? Was it possible he was lying to her, playing her, seeing other women, betraying his country, and could still come off this sincere without sounding smarmy? She couldn't imagine. "How's it going? It's what, the middle of the night over there?" Had he just come in from seeing someone else and called her out of guilt? She had to admit, it didn't sound that way.

"Oh, couldn't sleep. But I'm making some progress. It's slow. Can't talk about it, obviously."

"I know. Any idea on a timetable yet?"

"No. I wish. Tell you what I really wish, Jae. I wish you could be with me here."

"I'd love that."

"Would you?" He sounded genuinely surprised.

"I would."

"You start your job Monday?"

"Uh-huh."

"Looking forward to it?"

"Not really. It'll help pass the time. I don't like being a single parent, Paul."

"I'm sorry. I won't stay any longer than I absolutely have to."

As they finished with incidentals and courtesies, Jae found herself incapable of allowing her resentment over what she'd seen on the screen today—not to mention the suspicion her father and his associates had tried to engender in her—to grab a foothold in her mind. Yes, someday she had to tell Paul that she was aware of Trina Thomas. Jae wanted, needed, to know that that predated the new Paul. If she discovered any evidence that he was still fooling around behind her back, Jae had no doubt her forgiveness reserves would be spent.

His mention of her joining him in Europe was only wishful thinking, she knew. But the more she thought it out, the more it gained purchase. Paul couldn't do his work with her there as a distraction. And he had not been serious in the least. But it was fun to think about.

• • •

As much as Paul hated the idea of Jae's being exposed to her father the whole time he was overseas, he had to admit she had sounded good. She had a quick mind, strong character. She thought for herself. Maybe Ranold would have less influence on her than Paul feared.

And the kids sounded good too. Jae had told him they resisted the move as the time came for it, and he had hoped maybe that his and Straight's opposition would have changed her mind. But maybe this was all for the best. He had prayed fervently for her and had to believe that if her being in Washington was against His plan, God would have prevented it.

Having had such a warm conversation with her made Paul miss Jae all the more. He had to concentrate.

• • •

By 9 a.m. Paul had caught a few more hours of sleep, shaved, showered, dressed, and eaten. When he couldn't get Chappell Raison to answer his phone, he called Lothair. "Chapp and I have to get together."

"He's not ready."

"He'll never be ready, but time is running out. Has Magnor made any more attempts to reach him?"

A significant pause.

"Chapp's not taking calls," Lothair said.

"That wasn't my question, and you know it. Magnor has called, hasn't he?"

Silence.

"Lothair, do you realize how important this is?"

There was a whine in the man's voice. "Do you realize where my loyalty lies?"

"Of course! But all of us owe our highest loyalty to God. This is life-and-death stuff, Lothair. Confirm that Magnor has called, and I'll take responsibility for your telling me."

Silence.

"You know, Lothair, I wish we were all still teenagers and that this was some silly game. Is Chapp right there? Is that the problem?"

"Yes."

"Listen carefully. Yes or no. Can you tell me categorically that Magnor has not tried to call Chapp?"

"No."

"You understood me?"

"Yes."

"So he has called."

"I understood you."

"Good, then I understand you too. Chapp and I must meet as soon as possible. For one thing, it's Sunday. Is he going to deprive me of the privilege of meeting with fellow believers on the Lord's Day?"

Lothair snorted. "You want me to ask him that?"

"I want you to tell him I'm coming. For safety's sake, let's not meet in the same place, hmm? Where is your secondary meeting place?"

• • •

Paul set his room timers and took another labyrinthine escape route, hurrying toward his rental car, when he froze. Parked at the curb across from his hotel was a sedan identical to the one Karlis Grosvenor had used to ferry him around Paris. It also matched the sedan Paul had been issued for official use. Coincidence?

He didn't want to be obvious, but he needed to know who was who on the street. Was he being watched? Followed? He didn't dare proceed to his rental. He had to either get in the car issued to him, keep walking as if just sightseeing, or make his way back into the hotel.

Paul chose the latter and ran into Grosvenor as he was coming out. "Chief!" Paul said, shaking his hand. "What brings you my way?"

"Just dropping off your boss. You didn't tell me she was coming."

My boss? "Didn't know you needed to know."

Grosvenor was not amused. "Would have been nice to have a little warning. Gave her the cook's tour of Champ-de-Mars."

"My apologies. I didn't expect her to take up much of your time."

"Any time is too much," Grosvenor said. "I spend more time entertaining foreigners than I do trying to get my own work—"

"I've stayed out of your hair; you have to admit."

"Yeah, well, thanks," the chief said. "You getting everything you need?"

"Yes, thanks."

"Think you can run her to the airport in the morning? Save me a trip?"

"Sure," Paul said.

"Any reason you couldn't have picked her up? I mean, come on, it's Sunday. I haven't had a day off in weeks."

"I just do what I'm told, Chief."

"Yeah, me too," Grosvenor said. "But you're on for airport duty in the morning, right? Orly."

"Got it." *What in blazes?*

Paul went inside to the counter and asked for messages. "Yes, sir. Bia Balaam just checked in and would like to see you."

Paul phoned her and arranged to meet her in the lobby. She approached smiling and actually embraced him. As usual, she seemed overdressed, over made-up. They sat in overstuffed chairs in the middle of an atrium that looked out on the city.

"Surprised to see me?" she said.

"That's fair," he said. "What brings you?"

"Oh, don't worry. I'll stay out of your way."

Too late.

"I'm representing USSA NPO at the ceremonial announcement in Bern tomorrow. Thought I'd come early and see the Eiffel site."

Paul nodded. *I'll bet.* "What did you think?"

Her smile died. "Tragic. Tragic."

Well, there was some insight for you. Paul struggled to remain cordial. Did she, did Ranold, think he was a complete imbecile? Sending her to keep an eye on him, ensconcing her in his hotel, blaming it on her interest in the attack site and her attendance in Bern? Please. If this wasn't a blatant attempt to remind him who was in charge, he didn't know what was. Now Paul was going to be late getting together with Chapp, if he was able to slip away at all. He couldn't risk leading her to the underground.

Balaam was as intimidating as she looked, with her silver hair and eyes, the unusual height, the coldness she tried to hide with the occasional toothy smile. She creeped Paul out in business settings, but the social thing never worked at all for her. She was clearly not in her element. Bia's claim to fame—and a fast, recent rise within the NPO—was that she was a leader of men. This chitchat was disconcerting, but it did make Paul wonder if there was another dimension to the woman. He couldn't imagine.

He told her he had run into Grosvenor and had been handed the baton for her ride to Orly in the morning.

"Oh, good," she said. "Did he give you the particulars?"

"No."

"You might not have been so willing."

As if I were willing at all. "How early?"

"I need to leave the hotel at five, I'm afraid."

"Ouch."

"I'm sorry. I can tell Grosvenor—"

"Happy to do it," Paul said. Still able to lie. "Why so early?"

"Flying the government charter. And I want to be in Bern in time for the actual announcement. They're trying to schedule it so it hits most time zones at the best hour for network news. It'll be taped and replayed for the sleeping countries, of course."

"Of course."

Paul was antsy, wanting to get going, hoping he could figure a way to elude her, to get to his rendezvous without being noticed. But she was saying something about her son. Her son? Paul didn't even know she had a family.

"I'm sorry," he said. "You have a son?"

"And a daughter," she said. "I'm long divorced. Not a happy story, though the kids are good. Leya is a professor. Taj goes back to Georgetown tomorrow. He's doing well."

Paul studied her. She actually did seem to soften when speaking of her children. Who would have guessed? "Well, listen," he said, "had I known you were coming I would have arranged for dinner tonight, but—"

"Oh, no," she said, "don't change your schedule at all for me. I have tons of work and want to turn in early because of the, well, you know."

"Early flight."

And with that she was off, pretending to simply be in town on her way to Bern. Paul wondered if she had staff with her, crack tails he would have never noticed as they followed him into the French countryside and directly to the underground. Well, if such animals were there, Paul would make them work.

On his way to the Paris bureau staff car, Paul called Lothair and updated him on his estimated time of arrival. He chose not to tell him why. The last thing Chapp needed was another reason to be spooked.

Paul drove around Paris, watching for any shadows. Seeing none, he returned to the hotel, went to his room, left by yet another route, called Straight, learned the location of another car-rental agency—this one a long walk. Enjoying a pastry in a fountain square and again certain he was not being watched, he rented another car under another alias and drove a circuitous route out of the city. Finally he was on his way to see Raison, in the same general area where he had met him before, but in a new hideout.

21

"SO, WHAT DID HE HAVE TO SAY? What's the deal? What's going on?"

"Why didn't you listen in like you wanted to, Dad?" Jae said. She had stayed in her room rather than running down to report the phone conversation to him. She hoped her mother would bring the kids up so she could busy herself putting them to bed and avoid the third degree. No such luck.

"I was just hanging up the phone," Ranold said. Past retirement age and he still couldn't tell the truth.

"He's fine, I'm fine, we're all fine."

"You were able to keep it together, not give away that—"

"That what? That I've been told he's the same promiscuous rascal he's always been, and on top of that, a traitor?"

"What's the matter, Jae? Losing your resolve?"

"What made you think I had any resolve to start with, Dad?

You think this is easy? That I would hear a few disappointing details and then just sign up with the vigilantes to do in my own husband? That wasn't very insightful—"

"A few disappointing details? Do you realize that the man you married may be the biggest enemy to freedom the United Seven States has ever seen? Worse than Benedict Arnold. Worse than Alger Hiss. Worse than—"

"You call him the man I married as if I should have seen this coming. You forget how high you were on him when we were dating and engaged, Dad. You even beamed at the wedding. Not that long ago you sat on the stage at the Pergamum Medal ceremony, busting your buttons like the award was going to you."

Ranold sighed. "He was that good, Jae. He's not going to be easy to bring down. But we're trying. And we need your help."

Jae wanted to reiterate that she hadn't been close to convinced yet, but she didn't want to get into it. She heard her mother and the kids on the stairs and excused herself.

"As you're going to be part of the team now," Ranold said, "I should tell you we have a scheme in the works right now over there."

Jae hesitated but she wouldn't bite. Her father wouldn't be able to keep it from her anyway. She could get back to the subject anytime she wanted.

• • •

The idyllic setting for the Sunday midday meeting reminded Paul of country farms in the Midwest. It seemed incongruous to see several cars parked under the trees, a pleasant clapboard house in the shade, the winter fields lying fallow in the sun.

Chappell Raison and his leadership team met in the parlor, and this time Paul faced a much tougher crowd. Whatever it was in Chapp's bearing that so endeared him to these people, they rallied round him now, eyeing Paul with suspicion. Paul realized immediately that an all-out offensive was his only hope.

The little group began by singing choruses and praying, but it was all Paul could do to keep from interrupting. Even talking to God, they sounded defeated. Rather than asking for wisdom and guidance and courage, all they pleaded for now was protection and peace. There was going to be precious little of that soon enough. When the worship segment was over, Paul stood and faced wary eyes, except for Chapp's. He apparently couldn't bring himself to look at Paul.

Paul began quietly, earnestly, planning to warm to his topic as he took cues from the body language of his audience. "Chappell," he began, "what's happened to you? I was told one thing about you before I got here, that you were intense. That suggested I might have a hard time keeping up with you, that you would set a pace and a tone that would inspire me to do what I had to do in a tough and dangerous situation.

"At first I found you that way, talking fast, thinking fast, earnest, passionate. I give you some inside information, tell you what's coming from the government tomorrow, expect you to lead by example, get your troops fired up, lead the charge in the name of Christ, and what do I get? You're folding your tents, man."

Chapp had at least raised his head and was looking at Paul now.

"And then I hear of the tragedy that has befallen the body here. It's awful. It's maddening. It's enough to make you want to kill or quit. Well, frankly I expected the former, not the latter. Nothing we can do will bring that young woman back, but we can conduct ourselves in such a way that she will not have died in vain. We can, in her memory, get our backs up and oppose this evil world system, can't we?

"Chapp, are you done? Are you finished? Should the torch be passed to Lothair or one of these other younger, braver, brasher people? Because your intensity is just a memory now. If I were part of the leadership team here—and worse, if I were part of the rank and file—your example would inspire me to do what? Oh, I don't know. Quit?"

He was making Chapp mad now; Paul could see that. That was better than nothing. "If you'll all bear with me, I want to tell you the story of what happened in Los Angeles." Paul could tell he finally had their ears. They had been scowling at him, and some still were, probably out of loyalty to their besieged leader. But they were plainly interested now.

He told them of the underground factions in L.A. and how they had been beaten down again and again, suffering losses, even slaughter. "It would have been easy to cave, to give in and give up. No one, not even I, would have faulted them if they had. How much should people be expected to take?

"That's what I wondered when I heard your story, Chapp. I don't know where I'd be if I had lost my wife and kids simply because I wanted to exercise a right that was privileged in my country—and yours—not so many years ago. I have to wonder if I would still be a part of the underground, of the resistance. Well, here you are. You're still here. But are you leading the charge, or are you in the way?

"From a human standpoint, the L.A. underground was whipped. This wasn't even Gideon against the Midianites anymore. Those would have seemed favorable odds compared to a bunch of loosely organized, petrified, clandestine groups facing the military strength of the United Seven States of America. And so they did the only thing they could think of. They called on their one final resource, the unconquerable King.

"They prayed that God would smite their enemies. And then

they told their enemies they had prayed that and warned them that if they didn't stop killing believers, God would act. And He did. Do you know what the USSA has done about Los Angeles? They have abandoned it. No one but a believer can survive there anyway, so the government pretends it doesn't exist.

"Chapp, listen to me. I'm in no position to tell you how to feel or react. But I am here as your brother, telling you that come tomorrow, the clock begins ticking toward the end of the underground resistance as we know it. Maybe that's a good thing. No longer will we have a choice. Within sixty days, remaining underground will not be an option. Shall we put the chairs on the wagon 'cause the meeting's over? Or do we carry our colors into the public square and declare ourselves?

"Frankly, I'm no more eager to do that than you are, except that I know we have the victory in hand. I don't know how God is going to do it; I know only that He has to, because we can't. Chapp, if you could ask God to do in Europe something like He did in Los Angeles, what would it be?"

Paul sat and let the question hang in the air. If anyone but Chapp began to speak, Paul was prepared to shush them. The question had been put to their leader, and Paul wanted an answer.

"Well, one thing I *wouldn't* do," Chapp said, his voice tight, "is ask Him to help me flush out Styr Magnor."

Several nodded, but Paul sighed through his nose. "That wasn't the question. We'll deal with that in a minute." Starting over, slowly and articulately, and yes, he realized, condescendingly, Paul asked the question again: "Chapp, if you could ask God to do in Europe something like He did in Los Angeles, what would it be?"

"It's not going to sound loving," Chapp said.

"And why should it?" Paul said. "Do you think God's shutting off the water supply to Los Angeles was loving? That was vehemence. That was judgment."

"I don't know if He even still does things like this," Chapp said.

"'Jesus Christ is the same yesterday, today, and forever,'" Paul said. He could tell he had caught Chapp's imagination at last. But then, just as it seemed Chapp was about to speak, he sat forward and buried his face in his hands, shaking his head. "This is just an exercise, brother," Paul added. "There's no wrong answer."

"Yes, there is," Chapp said. "All I can think of is mayhem and ruin. There's nothing loving about what I am thinking."

"Again I remind you of Los Angeles, friend. God woos His own in love, but He judges His enemies in wrath and anger. Who are we to say which is preferred?"

Chapp looked up again, his face red and wet with tears. "I feel such rage. I want God to act. I want Him to take a stand on the part of His people. I want Him to deal a blow to the enemy."

"Say it, Chapp."

"I want Him to rain down judgment on those who punish us for believing in Him."

Paul said, "Have you considered that you have not because you ask not?"

"I don't know that I dare to ask."

"Tell *us*," Paul said. "Let us decide whether we want to pray with you for this."

"Yes," someone else said. "Tell us, Chapp."

"Yes."

"Yes."

"Please."

"All right," he said. "But I confess it does not make me feel better to think it and can likely only make me feel worse to express it. I compare the International Government to Egypt and us to the children of Israel. Chancellor Dengler is Pharaoh. . . . "

The rest glanced at each other, and Paul was getting the drift.

"What I want," Chapp said, "is a plague on the house of our oppressor."

"A plague?" someone said, making a face. "Chapp, that's awful."

"You see?" Chapp said. "You're right. I'm in the flesh. This is no good."

Paul sat silent. It had rocked him too, but he had been the one who encouraged this thinking. Was God really the same yesterday, today, and forever?

"I am not willing to pray for that," Lothair said.

In the midst of some murmuring, another said, "Neither am I. It sounds more mean than just."

"'I will take vengeance,' says the Lord," a woman said.

"Then it is for Him to accomplish and not for us," Chapp said.

Paul nodded. "Now you're talking." But what was Chapp talking *about?*

• • •

"She's *in* Europe now?" Jae said. "That's what you're telling me? If I'm such a crucial part of this new team, why would I not have known that?"

She and her father sat in the living room while Jae's mother made breakfast for the kids.

"Not all members of the team are required to approve every decision," Ranold said. "Chief Balaam is my designee for this operation, as well as our choice to represent us in Bern for Chancellor Dengler's announcement Monday morning."

"And Paul didn't know she was coming?"

"Of course not."

"But he does now?"

Ranold looked at his watch. "By now, he should. And the bug should have been planted."

"What are you talking about?"

Ranold looked self-conscious again. Jae hated when that happened. That meant he had something he knew she ought to know but was sheepish about telling her. This from one of the most powerful men in America. When he got this way, especially with her, she came as close to hating him as a daughter could hate her father.

"When, ah, Chief Balaam greets Paul, she will plant on his person, probably his jacket or whatever piece of material she touches, a microscopic device that will transmit to a receiver she can use to record anything useful."

"Such as?"

"Conversations."

"With?"

"With whomever, Jae. If he is behaving, he should have nothing to worry about."

"I want to know if you are hoping to catch him in subversive activity or an infidelity."

"Frankly, I don't care, Jae. Either will confirm my suspicion that he is not the new man you believe him to be."

"But the latter is my business, not yours, not the NPO's, not Bia Balaam's, and certainly not the USSA's."

"It will go a long way in solidifying your role on the team though, won't it?"

"Your pursuing it might cost having me on the team at all."

"I don't believe that, Jae. I admire your loyalty to Paul; I really do. I confess I don't understand it. If I thought your mother was unfaithful to me, I'd be homicidal."

As she should have been, rather than averting her eyes so many times?

"But this," Ranold continued, "is intended merely as a monitor. Maybe it will record Paul doing what he is supposed to be doing, and it will go in his file as another stellar example of great work."

"Yeah, right. That'll happen."

"But if in setting him up to see how he responds to an interesting situation we also find that he is fraternizing with the enemy, that could prove very beneficial as well."

"You set him up?"

Her father's gaze was darting again, and he actually reddened.

Jae stood. "Just tell me. You know I'm going to be steamed either way, so just put it on the table."

• • •

Paul remembered the sweet hours of prayer with the underground in Los Angeles as he and the other members of the French underground knelt. He had to admit, this was not the same. Singly, in pairs, and sometimes all at once, they poured out their hearts to God, beseeching Him to act. Some prayed that He would unleash judgment as He had in the book of Exodus to persuade the evil world leaders to let His people out from under the tyranny of religious persecution. Others pleaded with Him to show mercy and patience, to use some other means to get through to the hard hearts in Bern.

"All we want is to serve You," someone prayed. "All we want is the freedom to tell others the news of Your salvation and see them come to Christ."

When they finished praying, Chappell had a concrete, practical idea. "Just like in Los Angeles, we need to publish our response to what the government is doing. Once the announcement is made in Bern, we need to circulate far and wide our warning that if any believers suffer because they refuse to sign the decree—obeying man rather than God—we are praying that God will make the government regret it."

"Frankly," one of the older men said, "I will be praying at cross-purposes to that."

"So, God was wrong in Exodus?"

Paul knew God was never wrong, but he didn't know how to pray either. He stood and approached Chapp. "You and I need to talk in private about what we're going to do about Styr Magnor. I know that soon enough I will have to declare my true loyalties publicly, and that will mean the end of my tenure within the government. But if we can buy even a few days in the meantime by delivering this terrorist, it will also serve to protect the world from mortal danger."

22

JAE COULDN'T PUT HER FINGER on what was happening to her. She didn't know if it was the stress of living under her parents' roof again, the shock of knowing that her husband was suspected by the very people he worked for, the fear that he might again be straying from her, or what she had allowed into her mind by listening to the New Testament. But something was wrong. It was as if she were losing her mind.

She was all right with the kids, but she found her mother more maddening than ever—her docile take-life-as-it-comes attitude, letting Ranold get away with whatever craziness he dreamed up. And her father! Jae scolded herself. No way anything Ranold said or did should have come as a surprise to her. He was what he was, always had been, always would be. He had said as much himself when telling her the story of what his own mother had said on his fiftieth birthday.

Jae was impatient, angry, frustrated, unable to concentrate

for two seconds. And now, early in the morning, her father was telling her about the woman the NPO—the NPO!—was putting in Paul's path for the express purpose of entrapping him.

"She's good," her father said with obvious admiration.

"Oh, that makes me feel better," Jae said, feeling the blood rise in her neck. She was not about to defend Paul, and if he succumbed, she didn't think she could forgive him again either. But she believed the man was trying. She believed he had quit putting himself in compromising situations, and she wished no one else would either—especially while he was trying to develop some moral muscle in that area.

"Name's Calandre Caresse, and we've used her before. She's—"

"Come on, Dad. That's not her real name. That's a stripper's name."

He cocked his head. "Far as I know, that's her name. She's classy, discreet, and can be trusted."

"Listen to yourself!" Jae said.

Ranold looked genuinely puzzled.

"All right," she said, "let me ask you something. How would you describe me?"

"Smart, pretty, loyal."

"You've said that before. Be more creative. Am I classy?"

"I've always thought so."

"Discreet?"

"Sure."

"Trustworthy?"

"You bet."

"Dad, you just described a woman who lures men to her bed for a living the same way you would describe me."

He shrugged. "Well, okay. Maybe I should have qualified that. For a woman in her game, she's classier than most."

"That helped. So, what's the plan? What's she going to do? Does Paul have a chance?"

"I don't know the details," Ranold said. His eyes twinkled as if he couldn't wait to hear the results. "But if he has eyes in his head, he's as good as done for. She'll get him. And you'll have all the ammo you need."

"So what if he's just lonely, missing me, trying to stay true? You don't see this as totally unfair to him? to me?"

"You deserve to know what he really is, Jae! All this phony Paul's-a-new-man malarkey . . . if we do decide to send you over there, I want you clear that Paul is the target, the enemy."

"Send me over there? Are you serious?"

"Well, for sure not until you get your mind right about him."

From that very second on, Jae became obsessed with going, even if it meant convincing her father that she believed Paul was the enemy personified.

• • •

Only Paul and Chappell Raison remained in the little farmhouse nestled among the trees. "I apologize for coming on so strong, Chapp."

"I understand. I needed it."

"It's just that all I'd heard about you was your intensity and drive, and I saw that ebbing."

Chapp stood and moved to gaze out a window. "Frankly, it has ebbed, my friend. But if I understand what we're doing now, my intensity has nothing more to do with this. We are trusting God to act, because in ourselves we are not capable of competing anymore. We probably never were."

"You're still going to need some fortitude to get Magnor."

"I'm spent, Doctor."

"Look at it this way. The death of your friend has rekindled your desire to work with Magnor. He might have been suspicious if you finally started returning his calls all of a sudden, but this gives you cause."

Paul waited. He had pushed Chappell so hard today that he feared the man was at his breaking point. This had to come from him.

"So I call him? Or I wait for him to call again?"

"What's your gut tell you, Chapp? Have you rebuffed him so many times that he will give up? Or might he call again?"

"He called last night and again this morning, and Lothair told him I was grieving, too upset to talk."

"He told me the same thing."

"It was true, brother Paul."

"Actually, it's perfect. Without even intending to, you're forcing him to play into our hands."

"How?"

"You don't ever want to appear too eager. To sting him, you have to make him come your way. No doubt the reason he has begun calling again is because of the death in your group. News like that spreads fast in the underground. He has to be thinking that if today you are too upset to talk, tomorrow you might be mad enough to join forces with him."

"So if that is his proposal, I accept?"

"No."

"No?"

"No, you force his hand. Tell him you're defeated, whipped, through, and you're convinced he can't do anything to turn the tide either. Then hang up on him."

"Are you sure?"

"Absolutely. We want him certain that you are dead set against the idea that there is any value in your associating with him. Make him beg."

"But what if he believes me? What if I convince him I mean it?"

"So much the better. Play hard to get. It will keep from his mind any vestige of suspicion that you are too eager."

"Because?"

"Because if you come off too eager, it might be because you are cooperating with agencies that can bring him down."

Chapp sat back down, and Paul had the impression he was getting into this. "So how many times do I turn him down before finally agreeing?"

"That's entirely up to you. Use your intuition. Take him right to the breaking point where he's convinced it's hopeless. Then make him offer a show of good faith."

"Such as?"

"Meeting on your terms, at your place."

"He'd be a fool."

"Of course he would, but we're going for a compromise here. He has to win one somewhere along the line. You insist to the end he needs to come and see you where you are, and of course he'll have to flat refuse that. Just before letting the whole thing fall apart, he'll likely suggest a neutral spot, closer to where he is. That's where you make your most important move. You name the place."

"Where?" Chapp said.

"What would work?"

"The question is, what would work for you, Paul? I imagine you're not going to play this out long. Once we know where he's going to be, I'm going to disappear and you're going to come in with the authorities, no?"

"Now you're thinking."

"So, you tell *me* where," Chapp said.

"London."

"London? He'll never come to London."

"Says who?"

"Says me," Chappell said. "Would you if you pulled off a terrorist attack there?"

"I might, if I was as full of bravado as Magnor. He may just rise to the challenge. He'll be giddy that he finally has you on board, if he can just see his way clear to get to London. And then he'll think, why not? Later he can crow that he was in the very city he attacked."

Chappell raised his eyebrows and for the first time that day, Paul saw his smile. "Doctor, is thinking like a criminal required for your job?"

• • •

They left it that Chapp would check in with Paul anytime he communicated with Magnor. On the way back to Paris Paul grew suspicious of two different cars that could have been trailing him. To be sure, he drove a hundred miles out of his way and stopped at various tourist sites. Eventually he convinced himself it had been only his imagination, but he felt more secure when he finally reached the city after dark.

Along the way he felt a sudden, deep urge, a compulsion to pray for Jae. Straight had told him about feelings like this. He didn't even know what to say or whether he should try to pry from her later what might have been going on with her during that time. He simply prayed that God would protect her and be with her and give her whatever she needed right then.

• • •

Half an hour later Paul parked the second rental car a couple of blocks from his hotel. As he got out he became aware of a dark, attractive young woman heading for the door of Le Hotel Boutique across the street. She was trying to protect her long, brown hair from the cold wind. Paul was passing just as she reached the top of the marble steps leading to the entrance, and out of the corner of his eye he saw her fall in a noisy heap.

"Whoops!" Paul said, charging up the steps and reaching for her, but she was holding one ankle with both hands.

"I think I sprained it," she said with a slight French accent. "Can you tell?"

She reached for his hand and put it on her ankle. Her foot trembled, but Paul didn't notice any bruising or the telltale immediate swelling that usually came with a sprain. "Maybe you just twisted it," he said. "Want to try to stand on it?"

"In a second," she said. "Your hand is so warm."

Paul hadn't minded kneeling there with his hand on her, but when two bellhops hurried out, he stood, and she told them she was all right. As they moved away, she reached for Paul's hand again, and he helped her up. She stood gingerly and mince-stepped around. "I hope it's not sprained," she said. "But it hurts. Help me in, would you? I owe you a drink at least."

"Not necessary," he said, extending his arm. As she leaned all her weight on him, they moved inside her hotel to a tiny round table outside the lobby bar. She ordered wine, he a decaf coffee.

"I feel like such a fool," she said.

"Not at all. It happens. I've always been a klutz."

"Oh no!" she said. "Not you. You carry yourself with such grace. You must have been an athlete."

"Played a little ball."

"See?" she said. "I knew it. I'm Calandre. Calandre Caresse, and yes, I know what that means in English."

"*Calandre* or *caresse*?" he said.

She laughed. "I meant *caresse*."

"Everybody knows what that means," Paul said. "What does it mean in French?"

"'Endearing.'"

"And *Calandre*?"

"'Lark.' So you were caressing a bird."

"Was I?"

"You were. And I'm already feeling much better, sir."

"Ray," he said, shaking her hand. "Ray Decenti."

"Are you staying at Le Boutique too, Ray?"

"No. Nearby."

As she bantered with him, Calandre frequently leaned into him, touched his hand and arm, and became more and more familiar. Paul did not reciprocate but couldn't say he found her touch unpleasant. He had been away from home too long.

"Are you in Paris alone?" she said.

"I am. You?"

"Yes. I live in Toulouse but must come here for my work occasionally. I am an editor of a fashion magazine, and this is the fashion capital of the world."

"It is that," Paul said.

"And what brings you here?" she said.

"Just business. Sales."

"Interesting," she said, and he almost believed her.

When the check came, Calandre insisted on putting it on her room. Paul moved as if to leave. "You don't have to rush off, do you, Ray? No one will know if you are late getting back to your lonely room, will they?"

He smiled and shook his head.

"You must let me show you the magnificent view from my suite," she said. "But maybe you have a bigger one and on a higher floor at your place."

"I doubt it. Standard-issue for salesmen, you know. Budgets and all."

"Thankfully that is not true of our magazine. Come, you must see it."

Paul hesitated. "I have an early morning."

"I won't keep you long. Please. I might not be able to make it all the way with my injury."

He laughed at her obvious teasing, and against his better judgment walked her to the elevator. She leaned on him and limped as if her ankle still hurt.

When they got to her suite, she handed him the pass card and he opened the door.

"Wow," he said. "It *is* palatial."

"Come see the view."

He stepped inside, but the door shutting behind him seemed to bring him to his senses. "I really have to get going."

She passed him and threw the draperies open wide. "Just look at this," she said, slipping her coat off and draping it over a chair. She reached back for him and tugged him to the window. "The City of Light."

"Spectacular," he said.

As he stood there she lifted her sore foot off the floor and leaned fully into him so he was supporting her. He carefully stepped away and held her with both hands. "Okay," he said. "Thank you. You all right now?"

"You're not leaving, are you?" she said.

"I really must."

"You won't allow me to thank you for your kindness?"

"The coffee was more than enough."

"Aw," she whined, "surely not." And she moved toward him, reaching for his coat. He moved away. "You don't fancy me?"

"Actually, very much. You're really a beautiful girl."

"I am more than a girl, Ray."

"You know what?" he said. "I'm not going to do this. Don't make me insult you or appear ungrateful for the offer, but I'm leaving. Thanks again and good night."

As he strode to the door she called after him, "You know where I am. If you change your mind, any time of the day or night, I'll be here."

. . .

The phone rang at the Decenti home at about 3 p.m. Sunday. The kids were at the football game with their uncle and aunt.

The call was from Bia Balaam for Ranold. "Hold a minute, Chief," he said. "Is this something Jae might want to hear?"

He waved her to the phone, and as soon as Jae realized what she was about to hear, she was tempted to leave the room. But she could not pull herself away. She sat next to her father as he switched the phone to speaker mode.

"This is all you've got on him, Ms. Balaam?"

"Yes. I fear the bug was either malfunctioning or he was out of range all day. You're going to find this strange and out of character, General, and you, Mrs. Stepola, may be encouraged by it. But don't be fooled. One bit of intelligence we did pick up from Ms. Caresse is that Paul emerged from a car that was not issued to him by the French bureau."

"Is that so?" Ranold said.

Jae was still stewing about Paul's being out of character and her being expected to be encouraged by that. Maybe he had been *in* character; had they thought of that?

"Ms. Caresse feigned a fall in front of Agent Stepola to get his attention," Bia explained. "The first thing we hear from him is in response to that."

"Whoops!"

"I think I sprained it. Can you tell?"

Jae rolled her eyes. How transparent, and how weak of Paul to not see it.

"Maybe you just twisted it. Want to try to stand on it?"

"In a second. Your hand is so warm."

Oh, please! Jae listened as the woman got Paul to walk her to a table, insist that she owed him a drink, and then respond to Paul's self-deprecating comment about always having been a klutz.

"Oh no! Not you. You carry yourself with such grace. You must have been an athlete."

"Played a little ball."

Jae shook her head. He was biting. The drivel about the woman's name sickened Jae.

Then: *"So you were caressing a bird."*

"Was I?"

"You were. And I'm already feeling much better, sir."

"Ray. Ray Decenti."

Jae had to cover her mouth to hide a grin as her father appeared to nearly choke.

Finally the woman got to the part about being alone.

"You don't have to rush off, do you?"

Bia Balaam said Jae would be encouraged. Did that mean Paul would resist this obvious come-on?

"I won't keep you long. Please. I might not be able to make it all the way with my injury."

Laughter. Footsteps. Elevator noises. A door opening.

Jae was dying.

"Wow. It is palatial."

"Come see the view."

A door shutting.

Gag me, Jae thought.

"I really have to get going."

Attaboy, Paul!

"Just look at this. The City of Light."

"Spectacular. . . . Okay. Thank you. You all right now?"

"You're not leaving, are you?"

"I really must."

"You won't allow me to thank you for your kindness?"

Jae held her breath.

"The coffee was more than enough."

"Aw, surely not. You don't fancy me?"

"Actually, very much. You're really a beautiful girl."

"I am more than a girl, Ray."

Jae closed her eyes and actually wished for the first time that she was a praying woman.

"You know what? I'm not going to do this. Don't make me insult you or appear ungrateful for the offer, but I'm leaving. Thanks again and good night."

"You know where I am. If you change your mind, any time of the day or night, I'll be here."

"That's all there is," Bia said. "A bit of TV noise in his room after that, but that's all."

Jae felt as if she could fly.

"No phone calls?" Ranold said, sounding disappointed. "Is he not in contact with anybody?"

"If he's making calls," Bia said, "it's from outside the hotel. And this bug is not long range, you know. General, hold on, please. I'm getting something right now. Here it is."

"Hey, it's me. . . . Good. Had a long discussion with Raison's people today. It's time to marshal the international underground church, everybody, to again pray that God will act."

Silence.

"We can't hear the other guy?" Ranold said.

"Apparently not."

"Who is it anyway?"

"No idea."

Then they heard more: *"Thanks. He's finally ready to help me with Magnor."*

Silence.

"You're recording this, right, Chief?"

"Of course."

"This could be huge."

"You bet."

"You're kidding. . . . You did? I know you told me God puts it on someone's heart and—it's just that when He was prompting you to pray for me, He was prompting me to pray for Jae. Go figure. . . . Yeah, well, maybe He is working in her life. Nothing would make me happier. . . . I'll talk to you tomorrow. The old man sent Bia Balaam over here, pretending she's here for the announcement in Bern tomorrow. She just happened to check into my hotel, so she could see the attack site, of course. . . . Yeah, that's what I said. Anyway, I'm running her to the airport first thing in the morning. That's what, about 10 p.m. your time? I'll call you."

"Have we all heard enough?" Ranold said. "I have."

"More than enough," Bia said. "Guess I'd be disappointed if he bought everything I said. What kind of agent would he be if he couldn't see through this?"

"Big question now is, has he flipped, or is he infiltrating the underground?"

"Sounded pretty convincing to me," Bia said. "All that prayer business. What do you think, Jae?"

"I hope he's just playing up to the underground," she said. "But it didn't sound like it." All Jae cared about was saying enough to get herself sent over there.

"You realize what you're saying, honey?" Ranold said.

"Yes."

"That'd be treason."

"I know. Or, like you've said, he's that good. He'd have to be to succeed, wouldn't he?"

"You may have liked that he didn't fall for the woman, but—"

"But that's nothing, Dad, compared to—"

"What he may really be about. You ready to go help us find out?"

"I don't know. Do you really think I could help?"

"Of course you could."

"I agree," Bia said, convincing Jae that she could play elusive a little longer and still get to go.

"I don't know. I hate to leave the kids right now, and I'm not trained in this."

"We can give you a crash course," Bia said. "We've got to find out who this Raison is, where they meet, how many there are, and especially what your husband meant when he said Raison was willing to help with Magnor. Is he going to protect Magnor, work with him, what?"

"I'm willing if there's really something you think I can do," Jae said.

"I'll arrange a flight for the morning," Ranold said.

Before Jae went to start packing, her father asked her if she thought Paul had been talking to Stuart Rathe. In truth, that's exactly what she thought, and her mind was racing with all the implications. Paul wasn't trying to play up to anyone; he seemed to be talking with a friend who shared his views.

"I have no idea."

"Put that on your list. He mentioned the time difference, which sounds like the Midwest to me. Let's see if we can find out who that is. That'll tell us how legit Paul's underground contacts are."

Jae packed her New Testament discs with her other stuff and

thought how easy it had been to boldly lie to her father. He had always claimed he could tell someone was lying by watching their pupils and detecting other "tells." But when she had told that whopper, that she had no idea who Paul had been talking to, she had been looking at Ranold dead-on.

23

PAUL KNEW THAT IF HE DIDN'T GET TO BED before midnight, he would be good for nothing, having to rise the next morning by four-thirty to get Bia Balaam to the airport. But he had a chore that wouldn't wait.

He sat on a couch overlooking the city, his laptop on his knees, crafting a response to the government's announcement. This he would send to Straight, who would run it past the underground leadership in Detroit, Washington, L.A., Bern, Rome, Paris, and all the other contacts around the world. Each faction would be free to copy, forward, and disseminate the document as far and wide as they dared, including to all the major news organizations in their respective countries.

It read:

To: *The Honorable Baldwin Dengler, Chancellor of the International Government of Peace, Bern, Switzerland*

From: *The worldwide church of believers in the one true God of Abraham, Isaac, and Jacob, and God's Son, Jesus the Christ*

Re: *Your decree, announced this Monday, January 21, 38* P.3., *which we call the year of our Lord,* A.D. 2047

Chancellor Dengler:

We aver that the current world system, which has banned for nearly four decades the practice of religion by people of faith, is an abomination in the sight of almighty God.

We believe that you and your government, as well as most of your loyal citizens, are unaware of the size and potential influence of a people that has, by your actions, been pushed underground and forced to practice their faith illegally.

We ask that you rescind immediately the decree announced today and put a moratorium on laws prohibiting the practice of religion until you can determine how people of faith can peaceably live in this society without fear of reprisal.

We are beseeching our God to act in judgment, should this request not be carried out within forty hours of when the decree is announced, or midnight, Bern Time, Tuesday, January 22. We believe that He will act to deliver us from you, our oppressor, as He did in Los Angeles, California, last year.

We respectfully warn that you will regret ignoring this request, as we are calling upon God to specifically act as He did thousands of years ago against Pharaoh in Egypt, when Pharaoh refused to let the children of Israel flee his domain.

We refer you to the Old Testament account of the ten plagues God unleashed against Egypt. There are those among us who are asking God to eschew the first nine plagues and to refrain from hardening your heart, and it is our heartfelt wish that you avoid the dire consequences of the tenth plague at the forty-hour mark. Short of this, we fear that God may not limit this plague to the seat of the government but rather that it will affect the entire world.

To our brothers and sisters around the globe, we remind you that you need not feel bound by the Old Testament caveat of protecting your own households by sprinkling blood on your doorposts to identify yourself. We believe the blood of Christ has already been shed on your behalf and that God knows His own.

In conclusion: Rescind the loyalty decree, lift the laws against the practice of religion, or proceed at your own peril.

For your reference, following is the text of the carrying out of the tenth plague on Egypt, which we fear God may administer upon those who turn a deaf ear to our plea:

So Moses announced to Pharaoh, "This is what the Lord says: About midnight I will pass through Egypt. All the firstborn sons will die in every family in Egypt, from the oldest son of Pharaoh, who sits on the throne, to the oldest son of his lowliest slave. Even the firstborn of the animals will die. Then a loud wail will be heard throughout the land of Egypt; there has never been such wailing before, and there never will be again."

. . . And at midnight the Lord killed all the firstborn sons in the land of Egypt, from the firstborn son of Pharaoh, who sat on the throne, to the firstborn son of the captive in the dungeon. Even the firstborn of their livestock were killed. Pharaoh and his officials and all the people of Egypt woke up during the night, and loud wailing was heard throughout the land of Egypt. There was not a single house where someone had not died.

When Paul had polished the manifesto, he checked his watch and realized it was late afternoon in Chicago. He called Straight but got his machine. "I want to read you this thing, Straight. Call me as soon as you can."

Paul sat hanging his head. Was it possible God would do this? Would He finally lose patience, run out of mercy, act as He had in the days of old? Paul didn't know how to pray—that God would do it or not do it. Such a catastrophe would eliminate any hope of these millions of slain firstborns ever entering the kingdom.

Seconds later Jae called, speaking quickly. "Paul, don't say my name. Say as little as possible. You have been compromised. Listen, I couldn't call until I was able to break away from my parents' house under the guise of a last outing with the kids before I leave for Europe."

"Eur—?"

"Just listen. I've been enlisted to help bring you down, and I'll be there late tomorrow afternoon."

"Is—?"

"Paul! Listen! Balaam planted a bug on you. Probably on whatever jacket you were wearing when you greeted her. It has a short range, but she picked up your whole conversation with the young woman. You were set up."

Oh no! "Yes," Paul said. "Thank you, sir. I'll pick that up at the desk then?"

"And she played for Dad and me your side of the conversation with Straight."

Paul shuddered. They had talked about prayer and the underground, and he had even mentioned Raison. "Yes, I'm leaving the hotel early tomorrow morning, so I'll stop by."

"You didn't mention his name, but you said something about what time it would be where he was, and Dad assumed the Midwest. Paul, hear me. I'm on your side. I believe you're playing up to the underground to infiltrate them. If I'm wrong, well, then you're going to take me down with you. I've got to go, but I wanted to warn you about the bug. I love you, I miss you, and I'll see you tomorrow."

"Same to you, sir, and thank you very much. Good night."

As soon as Jae hung up, Straight called. "Hey, it's me. What've you got?"

"Yes, I already got that message. I'm picking it up in the morning."

"What?"

"Thanks for letting me know."

"What's going on, Paul?"

"I appreciate it, and can you call me when you know anything about my laundry?"

"You want me to call you back?"

"When you have it figured out, yes."

"I'll call you back."

"Thanks."

Paul paced for five minutes, hoping Straight would put two and two together. The tone sounded in his mouth. "Stepola."

"You're being bugged; is that it?"

"Yes, thank you. That'll be fine."

"You finished the document, but now you can't read it to me."

"Right. No, late morning will be fine."

"Can you transmit it to me?"

"Sure."

"And when you're somewhere secure, you'll get back to me?"

"That works for me. Thanks again."

• • •

Paul knew he would never sleep. This was as close as he had ever come to being found out, and he racked his brain to recall if he had totally given himself away.

His overcoat had to have the bug. Would he be able to find the bug without making so much noise that it was obvious he was looking for it? Better than destroying it, he decided, was to use it to his advantage. He opened the closet door where his coat hung so the transmission would be even clearer. And he would be wearing the same coat in the morning on the ride to the airport. Bia would be asleep by now, but she would check the recording when she rose.

Paul added a line to the cover page of the manifesto, reminding underground factions to hold it until after the decree had been announced in their time zones, and then to get it to everyone they knew.

Then he phoned his boss, Bob Koontz, in Chicago. "Sorry to bother you at home, Bob. Just wanted to check in and thank you again for releasing me for this assignment."

"Yeah, how's it going, buddy?"

"Frankly, it couldn't be better, Bob. I'm good, you know that?"

Koontz laughed. "I've been trying to tell you that for years. So, what's happening?"

"I've got the patter down, Bob, the lingo. I've infiltrated the underground here and in Rome, and I've got enough on these people that I think they're going to lead me to Magnor himself."

Bob swore appreciatively. "You serious?"

"I'll keep you posted. The Rome people meet in an abandoned cathedral about an hour south of the city. They're small and ineffective, but there is some tie to Magnor. They say he's headquartered in Germany. In France the biggest zealot underground faction is based in Marseille. I'm in good with them. Guy named Raison Arnaud is their top guy. He was mentored by Magnor."

"Man, you've really made progress. How soon before you can get to Magnor himself?"

"I'm hoping within two weeks."

"Wow."

"Yeah, wow."

"This will be a major, major deal for you, Paul."

"I hope so."

"Oh, it will," Koontz said. "Guess you know what's coming down tomorrow."

"The decree? Yeah. Can't wait. It's about time we started turning the screws on these people."

"I hear Balaam's over there."

"Yeah, she's here. I know Decenti sent her to keep an eye on me, but the more I think about it, the less it bothers me. She's good people, and if I were in the old man's shoes, I'd probably do the same. Did you know she's got kids?"

"I didn't, Paul."

"Yeah. A grown daughter and a son at Georgetown. Pretty proud of 'em, and rightfully so. Well, hey, just wanted to keep you in the loop, Bob."

"You didn't have to do that, but I'm glad you did. Proud of you, Paul."

"Well, you ain't seen nothin' yet."

24

JAE WAS ABLE TO PLACATE the kids about her trip by taking them out for ice cream Sunday, listening to their excited chatter about the football game, and assuring them that her main mission in Europe was bringing their dad home earlier than planned.

By the time she got them to bed and had endured her father's endless reminders of what to do and not do, and what to say and not say, she was exhausted and hoped she could sleep despite her excitement. Jae had no idea what was going on with Paul. She was thrilled with how he had handled the planted woman. But though she had told him she believed he was playing the underground as an infiltrator, she was no longer sure. He had sounded so real, especially with Straight.

Warning Paul about the bug had been the right thing, regardless. Jae was his wife, first, and even if it turned out he was guilty of treason, she owed him the benefit of the doubt initially. Would she turn him in? She didn't want to think about it.

Having already packed, Jae found herself digging through her bag to retrieve the New Testament discs. She had left off at the end of Philemon. Next came Hebrews. If nothing else, listening to a chapter or two of that might help take her mind off everything else and allow her to sleep.

Long ago God spoke many times and in many ways to our ancestors through the prophets. But now in these final days, he has spoken to us through his Son. God promised everything to the Son as an inheritance, and through the Son he made the universe and everything in it.

How Jae wished God would talk to her that way, and even wishing it made her realize she was making a huge assumption: that God was real. She couldn't deny there had been times, especially as a teenager, when she secretly wondered if someone wasn't behind all that she saw in nature. But Jae had never dared mention that, even to her friends.

The Son reflects God's own glory, and everything about him represents God exactly. He sustains the universe by the mighty power of his command. After he died to cleanse us from the stain of sin, he sat down in the place of honor at the right hand of the majestic God of heaven.

This shows that God's Son is far greater than the angels, just as the name God gave him is far greater than their names. For God never said to any angel what he said to Jesus: "You are my Son. Today I have become your Father." And again God said, "I will be his Father, and he will be my Son." And then, when he presented his honored Son to the world, God said, "Let all the angels of God worship him." God calls his angels messengers swift as the wind, and servants made of flaming fire.

But to his Son he says, "Your throne, O God, endures forever and ever. Your royal power is expressed in righteousness. You love what is right and hate what is wrong. Therefore God, your God, has anointed you, pouring out the oil of joy on you more than on anyone else." And, "Lord, in the beginning you laid the foundation of the earth, and the heavens are the work of your hands. Even they will perish, but you remain forever. They will wear out like old clothing. You will roll them up like an old coat. They will fade away like old clothing. But you are always the same; you will never grow old." And God never said to an angel, as he did to his Son, "Sit in honor at my right hand until I humble your enemies, making them a footstool under your feet."

But angels are only servants. They are spirits sent from God to care for those who will receive salvation.

• • •

Paul was only guessing that Bia Balaam had heard his call to Koontz, of course, but it seemed she was mellower this morning. They met in the lobby at five, and Paul had arranged to have his Paris bureau car at the curb.

"You look great," he said, and she did, especially for that time of day. She was not a young woman but her unusual height made her look perpetually trim.

"Why, thank you, Paul," she said, apologizing again for his having to rise so early.

"I have a big day ahead anyway," he said. "Might as well get at it."

"Making inroads, are you?"

"You bet," he said, opening the car door for her. "It's interesting to know something my targets don't know: about the decree today. That should put them in a tizzy."

"I just hope it silences them," she said, "once and for all."

"We can dream," Paul said. "My biggest fear is that the clampdown might spook Magnor. I've got a pretty good idea where we're going to find him, and I'm very optimistic about getting to him."

"You have been busy, Agent Stepola. I'm impressed."

As they headed south toward Orly, Paul said, "I'm always a little skittish at this point in an operation, especially when things seem to have been going so well. It's as if the luck has to change."

She nodded. "Bumps in the road. Can't avoid them. But if you go by the book, they'll even out. You have a reputation for turning bad situations into good ones."

• • •

After dropping Chief Balaam off, Paul found himself whistling as he drove back to his hotel to switch to the second of his rental cars. Then it was off toward Tours. He had hardly slept, and that would catch up to him eventually. But he fully expected Chappell Raison to hear from Styr Magnor again this morning—if not before the 8 a.m. announcement, then surely once the underground manifesto made the news.

Niggling at his brain was the prospect of Jae's showing up late that afternoon. He longed to see her, to hold her, touch her, kiss her. What he really wanted was to tell her the truth about himself. But he had no idea whether it would be prudent. Was she really believing in Paul at this point, or was that just something she had to say? She had saved his life by warning him of the bug, but she remained the most dangerous person in his life. He prayed for her as he drove.

Paul reached the original chicken-coop-cum-meeting-place at a little after seven in the morning. Lothair sat in a chair by the stove, barely moving, apparently hardly awake. On his lap lay a late-model, high-tech radio receiver, tuned to an all-news station.

Chappell was pacing and looked stony. "I don't like this, Paul. I really don't. I hung up on Magnor last night, just like you said. And there's been nothing since."

"Patience, man. He'll call. He needs you. What'd you think of the manifesto?"

"Brilliant. That your work?"

Paul nodded. "Your people ready to disseminate them?"

"As soon as we hear the proclamation from Bern," Chapp said. "All our groups get printable versions, our e-mail contacts get a Net version, and all our press contacts get both."

"Perfect."

"Not in my book," Lothair said. "And I'm afraid I speak for everybody but Chapp. Fact is, we're praying God won't do this."

"We'd better come to some conclusion," Paul said. "The thing is ready to go. Do we threaten the government with the power of God and then pray that God won't deliver?"

Lothair nodded.

Chapp shook his head.

"God's going to do what God's going to do," Lothair said. "We have to trust He knows best, even if we seem to be obligating Him to something He might not do."

"As for Magnor," Chapp said, "he is not going to call back, Paul. I was too convincing, too dead-on."

Lothair nodded. "He was, Doctor. If I were Magnor, I wouldn't call him again."

But Chappell was waving wildly, shushing them. "Hello, Styr," he said, as if he'd just lost his best friend. "Not bad, and you?" He hit a switch on his earphone that allowed Paul and

Lothair to hear without it sounding to Magnor as if he was on a speakerphone.

"You don't sound that well," Magnor said with a distinct non-Norse accent. Paul immediately thought he sounded familiar. Where had he heard that voice? What was that accent? Welsh?

"I'm really no better today than yesterday or the day before," Chapp said. "And I thought I was clear with you last night."

"Clear? My friend, I thought we got cut off! Are you telling me you were so rude as to hang up on me? Surely not."

"And I will again if you keep wasting my time."

"Raison, Raison," Styr cooed, "please. Did I not avenge the loss of your family? London was for your wife. Rome for your son. Paris for your daughter. What more must I do to show we are compatriots? The loss of the young woman is nearly as personal to me as it was to you, even though I never knew her, because she was your friend. And because it was so heinous. How dare Dengler and his lot attack us for a basic human right?"

The way he says Dengler, *Paul thought. I have heard this voice before. He hates Dengler personally. Why?*

"I want to take the offensive yet again, Chappell. Can we not work together? Can you not connect me with others in the underground? We must persuade Bern that the rebellion is widespread, not concentrated."

Chapp sighed and looked at Paul, shrugging and pantomiming hanging up.

Paul shook his head and rolled his fingers, encouraging Chapp to let Magnor talk. Meanwhile, Paul was desperately trying to remember the name of the Scandinavian cell group that vehemently opposed Baldwin Dengler's appointment as head of the International Government.

"That's all you want?" Chapp said. "Introductions?"

"That's a start," Styr said. "My dream is to have you as a colleague, a decision maker."

"Not interested."

Paul gave him a nod and an okay sign.

"Chappell, what will it take? What do you want?"

"An end to the bloodshed."

"That is my goal too."

"You bomb three major capitals and tell me you want to end the bloodshed?"

"Think of your history, Chappell. Remember the United States once dropped atomic bombs on Japan to save even more lives in the long run."

Paul shrugged and nodded at Chapp.

"That was the exception rather than the rule, Styr."

"That is precisely what such dire times call for. Our target? Bern. Infiltrate the government headquarters when all the top people are there. One more explosion, and we can start over."

And it came to Paul. Angry Storm the group called itself. They had pushed for the mayor of Oslo, Erik Buri, to assume leadership of the International Government, and he had come within a few votes of recalling Dengler and doing just that. They vowed revenge, even though the Dengler choice proved providential, as Buri died two years later.

Paul grabbed a pen and a notepad and scribbled *Angry Storm* to show Chapp. But as he wrote it, something else hit him. He played with the letters. Styr Magnor was an anagram of Angry Storm. Paul crossed it out and wrote, *CR, ask the origin of his name.*

Chappell read the note and squinted at Paul as if bewildered.

Paul nodded and urged him on.

"I've been meaning to ask you, Styr. What is the origin of your name?"

A pause. Then, "Why do you ask? Is it so unusual? There are many Styr Magnors."

"Just curious. You're the only one I know."

Paul worried now that Chapp had pushed too far. He didn't want to lose the prey over this. Paul drew a finger across his neck to tell Chapp to drop it.

"*Magnor* means 'fighter.' It describes me perfectly."

"And *Styr*?"

"I don't know. It's from Norse legend." It was clear Magnor was bored with this and maybe even suspicious. "Well, if you're not going to help, you're not going to help. I can't keep knocking on a locked door."

Paul looked quickly to Raison, who appeared to share his fear that they were losing Styr. Chapp looked as if he was about to apologize and move back to the subject, but Paul was afraid that would shift the balance of power. He repeated his finger across the neck, this time with more gusto.

"So you finally get it that I'm out?" Chapp said.

"Regrettably so. If you change your mind, you know where to find me."

"No I don't."

"Well," Styr said, humor in his tone, "at least where to call me."

• • •

Jae rose while the kids were still in bed and left them notes. Her mother was already up, making a big breakfast and going on about how excited she was to be taking the kids to their new school this morning. Of course, Ranold was camped out in front of the television, monitoring the replays of the great announcement from Bern and swearing about the immediate response from the underground.

"They want to play," Ranold fumed, as Jae wandered in. "They think they're going to fight fire with fire by what, killing our firstborn sons? Well, I say bring it on."

• • •

It was after noon in France, and while Chapp and Paul snacked on fruits and cheeses Lothair had brought from home, Styr Magnor had been back in touch with Chapp several times.

"This manifesto is your work," Styr said. "I'd know it anywhere. No wonder you don't think you need me. Well, who's going to pull this off for you? Dengler and his people will never cave in to this, and then you're going to have to put up or shut up. I have the manpower to start committing these executions, Chapp. And I'd start with Dengler's own son."

Paul was nodding, urging Chapp to keep him talking.

"You would?" Chapp said.

"For sure. Cripple the head, and the tail soon dies. Listen, are you going to take credit for this manifesto? Because if you're not, I am."

"The manifesto is what it is. We're all behind it."

"That's all I needed to know." *Click.*

Within moments the news carried the report that Styr Magnor had claimed responsibility for the underground manifesto, and the international vitriol began. All over the world citizens who feared a repeat of the L.A. fiasco went to the streets, demonstrating, pleading with the government to negotiate with Magnor. Others called radio and television stations and newspaper and magazine offices, urging Dengler to laugh in the face of this ridiculous threat, to never negotiate with terrorists, and reminding the chancellor that within forty-eight hours, the underground would be the laughingstock of the world.

Paul surfed the Internet, studying name origins, and found

that Magnor was indeed a name from Norse legend. Specifically it meant "supporter of Erik." That cinched it for Paul.

He knew who Styr Magnor was.

"When Styr calls back, Chapp, let's reel him in."

25

"RANOLD," MARGARET CALLED OUT, "the message light is blinking on the phone."

Jae followed him into the kitchen, where he mashed the speaker button and played a long message from Bia Balaam:

"General, I know it's after midnight there and you're not likely to get this until morning, but you may want to rethink sending Mrs. Stepola. I know this will sound strange, but instinct tells me Agent Stepola may be legit. I have too many years' experience to go off half-cocked, but unless he's the best I've ever encountered, he's convinced me. I got a brief update from him on the way to the airport this morning, and I fear his wife might be in the way as he closes in on Magnor and the underground. It's your call, of course, but that's my professional opinion. I've got to get on a plane here in a second, but let me play you this recording of a call he made to Chief Koontz in Chicago last night and also of our conversation today, and you be the judge."

Jae's heart sank as she listened. She could tell what Paul was up to. Once she had told him of the bug, he used it against Balaam. He was a master, but if his brilliance had cost her the chance of seeing him over there, she was not going to be happy.

When the recording finished, Bia rang off.

Ranold was preoccupied. "I don't know what to think," he said. "Maybe he's onto us. Didn't she think of that?"

"Frankly, Dad—and this is not easy for me to say—but I trust your judgment on this. He's always had a way with women."

"He has, hasn't he? Let's get some grub and get you in the air; what do you say?"

. . .

Paul and Chappell sat listening to news reports over Lothair's radio. International response to the threat from the underground reminded Paul of the reaction the Los Angeles warning had generated. Only the California result seemed to temper this a bit. There were pockets of atheistic loyalists who didn't want the government to test these waters. Callers to talk shows ran the gamut from hysterical laughter to mockery to disdain, but also included cooler heads. These were the ones who said, "Maybe if religion were not outlawed but rather ignored or even tolerated, it wouldn't have such an appeal to weak minds. Let them be."

Others said they were convinced now that Styr Magnor and his international cabal of terrorists would target firstborn sons around the world and try to make it look as if some angry God had acted. "This man," one woman said, "wants to inflict terrorist attacks on families one at a time. I agreed with Chancellor Dengler's initial response of never negotiating with terrorists, but isn't it time for at least a sit-down, a meeting of the minds? Find out what has this man and his followers so upset."

When Dengler's official response came on, Paul was particularly intrigued. He had gotten to know the man somewhat and was persuaded that the chancellor was well-intentioned. He was a man of character and principle, and while Paul was diametrically opposed to his worldview, it had not always been that way. Baldwin Dengler personified what Paul had once believed with his entire being, and the man articulated it better than anyone. He truly seemed to believe that a government and a society of peace depended on the abolition of religion, racism, and—of course—terrorism.

As Dengler approached the podium at the International Government of Peace's assembly chamber, Paul could picture it, hearing the cameras of hundreds of journalists.

Chappell Raison's phone chirped and he put Styr Magnor on speaker.

"You watching this?" Styr said.

"Radio," Chappell said, "and I don't want to miss it."

"Me either. I just wanted to make sure you knew he was on. You see, Raison, this is when we should have sent a devout rebel carrying a megaton bomb on his back. *Wham, bam,* and we start over, ma'am. He's about to start. I'll call you back."

"Ladies and gentlemen, International Chancellor Baldwin Dengler. Mr. Dengler will not field any questions this afternoon, and his remarks will be brief."

"Thank you," Dengler said. "As the world knows by now, Styr Magnor has taken responsibility for this latest threat to the security of our global village. As I stated when he wantonly attacked innocent civilians in London, Rome, and Paris, there will be no negotiating with terrorists.

"That remains the stance of this government. As for those citizens Mr. Magnor claims to represent, we maintain that they are a much smaller rebel faction than he claims. And as for his assertion that they believe they have the ear of almighty God, I remind you that it is this very belief that caused the wars that led to World War III, the establishment of a New World Order, and the banning of religion.

"If the last nearly forty years have not proved there is no God, surely they have at least proved that society is the better for not acknowledging that there is. I personally reject the idea, and this government unanimously asserts that we do not believe there will be any mass supernatural deaths resulting from our refusal to cower in the face of this warning.

"I am not so naive as to doubt that Mr. Magnor, in his frustration with our refusal to capitulate, will attempt some terrible affront against people of goodwill. I can assure every citizen that we will respond forthrightly and with swiftness to avenge any such attack.

"If Styr Magnor were a man of honor and dignity and intelligence rather than a coward, he would come into the open and compete in the marketplace of ideas. That is my challenge to him. Show yourself and stop lobbing your bombs of cowardice against right-thinking people."

Again the airwaves filled with the responses of the people, many lauding the courage of the chancellor, others horrified at his reckless challenging of a madman.

Within minutes, Magnor was back on the line with Chappell. "I have connections all over the world," he said. "But I need more manpower if we are going to carry out this threat. I have learned that Dengler believes his own rhetoric when he makes these pompous public statements. But now we have to call his bluff. Do you have people willing to effect this action?"

Chappell hesitated, looking to Paul, who nodded. "I might."

"Now you're talking, Chappell. Come and see me and we'll make our plans. Time is short. We're already down to fewer than thirty-six hours."

Paul vigorously shook his head.

"I'm not coming to see you," Chapp said.

"Well, there's no way I'm going to France."

"Where then? You name the place."

"Somewhere neutral. But not too far from either of us, eh, Chappell? And no lieutenants. Just you and me."

"I would insist on that."

"Let's get this done today, friend. You say where, and I'll be there."

Paul scribbled, *Suggest somewhere totally impossible.*

"Alaska," Chappell said.

Magnor laughed. "You're serious?"

"Dead serious. No one knows either of us there. We'll have total privacy."

"We don't have the time, man!"

"If time is the enemy, let's meet in London."

"London!" Magnor said. "You *would* suggest London. What's that, three hundred kilometers from you? Naturally I'm public enemy number one there."

Paul gave Chapp the cut sign again.

"You know, Styr, I didn't want to be involved with this—or you—in the first place. If London doesn't work, and you won't do Alaska, find someone else."

A long pause. "Tell me something, Chappell," Styr said, his voice cold now, "what were you going to do? How would you carry out this manifesto without me?"

"We're trusting God to act."

Styr howled. "I love it! Well, go ahead, but when God decides your battle isn't His battle, then what? Then can I expect a call from you?"

Paul put a finger to his lips.

Chappell said nothing.

"Thinking, Chapp? Your faith a little thin today? Worried how you're going to look and what will become of all your followers when the big firstborn wipeout doesn't happen?"

"It might not hurt to have a Plan B," Chapp said.

"Ah, the voice of reason at last. Listen, Chapp, I'll meet you in London, but I get to pick the place. And while I won't have anyone with me, they will be close enough to see whether you're alone too. If you're not alone, you'll never see me."

"Same here."

"All right, hear me. I'll say this only once. In the northeast corner of central London, in the Shoreditch area—do you know it?"

"I can find it."

"There's a noisy, crowded place called Horsehead's Pub. Got it?"

"Got it."

"Eight o'clock this evening. I'll make sure I get the table in the corner by the back door that leads to the alley. You'll come in and leave from the front door. I'll come in any way I well please and leave by the back. Any funny stuff and you'll find yourself in the alley for the rest of your days, follow?"

"You don't have to threaten me, Styr."

"I know I don't, friend. We'll be just over twenty-four hours from Operation Firstborn, eh? We've got a lot to cover."

"I'll be there."

"I'll be there first."

No, he won't, Paul decided.

RANOLD DROPPED JAE off at Bush International at 8 a.m. for the two-hour 8:30 flight to Paris. "I wouldn't let Paul know you're coming until you get there," he said. She nodded. "And let me give you this."

He reached behind him on the floor of the backseat and produced a box the size of a deck of cards. "This goes in your purse or anywhere within half a mile of whomever you're trying to record. And this—" he pulled from the box a tiny, waxed-paper envelope that appeared empty—"this is the bug itself. You have to turn it to the light to see it. Magicians use this kind of wire. Lean here, look close."

Ranold slipped his index finger into the envelope and pulled out two inches of the finest fishing line Jae had ever seen. It glinted in the light, then disappeared again. "I have to be careful," he said, "because I can't really feel it. See, in the middle there, it looks as if it's been tied in a knot."

"No," she said, moving her head, trying to get the length of wire to come into focus. "Wait . . . there, yes, I see. It's smaller than a piece of lint, Dad."

"And it's been treated. Not only is it tacky, to keep me from dropping it, but it's also got a magnetic charge, like static electricity that makes it adhere to clothing or whatever. Here's how it works."

Carefully placing the "knot" just above the palm of his left hand at the base of his middle finger, Ranold delicately extended the opposite ends of the line so they lay between his index and middle fingers and between his middle and ring fingers. It was as if he were wearing a microscopic ring backward on his middle finger.

"Notice," he said, "it's fairly secure there. Until I do this."

Ranold leaned over to embrace Jae lightly, putting a hand on each of her shoulders. She was struck at how odd and awkward this felt. Her father had not embraced her since she was Brie's age. When he pulled away, the bug attached to her coat. He held his hand up to the light. "See?" he said. "It's gone. You have it."

She looked for it on her coat. "No way I'd ever know it."

"And believe it or not," he said, "the guts of the transmitter, microphone and all, are embedded in that little knot." He gently felt for it, removed it, and placed it back in its waxed sleeve.

"And you want me to bug my own husband?"

"I want you to do your duty to me and to your country."

"And what about my allegiance to Paul?"

Ranold sighed. "If he proves worthy of it, then it's not misplaced, is it? If you find he's *not* worthy of it, I'm trusting you to act the way you would with any other traitor to the cause of liberty and freedom."

Cue the theme music.

• • •

On the way back to Paris, Paul pulled over at a remote spot, opened his door, and sat with his feet outside the car. He dialed the hotline number Dengler had given him with his fingertips. To his dismay, the chancellor's chief of staff answered the phone.

"I was told Dengler himself always answers this line," Paul said.

"Who's calling, please?"

"That's confidential, as you must be aware."

"How do I know you didn't get this number by accident?"

"You don't, except that I know it's the crisis line to the chancellor, and he will not be pleased if urgent business is delayed."

"My apologies. May I please know to whom I am speaking?"

"NPO Agent Stepola."

"Thank you, sir. And I don't mean to insult your intelligence, but you must understand the crush of media on a day like this. The chancellor is in interviews right now and has several high-level meetings scheduled for the rest of the afternoon. But if you tell me you must talk to him immediately, I'll fetch him directly after the current TV interview."

"Actually, I need to talk to him right this second."

• • •

Jae had learned from Paul how to travel light. Once settled on the transport, she tried to read and, failing that, to watch a movie. But she couldn't concentrate. Her mind was a mess. Paul knew she was coming, of course, and would be waiting for her if the business of this historic day didn't interfere. Would she really have the gumption to plant a bug on him when it was she who had warned him of the other one? Maybe he was suspicious now and would run a bug-sweeping device over his clothes. Wouldn't it be something if he discovered *she* had bugged him?

Maybe she wouldn't do it. Maybe she would tell her father she lost it or that it malfunctioned or she chickened out. Could—should—a woman be expected to entrap her own husband? There used to be laws against that. Weren't there still?

Jae busied herself watching the scenery below as they lost sight of the East Coast in what seemed like minutes. She set her watch six hours ahead and calculated they would reach Paris sometime before five. By the time she rented a car and found Paul's hotel, it should be around six.

Jae thought about listening to more of the New Testament, but she feared she wouldn't even be able to concentrate on that. And yet she was restless. What was it? She missed the interaction with the ancient texts. It was almost as if God was speaking to her. Had *she* ever spoken to *Him?* Not in so many words. What form would that take?

People around her were dozing. No one would know if she prayed silently. But what would she say? Jae folded her arms and lowered her head, tucking her chin to her chest. Closing her eyes, she felt fatigue wash over her and was tempted to let sleep invade. Instead, she spoke silently, inwardly. *God*, she said, *if there is a God, would You reveal Yourself to me somehow?*

Jae didn't know what else to say. In her listening one night, a verse had flown by that struck her as odd. Well, they all struck her as odd, but this one in particular. It was something about never being able to please God without faith. And that anyone who wanted to come to Him had to believe there was a God. She would have to find it and listen again, because she was certain there was some kind of promise about how God would reward those who sincerely looked for Him.

Was that possible? Could it be true? And if there was a God, would He have heard her prayer just then? Jae had added the condition "if there is a God," and she wondered if that proved she *didn't* have faith, that she *didn't* really believe there was a God, that she was, in essence, hedging her bets. But what about that promise? Wouldn't God reward her if she sincerely looked for Him?

Just before Jae dozed off she told herself that if she were God, she would not be able to ignore a prayer like hers. *I was raised to not believe in You,* she said. *I'm just asking You to prove me wrong somehow.*

• • •

Dengler seemed high from the attention and import of the day. "I trust, Doctor, that you are not abusing the privilege of this line. I have not taken a call on this phone from anyone for more than two years, not even after the terrorist attacks and not today."

"I understand, sir, and I assure you I respect the nature of the security."

"There are not but a handful of people who even have this number, and you are the only one who is not a head of state or a member of my inner circle."

"I believe you will conclude that entrusting me with it was wise."

"I hope so," Dengler said. "What do you have?"

"First, sir, I know that you understand many of the intricacies of international intelligence and espionage, but I would like the liberty of walking you through a few reminders. May I?"

"Please."

"What I am about to tell you goes to the heart of the security of the International Government and its citizens. It must not be shared with even one person not on a need-to-know basis. For instance, I have told neither my superiors nor my colleagues within the NPO, either USSA or International. I would advise that you not tell anyone on your staff unless they will be personally involved or overseeing the operation that results."

"I understand."

"Not your secretary, assistant, chief of staff—"

"I said I understand, Agent Stepola."

"You did. Forgive me. Sir, I assume you are aware of the name Steffan Wren."

"Of course. The Welshman who led the opposition to me when Erik Buri sought to unseat me. He and his group called themselves Angry Storm."

"Are you sitting down, sir?"

"Yes."

"Steffan Wren is Styr Magnor. And Styr Magnor is an anagram of Angry Storm."

Silence.

"You still with me, sir?"

"I certainly am. I will not ask how you came to this conclusion, given that my own virtual army of intelligence and security officers have been on the case for days."

"I know where Magnor/Wren will be this evening. My suggestion is that you put me together with your top military strike-force leader so his people can be in position long before Wren arrives. Again, sir, I know you know this, but leaks being what they are, I would tell absolutely no one else."

"How many personnel will he need?"

"I recommend letting him decide."

"And where would you like to meet him?"

"Ditto on that, sir. If you trust me, I believe the less even you know the better."

"I will have him call you on a secure connection within minutes."

"Mr. Chancellor, I believe Styr Magnor will be in custody or dead before midnight tonight. Can you conduct the rest of your day's business without letting on that we are close on this?"

"I shall do my best, Doctor. Keeping the smile off my face may be the most difficult."

"These operations are never easy, sir, so I am loath to make promises. But I believe the world will be safer."

"Primarily, Doctor, we will remove the threat that looms at midnight tomorrow."

Well, I wouldn't go that far.

• • •

Knowing Jae was en route, Paul called her phone and left a message. "Darling, an unavoidable bit of business makes it impossible for me to greet you upon your arrival. When you get to the hotel, ask for a message. I will leave you a pass card for the room. Enjoy room service and whatever else you want. I'm afraid I will not be back until late. Watch the news."

A few minutes later Paul took a call from a man with a lilting Indian accent who identified himself as Garuda Vibishana, "major general of the International Government of Peace, in charge of special weapons and tactics."

"How shall I address you, sir?"

"The same way you would like to be addressed, Doctor."

"Paul is fine for me."

"Then Gary works for me, though you will find I look more like a Garuda than a Gary."

"First order of business, Gary, is that we need to meet soon. Where are you located?"

"I am in Bern. I was here for the announcement and had planned to leave in the morning for my post in Belgium. I am at your disposal, sir."

"The operation site is London, Gary. Do you have adequate personnel there?"

"That is providential, as we are well staffed in all major cities, especially capitals. And if that is the target site, that is where we should meet. What section of London will be ground zero?"

"Northeast."

"And the time?"

"Eight p.m."

"Today." Vibishana said this with defeat in his voice.

"You like a challenge, don't you, Gary?"

"We will succeed, Paul. Let's meet in the northeast of London as soon as both of us can get there. I'll pick you up at Gatwick."

• • •

Paul called Chappell and Lothair and swore them to secrecy.

Chappell said, "So I'm going to London with you?"

"No. I am not about to expose you to the head of the government's SWAT team."

"But don't I have to make an appearance at Horsehead's?"

"Hardly. Magnor said he would be there waiting for you. I know what he looks like and where he said he'd be. I'll give the signal, and the government will take him down. You don't want to be where the media will be swarming within minutes, do you? And you don't want to be associated with him in any way."

"Of course not."

• — •

Paul raced to his hotel, dug through his supplies until he found the perfect raggedy clothes and shoes for the assignment, stuffed them in a bag, and headed to the airport. An hour later he was at Eastwick, where Garuda Vibishana picked him up.

The major general was about six feet tall and two hundred

pounds, bald, very dark, with a prominent nose and piercing brown eyes. He wore a suit and tie that seemed out of place, especially with his high lace-up, military-issue boots. "I will change into work clothes," he said, shaking Paul's hand. "As I assume you will."

Paul nodded.

Vibishana drove to a fire station in Denham, where he strode in carrying a leather briefcase and nodded to a man he called Scotty, a diminutive man in a T-shirt, firefighter pants, and suspenders, chewing a rubber band and eyeing Paul warily. "Friend of mine," Vibishana said, nodding at Paul. "He's okay."

"Yeah, well, I'm a friend of yours and I'm not okay," the firefighter said, laughing. He tossed the Indian a key.

Gary led Paul to a small back room. He locked the door and ran a bug sweep. "Secure," he said. He then pulled from his case a sheet of onionskin paper folded in fourths. When he spread it on the table, it was about two feet square. He slapped down half a dozen soft lead pencils and said, "Draw me the pub."

Paul sat back. "I'm sorry, Gary. I don't know the place."

"What?"

"Horsehead's was Magnor's idea. I can tell you what he said about it. He said it was crowded and noisy with an entrance in front and back, the back one leading to an alley, which is the way he plans to leave. He said he would take a table in the corner in the back."

"He's going to leave in handcuffs or a body bag," Vibishana said. "But we can't carry this out if we don't know the layout. Just a minute."

He left the room and brought back Scotty. "What do you need?" the little man said.

"Horsehead's Pub. You know it?"

"Seen it. Northeast off the Great Eastern Road."

"Ever been in there?"

"Nope, but I bet I know someone who has. Jessie."

"Who's he?"

"She. Firefighter. A lush. Knows every pub in London, she does."

"She on duty?"

"Sleepin'."

"You got a pint around anywhere?"

"For what?"

"I'll buy it from you."

"Not supposed to have a stash here, you know."

"So do you have one or not?"

"'Course I do."

Vibishana pulled a large bill from his pocket. "Bring the booze, and get her in here."

Scotty delivered the bottle and went to get Jessie. As they heard heavy footsteps up and down the staircase above them, Vibishana whispered to Paul, "Got to make sure she's in no condition to mention to anyone that we even asked about Horsehead's."

Jessie proved a bit worse for wear. A dyed blonde with too much makeup and her hair going in several directions, she looked unhappy to have been roused.

Vibishana cut to the chase. "Draw me a picture of Horsehead's Pub and there's a pint in it for you."

"That's easy," she said, breathing through her nose. She leaned over the table and sketched the place like an artist. "Bar's here," she said. "Tables up and down this way. WC's in the middle. Back door. Alley. Where's my hooch?"

"You want it right now?"

"What do you care when I want it? You gonna turn me in if it helps me sleep? I'll be better on the job in the morning."

"Just hope we don't get a fire tonight, doll," Scotty said.

She greedily accepted the bottle and was cracking the seal as she left. "Don't wake me if we do, Scotty. We got plenty of man-power."

"Good idea," Vibishana said when she was gone. "Let her sleep. Will she drink that tonight?"

"It'll be gone before you are," Scotty said.

27

IT HAD BEEN TOO LONG since Jae had been in Europe. She was disappointed to see the deterioration of Paris. As the late-afternoon sun descended, the lights came on all over the city, highlighting the indecency and excess that made her glad she was raising her kids in Illinois. Downtown Chicago may look a lot like this, but she was able to shield Brie and Connor from much of it. There were those who would chide her that this was the price of true freedom, but her views had changed when she became a mother.

Jae found Paul's hotel and picked up the envelope at the desk without a hitch. Soon she was settling into his room and enjoying the view. As she hung her clothes, she looked for his overcoat, but of course he had taken that, wherever he was. "Watch the news," he had said. She turned on an all-news television station, changed her clothes, ordered dinner from room service, and sat in front of the TV. She hoped Paul would not be too late.

Her meal was just okay for such a palatial hotel, and after a while the news tended to repeat itself. She didn't know how many times she had seen and heard the loyalty decree announced by Baldwin Dengler. Certain shots showed dignitaries in the background, and she saw Bia Balaam. Then came the demonstrations from around the world, expressions of support and criticism from various leaders, and Styr Magnor taking responsibility for the underground manifesto.

Finally came the coverage of Chancellor Dengler's forthright response to Magnor, and of course all the international reaction to that. As the news cycled through the same stuff over and over and so-called experts added their conflicting commentaries, Jae was tempted to watch something else. But Paul would have told her to watch the news for a reason. He had to be on some assignment that would wind up being covered.

She noticed his laptop on a TV tray near an easy chair. She settled in behind it as the news droned. The keyboard was locked and required a password. She shouldn't be snooping, Jae decided, but on the other hand she was here on the NPO's nickel, and that was what they expected of her. That was, plainly, rationalization, because she had already scotched her assignment by eliminating the element of surprise and even tipping Paul off that he had been bugged.

But still, she wanted to know what he had been working on, and nothing was going to keep her from trying. A distant memory made her wonder if Paul had ever changed his password. He had once used her first name, followed by the last digit in the year of each of their births—his, hers, Brie's, and Connor's. She tapped it in. Bingo.

All Jae saw on the desktop were various programs, expense

spreadsheets, notes, games, Web links, and a documents folder. She clicked on that and saw that the most recent files were numbered one through four and titled ManDraft. What could that mean? She opened the first and a chill ran down her spine. Christian Manifesto, first draft. Fingers trembling, she opened the second, third, and fourth and told herself she was just curious about how Paul thought, why he made the small changes he had made.

Jae tried with everything in her to find an explanation for this, other than that Paul himself had written the manifesto. She couldn't make it compute that he was a mole, an infiltrator into the rebellion, and yet himself wrote their manifesto. She could come to no other conclusion than he had flipped. He was part of them, believed in the cause, and had already become enough of a leader that he would be called upon to craft their policy.

Was that what he meant by telling her to watch the news? Was he not really returning until midnight the next night when this warning about the firstborn sons either came true—as had the one in Los Angeles—or proved false and proved these people's faith in God was misplaced?

Jae couldn't sit still. She wanted to call Paul, but she knew he wouldn't even answer if he was in the middle of an assignment he couldn't tell her about. But was he working on NPO International business, or was he on some caper for the underground? What she had discovered was exactly the type of evidence on Paul NPO USSA was looking for. Her father would worship the ground she walked on if she brought him this chestnut. *It'd be just like him to assign me to assassinate Paul.*

And should she? If it was true, if he was a traitor, a turncoat, a renegade, a maverick, a threat to the USSA, a mole within the NPO, was it not the responsibility of any honest citizen to expose him? to eliminate him?

Jae moved in and out of the various rooms in Paul's suite, banging the walls, pulling her hair, grunting in frustration. Why couldn't he be here? Why did he have to be gone? Why could she not know where he was?

Of one thing she was certain, there would be no more cat-and-mouse games between them. As soon as he walked through that door, she would put it to him. She wanted to know. He had to tell her. Was he the best infiltrator of the underground the NPO had ever produced, or was he a believer, wholly dedicated to the cause of the enemy of the state?

Jae had no idea what she would do with whichever answer he gave her, but she wouldn't sleep tonight without knowing one way or the other.

• • •

"I don't suppose I need to tell you," Vibishana said as he drove to a regional International Government office, "but this is a very difficult operation. It will be quick and dirty by design. We have to assume that Magnor/Wren will come into the pub alone as he promised, but that doesn't mean he will not have already planted compatriots in there."

"As you will have."

"Exactly. And while you have to be one of them, Paul, because you will identify him, I cannot be unless there are customarily people of color in that establishment. I'm guessing there are not, and thus I would stand out."

"I'm afraid that would be an understatement," Paul said. "A blue-collar pub would likely be a holdout against political correctness and diversity."

"I will run the point from outside," Vibishana said. "And Magnor will undoubtedly have people out there too, watching for people like us. We must be thoroughly invisible."

Paul dug through his stuff and pulled out the bag containing what he called his drinking outfit.

"Perfect," Vibishana said. "It even smells."

"That's from wearing it during half a dozen workouts and never washing it."

"My best camouflage is a slight limp," the Indian said, "making me look less than masculine. Harmless."

"And yet you will be carrying."

"Of course. The most powerful handheld weapon in history, as will all thirty of my people."

"Thirty?"

"Does that sound like overkill to you, Paul?"

"A little."

"As I said, this will be difficult, dangerous—too many variables. Lots of things can go wrong. I intend to assure that nothing does. Once we get the signal from you that Magnor/Wren is where he said he would be, we will not hesitate. We will storm the place, knowing he will also likely have armed personnel there. He will be agitated that he has not yet seen this contact person he expected, and he may try to bolt. That's why we need your signal as soon as possible after he is seated."

"And what form would you like that signal to take?"

"Let me put it this way, Paul: Regardless of how hard we work at making you invisible, you will never feel more conspicuous in your life. You need to trust yourself, trust your disguise, trust the situation, trust human nature, and trust us. You will likely assume you have been made and may opt out of giving the signal, fearing Magnor is onto you and that his people will respond before you do. That's a good reason to make the signal easy, clear, and totally normal. Think about it and be prepared to let me know when we're briefing our people."

When they arrived at London's NPO headquarters, the

assignees were already making their way to a meeting room in the back. The breakdown appeared to be about three-to-one men to women, but the women looked roughly the same size as the men. All wore black boots, black cargo-style pants, black T-shirts, and thick leather belts containing weapons and ammunition. They carried duffel bags and helmets with visors.

Vibishana spread the drawing of Horsehead's Pub on a flip chart, called the meeting to order, and outlined the mission. "You can leave your helmets here. Only these six"—and he read the names—"will wear the all-black outfit you have on now, as you will emerge from the command van on my signal and will be the last on the scene. The rest will dress the parts of street bums and pub patrons."

As if on cue, the SWAT team began riffling through their bags and pulling out appropriate clothes and shoes. Paul found it eerie that there was no talking and very little noise, but the personnel—men and women—immediately stripped to their underwear where they sat and changed into their getups. Paul was intrigued by where they found to hide their firepower.

The conspicuousness Vibishana predicted began right then as Paul felt obligated to change his clothes too. He wore a stained, sleeveless, ribbed T-shirt, cheap, raggedy suspenders, filthy woolen trousers, and faded, scuffed brown boots with no laces and no socks. Over this he pulled on a grimy denim jacket, too thin for the weather, his built-in reason for camping out in the pub for the better part of the evening. He finished with a floppy, flat hat that he pulled down over his ears and almost over his eyes.

"The key, as you know," Vibishana lectured, "is that we cannot overplay this. No acknowledgment of each other. No obvious studying of the area. We're street people; this is our home. We're bored, listless, barely conscious. We stare, we tune out, we respond slowly. But be aware of people in the area who don't appear to belong. You should be able to recognize Styr Magnor, aka Steffan Wren's people because they are not likely to be disguised.

"Magnor himself might be disguised, Agent Stepola, and it's entirely on you to identify the right man. Whoever is sitting at that back table when you give the signal has about a 50-percent chance of dying before he hits the floor. So—"

"—be sure," Paul said.

"Be sure."

Vibishana explained that Paul would be the first of the team in the pub, a little more than an hour before the rendezvous was scheduled. "We will drop him off six blocks from the place, and we will watch for curious eyes. Unless we stop to pick him up because of some suspicious activity, he will go in, settle, and appear to anyone who comes in after him as if he has been drinking for hours. His goal is to have an unobstructed view of the table in the back and be utterly unnoticed.

"A dozen of you—"and Vibishana listed them—"will wander in over the next half hour, blending in and finding spots where you can see Agent Stepola.

"Another dozen—" again he read off the names—"will be in the neighborhood—some in front, some in back—ready to move on my command, which will come through your earpieces. The remaining six will be in the command vehicle with me, and we will move out together at the appropriate time."

The major general explained that upon the signal from Paul, one of the personnel inside the pub would trigger a signal to him in the van and ignite a flash incendiary between Paul and Magnor/Wren, which should cause a stampede toward the doors. The rest of the inside SWAT team should stay out of the way of the panicked people. "Stay near the walls where you will have the freedom to charge toward Magnor. He will bolt for the back door, where the outside personnel will be on their way in. Now get this. This man is number one on the international most-wanted list. We may terminate him with the least provocation. Allow me to outline what form that might take. If he is armed, shoot to kill, even if he doesn't reach for his weapon. If he attempts to run through our armed personnel coming in the back door, shoot to kill. If any of his people reach for, point, or fire weapons, shoot to kill—Magnor first. If you hear gunfire—friendly, otherwise, or undetermined—shoot to kill. This man may survive, but dead or alive, he will be in our custody. Understood?"

SWAT personnel nodded.

"Now, Agent Stepola, what will be your signal?"

"I'll knock an empty glass to the floor."

Vibishana smirked. "Okay, Doctor. But if you should accidentally drop one early, the place is going to get a lot noisier a lot quicker."

• • •

Jae had to wonder: Was this how God revealed Himself to her? By discovering that her husband was a secret believer? And what did that prove? Because Paul had turned, did that make it true? Did that make God real? What if Paul was wrong?

What if *she* was wrong and Paul had not turned at all? Could the manifesto on his computer mean something else? Could he have infiltrated the rebellion so deeply that they trusted him to write this for them, not realizing that he didn't believe it himself? What would become of him—and the resistance—if the threat fizzled at the zero hour the next night?

And if Paul believed, for how long had that been true? Was he in with the underground in Los Angeles? Did he believe the drought was the work of God Himself? Or did he *know* it was?

28

PAUL BEGAN SECOND-GUESSING HIMSELF from the moment he left Garuda Vibishana's van and started ambling for Horsehead's Pub in Shoreditch. Would he recognize Steffan Wren? Sure, if he looked as he had looked when he had been a public figure. But now, his life depending on not being known as Styr Magnor, would he be disguised? Might he send a double, just to test the waters? He wasn't a stupid man. Had all the elusiveness Paul had coached into Chappell Raison done its work? Could they really sting the world's leading fugitive?

Paul tried to tell himself that all worthy ventures like this carried heavier-than-normal risk. The worst part was, as he watched Vibishana's taillights disappear in the distance, Paul was in league with the sworn enemy of his soul. Regardless of where he stood with the USSA, with International, with the NPO, and even with his compadres in this effort tonight, ridding the world of Magnor was the right thing to do. His work, his life, had resulted in these strange bedfellows, but he would not feel bad for working with this SWAT team in this endeavor.

Paul had left his watch with the rest of his belongings at the London headquarters, but his innate sense of time told him he would arrive at Horsehead's a little before seven. He would have to work at not looking around, gawking really, to be sure the SWAT team was in place. He was going to feel vulnerable and exposed, but it would sure help to be reassured that he was not alone.

The tone in his mouth told him he had a call and that he should have blocked the device. He knew it couldn't be Jae. She knew better. But Paul thought he'd better take it. He looked right and left, ahead and behind; determining no one was within earshot he pressed his fingertips together. "Stepola," he said.

It was Lothair.

"Man," Paul said, "you know I'm on undercover assignment."

"If you can't talk or even just listen, hang up on me."

"I've got a few seconds. What is it?"

"Do you believe God sometimes gives messages to us through other people?"

"I don't know . . . sure. Why?"

"'Cause I believe He gave me something for you. I don't get it, don't know why, but Chapp agreed it was worth sharing with you if you had time to hear it."

"How long is it?"

"Just two verses."

"Go ahead."

"It's from First Kings eighteen, verses thirty-six and thirty-seven. I just feel the Lord led me to the passage and wanted me to read it to you."

"Hurry, Lothair," Paul said, feeling rude but worried because he was coming into the busy section a few blocks from the pub.

Lothair read: "'O Lord, God of Abraham, Isaac, and Jacob, prove today that you are God in Israel and that I am your servant. Prove that I have done all this at your command. O Lord, answer me! Answer me so these people will know that you, O Lord, are God and that you have brought them back to yourself.'"

Paul felt his knees weaken and he almost stumbled. That would have been all right, he decided, because he was to look unstable anyway. "That is powerful, Lothair. Thanks for that, and forgive me for being short."

"Believe me, man, I understand."

"And could you do me a favor, friend?"

"Sure, Paul."

"Could you and Chapp and anyone else you're in contact with pray for my wife, Jae? I'm going to reveal the truth about myself to her, probably tonight—if I survive this. And I have no idea what will come of that."

• • •

Jae had grown so restless that in spite of herself, she switched channels between the news and vapid entertainment. Too much television was inappropriate, even for her, but she couldn't stand hearing the same news one more time. Once, however, when they were rehashing the underground manifesto, she made sure she was at Paul's computer and followed along. His last draft matched word for word what was read on the news.

Suddenly Jae found herself prostrate on the couch, compelled to pray for Paul. It was the strangest feeling she had ever had, and she was conflicted over whether she dared pray to a God about whom she had not come to any conclusion. *If He rewards those who seek Him, but they have to believe that He exists, will He hear my prayer about something else?*

Jae didn't know. All she was sure of was that she had to pray for Paul. "God, protect him. Be with him. Bring him back to me." Tears welled and sobs racked her throat. Jae couldn't stem the tide. "God, please!" she wailed. "Please!"

· · ·

Paul noticed the pub from a distance but kept his face pointed at the pavement. When he was sure no one was watching, he lifted his eyes to the faded, creaking sign with the rudimentary horse's head and glass of ale depicted on it. He slowed as he passed, as if thinking about going in, then went around the block.

Seeing nothing and no one out of the ordinary, he reminded himself to draw zero attention and followed three rowdy young men through the front door.

The place was already wall-to-wall people, mostly drunk men and a few women who had seen better days. To not appear new to a place like this, Paul forced himself not to cough, despite the thick blue cloud that permeated every inch of breathable air. Pipes, cigarettes, and cigars contributed, and the occasional opening of the front door seemed to have no effect on the haze.

Paul pushed a crumpled bill onto the bar and ordered a dark ale, taking it to a tiny table on the sidewall, facing the back. Near him a tableful of men rose to leave, and Paul surreptitiously grabbed two of their empties and pulled them alongside his full glass. He leaned into the wall and appeared to doze.

Paul sat there, barely moving, for more than half an hour as people came and went. When he had the chance, he grabbed empties from here and there and settled back into his repose. By now, a dozen of Garuda Vibishana's agents had to be among the patrons, but Paul didn't look closely enough to guess. He just trusted that they were here and would not let him down.

A giant clock showed 7:45 when two women and a man

started a dart game that seemed too close to other patrons for Paul's taste. But no one seemed to mind. If someone was walking through when it was time to throw, either the thrower or the walker waited. In the front, a group of boozy people started a sad drinking song.

And as Paul appeared to doze, shoulder and head resting on the wall, eyes barely open, Steffan Wren strode confidently through the back door. He looked to see that his table was empty, then went straight past Paul to the bar. He was a big but compact man, probably five-ten and two hundred and twenty-five pounds, wearing tan boots, brown corduroy pants, a horizontally striped sweater, an unbuttoned peacoat, and a matching stocking cap with blond curls poking out. Wren had a ruddy complexion; bright white, even teeth; and green eyes. He looked confident, self-assured, and as if he knew where he was going and what he was doing.

Paul nearly panicked, wondering if he should immediately give the signal. But no one else knew what Wren looked like. All they knew was where he was supposed to sit. But as Wren paid for his pint, Paul noticed a couple of men sit at his back table. Were they with him, or would there be trouble? A confrontation could throw the whole operation out of whack.

Paul couldn't imagine what Wren would do. It didn't make sense for him to draw attention to himself, but he didn't seem the type who would sit somewhere else or hang around waiting for the other two to leave. When he was halfway back to his table, Paul could tell Wren noticed the interlopers. He reached into the pocket of his peacoat, and Paul was again tempted to give the signal. Was Wren armed? And what was he going to do, threaten men for choosing an empty table?

Paul heard him call the men "gentlemen," but it was also clear he was asserting his right to "my table."

One of them stood and asked what he planned to do about it, and Wren produced a bill from his pocket. The other man stood quickly and grabbed it, and both men tipped their caps and took their drinks elsewhere. Looking satisfied with himself, Steffan Wren pulled the table a few more inches from the wall and settled himself behind it where he could survey the entire place, all the way to the front door. He didn't seem to notice Paul, and if he did, he didn't appear suspicious. He took a foamy swig of his brew, set it down, and wiped his mouth with the back of his hand.

Still appearing unconscious and propped against the wall, Paul moved languorously and caught one of his empties with his elbow. As he straightened his arm, the glass hit the floor with a crash. No one seemed to notice, except that in the next second a flash bomb went off and the place went up for grabs.

As Paul's eyes readjusted to the light, he expected to see Wren ducking out the back door into the waiting arms of Vibishana's team. But no. He had stood so quickly that the table and his drink went flying. And here he came, directly past Paul toward the front door. Could he be that fast a thinker, realizing his escape route was blocked?

SWAT team members poured through the back door, and as Wren produced a handgun and lowered his shoulder to ram the crowd already backed up to Paul's table, Paul reacted instinctively. Though unarmed, he rose and bent both knees. As Wren came within range, Paul sprang toward him, hands clasped at his chest, arms akimbo. Before Wren even noticed, Paul smashed into the man's face with his forearms, knocking him off his feet.

"Gun!" one of the SWAT team members yelled, and two opened fire, riddling Wren with bullets.

• • •

Jae's distress and helplessness had exhausted her, and she had not even realized she was dozing until she heard the high-pitched tone from the television and looked up to see BULLETIN . . . BULLETIN . . . BULLETIN . . . scrolling along the bottom of the screen.

"We have late-breaking news from London at this hour, where International Government intelligence and security personnel report the capture and shooting death of Styr Magnor. Chancellor Baldwin Dengler is about to speak live from Bern on this development, and we will take you there as soon as we get word.

"Reports from Great Britain say Magnor was a pseudonym for longtime Dengler nemesis Steffan Wren of Wales. Officials say Wren was set up in an elaborate sting operation by a crack antiterrorist, antirebel agent of the USSA's National Peace Organization. The name of the agent is, of course, being withheld to protect the security of his future assignments.

"Here now is Chancellor Baldwin Dengler, live from Bern."

Dengler stood at the lectern as reporters adjusted microphones and lighting, and as soon as the stage was clear, he began. "Ladies and gentlemen of the worldwide community of peace, I bring you good news. Styr Magnor is no more. As news outlets have already reported, it turns out he was none other than political activist and gadfly Steffan Wren. In cooperation with international peace forces, our own intelligence and security personnel were able to lure him to a pub in London within the past hour.

"As was feared and for which we were prepared, Wren did not allow himself to be taken alive. He has been positively identified as the mastermind behind the terrorist attacks and widespread loss of lives in London, Rome, and Paris, as well as tomorrow night's threat to the world contained in the so-called underground manifesto. We are confident that the danger to our firstborn children predicted for a little more than twenty-four hours from now has died with Steffan Wren. The decree calling for a written pledge of loyalty from every citizen within the next sixty days remains in force.

"I know you share my grief over the tragic loss of a misguided and misdirected life, but that you also share my satisfaction and joy over the successful conclusion to a most difficult and complicated operation that puts to an end a reign of terror we have not seen since World War III.

"As we celebrate this victory and applaud the cooperation between law-enforcement agencies of various nations, let us not forget the grief of the families who lost loved ones in the attacks. And let us live on in freedom and peace so these will not have died in vain. Thank you."

There was not a doubt in Jae's mind that this was Paul's mission. But how did it jibe with what she believed she had discovered about him? If the underground had anything to do with the terrorist attacks, they all deserved to die. And if Paul was behind this campaign to bring down Styr Magnor, did it mean he was only pretending to be part of the rebel faction?

She called him but got his answering device. "Call me as soon as you can, Paul. I'm going crazy waiting for you here."

• • •

Paul was on his way to the airport with Garuda Vibishana and on the phone with Baldwin Dengler. "How soon can you get to Bern, Agent Stepola? I insist that though we cannot make it public, you be adequately rewarded for your part in this."

"Oh, that's not necessary, sir. I share your pleasure in the outcome, but—"

"Did you not hear me say that I insist?" Dengler said, a smile in his voice. "Somehow I do not believe you have a choice when the boss of your boss's boss makes a request like that. Am I right?"

"Right, sir."

"Can you be here tomorrow?"

"My plan is to sleep in Paris tonight. As you can imagine, I am exhausted."

"Then I'll send a plane for you in the morning. Shall we say ten o'clock? We will schedule a private ceremony for noon. I will be sure that Ms. Balaam will be there. And Major General Vibishana, as well as my cabinet and staff."

• • •

Paul decided there was no way he could discuss anything with Jae on the phone and that she would just have to forgive him for not calling before he returned.

As he was getting on the plane, a call came in from Ranold. "I just got the word, boy, and are we proud of you!"

"Thanks." It was all Paul could do to remain civil, but he didn't want to compromise himself or Jae. He'd love to ask Ranold about setting him up, bugging him, even sending Jae to see what she could get out of him.

"I got to say, Paul, that frankly there were times when I was worried about you, wondered about you. But what I hear from every side is simply that that's how good you are at infiltrating. Good enough to make your own shop scratch their heads. Jae there with you?"

Paul told him he hadn't seen her yet and that he was on his way to her now.

"Well, I'll call her directly. Get pictures at the ceremony tomorrow and tell Bia to take good care of you, hear? And you and Jae get yourselves back here soon as you can."

"Hug and kiss the kids for me, will you, Dad?"

"Oh, sure."

. . .

"You just talked to him?" Jae said. "Why hasn't he called me? I left him an urgent message."

"He's getting on the plane right now," Ranold said. "You'll see him in no time."

"His phone works from the plane. I'm going to call him."

"He may have a reason, Jae. Let him be. He's on his way."

Then I'll call Straight.

But Straight wasn't answering either. That was good for him, Jae decided. She had planned to ask him flat out whether he was a believer. Was Paul? And what did that mean for her, for her kids, for their marriage, for their future?

29

BY THE TIME PAUL reached his hotel it was nearly midnight. On one hand he couldn't wait to see Jae. On the other he was as petrified as he had been when Steffan Wren had come through the back door of Horsehead's. Tired as he was, he was through playing games. Jae was going to get it all, both barrels. She could turn him in, leave him, or whatever, but he was no longer going to live a lie with her.

He took a deep breath when he got off the elevator. He could hear her hurrying to the door when he slid the pass card in the lock. Paul pushed the door open, and she caught and held it, locking eyes with him. He had never been so happy to see someone, come what may.

Jae grabbed his arm and pulled him in, letting the door slam behind him. They held each other silently for several minutes, and she led him to the couch. She turned off the television, but

Paul could see that his computer was open and the manifesto was on the screen.

"Where do we start?" he said.

"Tonight," she said. "What happened? Were you in there?"

He told her everything, from setting up Magnor through Raison to calling Dengler to meeting Vibishana. And he told her every detail of what had gone down at Horsehead's.

At times Jae covered her eyes. Paul had no idea how she was receiving all this. She had to wonder where he was coming from: supersleuth or secret believer? That he would make plain soon enough, but meanwhile, she leaned over on him, laying her head against his chest as he talked. Had she already made up her mind? Did she already know or think she knew? Or would she tear herself away when the truth came out, threatening to expose him?

When the story was spent, they sat there, entwined physically if not mentally. "I'm glad I didn't know how involved you were in the actual event," Jae said. "I was worried enough thinking you were just an adviser."

"I'll have a bruise or two in the morning," he said.

"Poor baby."

A long silence. Paul searched for words, praying silently.

• • •

Jae knew Paul had to be scared. He couldn't know what she was thinking, only that she had questions. She still wasn't entirely sure about him, but she had known him too long to be totally in the dark. She had seen the change and now too much evidence. Jae decided to make it easy for him, and if she was wrong, he could tell her so.

"I know, you know," she said.

"You do?"

She pulled back and nodded. "You're a good mole, Paul. Maybe the best there ever was. But you're not that good. You've turned, changed, flipped, haven't you? You're a believer."

"Couldn't fool you, could I?"

She shook her head. "I know a different man when I see one."

"So what does this mean for me, Jae? for us?"

• • •

When she stood and moved away from him, pacing and looking everywhere but at him, Paul died inside. *She doesn't know what she's going to do about me*, he decided. *And that can't be good.*

"Let me tell you something," she said. "I know the predicament you're in, or at least I think I do. But can you see that I'm in as bad a spot as you? I found the letter from your father, Paul. And I showed it to my dad. I've never felt more guilt, and I'm so sorry about that. I hope you can forgive me."

Forgive her? Paul nodded. Sure, he'd forgive her, but did she realize what that could mean for him? Had his success with the mission really erased any suspicion from Ranold's mind? and Balaam's? and maybe Koontz's by now? Had word gotten to Chancellor Dengler that the USSA NPO suspected their own man? Surely they couldn't have been that monumentally short-sighted.

"Paul," Jae continued, "I was sent here to find you out, trip you up, turn you in. And now I'm the only one who knows they were right about you. As always, you pulled a rabbit from a hat at the last minute and have convinced the best espionage minds on the planet that you're not what you appeared. No, you were so adept at infiltrating that you made your own people think you were a traitor.

"So where does that leave me, Paul? As a loyal citizen, a

dutiful daughter, do I leave you, divorce you, expose you, see you taken from me, from our kids, and perhaps executed?"

She finally stopped pacing and leveled her eyes at him.

He stared back at her. "I don't know, Jae. What *do* you do?"

"First," she said, "I want to understand this. I want to know your thought process. I want to know how you went from what you were to what you are. When did it happen? How did it happen? Is there no turning back? Are you in for the long haul?"

And so he told her. It began with his disillusion over what the NPO and the USSA did to people of faith. Yes, there were clear laws against what the rebels were doing, but the more he was exposed to them, the more he persecuted and yes, even killed some of them, the more he wondered what was so wrong about wanting to believe in something beyond one's self.

As he studied these people, he said, he realized what they really believed. That God was real. God was alive. God was the creator of mankind and the world. That mankind was evil, sinful at its core. "That was the hardest thing for me," Paul said. "I had always believed in the basic goodness of people. That was rarely borne out in real life, and I was no example of it, but it sure sounded better than that we were all born in sin.

"And then when I was injured and met Straight and started listening to the New Testament, I discovered the biggest surprise. I had always thought religious people lived by a certain code of conduct so they could earn their way to heaven. But that's not it."

• • •

Jae was amazed when Paul began quoting verses about salvation by grace through faith, and that it couldn't be earned by works so no one could boast. The same verses had jumped out at her.

"My sight was restored miraculously, Jae. That was God, and

no one can ever convince me otherwise. But even better than that, the blindness of my spirit was healed too. Once I allowed myself to believe that God was, and that He was alive and real, I needed Him in my life. Everything in life, my whole life, made sense only after I acknowledged that God made me and loved me and wanted to connect with me."

Jae returned to the couch and sat near Paul. "I don't know where I am with all this yet, Paul, but your father's letter first started working on me. And then I took the New Testament discs you left at home, and I've been listening to them for days. They puzzle me, they intrigue me, they mess with my mind, but I keep coming back to them. I even asked God to reveal Himself to me if He was real. I don't know if that's what He's doing now, or if we're both just crazy as loons."

• • •

She was close, Paul could tell. But she was not the type of woman who could be pushed. He'd learned that well enough over the years. Besides, this kind of an epic decision was personal. Trying to sell her on it, to browbeat her, would be futile, even if it seemed temporarily successful. Jae would resent it if she was badgered into it. Anyway, she was a woman with her own mind. If she came to this on her own, she would never waver. And that was the kind of faith she would need to survive the onslaught of life changes that would come with it.

"I need to ask you about the manifesto, Paul," she said.

"Sure."

"That was your work? your idea?"

"My writing. I worked with the French underground on what they wanted. The idea to pray for the Old Testament plague was their leader's, but after I saw what God could do—in Los Angeles—I wasn't sure I supported it. The whole underground church around the world is praying about this, Jae. Mostly against it, I presume."

"I need to tell you, Paul, that this alone is enough to make me doubt the existence of God. Do you really, seriously, believe He would slay the firstborn males of unbelievers throughout the whole world? I mean, besides sounding ludicrous, does it sound like a loving God?"

"I'm no expert, Jae. I'm new to this, and I don't want to sound glib, but it sounds like a just God who has finally lost patience with a disbelieving and mocking world. This story from the Old Testament is not a fairy tale. It happened before. And it was preceded by nine other plagues. You want to read about it?"

"I'm not sure."

Paul found the Bible Straight had given him and turned to Exodus. "When you're ready, if you're curious, this is the precursor to what we believe God could do twenty-four hours from now if the international leaders don't listen."

Jae took the Bible, with her finger in the pages, which was encouraging to Paul. "But aren't they going to assume Styr Magnor was behind all this craziness, and now that he's gone, so is the threat?"

"Yes. The government deserves to be told that that isn't true. They need to know that Magnor was a charlatan, not part of us, and that the real threat comes not from a crazy man but possibly from God Himself."

"And who's going to tell them that?"

"I am."

"Oh, Paul, no. Now, please. Even if you believe this, and even if I am considering it, I could never agree to letting you declare yourself before the chancellor of the world."

"Someone has to warn him, Jae. And who else is in a position to? I know the man. He likes and trusts me."

"He won't if you tell him that."

"So I just let it happen? Let him think the threat is gone? I owe him that much, Jae. A warning. So if it does happen, at least he'll know I have credibility."

"By that time you'll be in an asylum or solitary confinement."

"Where will I be in sixty days anyway, Jae? There's no way I can sign a declaration of loyalty to atheism."

• • •

They stayed up most of the night, reading, discussing, arguing. Jae was unable to get past the unloving, spiteful (her word) nature of the plague some believers were asking God to mete out to His enemies. Paul tried and tried to explain that if it happened it would be a last-ditch effort, that after decades of mockery and scoffing, God may resort to desperate measures to get people's attention.

"Do you expect to drop this on Dengler and then just waltz out of there and back to me?"

"I haven't thought that far ahead, Jae."

"Well, don't you think it's time you did?"

"One of us has to remain free; that's for sure," he said. "I propose you accompany me to the ceremony, whatever form that's going to take. Then I'll ask Dengler if you can be excused so he and I can talk business."

"Yeah," Jae said. "I can plan my escape back to America in case my husband slips and reveals himself as a lunatic before the one man who can do something about it."

"I plan to be diplomatic."

• • •

"Paul, there's no way in the world I will be able to do anything but sit in fear while you're in there." And then it came to her. "I could listen in. That way I'd know whether you were coming back to me or if I should fly home and try to tell the kids what's become of you."

"And how would you do that?" he said. "Wait, don't tell me."

Jae went to the closet and showed him the bugging device. "I said don't tell me," Paul said. "Well, I've got to hand it to Ranold. Nothing but the best for his newest special agent."

30

PAUL WOULD NOT HAVE BEEN ABLE to say whether he actually slept or spent the rest of the wee hours praying and crying as Jae stayed up reading. Never had Paul wanted and ached and longed for anything more in his life than that she would come to the truth as he had and that she would become his partner in the faith.

By the time they got to Bern, both were bleary eyed and quiet. "I know my role today," Jae said. "I'm the proud, dutiful wife. Your role, or at least your goal, is to somehow return to me when it's all over."

"I'll do my best," Paul said.

"Frankly, that's not terribly comforting. Paul, I don't know where I am in all this, but you must know by now that I am not going to turn on you. Whether or not we ever agree about God, I don't want to lose you."

"I can't go on long with the NPO regardless, Jae. Even if I don't reveal myself today, when I have not signed the loyalty document within sixty days, the truth will come out. You need to decide what kind of life that means for you and the kids."

• • •

Chancellor Baldwin Dengler was effusive when meeting Jae. "I only apologize that for obvious reasons, this ceremony cannot be public. You must be very proud."

"You have no idea," Jae said.

Bia Balaam pulled Jae off to the side. "What a relief for you, hmm? Our fears only reflect how expert he is. The less you say about our suspicions, the better, of course."

"Of course."

Jae enjoyed meeting Garuda Vibishana, who proved most courtly. "I've heard so much about you," Jae said.

"Oh, I am not so sure I would want to hear those details, madam."

The luncheon ceremony was attended also by Dengler's staff and cabinet, about twenty in all, including the Stepolas, Balaam, and Vibishana. The chancellor presented Paul with the International Medal of Freedom "for exemplary service to the global community." He draped it around Paul's neck as a camera flashed, and the chancellor reminded everyone, "The photo is only for our files and Mrs. Stepola's scrapbook."

At the end of the meal, Paul leaned close to Dengler. "Sir, if I may have a word. I'm wondering if I might have a few minutes with you alone."

Dengler looked at his watch. "We have arranged for your charter flight home, leaving about one-thirty. Does that give us enough time?"

"Yes, my wife could arrange to have our things delivered to the plane."

The protocol of the congratulations and good-byes alone took longer than Paul expected, and when he and Jae embraced, she planted the invisible transmitter on the arm of his suit coat.

• • •

Jae worked with a purser to have their luggage delivered to the charter, and then was told where she could wait outside for their ride to the airport. She found a bench in the bright sun, yet still sat shivering as she adjusted the earpiece and monitored Paul's conversation. Here was a story for her grandchildren someday. Who would have ever guessed her life would have come to this?

"Do you wish anyone else to join us, Doctor?" the chancellor said. "The major general or Chief Balaam?"

"No, this is a private matter, sir."

"Very well."

Jae heard them walking, doors opening and shutting, pleasantries, and finally Dengler telling his secretary that they were not to be disturbed. Then she heard Paul whisper, "Sir, if I may be so bold . . . may I assume that all conversations in your office are taped?"

"Why do you ask?"

"Because I would like to respectfully ask that any recording device be turned off for this conversation."

"That is highly irregular, Doctor. Those tapes are used exclusively for my reference, specifically for my memoirs."

"If I may say, sir, you will have no trouble remembering the particulars of this conversation, and I really must insist."

"Very well."

Jae heard nothing, but she assumed Dengler was instructing

his secretary to accede to Paul's wishes. Finally it sounded as if they were settling into Dengler's office.

"Thanks for taking the time, sir," Paul said.

"Not at all. I think you have earned it." Dengler chuckled.

"Mr. Chancellor, I want to come straight to the point. My investigation determined that Steffan Wren was not behind the underground manifesto and should not have taken credit for it."

Silence.

"In fact, sir, he was not really part of the rebel underground and was seen even by them as a charlatan who gave their cause a bad name."

Dengler cleared his throat. "He certainly did that."

"Yes, but do you see the implications of what I'm saying?"

"I hope not. If he did not write the manifesto, who did?"

Jae held her breath. Did Paul have to say?

"That came from devout members of the true underground, sir."

A long pause. "So we did not eliminate the threat by eliminating Wren."

"That is what I am trying to say, sir. He needed to be eliminated, there is no question of that."

"Of course. For the attacks alone."

"Yes, and for potential attacks."

Dengler sniffed and shuffled in his chair. "Does the underground, without Wren, have the wherewithal to carry out this midnight threat?"

"Sir, this is why I wanted to meet with you. The manifesto, to the best of my knowledge, is a sincere document."

"And by sincere, you mean . . . ?"

"That these people believe it word for word."

"I am not following you."

"They will not be carrying out this threat by trying to kill anyone. They literally believe this could happen as an act of God, the same as it happened in the ancient passage they cited."

"Oh, nonsense."

"I just thought you should be made aware, sir."

"And for what purpose, Doctor? I appreciate knowing that Wren may have been on the fringes of the underground, not taken seriously there. But with him gone and the rest counting on God to do their work for them, need I worry?"

"Whether or not you worry is up to you, sir. I just felt it my duty to be sure you were fully apprised."

• • •

Paul could only imagine how this sounded to Jae. She had to be encouraged that he had not revealed himself.

"Well, thank you, Dr. Stepola. I do feel better informed. Tell me, do you believe this will happen, the way the puzzling drought in Los Angeles happened? That the firstborn sons of everyone other than believers in God will be spontaneously slain by Him at midnight?"

Paul stared at him, praying silently. "I have never been able to explain away the L.A. phenomenon, sir. And regardless of what people think about it, it happened the way the underground there warned. As to whether the same might happen in this case, I guess we will know in less than twelve hours, won't we?"

Dengler laughed. "Yes, I suppose we will. You did not anticipate that I would announce this, did you, Doctor?"

"I never try to predict your actions, sir."

"Well," Dengler said, standing and reaching for Paul's hand, "I have already announced that the threat ended with the death of Styr Magnor/Steffan Wren. I still believe that, and I would not want the world to needlessly fear otherwise. Would you?"

"Want them to *needlessly* fear otherwise? No, sir."

• • •

On the plane, Jae told Paul straight-out, "I do not believe this slaughter is going to take place. If it doesn't, it will tell me a lot about your fellow believers and the effectiveness of their prayers. If it does, besides being the most shocked person in the world, I can't promise how it will make me feel about God. I suppose I will have to believe He is real, but I would have a hard time understanding Him or liking Him much."

Paul worried about Jae, of course, and he couldn't quit looking at his watch. Midnight in Bern would be 6 p.m. in Washington. With the time change they expected to touch down in D.C. midmorning. Stretched way past his level of endurance, Paul didn't know what else to say or do. He let his head fall and he slept the entire flight, not rousing until touchdown.

• • •

Jae was spent too, but she could not sleep. She wanted to find the verse that had been bugging her. She put the Hebrews disc back into the player and listened straight through until it jumped out at her:

You see, it is impossible to please God without faith. Anyone who wants to come to him must believe that there is a God and that he rewards those who sincerely seek him.

She prayed, *I want to believe that there is a God, and I am sincerely looking for You.*

• • •

Jae's mother picked them up at the airport. The kids were in school and, she said, already enjoying it and making friends. "Your father is at work, of course. But he can't wait to see you both. Berlitz and Aryana are coming for dinner at six-thirty."

Jae felt as if she had come out of a haze of craziness into some semblance of sanity.

When the kids got home from school that afternoon they attacked Paul and wrestled with him on the floor, telling him about everything they had been doing, friends they had made, and their teachers.

"Do we have to go back to Chicago now that you're home?" Brie said.

"I thought you *wanted* to," he said.

"We do, but not yet."

Ranold pulled in about five, hurrying into the house in his nicest suit but already pulling off the tie. He squeezed Jae's shoulder and vigorously shook Paul's hand. "I want to hear everything, son," he said. "Everything. Let me get out of these clothes. Your mother tell you Berl and the new wife will be here for dinner?"

Paul nodded as the kids screamed, "Yay!"

Ranold bounded upstairs with more energy than Jae had noticed in ages, and he soon returned in a flannel shirt, wash pants, and white socks. "Pardon the informality," he said, "but I didn't need one more minute in that monkey suit. Paul, come on into the den and join me in a stiff one. You can debrief me and we can catch the news before the other kids get here."

• • •

"Just give me a soda, Ranold," Paul said.

"You sure? You deserve a belt, man."

"I got a little shut-eye on the plane, but alcohol would probably put me out for a week."

Ranold poured himself a hard drink and Paul a soft one, and they sat. "Tell me the story as if I know absolutely nothing," the old man said.

And so Paul did. He even added what he had told Dengler.

Ranold finished his drink with a huge gulp, rose, and poured himself another. "You believe Magnor was *not* behind the manifesto?"

"I'd stake my life on it."

"Well, so we've eliminated Magnor, and when the big threat fizzles, the resistance loses its steam."

"That would certainly be the case."

Ranold leaned over and clapped Paul on the knee. "And we have you to thank."

You just might.

Paul kept glancing at his watch, and Ranold finally noticed. "Almost time for the news." He switched on the TV. The last couple of minutes of a five-thirty sitcom were playing.

Paul drummed his fingers on the arm of the chair.

"Couldn't be more proud of you," Ranold said. "Hey, you haven't touched your Coke."

"Not thirsty, I guess." In truth, he wanted to be with Jae right now. He could hear her talking with her mother and the kids playing in the other room.

At six straight up, it was as if the power went out in the house. Everything went black—every light, the television, everything. Brie screamed.

Ranold said, "What the—?" and Paul heard him rise and move to the window, pulling back the curtain. "Streetlights too," he said. "Power outage."

And just like that, the lights came back on. The kids laughed. Margaret said something in a high-pitched, relieved voice. The TV picture sprang back to life, showing the anchorman slumped over the desk and his partner, a woman, standing, screaming for help.

"Would you look at that?" Ranold said, leaning forward. "Guy looks like he passed out. Heart attack or somethin'."

The phone rang, and Paul heard Margaret answer. "Aryana," she said, sounding alarmed, "what's wrong?"

• • •

Jae looked up at her mother as the kids came bounding into the kitchen. "The lights were off!" Connor shouted, just as Margaret slumped to the floor, the phone clattering away.

"Daddy!" Jae called, and the men came in from the den as she picked up the phone. "Aryana?"

The woman was hysterical. "He just collapsed!" Aryana said. "When the power went out, or whatever happened, even our headlights went out. I told Berl to stop, but I could tell he wasn't steering. I grabbed the wheel and could feel him just sitting there limp. I was able to get my foot on the brake when we hit the curb. Then the lights came back on. But, Jae, he's dead!"

"What?"

"He's dead! No pulse, nothing!"

"Dad!" Jae said. "You need to talk to Aryana."

Jae took over trying to rouse her mother, who had fainted at the news, while Ranold took the phone.

"That can't be, Aryana!" he said. "He's a young man! Call the paramedics!"

Paul's molar vibrated with a tone, and Ranold turned away as if also taking a call. "I've got to take this, Aryana," he said. "Get help and call us back."

• • •

Paul answered his phone. It was Enzo Fabrizio from Rome. "It's happened, Paul. Are you watching the news?"

Ranold, pale, answered his private phone again. "Oh, Bia! No!" he said. "My son too!"

He slammed his fist on the kitchen counter. "I've got to get to Berlitz and help Aryana," he said. "Paul, will you come?"

"Let him stay with Mom, Dad," Jae said.

"Ranold," Paul said, "it's happened."

"What's happened?"

"The curse. The plague. The warning from the underground."

"What? What!" Ranold looked wildly at everyone in the kitchen, his eyes finally landing on Connor. "But, but your son, *your* firstborn son is fine!"

The kids burst into tears. Ranold stormed out.

Jae helped her mother into a chair and fanned her. "You kids help me with Grandma. Now! Get me a glass of water. Paul, you'd better check the news."

Paul made his way back into the den, where news bulletins of millions of deaths poured in from around the globe. And knowing his and Jae's and the kids' lives would never be the same, Paul heard the report from Bern, where it was announced that International Government Chancellor Baldwin Dengler was mourning the loss of his own eldest son.

WATCH FOR THE NEXT BOOK
IN THIS EXCITING SERIES,
AND TURN THE PAGE FOR MORE
BOOKS BY BEST-SELLING AUTHOR
JERRY JENKINS . . .

TYNDALE HOUSE NOVELS
BY JERRY JENKINS

The Left Behind® Series *(with Tim LaHaye)*

Left Behind®

Tribulation Force

Nicolae

Soul Harvest

Apollyon

Assassins

The Indwelling

The Mark

Desecration

The Remnant

Armageddon

Glorious Appearing

Prequel—available fall 2005

OTHER NOVELS
BY JERRY JENKINS

The Operative

Rookie (Youngest Hero)

Though None Go with Me

'Twas the Night Before

Hometown Legend

Soon

Silenced

For the latest information on Left Behind products,
visit www.leftbehind.com

For the latest information on Tyndale House fiction,
visit www.tyndalefiction.com